THE VINES
OF
AMBERFIELD

THE VINES OF AMBERFIELD

Gina Stewart

Hodder & Stoughton
LONDON SYDNEY AUCKLAND

British Library Cataloguing in Publication Data
Stewart, Gina
  The vines of amberfield.
  I. Title
  823.914 [F]

ISBN 0-340-56815-1

Published by Hodder and Stoughton,
a division of Hodder and Stoughton Ltd,
Mill Road, Dunton Green, Sevenoaks, Kent TN13 2YA
Editorial Office: 47 Bedford Square, London WC1B 3DP

Typeset by Hewer Text Composition Services, Edinburgh
Printed in Great Britain by St Edmundsbury Press Limited,
Bury St Edmunds, Suffolk

To the winemakers of England
without whom this story
could not have been written

PART ONE

1

They waited together on the wet, windswept tarmac, Meriel and these people she scarcely knew, her new family. The bleak November day was only a few hours old, yet already it seemed to Meriel that the waiting would never end.

Earlier that morning a phone call had informed them that the flight would land as scheduled, and they had risen, exhausted after another sleepless night, and made their way to Heathrow. They arrived only to be told that there was a delay, due to weather conditions: a sharp, blustery wind interrupted by squally showers had replaced the heavy rain of the night before and had led to a backlog of planes waiting to land.

All they could do was wait. Meriel and the others stood where airport officials had told them they might stand, beside the two black limousines, and watched as aircraft after aircraft landed. To Meriel's left, Vivienne Barton held herself still as a statue, clasping her handbag in black-gloved hands, not moving even when a gust of wind snatched at her hat or threatened to dislodge a strand of hair. She showed no sign of the agitation evident in her fifteen-year-old daughter Hatta, who shifted restlessly beside her, twisting a crumpled handkerchief between her fingers and casting quick, nervous glances about her as though unable to grasp the reason for their being there. Vivienne, by contrast, appeared calm and composed, giving no hint of emotion.

In front of them, the tall, broad outline of Vivienne's son Adam – shoulders hunched against the cold, hands

3

thrust deep into the pockets of his coat – dwarfed Sophie Meyreuil, his fiancée, who stood beside him. Except for Hatta, everyone was motionless, gazing straight ahead, not speaking, seemingly unaware that around them, outside this small, huddled group of sombrely clad figures, all was noise and movement and flashes of unexpected colour contrasting with the greyness of the day. They did not hear the drone and scream of aircraft landing and taking off. They appeared not to see the luggage containers snaking their way to and from aircraft and terminals, the refuelling appliances like brightly painted beetles buzzing about from one place to another, the curious glances of passengers being bused to their destinations. Narrowing their eyes against the occasional bursts of rain and the bitter, stinging gusts of wind, they stared fixedly in the direction of the recently landed aircraft, each one of them secretly hoping that maybe, just maybe, there had been some mistake . . .

And then, suddenly, the waiting was over. A Boeing had landed and was taxiing slowly towards them. As it drew to a halt, airport workers gathered respectfully by the hold until an official clutching a sheaf of papers gestured to the men still on board to bring their cargo out, slowly, carefully . . . Then, as Meriel and the others watched, Simon's body in its expensive American coffin was lowered from the aircraft into the waiting hearse.

So it was true: there had been no mistake. That terrible phone call from Cindy Huber had not been some monstrous hoax, some sadistic prank.

"May I speak with Meriel Barton, please?" The voice had been cracked with emotion, the speaker scarcely able to get the words out.

"I'm Meriel Barton," she had replied cheerfully, assuming the caller had a head cold and that she wished to inform her that Simon's flight had been delayed.

"Oh, Meriel! We haven't met . . . I'm Cindy Huber . . ."

4

"Cindy! How lovely to hear from you!"

"Mark . . . my husband Mark asked me to call you . . ."

"Yes?" prompted Meriel, but already she knew from Cindy's voice that something was terribly wrong. "Is Mark all right?" she asked.

"Mark's . . . Mark's fine. He's just in shock, that's all. Meriel, it's not Mark, it's Simon. There's been an accident. Simon's . . ."

"*NO!*" Meriel had wailed, "No, no, no!"

"Meriel, I'm so sorry."

Meriel had then flung herself down on her bed, pummelling the pillow with all her might until, exhausted, she had buried her head in her arms and rocked herself, moaning and whimpering, as though by blocking out sight and sound she could also banish the knowledge that Simon, her husband of just a few weeks, was dead.

"Mrs Barton?"

"Yes?"

Meriel and Vivienne turned simultaneously towards the official. He was a young man, clearly unused to this sort of duty, and for a moment he was confused, not knowing which of the two women to address. Sensibly, he spoke to the elder of the two.

"I . . .er . . . I wonder if you would mind following the . . . er . . ." Perhaps he thought the word "hearse" was indelicate. At any rate, he gesticulated weakly towards the vehicle in question, which was now proceeding slowly towards them.

"What is it, Mother?"

Adam withdrew the consoling arm he had placed around Sophie's shoulders and approached Vivienne. The wind whipped and tugged at his black wool coat and he had to lean forward to catch Vivienne's reply. Meriel tried not to stare at him. He looked so much like Simon it was almost unbearable. Last night, when she had been shown into the lounge at the hotel where the family were staying, she had

5

exclaimed aloud at the sight of those familiar warm brown eyes, the sandy-coloured hair.

"Simon obviously didn't tell you that he and Adam could pass for twins," Vivienne had commented coldly, "despite the two-year difference in their ages."

"Not really . . . no . . ." Meriel had floundered, brought close to tears by this latest shock as much as by her mother-in-law's tone of voice. "We'd known each other so little time . . ."

"Yes." There was no mistaking the disapproval written all over Vivienne's face as she continued: "I expect there's an awful lot you don't know about us. Or we about you, for that matter. But there you are." Did Meriel know, for example, Vivienne went on, that Simon's father Edward had recently suffered his second stroke and would not be well enough to attend the funeral? Was Vivienne correct in assuming that Meriel would be staying on with them at Amberfield afterwards?

"If that's all right . . ." Meriel was hesitant, unsure of her position, not knowing what Simon's family required of her. "Until I've had a chance to sort something out . . . It's all been so sudden. I really haven't had a chance to think . . ."

"I feel sure Simon would have wanted you to spend some time with us," said Adam, "After all, we're your in-laws. Aren't we, Sophie?"

The girl's dark eyes, disproportionately large in the elfin face, lit up with kindness and she nodded briefly but emphatically.

"Oh, yes," she replied, in a husky and attractively accented voice. "Yes, I am sure that is what Simon would like."

Of course! Meriel had remembered. Simon had told her that Adam's fiancée was French – from the south, she thought, although she was unsure of the precise area.

"Quite honestly," Simon had said, "I'm surprised at old Adam falling for someone like Sophie."

"Oh? Why?" Meriel had queried.

Simon had considered the matter for a moment. "I suppose what I mean is . . . well, Sophie is really very nice. I mean *really* nice."

"Are you saying that Adam isn't really nice?" Meriel had laughed, but Simon had merely shrugged, and laughed in return.

"I'm not sure I know exactly what I mean," he had replied. "But I think Sophie could be good news for my younger bro, that's all."

A loud sob brought Meriel back to the present. The hearse had now drawn level with them and the sight of the coffin had proved too much for Hatta, who began to wail uncontrollably.

"You will ride in the first car with Henrietta and myself," Vivienne informed Meriel. "Adam and Sophie can bring up the rear."

They climbed into the waiting cars as instructed, Meriel and Vivienne taking their places on either side of the sobbing Hatta. The girl's entire body was given over to the tears that Meriel was trying so hard to contain; she wept as though her world had ended and Meriel's heart went out to her.

As the cortège edged away from Heathrow and along the M25, Meriel stole a look at her mother-in-law, sitting still and straight beside Hatta in her elegantly cut black suit. She was acting as though Meriel was not there, as if the two of them had nothing in common. Surely this grief, this appalling pain should be shared, thought Meriel. How else was it to be borne? Beneath the brim of the wide black hat she could discern the older woman's carefully tinted blond hair and the set, unyielding, features. For a moment, she experienced something akin to compassion for this woman, Simon's mother, whose upbringing presumably did not allow her to weep in front of a stranger.

Hatta's sobs showed no sign of abating. Meriel, unable to bear the sound any longer, gathered the girl to her and stroked the straight blond hair. For a while, until she calmed down and stopped crying, Hatta submitted to Meriel's arm around her; then abruptly she pulled away, after which she refused to look at, or in any way acknowledge, her new sister-in-law. She spoke only once during the slow journey to Kent:

"Are we going home now?" she asked her mother.

"Yes," replied Vivienne. "We're taking Simon back to Amberfield."

"Frankly," Simon had said when he asked Meriel to marry him, "I don't think Princess Di would have been good enough for me as far as Mother is concerned. She'd have criticised her for being too thin, perhaps, or for not having enough O levels. Something utterly irrelevant, at any rate."

"Are you saying she won't like me?" asked Meriel in dismay.

"Perhaps 'like' isn't quite the right word," mused Simon. "She certainly won't dislike you – who could? – but on the other hand, she doesn't really go in for liking people, either. Unless they're close family, that is. It's just not her style."

"But . . . will she approve of me?"

"Ah." Simon held her at arm's length for a moment or two and studied her closely before letting her go. "Approve. That's another matter. I'm afraid I can't say. There really is no telling with Mother. But don't worry! Sooner or later you'll win her over! You'll see!"

"Simon, why can't we spend some time with her at Amberfield before we get married? That way we'd both have a chance of getting to know each other a little. After all, if I'm to live under her roof . . . it would be so awful if we couldn't stand the sight of one another!"

"Darling, I told you, she won't hate you . . . I simply don't want to give her the chance of making trouble between us, and believe me, that is exactly what she will do if she gets you in her clutches. Within minutes she'll have you down as a heartless little fortune-hunter – "

"Thanks a lot! Besides, you told me you didn't have a fortune!"

"I most certainly don't! But that kind of small detail wouldn't deter Mother!"

"Even so . . ."

"And there's another thing. Mother's not particularly prudish about these things, but she is old-fashioned in certain ways. For example, sex before marriage is fine so long as it doesn't take place under her roof. She seems to have no objection to Adam and Sophie living together at The Lodge, but . . . her sense of what is proper would be deeply offended if we were to get married from the same house, after living together there publicly for a time. Does that make any sense to you?"

Meriel gave a deep sigh. "I think so. What you're saying is that she cares about appearances."

"Exactly. Particularly now that Father is ill."

"All the same, shouldn't she at least meet me? Just once . . . maybe here, in London?"

"*No!*" His expression was serious now, his voice more urgent. "Believe me, I know Mother! If she decides she wants to split us up, she could make things very unpleasant for us."

"Simon?" she asked, aware that he was avoiding her eyes. "Are you telling me this has happened before? Can't you tell me about it?"

He shrugged in that way he had when he wanted to wriggle out of something.

"It was nothing," he said uncomfortably. "Anyway, it was a long time ago." Then, continuing quickly, he said: "Really, it's best if Mother doesn't meet you until you're my wife. That way she'll have no choice but to accept you as an equal. You do see that, don't you?"

"I suppose so . . ." said Meriel uncertainly. She felt she should pursue the matter, but she so wanted everything to be right between her and Simon that she let the subject drop. "All the same, what if . . ." she began.

"OK, what if. If you and Mother genuinely do not get on, we can always find somewhere of our own in a few months' time. How would that suit you? But in the meantime I'd like you to give Amberfield a go, if you can bear it. Amberfield is both my home and my career. My life there would be blissfully simple and uncomplicated if I hadn't fallen hopelessly in love with a certain young lady called Meriel Devereux and if I didn't absolutely insist on marrying her." Simon now drew her to him and, burying his face in her hair, he added quietly: "I can't tell you how fed up I am only seeing you at weekends and for the odd night during the week if we're lucky. I want to be with you all the time."

"It's what I want too, Simon," she replied, in such a heartfelt tone that Simon drew back amused, before dropping a light kiss on her nose.

"Well, then! Don't you see? What point is there in putting us both through what is bound to be a bit of an ordeal when there's nothing to be gained by it? Trust me!"

"All right, then. I'll trust you."

"There's just one other teensy little thing . . ."

"Now what!" She pretended to be exasperated.

"When you do eventually get to meet my mother, whatever you do don't make any mention of British wine."

"What?" She had laughed aloud. "Why on earth not, if that's what you make for a living?"

"Because, my sweet, we are in the business of making *English* wine. That is, wine made from grapes grown in the UK and, in our case, bottled on our very own estate. *British* wine, on the other hand, is made from imported concentrated grape juice. It is reconstituted by adding water and tastes disgusting."

"I didn't know that," said Meriel, simply. "But then, what I know about winemaking would fit onto a postage stamp."

"Hah!" Simon pulled away sharply, with a sudden bitter laugh. "I shouldn't worry about that if I were you! Half the people who grow vines don't have much of a clue, either!"

"Simon?" Meriel asked, recoiling from this unexpected change of mood and searching Simon's face for some explanation. "What is it? What did I say?"

"Oh, God, I'm sorry, darling!" His apology came instantly, but it was belied by the anger in his eyes. "It's just that . . ." he hesitated before continuing. "I don't have it all my way at Amberfield, if you must know."

"How do you mean?" she asked.

"For reasons best known to themselves, my parents brought in someone above my head a few years back, and he and I don't exactly see eye to eye."

"Someone?" asked Meriel, confused. "What sort of someone?"

"He's our cousin, as it happens. Name of Daniel Courtney."

"But . . . why? I mean, I thought you were responsible for making the wine! You and your father!"

"Yes, well . . . that was in the good old days before Dan decided to return to the UK and muscle in on the family business."

Mention of his cousin always seemed to make Simon angry, thought Meriel. Wasn't it time he explained to her the situation at Amberfield? Soon, she would be living there. She felt she had a right to know what to expect. She walked over to where Simon was now standing by the window, and slid her arms around his waist.

"Talk to me, Simon!" she said. "Tell me about it!"

After a while, she felt him close his hands over hers. Then he said:

"Planting those vineyards was *my* idea, Meriel! My idea! And things were going perfectly well, as far as I'm concerned. I'm telling you, there was no need to bring Dan in over my head."

11

"No, I'm sure there wasn't," she said soothingly. "So . . . what made them do it?"

Simon seemed not to have heard her, and when he spoke he ignored her question. "Did I tell you we used to grow hops in the old days?"

"Yes. Yes, you did." She remembered the details clearly. How three generations of Bartons had grown hops on fifty acres of Amberfield land. How the demand for English hops had gradually declined as the fashion for Continental and Australian beers grew. How Simon had persuaded his parents to sell the hopfields and use the money to plant the vineyards.

"You see, Meriel, the thing is that we're not really a farming family. I found that out when I went to agricultural college and saw what was actually involved in running a farm. Even if Father had had the expertise to rear sheep or grow apples and pears, I realised by the time I finished at college that farming wasn't for me."

"But without the hops you had no income. Is that it?" asked Meriel.

"That's it exactly!" Simon replied. "And that's why planting a vineyard seemed such a good idea. You only need a relatively small acreage to get going – a mere five acres will yield thirty-eight thousand bottles of wine in a good year."

"Thirty-eight *thousand*?"

"In a good year. Assuming five tons per acre."

She wanted to ask him more. What kind of grapes did they grow? Did they sell all the wine they made? Did Simon's parents realise how deeply he resented Dan Courtney? But Simon seemed to have forgotten his anger of a few moments ago, and Meriel decided not to risk upsetting him. These were questions she could ask him another day, when he finally showed her round her new home.

Travelling eastwards along the busy motorway, Meriel closed her eyes and thought back to the day of her first meeting with her future husband. It was in London; it was June: a cold, wet day following unexpectedly after three weeks of blazing summer; and there was a transport strike. Meriel, driving to her job in the City from her flat in Battersea, was caught in traffic on Southwark Bridge when she noticed a young man carefully making his way along the pavement, carrying what looked like a very heavy box. On top of it, balanced so precariously that she expected it to fall off at any moment, was a briefcase. The young man would look around from time to time as though hoping to spot a taxi, but they were of course all taken.

On the radio that morning as well as the previous evening, there had been appeals for motorists entering London to offer lifts to less fortunate travellers. It seemed churlish not to do the decent thing, so Meriel wound down the passenger window.

At that identical moment, the driver of the car in front of her – an elderly man in a silver BMW – had the very same idea. Pushing the button that controlled the electric window, he leaned across his car precisely as Meriel was doing, and said:

"Can I offer you a lift?"

Meriel's identical words came simultaneously. The young man, who had waited for a taxi for half an hour with no success before deciding he had no option but to proceed on foot, was now faced with two offers at once. He looked in amusement from one car to the other, taking in first the sleek comfort of the BMW, then the cramped interior of the beautifully restored black MG that was Meriel's favourite possession.

"Sorry, mate, but this one's prettier," he said, opting for the MG, and clearly referring to both the car and its owner.

The BMW driver grinned, and hooted briefly on his horn in acknowledgment of an inevitable decision.

"I'm not sure that box will fit in the boot," said Meriel, suddenly worried.

"It's all right. I'd rather keep it on my knees, if you don't mind. That way I can make sure nothing happens to it."

"Is it fragile?" asked Meriel.

"Fragile and very precious," said the man. "In this box I have twelve bottles of wine from the vineyards at Amberfield. I'm on my way to see some buyers – the company's entire future depends on them liking the stuff, so wish me luck. I'm Simon Barton, by the way."

Meriel was amused. "And I'm Meriel Devereux."

"Are you by any chance Something In The City?" asked Simon, taking in Meriel's smartly tailored suit, glossy chestnut hair and her long legs in their almost black stockings.

"Yes, as it happens, I am. I'm a foreign currency dealer."

"Well, you're definitely Something. That's for sure."

That was how it had all started, a year and a half ago. And now it was ending, with a funeral in the corner of Kent Simon had loved so well. They had reached the village at last, and drove slowly down the near-empty main street, a typically Kentish mixture of timber-hung façades interspersed with pink- or white-washed Georgian flat-fronted cottages, and black-beamed Tudor houses now carefully converted into shops or offices. One or two shopkeepers, unable to abandon their premises, came out onto the pavement to pay their last respects to Simon Barton. Most of these people had known Simon since earliest childhood and their links with the Barton family stretched back even further. To lose someone like Simon was to lose one of their own.

The sad, muted tones of the organ and the almost overpowering scent of flowers struck Meriel with a dizzying intensity as she entered the church. Stumbling on the ancient, uneven flags of the central aisle, she might have fallen if someone, a man, had not sprung forward to take her elbow and escort her to her place in the front pew.

14

"Thank you," she murmured shakily as she sat down, and glanced briefly at the person who had helped her. She saw a man, tall, dark-haired, not much older than Simon, she supposed, with the clean-cut, tanned features of someone who leads an active, outdoor life. His eyes, serious and unfathomable, met hers for a moment, before he left her to take his place in the row behind.

Hymns, prayers and eulogies followed. First Adam spoke on the family's behalf, paying tribute to the man he described as his brother and his friend, and detailing their upbringing together. Adam handled the situation well: he must be used to making speeches, Meriel thought, but a tiny part of her balked at a certain glibness in his tone. What she wanted from Simon's family, she realised, was some evidence of the raw anguish that was eating away at her own heart, but, except for Hatta, they seemed determined to control their emotions at all costs.

The head of the Barton boys' prep school came next, recalling various long-past escapades and concluding:

"We at Frogmore House remember Simon as a good all-rounder: he was good in class, good at sports, and even good at being naughty. He will be fondly remembered by all those who knew him."

A silence, broken by a certain amount of scuffling and the scraping of a chair along the floor, followed the headmaster's remarks. Then the plangent tones of a cello rose from somewhere to Meriel's left, though she could not see the performer from where she sat near a pillar. He really was very good, she realised, as the first hesitant notes developed into a warmer, deeper sound and the cellist gathered confidence. There was something about the quality of the playing that exactly expressed the grief that Meriel knew was locked up inside her but which for the moment would not come out.

From all around her came the sound of subdued weeping. Even the previously impassive Vivienne dabbed repeatedly at her eyes and nose as the music drew to a

15

close. Meriel, twisting her head to discover the identity of the soloist, was astonished to see that it was Hatta who rose from the chair by the pulpit, laid down her instrument and, sniffing inelegantly, returned to her place next to Adam.

It was now the vicar's turn to speak, but Meriel scarcely heard him. Instead, she was experiencing a rush of rage so unexpected and so overwhelming that she shook with the intensity of it. *How could Simon do this to me?* she kept thinking. *He knew how much I loved him. How dare he hurt me like this?* Her anger was such that she felt only physical violence would assuage it. If she could simply scream and shout and tear her hair and give in to all those powerful primitive urges welling up within her . . . but even the tears that might have soothed her would not come. All she could do was twist her hands together, over and over, and try and force herself to listen to what was being said:

"Simon Barton and his family reminded us that winegrowing at Amberfield is by no means a new phenomenon. As we are now all aware, the Domesday Book has records of almost fifty vineyards in southern England at the time of the Norman invasion, and one of those vineyards was right here at Amberfield. Now that Simon is no longer among us to nurture the vines of which he, like ourselves, was so proud, let us hope that no one, for whatever reason, takes that source of pride away from us."

Was it her imagination, Meriel wondered, or did the vicar's closing words cause a rustle of unease to pass through the mourners in the front pews? Moving her head as little as possible, she glanced briefly at the faces on either side of her, but none of them conveyed anything unexpected. Still, she thought, something had been said – or perhaps left unsaid – that struck a chord with one or more members of the congregation. She could feel it; even through the cloak of anger and despair the atmosphere was tangible, unmistakable.

After the funeral service at Amberfield Church and the brief cremation ceremony in Canterbury, the family and other mourners made their way back to Amberfield House. To Meriel, this was yet one more ordeal to be got through. This was supposed to be a homecoming; she wasn't meant to be seeing her new home for the first time through a glaze of unshed tears.

She could not help feeling that she shouldn't be here at Amberfield without Simon, and more than once she stretched out her hand before remembering that he was not there beside her. She realised just how dependent upon him she had become over the past year and a half. And yet, when he first stepped into her car on Southwark Bridge, she had had no premonition, no sense that this was the man she would one day marry.

She had been a little disappointed when she dropped him off in Gresham Street that he made no attempt to obtain her telephone number. She had felt at ease in his company, and each of them had somehow found a way of letting the other know they were not entangled in other relationships. Over the next few days Meriel sometimes found herself thinking about Simon Barton, and hoping that his meeting with the wine merchants had gone well. Then, a week later, just as she had resigned herself to never seeing him again, the receptionist at Vere Lassiter buzzed her to say there was a parcel waiting for her.

Inside, Meriel found a presentation box containing two bottles of wine from Amberfield Vineyards. "*Meeting successful,*" said the accompanying card. "*Thanks due to stunning chauffeuse. Please dine with me very soon.*"

"Hello, what's all this?" asked her colleague Kath Smylie, who happened to emerge from the lift at that moment.

"It's a present from a friend," Meriel replied, holding out the box for Kath to inspect.

"Someone you picked up, if this card's to be believed," laughed Kath in her forthright Australian manner. She

17

took out one of the bottles and read the label disbelievingly.

"*English* wine? Well, I'll say one thing for this guy,
whoever he is. He's certainly got a sense of humour!"

Meriel accepted the dinner invitation with pleasure,
though when they met again she discovered that his
meeting had not been quite as satisfactory as she had
assumed. It turned out that the buyers had agreed to take
only one of Amberfield's wines and that, Simon informed
her curtly, had been made by "dear, oh-so-clever cousin
Dan, the apple of Mother's little eye".

"Next time I'm sure they'll take some of yours!" Meriel
told him, at which Simon shook his head abruptly and
said:

"Let's change the subject, shall we? Tell me about
yourself. I mean, everything about yourself."

To her surprise she found herself doing just that. In no
time at all she was describing her childhood in a small
terraced house in Mitcham with her long-suffering mother,
Dorothy, and, occasionally, her errant father.

"He sounds interesting!" Simon had remarked. "In what
way was your father 'errant'?"

"Probably not in the way you're imagining," laughed
Meriel, hesitating before going on. She was well aware
that the activities of Ricky Devereux were not always of
the most edifying and in the present circumstances she was
unsure how much she should say.

Besides, what was there to say about "Tricky Ricky"
Devereux, her handsome, charming father, a man who
was never able to hold down a job for more than a month
at a time, who lied his way in and out of one doubtful
situation after the next, who kept promising things were
going to get better and then failing to deliver the goods,
and who finally, with very little warning, announced that
he was leaving to work in Australia and that he would send
for his wife and child as soon as he was on his feet?

Meriel had been thirteen at the time and as far as she

18

was concerned, life after her father's departure continued much as before. He had never been a man to spend much time with his family, and was adept at finding good reasons why he simply had to be away from home when he was needed there. What Meriel failed to realise until much, much later was that Ricky's continued absence very nearly broke her mother's heart. Scoundrel or no, he was the love of her life, and the only thing that kept her going was the certainty that one day he would do as he promised, and write asking them to join him.

And in the end, after five long years of waiting and hoping, Dorothy's faith was justified. Shortly after Meriel's eighteenth birthday, Ricky at last sent for his wife. Her destination, it turned out, was not Australia but South America, and although Meriel was never quite able to fathom out the reasons for this change of address, she was pleased for her mother's sake that all seemed to have turned out for the best. Not without sadness, mother and daughter decided to go their separate ways, and although Meriel had spoken of Simon in her letters to her parents, she had not yet mentioned her impending marriage.

Prompted by Simon's evident interest, Meriel then went on to tell him about her years at the local girls' school, where, because of her mother's nervous terror at inviting visitors into her home, Meriel made few close friends. Besides, as one of the few clever children in an institution that was not used to dealing with this particular breed, she was always made to feel out of place.

"And now I suppose you've got thousands," Simon had said, gloomily.

For a moment she thought he was talking about money, and she was on the point of telling him it was none of his business when she realised he meant friends. The truth was that she lived a remarkably solitary existence, partly through necessity – her career took up much of her time – but partly too because she had never got into the habit of developing close relationships.

"No, I haven't, as a matter of fact," she replied, strangely affected by the question. "In fact, I'd say I was rather lacking in that department."

"But . . . you're *lovely*!" Simon told her. "You should be surrounded by friends! Dozens and dozens of them!"

It was when she looked up at him and saw he meant every word he said that she realised for the first time that she did not have to be like her mother, always waiting, almost always disappointed, not daring to show too much affection in case it was thrown back in her face. She also understood, belatedly, to what extent her former self-sufficiency must have made her seem cold and unapproachable to others.

When Simon asked her to marry him, she knew that here was her chance to belong to the real world, a world in which people loved and were loved in return. She accepted without hesitation, handed in her notice at work and flung herself joyously into the business of preparing for married life.

They had assumed that by the time they returned from their honeymoon in the Seychelles, the buyers of Meriel's flat would be ready to complete the purchase. She and Simon would then see to the disposal of the contents and would drive down to Amberfield together, as man and wife.

Quite how her future mother-in-law had responded to the news that her son was getting married, Meriel did not know. When questioned, Simon had merely said that things had been "difficult" but that she was not to worry: Vivienne had decided to accept the inevitable, and to welcome her son's wife into her home. Not for the first time, Meriel let herself be swept along by Simon's unquenchable optimism and enthusiasm, and cast any niggling doubts aside.

What in fact happened was that they returned from their honeymoon to find that the completion of the sale had been delayed by a week and that a call from one of

Simon's Californian wine-growing contacts awaited them. Mark Huber's new and phenomenally expensive space-age winery was finally up and running: the harvest of locally grown Chardonnay and Sauvignon grapes promised to be a good one, and Mark wondered whether Simon would be interested in inspecting the new machinery for himself?

"Darling," said Simon, "it couldn't be more perfect! A second honeymoon, straight after the first. And all for a legitimate business purpose. Why don't we go?"

But in the end it was Simon who went to the States alone, while Meriel stayed to dispose of her furniture and complete the sale of the flat.

"You'll only be gone a few days," she said. "Don't miss this opportunity because of me – I know what the wine-growing business means to you!"

"One day you'll get hooked by it too, just like me," Simon assured her. "Just wait till I've shown you Amberfield and the vineyards, and our own admittedly fairly modest winery . . . the bug will get you too, Meriel Barton!"

"Who knows?" said Meriel, not believing him. Then Simon's arms were around her and he was hugging her in his impulsive, boyish way, and telling her he could not bear the thought of being parted from her for so long.

"I'm afraid there's nothing for it," he said at last, surfacing temporarily from a lingering, satisfying kiss. "We'll just have to make up for our enforced abstinence in advance." And his mouth had closed on hers once more, as he swung her up in his arms and carried her through to the bedroom, negotiating the luggage and packing cases with more luck than judgement until they tumbled together, breathless and laughing, onto the bed.

As Simon had wanted Amberfield to come as a complete surprise to his bride, he had even refused to show her any photographs of the house. Meriel, not knowing what to expect, nervous at having to enter Simon's home without him, wished above all for some friend or relation to be with her at this time, but she was alone, locked into her cocoon of misery as Vivienne, almost certainly, was locked in hers. The car now turned out of the village and down a side road, before swinging right between a pair of high wrought-iron gates supported by stone pillars. Before them, at the top of a long, sloping drive that divided the fields on either side, was Amberfield House.

Because of the lie of the land the house, built of traditional Kentish red brick, seemed to loom up over them in the evening half-light. Three storeys high, and topped by a wide stone pediment, it sat comfortably on a stretch of level ground between the slope that fell away from the front of the house and the darker hills beyond.

Even at this bare, wintry time of year Meriel could see that Amberfield House was beautiful. It was also bigger than she had imagined it and more imposing than the sturdy, relatively modest farmhouse she had been expecting. Yet it was in no way daunting. There was a comforting, unpretentious elegance in the shape of the windows, in the small bricks pitted with age and the heavy door now opening to throw a gentle, mellow light onto the sandstone sill. Together these features tugged at her in a way she could not have explained. Maybe, despite the Barton family's polite coolness towards her, this was a homecoming after all. For a brief moment she experienced a sense of regret that she would not be staying here for long. Then she shook the feeling away. Nothing was as it should be. Thinking about what might have been could only upset her.

Before following Vivienne indoors she peered through the increasing gloom at the fields they had just driven past, but saw no sign of the vineyards for which Amberfield was apparently famous. She owed it to Simon, she felt, to visit them before she left.

2

"Jacinta will show you to your room." Vivienne, still seemingly composed, was standing in front of the massive hall mirror, removing the pins from her hat and taking care not to disturb her hair.

Meriel followed the maid up the stairs and across the first-floor landing where she was shown into an airy, chintz-hung bedroom with its own adjoining bathroom and, more surprisingly, a small sitting-room complete with armchairs and writing desk. A large bowl of bronze-coloured chrysanthemums stood on the sitting-room mantelpiece, their burnished petals reflected in the gilt-framed mirror behind them. Meriel, catching sight of her own reflection, removed her hat and set it on the writing desk.

"I bring you a cup of tea?" Jacinta asked, her every word and movement expressing her sympathy for the young widow.

"No, thank you, Jacinta. I ought to be getting back downstairs . . ."

"Is not easy for you, I know," said Jacinta. She was a plump, motherly woman whose accent and appearance immediately announced her as Spanish. "You come here, you know no one . . . and Mrs Barton, she not unkind but her heart, you know, it is hidden. She not always an easy woman. If you need help for anything, you ask me. I help you. Always."

Meriel was not at all sure that Jacinta should talk like this about her employer, but she was grateful for the kindness in Jacinta's words. They gave her the necessary courage to tidy her hair and see to her make-up before descending the broad staircase to face her new family.

"Now, I show you the way," said Jacinta, directing Meriel towards a room from which the low murmur of voices could be heard. As she stood for a moment on the threshold, the voices faded to silence as first one group then another turned to see who had just entered and realised it was at last the person they had all been waiting for. Slowly, but more quietly than before, the conversation picked up again.

"Meriel, my dear." Vivienne made her way over to her. "I hope you found your room satisfactory?"

"Oh, yes, thank you. It's lovely."

Vivienne summoned one of the waitresses hired for the reception. "What will you have to drink? Sherry? Red or white wine?"

"Just Perrier water, please," Meriel replied, helping herself from the tray.

"Come," said Vivienne without further preamble. "I want to introduce you to Edward."

She led the way through the groups of guests, who turned and fell silent at their approach. Several reached out to take Vivienne's arm, to offer their sympathy, but she brushed them aside, indicating that she would speak to them later.

"He's in the conservatory," she told Meriel. "We thought he'd be quieter in there, away from all these people."

As they entered the conservatory through one of the three sets of french doors that occupied one entire wall of the drawing-room, an elderly woman stood up from her chair and spoke to the man in the wheelchair beside her.

"Mr Barton," she said softly. "Mr Barton! There's someone here to see you. Someone you've been looking forward to meeting very much."

"As I expect Simon told you, Edward has no speech," Vivienne said, kissing her husband lightly on the temple, "but Miss Digby assures me he understands certain things . . . we don't really know."

"I've told him all about you," said Miss Digby to Meriel, "and I know how much it means to him to have you here . . ."

She stopped, halted by Vivienne's irritable frown and the sharp turn of her head. Clearly, Edward's wife did not like the nurse putting words into her husband's mouth. Trying not to flinch at the sight of the lop-sided, motionless features, Meriel leaned down to take the old man's hands in hers.

"I'm so sorry about Simon," she began. "I really am . . . so . . ." but she was too close to tears, and could not go on. In any case, she could not have found the words with which to communicate with this shell of a man. A tiny, almost imperceptible pressure on her hands caused her to look up at Edward's face in surprise. A moment ago she had thought there was nothing but blankness in his expression and she had been on the verge of forgetting this was still a human being. Now she clearly discerned sadness and compassion in the paralysed features. Tears were beginning to trickle down the old man's cheeks and the pressure on her hands increased. There was no doubt that he understood what had happened to his eldest child; and if he understood that, then he must know who she was, too.

"Well," observed Jonathan Fox as Vivienne and Meriel returned to the drawing-room some moments later. "Old Simon picked himself a corker, didn't he?"

Dan Courtney took a sip from his wine glass and gazed in the direction of the two women.

"Yes," was all he answered, after a moment.

The two men – the one tall and sleek and fair, the other darker and slighter – stood by the vast marble fireplace that was almost as tall as they were and surveyed the scene before them.

"I noticed you weren't slow to ingratiate yourself with the new Mrs Barton," continued Jonathan oilily.

"What are you talking about?" demanded Dan, with just a hint of irritability in his voice.

"Back there in the church. That gallant leap of yours across the aisle . . ."

"She nearly fell, Jon! What do you take me for? We've only just buried Simon, for God's sake!"

"So? You and Simon never got on particularly well, as I recall."

"We had our differences, certainly. But I always respected him, you know that."

"You could afford to, couldn't you? Vivienne always listens to you rather than to her own sons."

"If Vivienne has ever followed my advice it's because she knows it's sound. Anyway, whose side are you on? I'd have thought it was in your interests to make sure Amberfield is run as profitably as possible."

"Ah! But some of us aren't convinced that Amberfield *is* being run as profitably as it might be. In my opinion – " he broke off, interrupted by the arrival of a neighbour, Bryan Talbot.

"Sad business," said Talbot, shaking his head and snatching a full glass of sherry from a passing tray. "Very sad. By the way, does anyone know exactly how it happened?"

Jonathan shrugged. "All I know is that Simon's car went off the road. He was driving to the airport to catch a plane back to his beautiful wife when – *crrumph*."

"Sad. Very sad," repeated Talbot. "By the way, Jonathan," he continued. "Talking of beautiful wives, where is Bella today?"

"Couldn't make it, I'm afraid," said Jonathan. "She's still with her mother in Bermuda." Then, as Bryan moved away, he added so that only Dan could hear: "I notice *you* didn't see the need to enquire after Bella's whereabouts."

26

Dan took a slow, deliberate sip from his glass before replying coolly: "If you remember, I was with you when you passed on Bella's apologies to Vivienne."

"Ah!" The fact that this was the truth did not soften the dangerous edge in Jonathan's voice. He seemed on the brink of saying something more, then apparently decided against it. "Well," he said eventually. "Mustn't stand around exchanging pleasantries all day. Time for a little circulating, I think. Let's see if I can't bring a smile to poor old Hatta's mournful *visage*. What do you think, Daniel? Is your pretty little cousin ready for something a little more interesting than a cello between her legs? Or is she still too deliciously young?"

Dan did not reply. With a familiar mixture of amusement and annoyance, he watched the other man walk away. The irksome thing was that Jonathan Fox, family lawyer and long-time friend of the Bartons, probably would succeed in comforting Hatta where others – including Dan himself – had failed. Earlier, when he had tried to say something sympathetic to her, he had found it impossible to break out of the bantering, half-flirtatious manner in which he habitually addressed his young cousin. From her response, he knew at once that he had disappointed her. Hatta, her eyes again brimming with tears, had turned away and left him in mid-sentence.

Now she was sitting alone on one of the pale blue sofas that normally clustered around the fireplace, but which on this occasion had been pushed back against the drawing-room walls to allow more standing room. She stared disconsolately about her, and at first refused to acknowledge Jonathan when he sat down beside her, pressing a glass of wine into her hands. But before long she was talking to him in earnest close-up, and allowing him to tuck a strand of hair back into place behind her ear. Dan would have liked to know what the lawyer found to say to this gawky, gangling fifteen-year-old. More urgently, he wondered what lay behind his comment about Bella.

27

"Dan!" Vivienne slid her arm through his and led him across the room. "Let me introduce you to Meriel."

The man at Amberfield Church, thought Meriel; the cousin whose presence at Amberfield Simon had so resented.

"How do you do?" she murmured politely, surprised that she did not immediately, instinctively, share her husband's mistrust of Amberfield's winemaker. She had thought she and Simon agreed about almost everything, yet even from behind the plate-glass wall of misery that separated her from other people, it seemed to her that Daniel Courtney was not instantly loathsome.

Dan was equally polite in his reply and, if anything, even warier than she was. As a result, she could not tell if his expressions of sympathy were sincerely meant.

What remarkable eyes she had, thought Dan. At first glance they appeared similar in colour to Simon's, though a paler shade of hazel-brown. But it was those greenish flecks you saw when you looked into them closely that distinguished them so.

"How long will you be staying at Amberfield?" she heard him ask.

"I . . . I don't really know. It's all been so sudden. I haven't had time to sort things out." She felt close to tears again.

Dan seemed to be having difficulty dragging his eyes away from Meriel, a fact of which he was unaware until something in Vivienne's tone when she spoke warned him:

"Meriel doesn't have a home of her own at the moment," she said firmly. "She is to stay with us until she finds somewhere suitable. We believe that is what Simon would have wanted."

That night, when the formalities were all over and everyone had gone home, Meriel dined with the Barton family for the first time. They ate in the dining-room – oak-panelled, like all the ground-floor reception rooms – in an

28

atmosphere of subdued tension. The courses, served on antique hand-painted, gold-rimmed plates in a pretty pale green and peach design, followed one another without anyone paying much attention to what they were eating.

Much to Meriel's surprise, Edward was brought in his wheelchair to sit with the family through dinner, though he himself did not eat. Hadn't the old man had enough for one day, she wondered? But she had to admit he did not look particularly stressed, and Miss Digby appeared to care for her charge extremely efficiently. Edward's dark suit fitted him well, and the silver hair was neatly trimmed and combed. From time to time he would utter an unintelligible sound, or would appear to nod his head, and Vivienne would turn towards him politely, while Miss Digby occasionally hazarded an interpretation, but Meriel found it impossible to guess whether Edward was genuinely attempting to say something or whether the sounds he made were purely involuntary.

Dan, who, Meriel learned, lived in one of the cottages on the estate, dined with them on this occasion, though it seemed he did not regularly do so. He sat opposite Meriel, saying little but, she felt, seeing everything. Something about him – his watchfulness, perhaps – bothered her, though she was not sure why. More than once, when she let the conversation float around her and drifted off into her own thoughts, she was brought back to reality by the realisation that Dan's eyes were upon her, coolly, appraisingly.

"Mother tells me you're staying on here until after Christmas," said Adam, from further up the table.

"Well . . . I . . ." began Meriel. She would have preferred it if Vivienne had discussed the matter with her first, instead of going round telling everyone that this was how it would be. "I sold my flat when Simon asked me to marry him," she started to explain. "So for the moment I don't actually have anywhere to live."

"I expect in due course you'll start missing the bright

lights of London," said Vivienne, "but in the meantime we've more than enough space for you here. Adam and Sophie have The Lodge, you know."

Meriel thought that Simon had mentioned this fact, though what and where the building was remained a mystery to her. Closer questioning revealed that The Lodge originally belonged to another house – far bigger and grander than Amberfield – that had once, two centuries ago, stood on adjoining land but which had subsequently been destroyed by fire.

"The Bartons were wealthy people in my grandfather's day," Adam explained, "so when The Lodge and its grounds came onto the market the family was able to snap up a bargain."

"Just as well," put in Dan. "As I understand it, Amberfield had very little acreage of its own. For example, all the vineyards are on land that belonged to the old house."

The conversation threatened to come to a full stop, and Meriel struggled to find something to say.

"I really am very grateful to all of you for having me," she said eventually. "And for giving me the chance to get to know Simon's family."

Perhaps it was only to be expected that her husband's relatives should react warily to her. They were every bit as shocked and distressed by Simon's death as she was, and there was bound to be some lingering resentment at the fact that he had kept their relationship secret until the last moment. All the same, Meriel could not help feeling it would have been nice if one of them could have taken her aside and told her how pleased they were to know her, how much they appreciated the fact that she had brought Simon such happiness in what turned out to be his last months.

Looking up from her plate, she saw Hatta staring at her and forced a weak smile. But the girl who only hours ago had let her head be stroked while she sobbed her heart out, looked away sharply. Even Adam, who was so like his brother that Meriel thought he was bound to find her to his liking, just as Simon had, was clearly finding it difficult to make polite conversation.

"When are you and Sophie getting married?" Meriel asked him.

"Not for some time yet," replied Adam. "It looks like being early September, doesn't it, darling?"

"I think that is the best for my family," replied Sophie. She threw Meriel a small shy smile, full of genuine warmth. "So long as it is not during the *vendange*, or nobody will come!"

"The *vendange*?" queried Meriel.

"When we pick the grapes. Usually it is later in September."

"I hadn't realised your family were wine-growers too," said Meriel, wishing that the burden of making conversation had not fallen upon her.

"That is correct, yes. My family lives in Provence."

"I suppose things are done differently at Amberfield from the way they are in Provence?" she hazarded.

"Too right, they are," exclaimed Adam, in a tone which took Meriel by surprise and caused Vivienne to look up sharply.

"Of course, in our vineyards it is very different," replied Sophie pleasantly. "But just because we have the sunshine, and because we have made wine for many, many years, you must not think that is always easy for us. We too have our problems. Particularly with the common market, and with the wine lake . . ." she concluded, making swimming movements with her arms.

Dan, doubtless aware of the perplexed look on Meriel's face, spoke up at this point.

"Much of the wine being produced in Provence and Roussillon – and in parts of Italy for that matter – has traditionally been of poor quality. It was fetching very low prices because no one wanted to drink it, and much

31

of it ended up being thrown away after sitting around in the wine lake for months on end. So eventually the EEC had no option but to bring in tighter controls to improve the quality of the wines. The results, incidentally, have been spectacular."

"Can't see the sense in all these regulations, myself," said Adam. "People like Sophie's grandfather always managed to make a good enough living in the past. There were no complaints then about the quality of the wine. They just got on with it and drank the stuff."

"In the old days, before all the new machinery and new ways of prolonging the life of a wine, someone like Sophie's grandfather could only grow a small quantity of grapes, relatively speaking. There was enough demand locally for him to make an adequate living and everybody was happy. But things have changed. These days, the customer is rather more discerning."

"Still I preferred it when we could do what we wanted," insisted Sophie. "You know, I do not like all these rules, all these people who check on what we do, and who want to see exactly how we make each bottle of wine!"

"Sophie, surely you of all people must understand that a country like France simply cannot afford to develop a reputation for producing nothing but a lot of low-quality wines? Whatever my own reservations about the EEC's regulations, you've got to admit that some of them have been for the best. At least those growers who are willing to improve the quality of their product are being given every assistance."

"And what about here in England?" continued Meriel. "Do we have to obey the same EEC regulations?"

"Not all of them, no," replied Dan. "Though presumably we will have to in due course. For the moment the UK is rated as a small producer, which means that we're exempt from controls on what type of vine we're allowed to grow, for instance. But we're getting dangerously close to the limit of what we're allowed to produce, after which everything will presumably change."

"As a matter of interest – how do our wines compare with the ones Sophie's family are making?"

Alone among those gathered in the dining-room, Meriel was unaware that she had used the word "our". There was a short silence before anyone answered, then Adam said curtly:

"Quite frankly, at the moment we don't know what sort of wine we're producing – "

"Adam, please!" interrupted Vivienne, warningly.

But Adam ignored her and continued: "Some years ago our winemaker in his wisdom decided we should replace our original planting of Müller-Thurgau vines with a whole load of more fashionable varieties."

He endowed the word "fashionable" with the deepest contempt, provoking an instant rejoinder from Dan.

"It wasn't a question of being fashionable, Adam. It was a matter of growing the right vines on the right soil. As you will discover when we harvest the first of the new grapes next autumn."

"There was nothing much wrong with the old ones, if you ask me," said Adam. "We've always managed to make a perfectly adequate wine – as you can taste for yourself," he added, raising his glass in Meriel's direction.

Meriel, remembering the pride with which Simon had poured her first glass of Amberfield wine, sipped the drink before her.

"It certainly tastes all right to me," she agreed.

"All right isn't good enough, I'm afraid," said Dan. "If we want to survive, we simply cannot afford to let other producers overtake us in quality."

"That's rubbish, Dan – " began Adam angrily, then stopped as Hatta sprang up from her chair and ran out of the room.

"Adam! Daniel!" This time Vivienne barely succeeded in keeping her voice under control. "That's enough, do you hear me? This is neither the time nor the place, as both of you should know."

The atmosphere had suddenly turned from muted sorrow to undisguised anger. Meriel, aware that she had played an unwitting part in sparking off this display of hostilities, saw that Adam's eyes were fixed on Vivienne. In turn, she was staring down the table with anger in her eyes. Then Miss Digby laid her napkin on the table and pushed back her chair.

"Come along now, Mr Barton," she said, manoeuvring the wheelchair between sideboard and dining table and making for the door. "It's well past your bedtime, and we've all had a difficult day. Say good night to everyone, Mr Barton."

A sound, more like a croak than any recognisable word, issued from Edward's lips.

"There. He's said good night to you all," said Miss Digby.

"Good night, Edward." Vivienne rose and kissed her husband, adding, with a sad half-smile: "Sleep well, darling."

Was he trying to say good night, or was there something else he would have liked to express? wondered Meriel as the old man was wheeled away. It seemed to her that there were clear signs of agitation in Edward's demeanour and she felt certain he had understood the discussion round the dinner table and that he would have liked to make a contribution.

As she lay in bed unable to sleep, she wondered at herself for being able to sit at table with others, and eat and carry on a normal conversation on this of all days. She was aware that, almost for the first time since Simon's death, she had been thinking about something other than her grief, and the realisation caused her to feel momentarily guilty. Yet the fact remained that things at Amberfield were not as she had expected them to be. Beneath the surface of Amberfield's seemingly unruffled calm she

34

could sense rivalries and tensions that went far beyond the Barton brothers' dislike for their upstart cousin.

Was it her fault that she had failed to realise what lay in store for her? Had she neglected to ask the right questions? Or had Simon, for whatever reason, chosen to keep the facts from her?

She turned over with a sigh. What did it matter, in any case? The Bartons might be too well-bred to speak their minds openly, but they could not have made it plainer that they were opening their home to her under sufferance. Come the New Year she would be back in London; back at her frenetic, highly paid job on the trading floor at Vere Lassiter, the job that Rory Lassiter had already told her was hers for the asking.

Dan opened the door of his cottage and watched as the dogs shot out past him and were lost to view in the dark. After a moment, he decided he too could do with one last walk before bedtime and, pulling on his Barbour, followed the two black-and-white pointers down the lane.

Outside, all was quiet. The cold wind that had earlier chilled the mourners outside Amberfield Church had now died away; instead, there was a smell of rain in the air, heightening the odour of decaying leaves. Whistling quietly to the dogs, Dan wandered in the direction of Amberfield House, stopping only when he saw its dark shape looming against the slightly paler sky. There were no lights visible; Dan could imagine that all its inhabitants were exhausted by the events of the day, though how many of them lay awake miserably remembering Simon Barton was impossible to know.

When he reached the trunk of the great oak downed in the hurricane that destroyed almost a fifth of the woodlands of Kent, Dan sat down and peered through the dark towards the house he had first visited almost thirty years ago.

*   *   *

35

One of his clearest and most abiding childhood memories dated from the time when he was taken to Amberfield to bid farewell to his Aunt Vivienne and Uncle Edward before he and his parents emigrated to Australia. The visit had been memorable for two main reasons. The first was the unexpected emotion displayed by both Vivienne and Dan's father, Philip, in the face of their forced separation. Until then, Dan had not been aware how close brother and sister were, and however much they protested that they would see each other once a year, they knew deep down this was unlikely to happen. The distance and the expense were simply too great.

Even at that early stage in his life – Dan was not quite four at the time – he had the impression that, but for his mother's insistence, the family would have remained in England. Later, he discovered that this was indeed the case. It seemed that Sylvia had grown tired of living in a small, undistinguished house on the outskirts of Northampton. She was also bored with her marriage to a secondary school teacher with little in the way of prospects. To her, Australia represented a new and exciting challenge, one which she believed would give her life new meaning. Once she had set her heart on emigrating, nothing – and certainly not Philip – could change her mind. Then as always, what Sylvia wanted, Sylvia got.

After lunch, when the grown-ups adjourned to the drawing-room for coffee, Dan went off and explored the house. Quite simply, he had never seen anything like it, and to his young eyes it seemed to go on for ever. Seven, eight, nine bedrooms . . . he could not believe his uncle and aunt lived all alone in this place of deep, many-paned windows and not just one but two stone-flagged kitchens, one for the cooking and one for the washing up.

"Believe me, it won't seem half so big when Viv has her baby," Sylvia told her son in response to his amazed questions.

"What baby?" he had demanded, crossly, not realising he was jealous.

"Vi*vienne* is going to have a child, Dan," said his father, stressing the extra syllables in his sister's name. "Very soon, as a matter of fact. I'm only sorry we shall have gone by then."

"Dad," Dan had asked, instantly putting the baby out of his mind. "Is our new house going to be like Auntie Vivienne's?"

"Hah!" Philip had been vastly amused. "No, son, I'm afraid not! Unfortunately for us, there aren't too many Queen Anne houses down under. I think Queen Elizabeth II will be more our style."

Not for the first time, Dan Courtney cursed the bad luck that had led to his present impecunious, dependent lifestyle, when what he craved was the freedom to live his life exactly as he chose. *If* only his father had not died before he had the chance to make a success of his new life in Australia; if only he had not had to sell the family home so as to keep Sylvia, now suffering from Alzheimer's disease, in a decent nursing home.

But more than that, if only he had not lost everything – Laura, the house he had struggled so hard to buy, the first crop from the first vineyard he had planted – through his own appalling stupidity! After the house and the land and the vineyard had been sold, all for far less than their actual value, and when his considerable debts had all been paid off, Dan was brought face to face with the fact that, in order to live, he would have to seek paid employment. It was with a mixture of desperation and resentment, therefore, that he wrote to his uncle and aunt telling them he was intending returning to England, and asking if they needed an extra pair of hands at Amberfield.

To his relief and surprise, Vivienne telephoned almost immediately, telling him that Edward was in hospital recovering from a stroke, and that she would be delighted to employ her nephew. The salary would be low, she warned him, but a cottage was available for his sole use. She did not know it, but she did not need to offer blandishments. By then, Dan was desperate. Desperate enough not to inform Vivienne of the true reason for the failure of his first and last, vitally important harvest; nor did he admit to her that his dream was to build up the country's most successful wine-growing business before starting up once more in his own right.

But what were the chances of this dream becoming reality now that Simon was gone and Adam had automatically moved into a position of greater power? Adam was slower to come to a decision than Simon; more guarded; or perhaps more secretive, thought Dan. Like his brother before him, Adam bitterly resented Dan's influence over Vivienne and would be sure to try and thwart him at every turn. Things had never been easy for Dan at Amberfield: now they seemed set to become even harder.

Rising and stretching his lean limbs, he made his way back to the cottage, whither the dogs had long since returned. To his surprise, he found them already asleep in front of the remains of the living-room fire. On hearing him enter, they raised their heads briefly and Kipper, the younger of the two, thumped his tail weakly against the floor, causing the brass fender to rattle. Dan, who did not remember leaving the front door open, checked that it was now closed and locked and made his way up the narrow stairs to the bedroom, a slow smile beginning to crinkle his eyes and relax his mouth. Funny, though. He hadn't noticed the car.

The moment he opened the bedroom door he knew he was right: there was someone here already, waiting for him. Moving softly across to the bed he switched on the bedside light, at which the expression of mock-surprise on his face turned to one of genuine astonishment. No wonder there had been no car!

"Hatta!" he said in a tone of gentle exasperation,

catching sight of her intense brown eyes gleaming at him over the edge of the duvet.

"It's absolutely freezing in here," she said, wriggling out of her nightie and throwing a pair of red-and-white striped bedsocks onto the floor. "Thank goodness you've come at last."

"Sweetheart, what *are* you doing in my bed at this time of night?"

"I've come to a decision," she said, the nervous shake to her voice belying the confidence of her words.

"Oh?" Dan smiled in spite of himself. "And what decision might that be?"

"I'm sick of being a virgin," Hatta informed him. "And I've chosen you to do something about it."

3

Waking shortly before eight, Meriel lay for a while in the unfamiliar bed, listening for the sounds of a house coming to life. When she heard voices, and a distant door closing, she rose and wandered listlessly about her room. She seemed unable to make the slightest decision. What clothes should she wear? Should she bathe or shower? What did it matter either way?

She crossed to the window and pulled back the curtains and gazed, at first unseeingly, at what lay beyond. Spread out before her under the grey morning sky were lawns, a flower-bed or two and, beyond these, chalky Kentish hills studded with sheep and crowned with trees. Now at last she began to experience a reaction, as the contrast between this peaceful scene and the sight that normally met her eyes on weekday mornings made itself felt.

In Battersea, her bedroom window gave onto a high redbrick building identical to the one she lived in. During the morning rush hour the air in the narrow street that separated the two blocks of flats was thick with exhaust fumes, and the growl of traffic could be heard above the sound of running bathwater or BBC radio commentary. Yet most mornings she braved the cars and the pollution and set off early for a run around Battersea Park. If she enjoyed the exercise under those conditions, she thought, how much more pleasurable it would be here.

The urge to run, to breathe clean cold air, came over her in a rush. She pulled on tracksuit and running shoes and, moments later, let herself out of the house via

40

the kitchen door. She found herself in a large cobbled courtyard flanked on the left by the converted stables which served as garaging for the family's several cars and, on the right, by a former oasthouse which now clearly doubled as something else.

Although the two round oast chimneys with their slanting cowls still remained, and the white-painted timber cladding that covered the building's upper half was clearly original, it appeared that the structure had been considerably extended in recent times. New-looking double doors, made of steel, were not merely closed, but padlocked, Meriel noticed as she came closer, and there were no windows through which she could peer to find out what the building was used for.

A sign on the wall pointed towards the "Vineyard Shop"; walking in the direction indicated, she saw she was standing in front of a spacious two-storey barn whose door, even at this early hour, stood open. Entering, Meriel found herself in a bare, stone-floored room containing a desk, a chair, a telephone and precious little else. *Some shop!* she thought, although she supposed it was possible the wine-tasting happened elsewhere and customers merely settled their bills in these uninspiring surroundings.

A door led from the shop into another room, and as Meriel pushed it open she was startled to see an elderly, white-haired man perched on the edge of a table, engrossed in his morning paper.

"Oh, I'm sorry!" she exclaimed. "I didn't realise there was anyone here!"

"Jethro Weston," said the man, sliding off the table and holding out a brown, wrinkled hand. "Mr Courtney's assistant." His bright blue eyes were in stark contrast to his weatherbeaten face, and his smile was among the most infectious Meriel had ever seen.

"And I'm Meriel Barton."

"Yes, I know," said Jethro simply. "We saw you at the

church, my wife and I. You can't know how sorry we both are about Simon."

"Thank you."

"Were you wanting something?" asked Jethro. "Or are you just finding your way around?"

Meriel smiled. *Right first time!* she thought. "I saw the sign to the Vineyard Shop," she explained. "So I decided to take a look."

"Well, it's not much of a shop, as shops go," said Jethro. "Michelle – that's the girl who comes in from the village to help out – she does her best, but the place really needs taking in hand. As things are we're missing out on a lot of sales."

"And this room here?" asked Meriel.

"This is Adam's office. It's where they keep the invoices and all the other paperwork."

A single four-drawer filing cabinet, thought Meriel. Again, the room was furnished in the bare minimum. It was beginning to look as though business at Amberfield was not exactly booming.

Retracing her steps across the courtyard, Meriel rounded the old stable block and made her way through the walled kitchen garden that adjoined the east wing of Amberfield House, breaking into an easy, fluid run as she passed the rows of Brussels sprouts and late cabbages. The last of the outdoor tomatoes were ripening on plants whose yellowing leaves awaited the first frosts of the year before dying back altogether, and Meriel saw that rows of polythene tunnels, possibly used for bringing on early salad crops, were being dismantled and cleaned in preparation for the winter.

An arched entranceway in the high walls led her out of the kitchen garden and onto a lane, muddy after the previous night's rain. She passed a couple of greenhouses, in one of which grew a large vine heavy with small pale-green fruit. To her inexperienced eye, they looked like the muscat grapes she had so often enjoyed in France and Italy: at any rate she felt reasonably certain that these were a table variety, and would not be turned into wine.

Above her, the low grey clouds were breaking up, revealing occasional glimpses of a weak, pale sun. Meriel breathed deeply, regularly, astonished that she was able to enjoy the therapeutic quality of the exercise as she followed the lane upwards between greenhouses and other outbuildings. Soon she had left Amberfield House behind her, and found she was running along the ridge of a hill, with distant views to either side. Ahead of her she could see some woods, and smoke rising from a lone chimney.

Paussing to catch her breath at the summit of the ridge, she looked around her, admiring the view. To the north lay a steep pasture in which grazed a herd of cows, their breath rising in clouds in the cold morning air. Beyond them, about halfway up another hill, stood a house, smaller than Amberfield, and painted white. She guessed this must be The Lodge, Adam and Sophie's home, though she could not be sure. A maroon car, almost certainly a Jaguar, was speeding along the road that led away from the white house, and Meriel followed it with her eyes until she saw it swing into the drive at Amberfield, clearly visible from her elevated position. Was this Adam, she wondered, paying a visit to his mother?

She turned to discover what lay to the south. What she saw caused her to draw in her breath sharply. Before her, sloping gently away until halted by a broad, tree-lined stream, lay the Amberfield vineyards. Whatever Meriel had expected to see, her initial reaction was one of disappointment. The Bartons might well be among the biggest wine-growers in England, but compared to the vast expanses given over to grapes in France or in the Napa Valley in California, this was pretty unimpressive stuff. True, the vines were planted in regimented rows and supported on smart galvanised wires but most of the leaves had already fallen from the straggling canes and the plants had an unkempt, neglected air.

43

Leaving the muddy lane, and making her way down through the serried rows, she saw that the field consisted of two large blocks of identical-looking vines interspersed with smaller quantities of other varieties. Closer attention to the handwritten labels attached to the plants revealed that whereas many of the grapes had names she knew – Chardonnay and Riesling, for example – there were a great many more with which she was unfamiliar. She was unsure what to make of Gagarin Blue, for one, or the many varieties as yet unnamed and referred to only by a number.

Suddenly struck by the depths of her ignorance, she wished Simon could be with her to answer her questions. For despite the early morning chill and the numbing air of unreality that hung over much of what she did, she realised to her surprise that the vineyard was exerting a strong fascination over her. At that moment, a glimmer of pale sunlight, illuminating the slope before her, created a sensation of warmth – real or imaginary, Meriel could not tell – that caused her to stop in her tracks. Closing her eyes for a moment, she could almost believe it was deep summer, with the swollen grapes hanging on the vines and the drowsy hum of bees filling the air.

A sudden noise brought her back to reality. Opening her eyes and looking about her in alarm, she was relieved to see that it was nothing more serious than Hatta, running along the lane in the direction of Amberfield House. Did she jog too, Meriel wondered, setting off back up the field at a gentle trot? When she reached the ridge, she debated calling Hatta's name, but hesitated, remembering the girl's coolness towards her. Then, all thoughts of attracting her attention were dispelled when she saw that Hatta, apart from the seemingly obligatory Doc Martens, was wearing nothing but a white nightdress, though she seemed to be clutching a pair of stripy socks in one hand. Meriel decided she must have got her feet wet. As the girl sped away from her down the muddy lane, her straight blonde hair flying behind her, the outline of her naked, skinny body was clearly visible through the thin fabric.

Amused, Meriel wondered what on earth Hatta was doing out of the house at this hour of the morning, wearing such unsuitable clothing. What could be so compelling that anyone would risk catching pneumonia for it? Knowing that she was unlikely to find the answer to her question, she nevertheless set off along the lane in the direction of the woods, running properly now, lengthening her stride and ignoring the muddy splashes that marked her tracksuit.

Had it not been for the flurry of dogs racing down the path towards her, barking excitedly, Meriel might almost have missed the cottage hidden behind its high rhododendron hedge. As it was, the dogs brought her to a halt by blocking her way, tails wagging in welcome, close to a small, rickety gate that opened into a dripping front garden. Just as Meriel realised whose home this was, and tried to move away out of sight, the front door opened and Dan appeared on the threshold, calling to the dogs to be quiet and come indoors.

Suddenly catching sight of Meriel, Dan looked at her in surprise.

"I'm sorry . . . I didn't realise there was anyone here . . ." he began.

Why else would the dogs be barking, thought Meriel, unless . . .

"I was just out for a run," she explained. "I like to get some exercise before breakfast."

"Do you, now?" said Dan, a slight smile crinkling the corners of his eyes. "That sounds like an excellent idea . . ."

Meriel, uncertain what to make of his tone, turned away. "I must be getting back," she said tamely. "Jacinta said she'd make some coffee . . ."

"Wait!" Dan was pulling on his Barbour and closing the

door. "I'm just on my way to the house myself. Let me walk you back."

"Well, I . . ." Meriel had no choice but to submit. But, not for the first time, his presence bothered her, and she was annoyed with herself for being bothered. With Simon, she had always felt at ease; comfortable; safe in the knowledge that this was the right place to be. Already she was beginning to hope that being friends with Adam would give her the same sense of security.

Dan, however, made her nervous. Whether intentionally or not, he managed to convey disapproval in the way he addressed her and looked at her. She had noticed that critically appraising look in his eyes the previous evening at dinner, and she felt it was undeserved. What did Dan Courtney know about her, beyond the fact that she had, briefly, been Simon Barton's wife? What right did he have to judge her, if that was what he was doing, when only moments ago she had seen Hatta emerging from his cottage? Or had she imagined what she saw?

Glancing sideways at his lean, serious face, she let her eyes travel down to the hand – tanned, well-shaped – fidgeting with the edge of something stuffed loosely into his pocket. With a shock, she saw it was a red-and-white sock; without doubt it was the pair to the one Hatta had been clutching.

So, she thought, her suspicions were correct. Hatta had indeed visited Dan in his home. What was she to make of that? The girl was no more than fifteen – a child still. Even if she was infinitely more mature than she appeared, it was surely unthinkable that she had spent the night in Dan's bed. And as for Dan – was he the kind of man to take advantage of a girl that young? Apart from any considerations regarding Hatta herself, such behaviour would be a monstrous betrayal of his employer's trust. No, she decided. She must be making a mistake.

She stole another quick glance at Dan's face, but the strong features gave little away. Even if he were wholly

46

innocent of the deed of which she suspected him, he might at least have the grace to look sheepish! It must be obvious to him that she had seen Hatta and that she would draw certain conclusions. But of course the truth, as Meriel already realised, was that Dan simply didn't care what she thought. He looked up now, and the hint of a lazy smile seemed to be hovering around his mouth. If he had had Hatta in his bed last night, he was certainly showing no remorse.

When they reached the cobbled courtyard, they parted politely, with the minimum of words. Meriel strode swiftly towards the kitchen door while Dan continued on his way to the converted barn that served as office, boardroom and shop. On his way there, he stopped to peg Hatta's sock to a clothes line.

The following Sunday Adam drove Hatta back to her girls' boarding-school for the last weeks of term and Meriel breathed a sigh of relief. She found it hard to work out whether she was merely turning into a prim and prudish 24-year-old who had completely lost touch with modern youth, or whether she was in fact genuinely concerned for Hatta's well-being. After all, Hatta didn't like *her* particularly. She wondered whether she should tell someone – Vivienne? Adam, maybe? – what she had seen, but in the end she found she could not do so. She had no proof of anything untoward, for a start, and she was loath to upset or antagonise the family at this delicate time.

Over the next few days Meriel began acquainting herself with Amberfield House, though for the time being she concentrated chiefly on the ground-floor area. Apart from her own rooms there was little of interest to her on the first floor, and she was as yet not ready to explore the attic quarters – "the children's floor" – as Vivienne still referred to it, which included Simon's old room.

Although Vivienne had given her a whistle-stop tour of the house the day after her arrival, Meriel had been too dazed to take much in. Now she was remedying the situation. Among her first discoveries was the fact that, whereas the shell of the house was authentically Queen Anne, the interior had been considerably remodelled and extended over the centuries. The conservatory, for instance, had not been added until the mid-1960s, when a small inheritance came Vivienne's way. Two ground-floor music rooms, for performance and practice, had been built between the wars for Edward's grandmother, a violinist of some repute who had presumably passed on her talent to Hatta. When Edward became confined to a wheelchair, it seemed sensible to move him and Miss Digby into these conveniently located rooms, where the various family members visited him daily.

Because of the conservatory and music-room additions, Amberfield House was far more spacious at ground level than in its upper storeys. In its decoration and furnishings it was also far removed from her idea of a working farmhouse. But that, she soon came to realise, was because growing vines had nothing whatsoever to do with farming. It seemed that Edward was unusual among English *vignerons* in having grown a crop previously. As Vivienne had explained to her one evening over dinner, most English vineyards consisted of a mere half-dozen acres worked by retired colonels or City whizz-kids hoping to regain contact with their sanity.

This certainly explained the blue-and-gold drawing-room with its elegantly swagged curtains. It also accounted for the gleaming panelled hallway with its ever-changing bowl of fresh flowers – Christmas roses today, Meriel had noticed. Only the kitchens matched her expectations. Here Jacinta presided over a barn of a room in which an old and much loved Aga, a Victorian built-in dresser and scrubbed pine table held pride of place. The breakfast-room, a scullery twice the size of Meriel's Battersea kitchen and a vast walk-in larder led off from the main

48

room and together this area seemed to Meriel to represent the heart of the house.

As Meriel came to know the house better, she began to find tell-tale signs of the work that had been carried out over the years. Even small details such as door handles and a change in the width of the floorboards struck her as fascinating. She loved the way the various craftsmen had left their own individual imprint on everything they touched, even supposedly humble things like door frames or skirting-boards, and she would wander around admiring a fireplace here, a window-embrasure there, with such delight that she sometimes thought it was just as well Simon had not shown her his home before she agreed to marry him. Had he done so, she might never have known for certain whether she had fallen in love with the man or his house.

By the end of her first week she felt she had seen everything except for the winery, which seemed to remain permanently locked. When she asked if it would be convenient to be shown round, Vivienne promised to organise a tour, but so far she had done nothing about it.

After that first morning, Meriel had worked out a route to the woods which avoided Dan's cottage, and soon fell into the habit of taking her pre-breakfast run whatever the weather. The sense of well-being that came over her as she made her way down the leaf-strewn rides and mossy paths was more than merely physical. Gradually, Meriel felt herself being reborn after the sadness of the past few weeks. Sometimes, passing a holly bush laden with red berries, or touching the nascent, sooty buds of an ash tree, she felt a twinge of regret that she would soon be leaving all this for the noise and congestion of London.

Her early-morning run would be followed by a shower and then breakfast, sometimes alone, sometimes in the company of Miss Digby when she judged that Edward could safely be left unattended for half an hour. Generally, Meriel preferred to be on her own, so that she could read

49

the papers and catch up on the City news in preparation for her return to work, but when Miss Digby breakfasted with her, polite conversation was called for.

"First Monday in the month," remarked the nurse on one occasion early in December, when Meriel had been at Amberfield for almost three weeks.

"Is it?" enquired Meriel. "Does that have some special significance?"

"That's when they have their board meetings," Miss Digby told her.

"You mean here at Amberfield?"

"Over in the barn," Miss Digby answered. "Sometimes you can see the sparks fly a mile off . . ."

"I gathered there were problems . . . what exactly is going on?"

"Well, now. Some of them want to run Amberfield one way, some of them have other ideas. If you catch my meaning."

"Yes, but . . . what precisely is the bone of contention? What was all that the other night about not knowing what sort of wine we're producing?"

Miss Digby dabbed at her mouth with her napkin and leaned forward confidentially.

"If you ask me," she said, "it's that Mr Courtney that's causing all the trouble. I'm not saying he and Mr Simon didn't get on, but . . ."

"But he and Mr Simon didn't get on?" suggested Meriel.

"Well . . . you could say that, I suppose."

"And what about Adam?" asked Meriel. "How does he get on with Dan Courtney?"

"Adam? Well, now . . . Adam is – "

"Adam is right here behind you," said Simon's brother, opening the door to the breakfast room and causing Miss Digby to jump half out of her skin.

"Oh, Mr Adam!" she said, clutching her throat and turning a rather unbecoming shade of crimson. "What a fright you gave us!"

50

"Sorry, Diggers old thing. But we need Meriel over in the new barn. Can you spare us a moment?"

"Of course!" Meriel, surprised at the request, rose and followed Adam from the room. "What's all this about?" she asked as they made their way across the courtyard.

"Nothing remotely serious," said Adam easily. "Just a little matter for you to consider."

Meriel, suppressing a smile, thought she could guess what this "little matter" might consist of. Earlier that week Vivienne had emerged from a meeting with her son in a particularly preoccupied frame of mind. Meriel could tell from her mother-in-law's frequent, appraising glances that she had been one of the subjects under discussion, and she was curious to know what line the conversation had taken.

Vivienne finally gave her a clue.

"Meriel," she said, "Would I be right in thinking that you are having second thoughts about resuming your career?"

Meriel was surprised. "How did you know? I've only just begun to realise that myself!" It was true, yet at the same time she was starting to miss the stimulus that work provided.

"But you are aiming to do *something* in due course?"

"Oh, yes! Definitely! If, for example, there was anything I could do to help out here . . ."

"Yes, yes," murmured Vivienne, vaguely. "We'll have to decide what's to be done for the best."

So! thought Meriel as she climbed the stairs to the boardroom. *They've found a job for me!* There and then she decided that however menial it might be, she would take it, and that even if she was offered a salary, she would work unpaid. She had no need of money: at her request, Rory Lassiter had agreed to invest the proceeds from the sale of her flat, and she knew she could rely on him to provide her with an adequate income.

Adam ushered her into the room where, round a large,

modern table in pale oak, Vivienne sat between Dan Courtney and a man whose face Meriel recognised but to which she was unable to give a name.

"Ah, Meriel," said Vivienne, with a hint of impatience in her voice. "We need to have a word with you. You know Dan, of course, but I believe you have yet to meet Jonathan Fox, our lawyer."

Although Meriel remembered seeing Jonathan at the reception after the funeral, they had not been formally introduced. Jonathan, who had risen to his feet the moment Meriel entered the room, came over and grasped her hand in his, murmuring his condolences. All the while he spoke the approved, expected words, his pale eyes studied her with a calculating coolness. He was sizing her up, Meriel realised. Perhaps he was wondering whether she was capable of handling whatever it was they had in store for her. Feeling suddenly uncomfortable, she pulled her hand away from the lawyer's and sat down in the chair Adam held ready for her.

"It seems we have something of a problem," began Vivienne. "Well, perhaps *problem* is too strong a word for it, but we do have to come to some sort of a decision, and soon. Jon, why don't you explain things to Meriel?"

Jonathan, only too pleased to have an excuse to stare at Meriel, turned his chair fully in her direction.

"As I believe you are already aware, Simon died without making a will."

"Yes, I did know that." Meriel was taken aback by the statement. "We did talk about making our wills. We meant to do it before going on honeymoon, but somehow we never got around to doing anything about it."

"Perfectly understandable," nodded Jonathan. "All the same, the lack of a will does present us with a little difficulty, as Vivienne has mentioned."

"But what difference would a will have made, given that there was so little to pass on?" asked Meriel.

"It's true that Simon did not own his own house,"

replied the lawyer, "and that his banking accounts total no more than two and a half thousand pounds. However, you would appear to be unaware that Edward made over a percentage of the company – by which I mean Amberfield Wines – to each of his sons following his first stroke."

He paused to make sure that Meriel understood him thus far though, given her background in the City, he had a shrewd idea she followed him easily.

"How stupid of me!" exclaimed Meriel. "Yes, of course I always assumed Simon must have some sort of a share in the company." It was only to be expected, she thought, that Edward would have made arrangements to protect his family against death duties. He would have set up a trust in favour of his sons, and would have started making over the company to them. If she and Simon had made their wills, she would have known all about this aspect of his finances. Then, her mind racing on, she added: "Are you saying that I will be liable for inheritance tax on Simon's share of the company? Is that the problem Vivienne referred to?"

Because if so, she was thinking, *it really doesn't matter. I've got the money from the sale of the flat. I can use that to pay the tax!* Jonathan spoke before she had a chance to continue.

"Oh, no!" His laugh was almost dismissive. "Simon's estate is not of a size to incur inheritance tax. You need have no worries on that score."

"Then – " For a moment, Meriel was puzzled. Then the implication of what Jonathan Fox was saying struck her with its full force.

"You mean . . . what you're saying is that I . . .?"

Jonathan Fox smiled slowly.

"That's right," he said. "Following Simon's untimely death, you are at this moment a shareholder and full board member of Amberfield Wines."

"Heavens!" Meriel was temporarily lost for words. She had been expecting to be offered a position of some sort, something temporary and undemanding, but

53

this! "That's . . . really amazing!" was all she could manage.

Amazing, she thought, and rather wonderful. She realised that ever since her arrival she had secretly longed for some reason to be able to stay at Amberfield, and here it was, being handed to her on a plate. But when she looked around the circle of faces, expecting to be met by smiles to match her own, she saw nothing but watchfulness in their eyes. They seemed to be waiting for her to say something, but she did not know what it could be, and the smile slowly froze on her face.

Vivienne, tapping the table impatiently with her pen, spoke up:

"I think, Jon, that I'd better take over at this point. I'm sure Meriel will understand that none of us could ever have foreseen the present situation. Our problem now is that we have a board member who wishes to relinquish her shares. I feel the most satisfactory solution would be to sign over these shares in equal parts to the remaining three board members."

The truth hit Meriel like a blow. *They don't want me here*, she thought. *They just want me to hand over my shares and go!* Her immediate reaction was one of such hurt that she might have meekly agreed to do as they expected had Dan not spoken up.

"You mustn't feel you're in any way obligated to stay. We all understand that a commitment of this sort must be the last thing you'd want right now."

"And that, as it happens, is where you'd be wrong." Meriel was surprised by a small rebellious surge that was beginning to well up inside her, gradually replacing the hurt.

Dan, realising he had misinterpreted Meriel's look of pain, spoke again.

"I'm sorry . . . we simply thought . . . I mean, this isn't exactly the sort of thing you're used to, is it?"

"Perhaps not," agreed Meriel. "But I do think you

54

might have done me the courtesy of asking my opinion first."

"I rather assumed that is what we were doing," put in Vivienne briskly. "But Meriel, really! What is there to discuss? The trust Jonathan referred to just now was intended only to protect the company against crippling inheritance tax. We all understood as much, and that included Simon. I'm quite sure he wouldn't have wanted you to be burdened with the daily business of running Amberfield Wines."

"I disagree!" said Meriel, heatedly. "Simon always said he wanted me to learn about the business. He used to say it was only a matter of time before I caught the winemaking bug, and now that I'm here I'm beginning to think he was right."

Vivienne's expression softened markedly as she listened to Meriel. It was almost as though she caught the echo of her son's voice in the words she had just heard.

"I have to admit, that does sound just like Simon," she said. "Always coming out with bright ideas before giving himself time to think about the consequences! You see, it seems to me you can have no conception of what our work here entails. Growing vines in Britain bears little relation to the sort of thing you've probably seen on television or read about in books. We don't live in a country where the sun shines for weeks at a time, and unlike our Continental friends we get virtually no support from the government. Wine-growing in England means hard work, and a great deal of it. The rewards, I might add, are risibly small."

"I know that!" Meriel assured her. "But in spite of all the problems I can see now that there is something glamorous about growing vines – "

She regretted the words the moment she had spoken them. How naïve she must sound!

"Glamorous!"

The exclamation – half amusement, half ironic disbelief – issued from Dan, who now stretched back in his chair,

55

linking his hands behind his head. Adam raised first his eyebrows and then his shoulders, before slowly shaking his head. Jonathan contented himself with a pitying smile.

"You see?" said Vivienne. "Simon simply did not prepare you for the reality of the situation. Believe me, it would be in your own best interests not to become involved with the company. And it goes without saying that we would pay the going rate for your shares."

Any remaining doubts Meriel harboured were finally dispelled by the murmured agreement that greeted Vivienne's last remark. *How dare they offer me money?* she asked herself. *What right have they to decide my life for me? I've as much right to be here as any of them!* Controlling her anger with difficulty, she turned towards her mother-in-law. "I know I have a lot to learn," she said. "Simon and I may not have discussed the business in detail, but you must understand that we weren't able to see each other every day, and we had so much else to talk about – and anyway, he always said there was plenty of time for all that once we were married. He wanted to show me everything himself, explain everything to me on the spot, so that it meant something to me. If only we'd known we had so little time . . ."

Vivienne sighed deeply. "Yes, yes. Don't distress yourself."

"I think," Jonathan put in tentatively, "that we're in danger of getting away from the point of this meeting . . . and I do have another appointment shortly."

"Meriel." She turned to hear what Adam had to say. "Now don't get me wrong but . . . well, Dan's right, isn't he? This isn't the sort of thing you're used to. I'm not denying your business expertise, but buying and selling Deutschmarks and yen isn't quite the same thing as growing vines. Even if you and Simon had discussed the business *ad nauseam*, you really have no experience that could be . . . well, of any practical use."

"So. Simon's wife – Simon's *widow*," she corrected

herself, "has to have some practical use?" She was openly angry now, but she was also shocked that the others were making so little effort to see her point of view.

"Adam didn't mean it that way," put in Vivienne. "It's just that we feel you'd be happier doing a job you know; a job you've been trained for, and which I'm sure you're very good at. My fear is that you will be so bored here."

Now Meriel understood the reasons for her mother-in-law's questions of a few days ago. There was never any intention of finding something for her to do within the company. Vivienne had simply been hoping that Meriel would take the opportunity to return to London sooner rather than later. But why should she go, she asked herself? She not only wanted to remain at Amberfield, she felt a powerful need to stay. Something told her that if she returned to London now, and resumed her old life as though nothing had happened, she would never get over Simon's death. Only by living in the home she should have shared with Simon, and experiencing life as he had led it, could she hope to heal the deep wounds she had so recently suffered. She would have liked to explain some of this to Vivienne and the others, but she sensed they were not in a mood to listen to her. It seemed safer to stick to practical considerations for the time being.

"If it's all the same with you," she said quietly, "I'd very much like the chance to find out whether I can bring anything to Amberfield Wines. It seems to me that this place could use a bit of business acumen – in particular, the vineyard shop which is, in my view, a complete non-event, and it would give me great pleasure to knock it into shape. What is more, I feel I owe it to Simon to try and make sure his interests are properly represented."

"How dare you!" said Vivienne in sudden anger. "How dare you presume to take over Simon's mantle when you know next to nothing about wine-growing or how we operate here!"

"It's not through want of trying!" exclaimed Meriel.

"I've asked you half a dozen times to give me a conducted tour, but you always manage to find some excuse!"

"Vivienne, calm yourself." This was Jonathan Fox, who placed a restraining hand on her shoulder, preventing her from speaking out again. "As I understand it, the board has no power to compel one of its members to relinquish their holding if they choose not to do so." He turned to Meriel, and added: "Am I to take it that you do in fact wish to hang on to your holding?"

"I . . . yes," replied Meriel, taking a deep breath. "At least for the time being. It was Simon's greatest wish that I should come and live here with him, and learn to love Amberfield as he did, and I think you owe it to him to let me find out for myself what his home means to me. Can't you see that the last thing I want from his family, from you, is money?"

Jon spoke again. "It was perhaps unreasonable of us to expect an instant decision from Meriel, under the circumstances. Would you like some time to think about what has been said?"

"My decision is made," replied Meriel firmly. "What I would appreciate, however, is a look at the documents relating to the setting up of the board, also the company articles, and, in fact, anything that might have a legal bearing on my position here."

This time, Vivienne seemed too startled to be angry. "Er . . . Jonathan?" she asked.

"No problem," said Jonathan smoothly. "I have copies of all the relevant papers in my office. After the Christmas break, as soon as you feel ready, why not give me a call and we can go through them together?"

"Thank you," said Meriel. "I'd like that." Then she turned to Vivienne. "And the shop?" she asked. "How would you feel about me trying to make something of that?"

"Why not?" agreed Vivienne after a pause. As far as she was concerned, the shop was a lost cause, but it was probably no bad thing to give Meriel something to do with her time. "Why don't you give it a try and see how things work out? In the meantime, I realise that I may have spoken in haste earlier on, and I trust you will accept my apology. Now. How about a tour of the winery at, say, ten thirty tomorrow morning? Would that suit you?"

It was a summons as much as a suggestion, but there was no earthly point in turning it down.

"Thank you," she said. "That would suit me very well."

Sophie Meyreuil opened the kitchen door to her fiancé, waited while he cleaned the soles of his shoes on the door-scraper, then kissed him perfunctorily on the lips.

"Hey!" protested Adam. "What sort of a welcome is that?"

"It is the welcome you deserve!" she told him sternly. "For being late for your lunch."

"Darling, I'm sorry. The fact is that the meeting went on a bit." Adam assumed a contrite expression and held out his arms towards her, but she was not yet ready to forgive him.

"Always you say the same thing! Always the meetings go on. When we are living in France, you will miss your lunch altogether if you do not come home at twelve o'clock."

"Ah. Yes. About moving to France," said Adam, shifting uncomfortably.

"What is it, Adam?"

"I think it might be best if we didn't say anything to Mother for the time being. Not while she's still so upset. She needs me here, Sophie."

"Of course you are right!" exclaimed Sophie. "But I hope that does not mean you have changed your mind? Always you have promised me we would go to Provence!"

"No, no, of course I haven't changed my mind. But

I'd rather you kept it from Mother. At least for the foreseeable future."

Adam watched as Sophie ladled soup into bowls – French pottery bowls, with handles – and bent to retrieve a baguette from the oven. As usual, whenever he observed his fiancée practising her astonishing culinary skills, Adam was overcome by a feeling that he did not deserve her. With her delicate, elfin looks she exactly matched his mental picture of his perfect woman and, dressed as she was now in black leggings and a cowl-necked maroon sweater that reached almost to her knees, she struck him as well-nigh irresistible.

He would dearly have loved to suggest abandoning the soup and proceeding directly to their yellow-curtained bed, but he was stopped by the knowledge that she had devoted a considerable amount of time to preparing his lunch. The least he could do was show some appreciation.

"Mmmm!" he exclaimed, tasting the rich, fragrant broth. "Sophie my darling, today you have surpassed yourself."

In spite of herself, she was beginning to smile as she sat down opposite him.

"So," she said. "Tell me about this morning. Did you have a good meeting?"

"Not really," replied Adam, his face clouding over at the memory of it.

"But why? What is wrong?"

Adam broke a chunk off the baguette and began tearing it into smaller pieces.

"In a word, Meriel."

"*Meriel* is wrong?" said Sophie in surprise. "That I do not believe!"

"The thing is that she has inherited Simon's share in the company – "

"Of course she has! But you know that already!"

"What I didn't know before was that she would want

60

to take up her seat on the board," said Adam grimly. "Mother and I, and Jonathan too for that matter, all assumed that Meriel would be only too anxious to sell us her shares and get back to London as soon as possible."

"And now you are saying she will be staying at Amberfield?"

"It rather looks like it."

"But . . ." Sophie gave the matter some thought before continuing in a puzzled voice: "Is that not something good? That Meriel will stay? For me, it is very nice that I have a friend here."

"Darling, I wouldn't be in too much of a hurry to make friends with Meriel if I were you," put in Adam quickly.

This brought a laugh from Sophie. "Not make friends with Meriel? Adam, why do you say that?"

"I just meant – " Adam hesitated and then went on. "She could change her mind, Sophie. Come to think of it, I'm sure she will. So it's probably best if the two of you don't get too chummy."

When Sophie did not reply immediately, Adam looked across at her and saw that she was watching him thoughtfully. With her elbows propped on the table, she was holding the soup bowl in both hands and her face had assumed that expression she had when she did not wholly believe him.

Adam, as always, was devastated by that look. More than anything else he needed Sophie's approval, and could not bear the thought that she might withdraw it if she knew the true reasons for his desire to see his sister-in-law safely off his hands. Still Sophie said nothing, and Adam decided some gesture was necessary on his part.

"Oh, Sophie!" he said at last, in the gruff, affectionate voice that only she had ever heard, and that never failed to win her over. "Forget what I just said. By all means make friends with Meriel. I just wouldn't want you to get hurt, that's all."

Still Sophie said nothing.

61

4

"What a wonderful place!" Meriel stood amazed in the doorway to the winery. The former oasthouse consisted of a spacious, high-ceilinged, white-painted room, into which the light came streaming through the long narrow windows along the far wall.

"Yes, we are lucky," agreed Vivienne, who seemed to have forgotten her anger of the previous day. "Most of our competitors have had to build wineries from scratch, and some of them are frightfully out of keeping with their surroundings. Not only that, but it's wildly expensive to put up any new building nowadays. Don't get me wrong – this one couldn't be described as cheap by any stretch of the imagination. But there you are. It's one of the many risks you have to take if you want to produce wine commercially."

"How old is the building?" asked Meriel.

Vivienne was not sure, saying it had always been assumed that, along with the house itself, the oasthouse dated from Queen Anne's reign. The barn, however, was older – perhaps by a hundred years.

Dan followed the two women indoors and drew the door shut. Then, to Meriel's considerable surprise, he locked it.

"We keep the winery locked at all times," he explained. "Only Vivienne and I have keys – and Customs and Excise, of course."

"You're not serious, are you?" laughed Meriel.

"Oh, yes, completely serious. The tax people have to know exactly – and I mean *exactly* – how much wine is being produced here. You see these tanks – " he gestured at a number of round, ceiling-high metal containers that lined one of the whitewashed walls. "Each of them has a number marked on it – that's how many litres of grape juice we have waiting to be processed. Customs and Excise have free access to any part of the winery at any time – and if at the end of the day the number of bottles we produce doesn't tally with the amount of grape juice, we've got a lot of explaining to do."

"And then I suppose there are all sorts of EEC regulations," said Meriel.

"Actually, no," Dan told her. "But all that's about to change. For the moment the British Isles are classifed as an experimental area in wine-growing terms. But the minute we exceed our quota of 3.3 million bottles we will come under Community rules. I can't say I'm looking forward to it."

Meriel gazed around her at the spotless array of tanks and machinery whose function she could only guess at. The shop, Adam's office, even the vineyard had struck her as worryingly amateurish. This was a different world.

"I was imagining something quite different . . . nothing so high-tech as this!"

"We are well equipped," agreed Vivienne. "Here, for instance . . ." she led Meriel across to the bottling plant which took up the entire width of the building, before listing some of the more puzzling items: "Destrigger – that's for taking stalks and suchlike off the grapes – Vaslin press, this rather splendid old wooden press . . . We're probably rather unusual among English vineyards," she continued, "in that whereas we make most of our wine using the most up-to-date technology, we also produce a couple of rather special vintages which are virtually hand-made, in the old, French way."

"So . . ." began Meriel, "is this where the grapes are brought when they've been picked?"

"That's right," replied Dan. "The grapes are picked

and put through the destrigger before going for pressing. After which the grape juice is sterilised and stored in these tanks."

"Sterilised? You mean, like milk?"

"Ah." Dan smiled at Vivienne before replying. "As it happens, you've hit on one of those questions that are giving us some pause for thought at the moment. Traditionally, the must – "

"Must?" queried Meriel.

"That's the correct name for the grape juice after pressing," put in Vivienne.

"Yes, the must has to be sulphured to kill off various bacteria and wild yeast spores. But . . ."

"But Dan has certain opinions as to how much sulphur dioxide we should actually be adding," remarked Vivienne. "Dan is becoming hooked by the idea of organic wine-growing."

"Oh?" Meriel looked at him with interest. He hadn't struck her as a "green" convert. "Is that actually possible?"

"It's happening all over the place – France, Italy, Germany. Even in England, to a small extent. And believe me, it's where the future lies. Both for health reasons and for the quality of the wines."

"I do hope you're right, Dan," sighed Vivienne. "Otherwise we shall all find ourselves in a very pretty pickle indeed. You could ruin an entire harvest by failing to kill off the wild yeasts . . ."

"Don't you need the yeasts for fermentation?"

"Yes, but what we use is a pure wine yeast. Come. I'll show you."

Selecting another key from the bunch he was holding, Dan led the way to a door at the far end of the winery.

"Downstairs we have the heart of the matter," he said. "This is where the grape juice is turned into wine."

The moment the door was opened, Meriel was assailed

by the unmistakable, heady smell of wine that rose from the fermenting room.

"Isn't it wonderful?" said Vivienne, smiling as Meriel closed her eyes and breathed in the potent, evocative scent. "If it weren't always so wretchedly cold down here there are times when I think I could almost live in the winery."

Meriel gazed about her, taking in the streamlined containers on metal legs, with their round doors like portholes, and their plumbing of taps, gauges and tubes. Beyond them, ranks of smaller yellow fibreglass containers reached almost to the far wall. Their sheer number took her by surprise.

"There's something I don't quite understand," she said. "I thought you told me the vines at Amberfield were too young to be harvested until next autumn. So how come these tanks are all full?"

Dan and Vivienne explained that the vineyards at Amberfield were originally planted with five acres of Seyval Blanc, six acres of Müller-Thurgau, and half an acre each of Chardonnay and Pinot Noir. Without going into details, they told her that the Müller-Thurgau grapes had proved unsatisfactory and had consequently been dug up and replaced with a number of other varieties.

"We now have plantings of Schönburger, Seibel, Triomphe d'Alsace, Léon Millot and Siegerrebe, all of which will be picked for the first time next year," Dan continued. "The thing is, we're experimenting all the time. Depending on how they turn out we'll either increase our plantings or abandon certain varieties. Of course, we still have our original Seyval grapes, God bless them, and they're coming nicely into their prime."

"The Seyval is what keeps us going," put in Vivienne, "though I for one will be very relieved to have the income from the new plantings."

"I assume that means all these tanks are filled with Seyval wine?"

65

"Oh, no, not by a long way!" replied Vivienne. "We get all kinds of grapes sent to us from other vineyards for vinification. Particularly now that Dan's reputation as a winemaker is beginning to spread."

The compliment brought a smile from Dan. "When you consider that it can cost thirty to forty thousand pounds to build a winery, plus probably twice that much for the machinery, you can see why there is such demand for our services."

"And is the liquid in the tanks – the must – is it still fermenting?"

"Ah, well, no, actually. Wine ferments pretty fast – it's all over in two or three weeks – even less sometimes. I've known it to take as little as five days. After that we have to remove it from the tanks leaving the sediment behind – that's known as racking off – then return it to the tanks after they've been cleaned. *That*'s what's in the tanks at present."

"You mean . . . real wine?"

"Yes, if you like. It's sitting in there, developing away, until we feel it's ready to be bottled."

Very carefully, Dan drew off a glassful of murky, opaque liquid and handed it to Meriel.

"Not very pretty, is it? But you just wait. In a few months' time, given a bit of luck and a few good frosts in January, all the tiny particles and hazes in suspension will plummet to the bottom of the tank leaving the wine brilliantly clear. This is our Seyval Blanc, by the way."

Meriel swirled the uninviting-looking liquid around in its glass, trying and failing to imagine it in its bright, clear state. "It sounds like magic," she observed.

Dan's smile was warm, enthusiastic; easy to respond to.

"Yes! That's what I always think! Winemaking *is* like magic. Every year the vines produce their fruit and every year the fruit turns into pure gold . . . or rosé or red, though we don't make so much of the latter."

66

"Dan," said Vivienne. "I have a million and one things I ought to be seeing to. Can I leave you to continue the guided tour?"

"With the greatest pleasure," replied Dan. Turning to Meriel when Vivienne had left, he added: "Now, why don't I show you something really special? Come with me."

Meriel followed him along the new concrete floor to the far end of the winery, past the stainless steel and fibreglass tanks, and round a previously concealed corner. She was in a vaulted room given over partly to traditional oak casks, and partly to tall wooden racks filled with downward-sloping bottles.

"I've seen pictures of these," she said, indicating the racks in surprise. "Surely you don't make champagne, do you?"

"We most certainly do," replied Dan. "Though we mustn't refer to it as champagne. This is Amberfield's very own *méthode champenoise*, or 'traditional method quality sparkling wine' if you prefer. As I mentioned earlier, Edward planted some Chardonnay and Pinot Noir grapes, which are the varieties traditionally used in the making of French champagne."

"And the casks?" she asked. "I didn't realise people still used these!"

"At two hundred quid a throw for a new French cask, which can only be used a limited number of times, not a lot of people do use them. But a wine matured in oak is something quite out of this world. Here, try this."

Taking a tulip glass from a wall-mounted rack, Dan again drew off a small quantity of wine.

"This is our special reserve Seyval," he explained. "In fact, we shan't be bottling this particular wine until June next year, so the flavour has yet to develop, but you might just get some idea of the glories to come."

He handed Meriel the glass. She sniffed at it amateurishly, and breathed in the honeyed aroma, before

67

risking taking a tiny sip. Already the brew was taking on the distinctive smoky flavour that only comes from maturation in oak.

"I always think of Seyval as the UK's Chardonnay," said Dan. "You wouldn't believe how much better it tastes here than in Germany, for example. You'll have to use your imagination to guess how good it will be by next summer – "

"Mmmm."

"Well? What's your verdict."

"Actually, I'm not really qualified to say."

"You don't have to be qualified. What matters is whether you can tell a halfway decent wine from the usual sort of rubbish. And I find that women often have a particularly fine palate. There are a couple of very good women winemakers in this country. Did you know that?"

Meriel, sniffing again at the fragrant liquid, experienced a twinge of unease. Even she could tell that what she was tasting now – and what she had tasted of virtually all the wines made by Dan – was greatly superior to those produced at Amberfield in previous years, when Simon was the winemaker. Why then had Simon (and Adam too, as far as she could gather) been so opposed to Daniel's plans for the company? Surely they would have instinctively wanted only the very best for Amberfield? The answers to her unspoken questions seemed to point towards criticism of Simon's decisions, and this was something Meriel was not prepared to tolerate from Dan Courtney.

"I'm sure it will be lovely," she said brightly, handing back the glass. "Really delicious. And thank you for showing me round."

"My pleasure entirely," said Dan, walking her back up the stone steps and towards the winery door. "If ever there's anything else you'd like me to explain . . ."

"Thanks," she said, "but I'm sure you're always very

busy. I can always ask Adam if there's something I don't understand."

Dan raised his eyebrows slightly. "Adam? Well, I wouldn't say he was the world's most knowledgeable wine-grower . . ."

"Whereas you are, I suppose?"

"Adam sees to the financial side of the business. He has his job and I have mine, that's all."

"I am aware of that," said Meriel quietly. Then, after a moment she added. "All the same, I'd appreciate it if you didn't criticise Adam in my presence."

"I'm sorry. I didn't mean to sound critical."

"And while I'm on the subject of my new family," she added, "I think it might be wiser if you kept your hands off Hatta. Particularly as she's your cousin!"

"Pardon me?" said Dan, stepping back in feigned astonishment.

"I'm sure you know exactly what I'm talking about," retorted Meriel, angry that he did not even have the grace to look embarrassed.

"Of course I do," he replied easily. "You're referring to the night young Hatta commandeered my nice warm comfortable bed and made me sleep on the chesterfield. Why?" he added disingenuously. "What *has* that silly girl been telling everybody?"

"She hasn't said anything," replied Meriel, uncomfortably aware that she had probably been jumping to false conclusions. "I just thought . . ."

"Look. Whatever Hatta thought she wanted from me that evening she came to my cottage, I can promise you she was pretty relieved to have her mind changed. And as for her being my cousin, I would have thought that was exactly why she came to me rather than anyone else. Sex between first cousins is legal, you know. But Hatta's not ready for sex, and even if she were she wouldn't be getting it from me. You can believe that or not, as you wish."

Everything Dan said had the ring of truth. Meriel did

not know whether to be relieved on Hatta's behalf, or annoyed with herself for making an unfounded accusation. But deep down she knew that sooner or later she would have had to find out the truth.

"OK," she said at last, "I'm sorry if I misread the situation. It's simply that I can't help feeling just a little responsible for Hatta. She's so young, and what with Simon, and her father . . ."

"I agree with you entirely," said Dan. She could tell he wanted to be allowed to get on with his work. She also sensed, with regret, that he thought less well of her following her outburst. But that was a small price to pay for the knowledge that Hatta would come to no harm.

Early in the New Year Meriel parked the MG in the village's grandly named Municipal Car Park, paid and displayed, and began making her way towards the offices occupied by Fox, Lambert and Lambert, Solicitors.

Christmas at Amberfield had been a quiet, subdued affair, as was only to be expected. After the midnight service at Amberfield Church they had slept in late, eaten a traditional Christmas lunch, then opened their presents around the drawing-room fire. They were loath to admit it, but each of them found the strain of the festive season, the knowledge that this should have been a time for rejoicing, almost unbearable. Now that Twelfth Night had been and gone, and the decorations had disappeared from shops and homes, Meriel felt she could begin to breathe again.

As had earlier been explained to her over the telephone, Jonathan's offices were located above the Kent and Canterbury Building Society, and Meriel had immediately visualised the dingy dustiness of the place, the scuffed brown lino on the stairs leading to the first floor, the worn leather seats and the dowdy, elderly, underpaid secretary. As it turned out, she was correct in respect of the secretary only, and here only in part. Ruth Protheroe was in truth seriously underpaid compared with her counterparts elsewhere, but since she was not aware of this fact her employer saw no reason to enlighten her; as to the rest, she was middle-aged rather than elderly, and her clothes were more conservative than dowdy.

Meriel's first reaction as she reached the top of the stairs and pushed open the door before her, was one of surprise that a solicitor in sleepy Amberfield should occupy such grand surroundings. Both Ruth's office and Jonathan's, into which Meriel was shown without delay, were fitted out with pieces of antique furniture of undeniable quality and the same could be said of the oil paintings on the walls and the thick dark beige carpets. It was clear that Fox, Lambert and Lambert, whoever the last two might be, did not rely on local trade alone.

"Meriel!" Jonathan's voice was a murmur, and his lips caressed the hand which, as on the occasion of their previous meeting, he held for too long. "How *very* good of you to come and see me! I thought," he explained as he settled her into a chair and placed a pile of documents in front of her, "it might make sense for you to go through these first, then ask me questions after. How would that suit?"

"That would be fine, Jonathan," said Meriel.

Meriel accepted the coffee she was offered and for the next two hours devoted herself to a thorough examination of the files Jonathan had placed at her disposal. While she read, and made notes, Jonathan carried on with his own work, making sure he did not disturb her, dictating quietly into the machine on his desk, even leaving the room from time to time to take phone calls and always looking up with a smile whenever she needed him to clarify something for her.

Right from the start it was apparent that Jonathan was a man who took great pains to keep his paperwork in good order. What was more, he had arranged the files in such a way that each one followed naturally upon the other, so that she was not forever having to hunt back and forth for additional information.

71

"*The property hereinafter referred to as Amberfield House* . . . *etc, etc,*" she read. "*the land bounded to the east by Hawthorn Lane* . . ." The discovery that the road in which Amberfield House stood had a name caused her to smile, though it was only to be expected. After the house and the land came details of the outbuildings: winery, barn, garaging, stores and greenhouses, all seemed to be correctly listed.

The same care had gone into the drawing up of the company articles. Meriel was intrigued to find that under the legal protection clauses was one protecting her from being sued if she unwittingly gave a false description of a product. Given her restricted knowledge of English wine, she decided that was probably just as well.

"Any questions?" asked the lawyer.

"I take it you would like me to sign the transfer document making Simon's shares over to me?"

"If you would be so kind," nodded Jonathan. "There will of course be a small broker's fee to be paid for the transfer. Plus my own fees, of course."

"Of course," murmured Meriel.

"Anything else?" queried Jonathan.

She hesitated. Something was causing a little antenna to twitch in the back of her mind, and she did not know why.

"Basically, I'm impressed," she said. "You seem to have gone into things pretty thoroughly."

"But?" It seemed that Jonathan never missed a trick.

Meriel consulted her notes once more, but virtually all the queries she had jotted down had been answered by the time she finished reading through the documents. She shook her head.

"There is something, I feel sure . . . but I'm afraid I can't think what it might be."

"You're happy with the fact that your own private money remains safe in the event of Amberfield Wines going bust?"

"Things aren't that bad, are they?" asked Meriel.

Jonathan merely smiled. "They're not good, Meriel. They're certainly not good."

"But surely the sale of the hopfields brought in enough money to keep everything going?"

"That was the idea, certainly. But when you consider that it costs around five thousand pounds to plant a single acre of vines, and add to that the sum needed to equip the winery, you'll appreciate that it's possible to get through an awful lot of money very fast. And that's without taking into consideration the matter of Hatta's school fees, and the wages paid to Dan and Jacinta and Jethro. You'll have to go through the accounts with Adam if you want a true picture of how things stand, but I'm sorry to say that at the moment expenditure far exceeds income. To put it bluntly, the capital generated by the sale of the hopfields has all but gone."

Meriel stared at Jonathan, appalled. She had expected to learn that Amberfield's finances were shaky, but she had not realised that the situation was *this* desperate.

"Won't things improve once the new vines start to yield?"

"Frankly, I doubt it. Don't forget, there are three properties to be maintained.

There it was again, that little twitching antenna, but stronger now. It was as though the computer in her head was busily filing away some potentially lethal virus in a place where she could not access it. Would this thing, this blip, pop up one day when she was least expecting it and wreak havoc?

"If you don't mind, Jonathan, I'd like to run through these papers again. Just in case there is something I've missed."

"Of course," said Jonathan. "Take all the time you need."

And yet, when she flipped through the files again, everything seemed so clear-cut, so above-board. She could find nothing to explain her sudden concern and could only assume that her brain was simply tiring of too much information.

She pushed back her chair and, to give her eyes a rest from all those words, took advantage of Jonathan's absorption in his own work to observe him more closely. From her vantage point across the large desk she took in the lawyer's narrow head and slicked-down fair hair, the pale lashes, the fine, almost too-thin features so typical of a certain kind of Englishman. He was handsome in his way, she had to acknowledge; very handsome if your taste ran to smoothies in navy double-breasted suits. With a sudden shock, she remembered that this was precisely the kind of man she used to go out with before she met Simon . . .

Quite suddenly, the question that had been bothering her came to the forefront of her mind.

"Well? Have you found it – whatever it was?" asked Jonathan.

"The Lodge!" she exclaimed. "Why are there no papers relating to The Lodge?"

Jonathan's eyes were razor-sharp as they met hers. Then he looked away. "As it happens, The Lodge does not form part of the company. It never has done."

"Why is that?" For some reason this struck Meriel as strange.

"I imagine the reasons are historical," Jonathan replied. "I believe the property was not acquired by the Barton family until shortly after the First World War, since when it has always been considered as a separate entity."

"So if the company – Amberfield Wines – does not own The Lodge, who does?" asked Meriel.

"Until a year or so ago, the property was owned outright by Edward Barton. It is now held in joint ownership by himself and Vivienne. I'm sure you are aware that it is normal practice nowadays for a husband and wife to own property jointly. It certainly strengthens Vivienne's position in the event of Edward's death. In my opinion, this was a sensible move to make, legally and in every other way."

"I'm sure it was," agreed Meriel doubtfully.

When Jonathan spoke his tone was firm: "I did not include the documents relating to The Lodge for your perusal because, strictly speaking, they are not connected with your membership of the board."

He was telling her to mind her own business, thought Meriel. Perhaps he was right. She was beginning to wonder why she had raised the matter in the first place. She smiled apologetically.

"I'm not quite sure what I'm trying to get at. Nothing, probably."

Jonathan studied her for a moment, then said:

"I'm not sure whether I ought to be saying this, but there is something on my mind relating to the company."

"Please go ahead," said Meriel.

Choosing his words with care, he went on:

"As you may or may not be aware, there were disagreements among the various members of the Barton family about the way in which the company was run."

"Yes. I am aware of that," replied Meriel.

"What you possibly do not realise is that this disagreement occasionally spilled over into a direct clash of wills. To such an extent that Edward sometimes felt his sons were not to be trusted and I'm afraid to say that applied to Simon as much as to Adam."

This was so far removed from Meriel's own line of thought that she was temporarily stunned into silence.

"No!" she exclaimed at last, "I can't believe that! You must be mistaken. Edward . . . I mean, what reason would he have to mistrust his own sons? Simon *lived* for Amberfield Wines! Everybody knew that!"

"I'm sorry," Jonathan was saying, throwing her an almost furtive look which Meriel hoped did not conceal a knowledge of other unpleasant facts. "I can see this has

75

come as something of a shock. Perhaps I shouldn't have spoken – "

He broke off as a woman came in, without knocking. She was tall, with endless legs emerging from the short skirt of her pillar-box red suit and on her head she wore a small round hat of silky black fur. She was so laden with parcels and shopping bags that she had to shoulder her way sideways into the room.

"Jonathan! I'm so sorry!" she exclaimed, the lengthened vowels instantly revealing her North American origins. "I didn't realise you had a visitor!"

"Bella." Jonathan rose, a mixture of pleasure and annoyance showing on his face. "Isn't Ruth – "

"I think she's playing with the photocopier, darling," explained the woman. "Really," she added without pausing for breath, "I never meant to interrupt anything, but I just got myself a lift from the station with that woman who runs the craft shop would you believe and I thought I'd drop by and see if you could run me home."

"It's all right," said Meriel. "I was just on my way out."

"Oh, but of course!" exclaimed Jonathan. "You haven't met my wife, have you, Meriel?"

The two women shook hands, Meriel's warm smile halted by the less than friendly expression in Bella's eyes.

"How nice to meet you," Meriel managed, after a moment.

"Yeah, sure, good to meet you too," replied Bella, but already she was pushing past Meriel, and dropping her collection of parcels about Jonathan's feet.

"Darling, I've had such fun at Harrods' sale," Meriel heard her say as she made her way back down to the street. "You should have come with me!"

She did not catch Jonathan's reply.

5

The stairs that led to the top floor of Amberfield House were narrower and steeper than the imposing flight that linked the entrance hall to the landing off which Meriel's room was situated. They were also cut off from the rest of the house by a door which tended to be closed when Hatta was in – she liked to maintain her privacy when in her own room at the top of the house – and open when she was out. Soon after her arrival at Amberfield, Meriel had been told that Hatta's was not the only attic room. The whole floor had for years served as the Barton children's quarters, with separate bedrooms for Simon, Adam and Hatta as well as a communal playroom.

Vivienne had already hinted that Meriel might wish to sort through the bits and pieces, as she described them, that remained in Simon's old room and Meriel had readily agreed. But each time she decided now was the moment to tackle this particular obstacle, she ended by changing her mind. Although one part of her longed to see the place that Simon had called his own from early childhood, another part warned her to be careful. She did not know what lay up there for her to find, whether looking into Simon's earlier existence might upset her. So far, she thought, she had done a pretty good job of not becoming too upset. Why spoil a good thing?

Shortly before Hatta's return to school after the Christmas holidays, Meriel finally decided to ask the girl to give her a conducted tour of the attics. That way, she couldn't chicken out at the last minute. But when she went in search of her, Hatta was nowhere to be found. Climbing to the first-floor landing, she found the door to the attic staircase open, and, on an impulse, decided to show herself around.

A weak winter sun angled through the dusty window at one end of a narrow, white-painted corridor, punctuated by varnished wood doors. Meriel made her way to the landing window and peered out. She had imagined she might be above her own room, but she was mistaken: instead, she found she was looking out over the cobbled courtyard with the converted barn and oasthouse beyond.

Unable to discern much because of the state of the window-panes, Meriel slid open the sash and leaned out, filling her lungs with the cold winter air as she surveyed the scene before her. Not that there was all that much to survey. The barn door was open: doubtless Adam was there, with the village girl who came in to help. By way of contrast, the doors to the winery were padlocked shut, their steel panels reflecting the pale sun. On the cobbles, sparrows were chattering and fighting over the crumbs Jacinta had thrown out for them, and faint sounds of chopping and stirring emanated from the kitchen.

Very gradually, Meriel became aware of something else. It was the sound of voices – quiet, careful voices – from the direction of the old stables. Leaning out as far as she dared and craning her neck, she saw a man she did not know – a tubby, grey-haired man who waved a cigar about as he spoke – engaged in earnest conversation with Adam, who was not in the office as she had assumed.

The two men stood in the shadow of one of the wide wooden doors, so that even from Meriel's vantage-point they were scarcely visible. Even so, it struck her that there was something furtive in the way they kept looking about them, as if checking that they were not being overheard. Suddenly, the quarrelling sparrows flew away and in the quiet that followed Meriel was able to hear snatches of the conversation going on beneath her.

"You've already agreed it's a wonderful sight!" she clearly heard Adam exclaim before continuing in a quieter, more urgent voice, as though attempting to persuade the other man that this sight was indeed worth seeing.

The other man listened carefully to what Adam had to say, then nodded and took out a pen with which he scribbled on the back of an envelope.

"Check it out for yourself!" he insisted. "For that sort of – " his voice was lost in the noisy rattling of Dan's pickup truck as it entered the courtyard. Rather to Meriel's surprise, she saw that Adam and the other man did not come out to greet the winemaker. Instead, they withdrew even further into the shadows, and stood quietly by the garage wall, out of Dan's sight, where they remained until the truck had been unloaded and driven away.

"I'll have the money in place by February or March," the other man was saying as they emerged into the now empty courtyard.

"That soon!" exclaimed Adam. "Does that mean you're definitely intending to go ahead this time?"

"Aye, more than likely. But it doesn't do to count your chickens before they're hatched. Things have got to get moving on the other front, too."

Meriel, pulling back from the window so as to avoid being seen, missed Adam's reply. Shortly after, she heard the sound of a car drawing away from behind the garages, then saw Adam stride briskly across the yard and spring up the couple of steps into the office. Meriel closed the window, aware of a feeling of curiosity mingled with mild embarrassment. How strange that Adam and his visitor had chosen to hide from Dan! she thought. On the other hand, what on earth had possessed her to eavesdrop on the two men in the first place? What concern was it of hers that Adam seemed to be interested in the other man's business affairs?

More than a little unsettled by this episode, Meriel

wandered back along the corridor, touching each door lightly with her hand to see if any were open. She did not want to commit herself by doing anything as positive as turning a handle. If the door gave, then she would go in. She was beginning to feel unexpectedly nervous, and had almost convinced herself that she would leave now and return with Hatta, when one of the doors swung gently open at her touch.

This was obviously Hatta's bedroom: her "space" as she liked to refer to it, although space was the one thing there wasn't much evidence of. Clothes, make-up, records, books, all lay strewn over the floor, the bed, the chest of drawers and other surfaces. The imprint of Hatta's body could be seen in the large bean bag she obviously occupied when watching the little television squeezed in-between a stack of sheet music and a parched houseplant. On the walls, posters of Marilyn Monroe, Mozart, Nigel Kennedy and Rob Lowe were plastered in a row, prompting Meriel to wonder what all these people would have made of one another.

She stepped out into the corridor and pulled the door to.

"What do you want?"

Meriel spun round. Hatta stood at the top of the stairs, watching her.

"I . . . I was just looking for Simon's room."

"Why?" demanded Hatta.

"I wanted to see it. He often talked about it."

"Well, this isn't it. This is my room. And this one next door's the playroom. Or, at least, it used to be. It was emptied out yonks ago. Once in a while it gets used as a spare bedroom, but that's all." She held the door open for Meriel to see.

Meriel, glancing briefly into the room, sparsely furnished with a bed, small wardrobe and chest of drawers, could see that this was so.

"This was Simon's room," continued Hatta, leading

the way back down the corridor and opening another door.

"You first," said Meriel. She was now very nervous indeed and stood with beating heart in the doorway for some moments before forcing herself to go in.

"It's all right," said Hatta, who seemed to have no trouble understanding how Meriel felt. "It's pretty innocuous, really. Simon didn't spend all that much time here, as a matter of fact."

Meriel entered the room and looked about her. Hatta was right. The room, with its pale grey walls and navy-and-red striped curtains and bedcover, did not appear to hold any terrors.

"Ouf!" she said with relief. "I don't know what I was expecting, but . . ." she shrugged and smiled.

"I think Mum wants you to decide what to do with these books – " Hatta gestured towards the shelves in the alcoves on either side of the bed. "Also Simon's wicked stereo system."

There was no disguising the note of envy in Hatta's voice as she ran her fingers over the sleek gunmetal tower.

"Why don't you have it?" Meriel asked her. "I'm sure Simon would have liked that."

"Well . . . I mean, I've got one of my own, but it's not a patch on Simon's. Oh, Meriel, are you sure? Don't you want it? And what about the compact discs?"

"*Please*, Hatta! Take them all. They should all be yours."

To her considerable surprise, Hatta flung her arms about her by way of thanks.

"You don't know what this means to me!" she said.

"If only you'd told me! You could have had it before!" laughed Meriel.

"No." Hatta was suddenly solemn. "That wouldn't have been right. Now's a good time."

While Hatta carried hi-fi components across the corridor to her room, Meriel turned her attention to the

81

contents of cupboards and chests of drawers. She began with the clothes, folding them neatly into black plastic bags ready for the next jumble sale. Coming across a thick brushed-cotton lumberjack shirt she went to see if Hatta wanted it, only to find that the girl had vanished, and that she was alone once more.

After the clothes came the books, mainly science fiction titles for which Meriel could not imagine ever developing a taste. These she packed into cardboard boxes which she placed in the corridor alongside the black plastic bags. Returning to Simon's room, she congratulated herself on making so much progress in such a short time. Surely the worst was now over? She had been afraid that these mementoes of Simon might cause her pain, and yet here she was, coping with this potentially traumatic task perfectly coolly and calmly.

She was on the point of giving herself a metaphorical pat on the back when a photograph, long trapped under a heavy dictionary, fluttered to the ground. When she bent to pick it up, she saw that the picture – cracked where it had been folded, brown at the edges – was of Simon as a small boy. Instantly she knew that here was her downfall; the breach in her carefully built-up defences.

In the picture Simon, who, judging by the missing front tooth, must have been aged around six, was dressed in outsize cricketing gear. With pads reaching up almost to his waist, and a cap that obliterated half his face, there was in fact not all that much of Simon to be seen. Yet there was no mistaking who it was. In his gloved hands he held an old-fashioned bat, and he wore an expression of such intense determination that Meriel first smiled then, unable to stop herself, fell down on her husband's bed and howled.

There was nobody to hear her in the quiet attic room, as Meriel wept for all that she had lost: not least, for Simon's child – surely it would have been a boy identical to the one in the photograph – the child she would never have.

But even as she wept for the man who had been her best friend as well as her lover, she began to understand the healing power of tears. For too long she had been trying to ignore her pain, with the result that she had suffered all the more. Now she gave herself up to her misery utterly, grateful that she was at last capable of doing so.

Then, when no more tears would come, she rose and crossed to the washbasin in the corner of the room, splashed cold water onto her face and, with Simon's picture safely tucked into the pocket of her jeans, turned her attention to the contents of a high, five-drawered chest.

Letters (though none from herself: Simon had kept those separately, and had taken them with him to Meriel's flat when they married), newspaper cuttings, school reports – all these she bundled together, having decided to take them to her room and sort through them another time. There was also, she noticed as she opened the largest drawer, a red-covered notebook which at first Meriel took to be one of Simon's school-exercise books. But when she opened it she discovered that it consisted of little more than the cover and a few loose pages of handwriting which, in any case, was not Simon's.

Even so, she was curious. Judging by the worn, grubby state of the notebook, it had fallen apart through overuse. Turning over the pages one by one, Meriel saw that they were densely covered in squiggly, untidy writing, which frequently departed from the printed lines. The text was punctuated with occasional poorly executed diagrams and, more rarely, rows of calculations. Peering more closely at the scarcely legible handwriting, training her eye to recognise the uneven, incomplete letters, she began reading. With a quickening interest, she realised that what she had before her was Edward Barton's own handwritten account of the planting of the vines at Amberfield. Smoothing the first sheet flat, she began reading.

Now, as I come to write the story of the wines of

Amberfield, I find I can no longer remember at what precise moment the idea of planting a vineyard first came into my head. Or rather, into Simon's head, for though my first-born son was no more than a callow teenager at the time, everyone is agreed that the suggestion was originally his.

I, alas, cannot remember. The stroke I suffered three years ago has left me unable to recall certain things, and there are irritating gaps in my memory which I would dearly love to fill. More worryingly, my estimable physician Dr Dinwiddy has indicated that I shall at some time in the future suffer a further, more severe attack which could leave me totally incapacitated. It is for this reason that I have decided to set pen to paper while I am still able. Both for my own satisfaction, and for the entertainment and instruction of those who will come after me, I have decided to write down as best I can recall the sequence of events that led to the harvesting of our first crop here at Amberfield.

From the start (whenever that was) the idea of turning *vigneron* in my old age appealed to me in a curiously romantic manner, though it should be stressed right away that the overriding considerations were hard-headed and commercial. True, I can remember standing on the site of what was to become the first of our fields to be planted with the new crop, closing my eyes and imagining the slopes of perfectly aligned vines, basking under a blazing sun in an improbably blue sky, the grapes ready for picking –

Meriel raised her eyes from the notebook, smiling as she recalled doing exactly the same thing herself. Then she bent her head once more to her reading:

– but I am anxious to dispel the notion, long held by the English drinking classes, that wine-growing in this country is no more than a quaint little hobby for

84

eccentrics. I also feel it necessary to explain to future generations of Bartons why the decision was made to abandon the growing of hops and thus break with a long and honourable tradition: a tradition that contributed to the continued prosperity not only of the Barton family but of the county of Kent as a whole.

It must have been a hard decision to make, thought Meriel, remembering Simon's account of the time the diggers and rotovators came trundling up the road and into the fields where the hops were grown. But, as Edward now reiterated, they had had little choice. What sense did it make to continue to grow a crop which was no longer required? Simon's suggestion that they should plant vines instead must have struck an immediate chord. And surely the discovery that viticulture was practised in their part of Kent almost two thousand years ago can only have reinforced the Barton family's decision to go ahead with the new scheme?

All the same, Edward made it plain there were some aspects of hop-growing that he missed. Among these was the annual invasion of hop-pickers from the East End of London. Each September, Amberfield played host to scores of pickers who arrived with wives and children and camped out in barns, stables and every other available outbuilding for the duration of the harvest. When the time came for them to leave, Edward and Vivienne watched them go with a mixture of relief and regret. It was good to have the hops safely gathered in; but how sad to think that these families, and especially the cheerful, grimy children, would not see the countryside again for another full year.

Then, Edward returned to the subject of the vines.

We now had to decide which varieties of grapevine to plant, and to this end we despatched Simon on a "recce" of other vineyards in the southern counties. The information he provided suggested that the varieties most

85

likely to succeed were the two vines most commonly planted in the United Kingdom: first, Müller-Thurgau and second, the vine now known as Seyval Blanc, though in those days I seem to remember it was known by some number or other. Both were recommended by the EEC commission on viticulture and the samples purchased by Simon showed us that, when blended, the two wines created a soft, almost muscat "nose" combined with a lovely fresh, flowery flavour that was more than palatable. At the same time, I was unable to resist ordering rather smaller quantities of Chardonnay and Pinot Noir grapes, without which it seemed to me no vineyard was complete. At last, the great adventure had begun.

There followed several more pages of details about pH readings, site preparation and the like before the text came to an abrupt end, in mid-calculation. Meriel, eager to read more about the story of Amberfield, searched through the remaining contents of the drawer, hoping to find the missing pages of the notebook, but there was no sign of them.

"Damn!" she exclaimed in frustration when a hunt through Simon's bedside table also failed to turn up anything of interest. Then the memory of what she had just read calmed her down somewhat. Picking up the notebook, Meriel hugged it to her for a moment. Whatever Jonathan Fox had meant the other day by his suggestion that Edward mistrusted Simon was surely disproved by what she had just read. Edward's gratitude and indebtedness to his son were there for all to see. Jonathan had got it all wrong. He must have.

Dan lay sprawled the length of the high-backed settee in front of the fire, a writing-pad propped against his knees and a pen in his hand. When the sitting-room door opened he raised his head briefly, then continued scribbling onto the airmail paper. The dogs asleep on the fireside rug merely opened one eye each to check that they had guessed correctly, then sighed mightily and carried on as before.

"Fantastic reception!" said Bella sarcastically. "Such enthusiasm!"

"Hi," said Dan.

"Hi to you too." She leaned over the back of the settee and sought out Dan's mouth with her own. "Mmmmm. Have I missed that! Jesus Christ but it's cold in here!" She made her way round to the other side of the settee and stood in front of the log fire, blocking the warmth from the dogs who shifted in disapproval.

"That's a terrifyingly large number of dead animals you're wearing," Dan observed.

"What is it with you Brits!" exclaimed Bella. "You all eat meat don't you? And you wear leather shoes?"

"The cow," Dan pointed out, "is not an endangered species."

"I'll have you know that without something like this to keep me warm *I'd* be an endangered species," retorted Bella. "Besides, I wouldn't be seen dead in New York without a fur coat. What else is a girl supposed to wear to a charity lunch? Anyway," she continued in a more seductive tone, turning to Dan with a smile and running her hands down the shining pelt, "aren't you going to ask what I'm wearing underneath?"

"Knowing you, it'll be another fur coat," said Dan.

"Daniel!" By now she was displaying a measure of genuine exasperation. Crossing to the settee, she lifted Dan's legs out of the way, sat down and began slowly massaging his stockinged feet. When he still failed to respond, she grasped a foot more firmly and slid it under the fur coat, moving it along her thigh and up, higher –

"You couldn't possibly give me another five minutes, could you?" asked Dan.

Bella threw the foot aside and stood up. "Oh, really,

87

Dan, you are impossible! Who is it you're writing to that's so much more exciting than me?"

"No one could possibly be more exciting than you," replied Dan suavely, "but I *would* just like to finish this letter."

Bella was now round the back of the settee again, leaning over, reading what he was writing.

"Paul? Paul who, may I ask?"

"Paul Greenberg. He's a wine-grower – "

"Surprise, surprise."

"– in Canada. If I play my cards right, I may be able to persuade him to let me have some vine cuttings."

"Vine cuttings!" exclaimed Bella. "Well, that certainly explains a lot. I should have known better than to try and compete with *vine cuttings*!"

"Ah, but these are special," Dan explained. "These are cool-climate red wine varieties. Note the colour. *Red* varieties. From Russia, as it happens."

"Gosh." Bella could not have sounded more unimpressed.

"Seriously," Dan assured her, "it's thrilling stuff. It means we may one day be able to make a decent red wine in the old UK. Tell you what. Why don't you make yourself useful and dig out an airmail envelope from the desk? After which, I'm all yours."

Bella, who never liked being asked to do anything for anybody, hesitated a moment before pushing open the roll-top desk.

"I have to say this, Dan," she remarked. "It would be nice if you could act like you were pleased to see me."

"Of course I'm pleased to see you!"

Bella guessed – rightly – that he had failed to notice that she was genuinely annoyed at his treatment of her and she was determined not to let him get away with it. After she had found the envelope, she continued picking up letters, postcards, bills, photographs, glancing at them then tossing them aside, making as much noise as she could and generally letting her impatience show.

"Well, well," she said after a while, her voice now drawling; teasing. "Who is this Laura who writes to you on scented paper . . . and who, incidentally, cannot spell?"

"Leave those, please," Dan asked her quietly.

"I will not! Tell me! Who is Laura?"

"Not *is*. Was. She's someone I used to know years ago."

"Uh-huh. Someone in deepest Australia, I suppose. Incidentally, you've never talked about all that . . . about when you had your very own vineyard. Did Laura – "

But by then Dan had sprung up from the settee and grasped Bella's arm.

"I meant what I said," he informed her with barely suppressed anger. "Those are private letters. Just leave them alone, will you?"

"Oh, Daniel, I've annoyed you!" said Bella in her most winsome and contrite manner. "Darling, I'm so sorry!" Her arms were around him and she was sliding out of the fur coat, revealing the figure-hugging one-piece catsuit beneath. "It's just that I've missed you so, and you obviously haven't missed me at all . . ."

"You know that's not true," he told her, his hands roaming over her, becoming reacquainted with her. "How could any man not miss these?" He was nuzzling her nipples through the stretchy stuff of the catsuit, then using his teeth to unfasten the zip.

"Aaaiiii . . ." was Bella's response, almost a moan, but her eyes over Dan's head remained open, her face without expression.

Some considerable time later, waking from a brief sleep in the creaky old walnut bed with inadequate springs, Dan cautiously removed his arm from across Bella's shoulders and hauled himself into a sitting position. As far as he could tell, she was still asleep, which at least gave him time to think how best to say what had

89

to be said. Then he saw her sharp, wide-awake eyes on him.

"Come on, Dan," she said. "Spit it out."

He gave a short laugh. He never could hide anything from this one. Maybe nobody could. Even so, he cleared his throat nervously before speaking.

"Listen, Bella, I was wondering whether maybe we shouldn't cool things down for a while."

Bella raised her head and studied him from between the curtains of her hair. "How do you mean, 'cool things down'?" she asked.

"It's just . . . well, I'm getting a bit worried about how much Jonathan knows."

"Jonathan knows nothing," said Bella.

"I wouldn't be so sure about that. He's taken to making veiled remarks. Like at Simon's funeral, for example."

"Oh? What did he say?"

"Can't remember, exactly. But it was clear he's suspicious. I just thought maybe we should be a bit more careful, that's all."

"Careful? Believe me, Daniel, I'm always *very* careful. You're not telling me you're scared of Jonathan, are you?" Her hand, which had been stroking the dark chest hair, began making its way slowly, skilfully downwards across the taut stomach muscles.

"No, of course not! On the other hand, I get the feeling he's watching me, and it bothers me. I think it might be wiser if you didn't come here for a while."

Bella sat up. "OK," she nodded. "How about us meeting somewhere else? Don't they have motels in this country?"

"I just think that for the time being . . . I mean, until things settle down . . ."

Without warning, Bella sprang out of bed and began wriggling into her catsuit and pulling on her boots. Ignoring Dan's last question she said:

"Daniel, I have to go now. How about if I call you on

Wednesday to see if it's OK for me to come by? Jonathan said he'd be very late that night."

"Bella, haven't you listened to a word I've been saying?" asked Dan in exasperation.

Bella paused by the doorway, then said:

"Oh, yes, Dan. I heard. But you seem to forget that I'm the one who calls the shots around here. *I* decide if and when I see you. Not you. Bye, now."

She was gone. Dan heard her running down the narrow stairs, pausing to pick up her coat from the sitting-room floor. What he did not know was that before she left she took the precaution of stopping by the desk and pocketing something that had caught her eye earlier that evening. It just might come in useful. And, as she had informed Dan only minutes ago, she believed in being careful.

91

6

The no-nonsense approach might work, Meriel decided
after struggling for some time with the heavy furniture,
though she had her doubts. Michelle, the village girl who
was euphemistically referred to as Adam's secretary, had
observed her struggles for some time without comment.

"As there doesn't seem to be much going on for the
moment, why don't you give me a hand?" she suggested.

"Actually," replied Michelle unenthusiastically, "I *am*
quite busy."

"No, you're not," retorted Meriel. "So, why don't
you shift some of Adam's belongings away from this
corner here, and help me heave this desk into position,
here . . ."

Michelle capitulated. "What are we doing this for,
anyway?" she asked.

"Hasn't anyone told you? I'm taking over the vineyard
shop, and I need somewhere to work from."

"Oh, yes. I think Adam did mention it. But don't you
think this room a bit small for two people?"

Meriel sighed. It was true. It was also, she supposed,
the reason for Adam's undisguised reluctance to have
her move in with him. Yet what choice did they have?
Of the two rooms on the ground floor of the barn, the
larger, outer one would have to continue serving as both
workplace to Michelle and as so-called sales area.

Meriel shook her head as she looked around. Amberfield, like all but a tiny handful of English vineyards,
relied on selling its wines directly to the public, at the
winery door. Only three or four of the biggest names in

English viticulture produced sufficient wine to sell through off-licences or supermarket chains. If these cramped and unappealing surroundings represented Amberfield's best effort to market their product, it was small wonder they were in trouble.

For a start, the office was left unattended for much of the time. As far as Meriel could tell, Adam went about his own affairs and kept highly irregular hours. She assumed he was generally engaged on Amberfield business, but there was no way of telling. Certainly Michelle rarely appeared to know what he did with his afternoons, and more than once Vivienne came in search of her son.

Sometimes, Meriel found herself harbouring the unworthy suspicion that Adam's appearances in the office were designed to keep his mother happy rather than to allow him to do any real work. During the couple of hours he spent at his desk before he returned to The Lodge for a long lunch, he would at most answer a letter or two and process the occasional order. One order for bottles and for corks, which Dan asked Meriel to pass on to Adam with the message that these were needed particularly urgently, had yet to be dealt with, despite Dan's frequent reminders. Meriel found Adam's attitude, both to the company and towards herself, hard to fathom. She supposed that was because she assumed he would resemble Simon in temperament as well as in looks, but it was not so.

Meanwhile, Michelle, though usually pleasant and well-meaning, had managed to avoid learning anything whatsoever about the product she was employed to sell, a fact which did not endear her to potential customers. She could also be distressingly absent-minded. Already this week Meriel had observed the girl fetching a bottle of Seyval Blanc for a visitor who wished to taste it before buying, then seating herself at her desk and resuming a long telephone conversation with a friend without thinking to provide the poor man with a glass. Had it not been for

Meriel's timely intervention the sale would have been well and truly lost. Clearly, there was room for improvement.

The sound of a car drawing slowly into the courtyard took Meriel by surprise.

"That can't possibly be Sophie already!" They had arranged to go shopping in Canterbury and Meriel had not realised how late it was. "That'll have to do for the time being, Michelle," she said, much to the girl's relief. "If anyone asks, I'll be back by three."

Grabbing her jacket and shoulder bag, she ran out to the courtyard and jumped into the waiting Renault.

"We go to my favourite shop, yes?" asked Sophie.

"Yes, of course! Anywhere you like!"

Sophie was leaving for France the following day, to spend some time with a sister who had just had another baby. The purpose of the trip into Canterbury was to buy presents for sister and family, and as Sophie pulled out of the drive she said:

"Woollies. That is where I buy the best presents. Do you go to that shop sometimes?"

"Not often, no," replied Meriel, astonished that someone as chic as Sophie should even consider shopping at Woolworth's. "Sophie, are you quite sure that's the best place to go? I mean, I'm sure they're very good value, but . . ."

Sophie, however, was adamant, and when Meriel discovered that Woollies was actually a boutique selling hand-made knitwear, and that a sale had just begun, the outing began to make a lot more sense.

Inside the shop, Sophie gave Meriel a brief run-down on her sister's family – how many people it consisted of, and roughly what sizes – and instructed her to dig out anything she liked the look of. Sophie then proceeded to whittle down the stack of possibles until she had chosen what she wanted.

Meriel, impressed by Sophie's efficiency, had only one further question.

"Isn't it too hot in your part of the world for some of these?" she asked as she stroked a thick, soft, heather-coloured jumper that was going to look marvellous on Sophie's nine-year-old niece.

"Absolutely not! In winter in Provence it can be so cold! *So* cold, you would not believe it! Now I take you for lunch. No?"

"No," replied Meriel. "Now I take *you* for lunch!"

Although the day was dull and grey, the town was busy with shoppers taking advantage of the January sales. Meriel found it easy to get along with Sophie, and more than once as they made their way towards the wholefood restaurant recommended by the French girl, they were able to share a joke about some particularly outlandish example of sale merchandise in a store window. Meriel began to realise that she would miss her new friend while she was away.

"How long will you be in France?" she asked.

Sophie shrugged. "That I do not know. First I stay with Natalie – that is my sister – and then perhaps I come back for a little, but then I must go again to my parents' house to make the arrangements for the wedding."

"But that's not until September!" remarked Meriel.

"Oh, but there is so much to arrange!" said Sophie. "Besides, I – " She checked herself, but Meriel, unable to guess what she meant, asked:

"What else besides?"

Sophie looked up at her guiltily. "I know I should not say this, when everyone here is so kind. But . . ." she admitted with a shrug, "it is the truth that I prefer to live in my own country."

"Oh, Sophie!" exclaimed Meriel. "I had no idea you were unhappy here!"

"It is not that I am unhappy in England. It is just that there is not always so much for me to do. In Provence I think perhaps I open a restaurant, but not here."

95

"Why on earth not?" asked Meriel. "I think that's a great idea. Have you suggested the idea to Adam?"

But Sophie seemed not to hear her, and after remaining lost in thought for several moments she leaned across the table and said:

"This sound stupid to you, I think, but Adam, he is a good man when we are in France."

The quaintness of the statement would have drawn a smile from Meriel if Sophie did not appear so deeply in earnest.

"I imagine Adam's a good man anywhere," she said simply, though for some reason the memory of his half-heard conversation in the courtyard came flashing into her mind.

"I hope you are right," replied Sophie. "Oh, Meriel, you do not know how much I hope you are right."

The following week, for the first time since Simon's funeral, Meriel dressed in city clothes: high-heeled black shoes, opaque black stockings and a new aubergine-coloured skirt with matching jacket, fitted and short. The clothes felt strange at first, and Meriel had to remind herself that for very nearly five years – getting on for a fifth of her life – she had worn outfits similar to this every single working day. But the world of work, and London itself, seemed to belong to some far-gone era which at times took on an almost dream-like quality in her imagination.

This sensation was not dispelled when she stepped out of the taxi outside the offices of Vere Lassiter and, with a sudden onset of nervous anticipation, pushed through the softly hissing revolving doors. She paused inside the glass atrium that had so impressed her when she first came to work at Vere Lassiter. To either side, trees in containers flourished as if in their natural habitat, their delicate, silvery-green leaves rustling in the breeze created by the constant movement of automatic doors; fountains surrounded by cushioned seats spurted and died down, then spurted and died down again, creating restful oases among the endless comings and goings. Way, way above her, a glass and steel roof arched over the open space below, protecting all within from the elements, its cunningly positioned lighting giving a permanent impression of bright sunshine. The truth, as Meriel was only too well aware, was that the January day was cold and overcast, the sort of day that made you long for sunshine and a crisp blue sky.

As she made her way towards one of the circular, glass-sided lifts that plied silently between the building's many floors, Meriel reminded herself of the purpose of her visit. She must be firm, she told herself. She had made her decision, and she intended to stick by it.

The receptionist, seated amid black ash desks and switchboard consoles that were reflected in the shiny grey marble floor, greeted Meriel with a smile and told her she was under instructions to show her in the moment she arrived.

"Would you like someone to take you through?" she offered.

"It's all right, thanks," replied Meriel, "I think I can still find my way."

Scarcely six months had passed since she had quit Vere Lassiter in order to prepare for her coming wedding, yet as she walked along the glass-sided passage that overlooked the trading floor, she felt she was inspecting a world she had never known. Although she knew that her mentor Giles Atkinson had recently opted for a quieter life on the board of a department store, it seemed that with only a couple of exceptions all her former colleagues had also moved on.

Nigel Starling was still there, she saw, eyes narrowed in concentration as, with a phone in one hand and a cigarette in the other, he studied his computer screen, analysing and assessing in his inimitably shrewd fashion. And the girl in the yellow blouse – Meriel thought she might have joined the company just as she herself was about to leave. But apart from these two, everyone she knew seemed to have left, only to be replaced by younger, fresher versions of themselves.

Even the Australian girl Kath, who had always struck Meriel as being the archetypical long-term employee, had relinquished her screen to a stranger. Meriel was sorry not to see her: she had been forthright, rough-edged and even frightening on occasions, but she was the nearest thing to a friend Meriel had had within the company. Once, Kath had given her good, if unasked-for, advice, though she had not heeded it at the time. Now, she knew better.

Meriel could not but be struck by this astonishing turnover in staff, though she knew she should not be surprised. Although she had not lost her job as a result of the stock-market crash of October 1987, many others had. Later, when the situation began to improve, new people were taken on. More recently, as recession began to loom, many of these new employees had in their turn been laid off. But even without the cataclysmic effects of Black Monday, the burn-out rate among dealers was dangerously high. It was a job for quick-witted, eager young people who lived and breathed work. Marriage and family commitments had no place here, as those who tried to combine these disparate elements discovered to their cost.

She knocked lightly on the door to Rory's office and went in.

Without a word Rory Lassiter, who was in the process of dictating letters to his secretary, sprang to his feet. With one bound he reached Meriel's side and swept her into his arms where he held her, hard, for what must have been quite a while to judge by the secretary's repeated throat-clearing.

"That'll be all for now, Vanessa," said Rory, without looking at the girl. "We'll finish the rest later." He placed a finger under Meriel's chin and tipped her face towards his. "So. Tell me truthfully. How are you?"

Meriel looked up into Rory's laughing dark blue eyes and found herself instantly captivated, just like all the other times; just like all the other women.

"I'm fine, Rory," she said at last. "Really I am."

"You've lost weight," remarked Rory. "How fortunate that I booked a table at Roper's and not one of these places where they try to pretend that two forkfuls of meat and a frilly tomato constitute a main course. Shall we go?"

For a moment, as she preceded Rory out of the office and made her way towards the lift, Meriel was nonplussed. Wasn't it just the tiniest bit crass of Rory to book a table at Roper's of all places? Surely he hadn't forgotten that was where he took her that first time, soon after she joined the firm, when as an inexperienced nineteen-year-old she had made such a fool of herself? Then, seeing his warm smile upon her, she felt her doubts vanish. Rory had probably taken scores and scores of women to lunch, dinner and heaven knows what else in just about every restaurant in town. Why on earth should he remember one silly, unimportant encounter with her?

As they descended to the ground floor in the glass lift, Meriel stole a look at her former employer. He must be thirty-five now, she calculated, recalling with amusement that he had struck her as quite old when she first came to work for him. Now, the gap in their ages seemed to have narrowed, though she was the one who had changed, grown up, whereas Rory was just as she remembered him. The permanent tan that accentuated the crinkles at the corner of his eyes had not faded, and he still sported the shock of black curly hair which he liked to wear just a fraction too long by City standards. Meriel had little doubt that he was well aware that women loved the contrast between his athlete's head and body and the fashion-plate appearance of his impeccable suits. Today's was pale grey, the pleat-fronted trousers pulled in by the supplest dark grey leather belt.

Meriel knew even before she looked that the shoes

would match the belt exactly. They would, indeed, have been fashioned from the same piece of leather, which Rory would have picked out for himself. He not only scorned off-the-peg footwear and other clothing, he also gave a wide berth to anything carrying a designer label. Everything he wore was made specifically for him, to his own instructions. Not for him the Armani suit or the Gucci loafers: his jackets bore no maker's name on the lining, and he was rumoured to have sent back the batch of shirts on which the manufacturer had had the temerity to embroider his own initials, even though the letters were tiny and hidden away on the back of the collar.

She suddenly remembered there was something she had entirely forgotten to ask him.

"Oh, Rory!" she exclaimed, horrified at such a glaring omission. "Weren't you about to become engaged as I was leaving? To . . . Andrea?"

"That's what comes of burying yourself in the depths of the country. You lose touch. Andrea and I didn't work out, I'm afraid."

"I'm sorry."

"Don't be. I think I knew from the beginning that we were wrong for each other. We postponed our engagement so often that the end came as a merciful relief. To both of us, I think. Andrea has started seeing a solicitor in Winchester. They sound ideal for one another."

"And you? Have you – "

Rory shook his head. "No such luck," he said. But he did not look very unhappy with his continuing bachelor status.

As they stepped out through the revolving doors Rory sprang forward to hail a taxi. Being empty, it stopped, but Meriel had the distinct impression that the driver would have had no compunction about throwing the occupants out in favour of Rory, if need be. He did seem to have that effect on people, she remembered. In fact, she was beginning to wonder how she could ever have forgotten.

100

The restaurant had undergone a facelift since Meriel's previous visit. Gone were the rose-splattered tablecloths and eau-de-Nil wall coverings. Instead, a minimalist look now prevailed, the severe black-and-white decor enlivened only by bottle-green accessories. The staff appeared to have changed, too. Either that, or Rory had not eaten here for some time, to judge by the lack of recognition in the waiters' faces.

"Will you join me in an aperitif?" Rory asked as he handed her the wine list. "I'll have my usual *fino*."

"It says here you keep a selection of English wines," Meriel said to the wine waiter. "Would any of them be suitable before a meal?"

"Meriel, my sweet!" Rory laughed in disbelief. "Surely you're not serious?"

"I most certainly am!" replied Meriel, stung by Rory's barely concealed sarcasm. "Quite apart from anything else, I want to find out what the competition is like."

The wine waiter coughed discreetly. "Ah . . . if I might make a suggestion . . . ?" he hazarded. "We do, as it happens, stock a first-rate Reichensteiner from a vineyard in Sussex . . . as supplied to the House of Commons and to British Airways, in fact. Would madam care to try a glass?"

Meriel smiled warmly at him. "Thank you. Yes, I'd love to."

"What can I say?" said Rory with an amused smile. "A glass of . . . what was it? Reichensteiner, for the lady and a dry sherry for me."

When the drinks arrived, and the waiter was out of earshot, Rory leaned forward earnestly as Meriel took her first sip.

"Well? Do British Airways buy this stuff to drink or do they put it in their engines?"

Meriel savoured the delicate, floral quality of the wine, enjoying its soft finish. Then she took another sip.

"Actually, it's truly delicious." She smiled at Rory who

101

still wore a sceptical look on his face. "No, really!" she insisted. "It is very, very good. Try it," she urged him. "Go on. Before you taste your sherry."

A cooler expression had crept into Rory's eyes. This used to happen, Meriel remembered, whenever anyone said something he did not agree with. The smile would fade from his face, his features would be put on "hold" while he considered his reaction, and then one of two things would happen. Either he would narrow his eyes and deliver a withering counter-attack in a far quieter voice than normal, or his entire face would relax and break out into a smile a mile wide. During that interval, his interlocutor would be in agony. Everyone, it seemed, and Meriel had been no exception, craved his approval. On this occasion, to her huge relief, the smile won. Rory took the glass from her and sipped from it before raising his eyebrows in surprise and saying:

"You're right. It's good. Very good indeed." He took out a snakeskin notebook from his breast pocket and held his pen poised.

"What did you say it was called?"

"Reichensteiner," Meriel told him. "But I'm afraid I don't know the name of the vineyard."

Rory called the wine waiter back, asked the name of the vineyard, then requested that his *fino* be taken away.

"I've decided on the Reichensteiner instead," he informed him. "Would you be so kind as to bring us another glass?"

This was also Rory's way, Meriel recalled. He knew how to play the "if you can't beat 'em, join 'em" game to devastating effect and, when it came to business, he frequently did so. She had not until now been aware that he employed the same tactics on a more personal level, but why should she object when he capitulated so charmingly?

He ordered *magret de canard* followed by coffee mousse for both of them, with only the most rudimentary glance in her direction to check that these choices suited her. Amused, she realised that it was her turn to capitulate.

"Now, tell me," he said over coffee, "when were you thinking of coming back?"

"That's what I wanted to talk to you about. I . . ."

"Money's no object," put in Rory. "You can name your price."

She shook her head. "That's not the important thing. The point is that I don't think I want to come back."

"Oh, not yet, certainly. I'm sure it's far too soon for you to be thinking about working full-time. But how about Easter? I thought you could maybe come in occasionally between now and then, get back into your stride as it were – "

"Rory!" she interrupted him. "You've missed the point. I've decided to stay on at Amberfield. Not just for the time being, but for good if things work out that way."

She had thought he might be annoyed with her, but he merely uttered a short laugh, and gently shook his head.

"I have to say, I can't see it, myself. Meriel Devereux mulching vines and treading grapes and whatever else they do in these places. Come on, now! Admit it! That doesn't sound like you, does it?"

"First of all, you're forgetting that I'm Meriel Barton now, not Meriel Devereux. I'm a different person, Rory. All that part of my life – working in the City – it's over. I need to move on to something else."

"OK. Fine. I can understand that, and in fact I'd be willing to back you in another area, if that's what you wanted. Maybe I could set you up in business on a freelance basis. As a financial consultant. How would that suit you?"

"That's kind, Rory, but no thanks. I've made up my mind. I've been given this opportunity to make a go of Amberfield Wines, and I've decided it's what I want to do. Simon would have wanted it too, I'm sure of that. Believe me, I'm deeply grateful to you for holding my job open. And I'm sorry it's taken me so long to come to a final decision, but that's the way it is."

Rory was studying her closely, but she had the impression he was not taking her wholly seriously.

"My worry is that you'll be throwing away your life if you stay on there. I'll admit that wine we drank was good, but one decent bottle doesn't make an industry. You must see that there's no future for British wine."

"For *British* wine, most certainly not," agreed Meriel. "At least, I sincerely hope so."

"I beg your pardon?" Rory's confusion was total.

"You see!" exclaimed Meriel, "even someone as knowledgeable and sophisticated as you doesn't know the difference between British and English wines!"

"OK, *English*, since you insist on being so parochial – "

"No!" Meriel interrupted him. "They're two completely different things, with nothing at all in common." She explained, briefly, what she meant, before concluding:

"*British* wines are the main reason why this country's wines have had such a bad press in the past. But they bear no relation to the real thing, I can promise you that."

"Well, well," murmured Rory. "I stand corrected. So," he went on, "you really are taking the whole thing seriously?"

"Yes, I am."

"And I'm to take it that you truly mean it when you say you don't wish to come back and work for me?"

"Yes, Rory, I do."

"Well, I can't pretend I'm not sorry. You were one of my best people, you know. I'd rather counted on having you back. But if you've made your decision, then so be it. I can live with that. There's just one thing . . ."

"Yes?"

Rory lightly drew a finger across the back of her hand.

"I'd like us to be friends," he said simply. "Can we go on seeing one another?"

"Friends? Yes, of course," she replied, after only the slightest hesitation.

"Then . . . it's all right if I phone you?" asked Rory.

"In a while, Rory. When things are more settled."

After putting Meriel in a taxi to take her to the station, Rory decided to walk back to the office. He wanted a little time to think before immersing himself in his work, and this seemed as good an opportunity as any. Besides, he knew he did not produce his best effort when he was angry, and, although he had managed to hide his feelings from Meriel, he was not best pleased with the outcome of his lunch with her.

What he had said to her was true: she had been an outstandingly able employee during her time at Vere Lassiter. She was, moreover, popular with colleagues and clients alike. He would certainly like her to take up her former position with the firm, but there was more to it than that. Indeed, there was a good deal more to it than Meriel appeared to realise, even though Rory had sought to jog her memory by taking her to that same restaurant again.

For Rory remembered that occasion very clearly. At the time, five years ago he recalled, it had suited him to play her game, to go along with her wishes. There was Andrea and his impending marriage to consider. But it was his habit to file away certain people, certain incidents for future use, particularly when there was a score to be settled. Meriel might not be aware of it, but she had not escaped this particular net. One day he would haul her in, willy-nilly . . . Rory smiled to himself. Something told him he would not need to pursue her. He had a feeling she would come of her own accord. It was simply a question of waiting.

7

Meriel was not quite nineteen when she first met Rory Lassiter. The previous summer, she had passed her A levels with good grades and had taken a crash course in shorthand and typing. She had already decided to apply for a place at university for the following year when Ricky's letter arrived from Argentina and changed both her life and her mother's.

"Fancy that!" Dorothy had exclaimed. "Ranch manager! After all this time, someone's finally seen what Ricky's made of! Here. See for yourself."

And Meriel, seeing her mother almost weeping with happiness, had not had the heart to point out that the duties Ricky described could not by any stretch of the imagination be referred to as those of a ranch manager. His job, plainly, was that of general handyman. And judging by the wheedling, sometimes petulant tone of the writing, even this job was his only on condition that he was accompanied by a wife to do the cleaning and cooking. But at least there would be employment for them both, and a *casita* thrown in. All Meriel could do was to pretend to share Dorothy's excitement.

"Of course," Dorothy had said, and probably meant it, "if you're going to be studying, I'll stay on until you're able to fend for yourself. Until you're earning a bit of money . . ."

But Meriel assured her she had not really set her heart on going to university. This was largely true. There were moments when she imagined herself enjoying the freedom and the intellectual stimulus of living among a group of like-minded young people, but most of the time the idea struck her as simply too scary. She had not fitted in at school: why should university be any different?

Dorothy scarcely tried to conceal her relief at Meriel's decision. After coming out top of her class in shorthand, and very near the top in typing, Meriel took a couple of temporary jobs, no more than two or three weeks each, before accepting a permanent position as a secretary with Beatty's Business Services, a company which specialised in storing office documents, shredding office documents, and shifting office documents from one place to another. The pay was suprisingly good, and for a short time, Meriel succeeded in persuading herself that if she worked hard and learned all she could, she might in time aspire to a more active role in the company.

Before long, however, she had to admit to herself that she was bored to death; Mr Beatty was pleasant enough, and the drivers liked to joke with her and tease her during their brief stops at headquarters between deliveries and collections, but it soon became horribly clear that there was no future for her in a company of this kind. An article in *Cosmopolitan* about careers in merchant banking roused Meriel's interest to such an extent that, on an impulse, she wrote to Vere Lassiter suggesting that they employ her. To her astonishment and delight, they did just that.

After Beatty's Business Services, the hectic atmosphere at Vere Lassiter came as something of a tonic. True, the pace of work was such that there was little time for any life outside the office – Meriel had to be at her desk long after and sometimes considerably before the hours agreed in her contract – but she found the world of wheeling and dealing, of foreign currency fluctuations and immense financial risks oddly stimulating. Her interest in current affairs grew apace, and she would devour the day's press for indicators of likely movements in the money market.

Given her looks and her undoubted ability, it was inevitable that she should at some point come to Rory

Lassiter's attention. She had been introduced to him, briefly, when she first arrived, as Rory made a point of taking a quick look at all new employees (he was good at remembering who people were, and he enjoyed the look of surprise on the faces of less important members of staff when he recognised them in the street, or waiting for the lift). Since then she had on one or two occasions needed to take documents to his office and there had been the occasional brief, polite exchange of civilities.

She did not realise that Rory kept more than half an eye on candidates he considered suitable for promotion, nor that she came into this category. So it was with trepidation verging on terror that she obeyed his summons soon after her mother's departure for South America and entered his office.

"I know I've had a lot of time off lately," she began, determined to have her say first, "but there's been so much to do, what with selling the house and the furniture and so on . . . I'm really very sorry. Anyway, it's all done now. It won't happen again." To her embarrassment, her eyes filled with tears.

"My dear girl!" exclaimed Rory, pulling a box of man-size tissues out of a desk drawer and pushing them across to her. "Believe me, I haven't called you in here to give you a ticking off! On the contrary. I've been hearing excellent reports of you."

Meriel blew her nose and looked at Rory in embarrassment.

"I'm sorry," she murmured, "I assumed you were cross with me."

Rory looked across at the girl before him and took in the skin like cream and those sensational eyes. Even the reddened nose and the pallor of exhaustion could not diminish the quality of looks like those, he thought. She was a bit awkward, perhaps, for his taste; a little unsophisticated. But in a couple of years, when she was in her twenties and the roundness of her face began to give

108

way to a sculpted, more refined look, she would be quite a looker.

Feeling him stare at her, Meriel grew hot and embarrassed, at which Rory, to spare her further confusion, dropped his gaze and began explaining the real reason for her visit to his office. She was to be promoted, he told her, and trained with a view to working in the dealing room.

"I'm sure you're sufficiently well informed to know that after what they're calling Big Bang, brokers will be allowed both to buy and sell shares, currencies, whatever – ?"

Meriel nodded. She was aware of the sweeping changes about to engulf the City: 24-hour trading, computerisation – already Vere Lassiter were foremost in adapting to the new system.

"Well," Rory continued, "the point is that we shall in future need a brand new kind of broker – or dealer, as they'll be called, I gather – young, adaptable, quick-witted, fast on their feet . . . and from what I've seen, you strike me as a likely candidate. So. What do you say?"

She stared at him in astonishment for a moment, before relaxing back in her chair and smiling broadly.

"I'd love to have a try!" she said. "If you're sure I'm up to it."

She was put to work with Giles Atkinson, a man who initially rebelled at this new responsibility. He was, after all, of the generation that could not fully adapt to the idea of women doing this sort of job at all. But teaching usually seems worth while when the pupil is able and attentive, as Giles discovered with Meriel. As always, she picked up new information quickly and found it easy to retain what she had learned.

She was working late at her screen one evening, waiting for an important phone call which Giles, who had a wedding anniversary to attend, deemed she was competent to handle, when she was startled by a voice behind her.

"Giles keeps telling me how pleased he is with your progress," said Rory, motioning her not to stand up. "I'm delighted things are working out so well. He's not an easy man to impress, our Giles! Has a reputation for being a bit of an ogre, I believe."

Meriel smiled. "Oh, he's just an old sweetie, really," she said, unthinkingly.

"Not so much of the old!" laughed Rory. "I'll have you know he's only a few years older than I am!"

"Oh, I didn't mean – !" Again, Rory made her feel embarrassed. What she actually meant was that Giles projected a more paternal, more middle-aged figure than Rory who was, it had to be admitted, altogether sexier.

The expected phone call came through, and Rory watched as Meriel effortlessly switched her full attention to the matter in hand. Within moments, the deal had been finalised, the Dutch guilders sold.

"Well," she said, "that's me finished for today."

"Lucky you," said Rory. "I'll be here half the night, by the look of things. See you tomorrow, then."

She wished him good night, fetched her coat and was on her way towards the lift when she heard footsteps approaching.

"Hi." It was her colleague, Kath.

"I didn't realise there was anybody still here," Meriel told her in surprise.

"Apart from Rory, of course," said Kath.

She was a few years older than Meriel, with cropped fair hair, a harsh Australian twang and a preference for dauntingly severe suits. Meriel was more than a little in awe of Kath, and of her formidable reputation in the dealing room.

"Er . . . yes . . ." said Meriel.

"Ask you out to dinner, did he?" inquired Kath.

"Rory Lassiter? Certainly not!" Meriel was amused at the suggestion.

Kath looked at her coolly for a moment, then she said: "I think you and I ought to have a little talk. Got time for a drink?"

"You mean now? Well, I . . ."

But it was evident Kath was not going to take no for an answer, and ten minutes later they were seated in Porky's Wine Bar with a bottle of chilled white wine and helpings of pitta bread and taramasalata.

"If you don't mind my saying so, you strike me as being particularly wet behind the ears," Kath informed her without beating about the bush. "I'd have expected someone with your looks to be more experienced . . . either that, or you're extraordinarily devious."

"I'm sorry?" Meriel was utterly perplexed. "I honestly don't understand what you're trying to say."

Kath lit a black Sobranie and slowly blew out a stream of smoke. "OK, OK. I'll try and put it as simply as possible. Rory Lassiter, our great and rather gorgeous employer, seems to think he enjoys *droit de seigneur* over female members of staff. Are you with me so far?"

"Yes . . . I think so, but . . ."

"In other words, he expects to bed people like me and you as part of our contract of employment. People like me and you, having been road-tested, so to speak, are then discarded in favour of a newer model. And that applies even if you passed your MOT with flying colours, as I believe I did. The trick of it is not to mind. Not to get upset. And definitely not to make the mistake of thinking Rory loves you, or vice versa."

Meriel shook her head. "You don't understand – "

"I'm telling you all this because it will sure as heck be your turn soon. Any minute now you'll be invited back to Rory's little Barbican love-nest and any reply beginning with 'n' and ending with 'o' will be met with considerable displeasure. The point is this: from what I hear, Vere Lassiter needs you. You're too good to lose. Or at least, you will be in a few months' time. So when Rory makes his move, do your stuff, lie back and enjoy it then put it out of your mind once and for all."

Meriel scooped up some taramasalata onto a strip of

111

pitta bread while she thought over what Kath had said. She certainly did not intend to take what she had heard at face value. Maybe Rory did sometimes make a pass at an employee, Kath included. Maybe Kath was still a little in love with Rory and had misinterpreted his friendly, innocent chat with Meriel as sexual interest. She was jealous, and she was using this rather clever tactic to try and warn off a potential rival. Meriel suddenly felt rather sorry for Kath.

"What you don't realise," Meriel said, "is that I've already got a boyfriend – "

"Ha!" Kath's laughter was explosive. "That's never stopped Rory in the past! What I've been telling you will surely come to pass, Meriel. Just be prepared, that's all."

Although she was certain that nothing Kath said applied to her, Meriel was none the less watchful in Rory's presence over the next few weeks, waiting to see if he did indeed "make his move". But his behaviour remained unchanged, and after a time she relaxed, and began to forget what Kath had said.

Then, in June of that year, Kath took a fortnight's holiday, and on her very first day away from work Rory called Meriel in to his office and asked her out to dinner.

At first, Meriel didn't even realise what he was asking. He started off by saying something about how pleased they all were with her progress and then went on to suggest they should have a discussion about her further promotion prospects. It wasn't until she had agreed to the day and the time – seven thirty, which she thought oddly late for an office meeting, but she assumed that was the only time he was free – that he named the restaurant where they were to meet, and the scales fell from her eyes.

"Oh, I . . ." she began in confusion. "I'm sorry, I didn't realise . . ."

Rory had a wonderful way with raised eyebrows, causing them almost to vanish under the shock of curly hair when

112

he wished. It was a habit that always made people – and women in particular – smile.

"What didn't you realise, Meriel?"

"I assumed you meant an office meeting . . ." she said, trying to sound more confident than she felt.

"At seven thirty in the evening?" he asked in mock astonishment. "When dinner is beginning to be served all over London? What an extraordinary idea!"

"It's just that . . ."

But now Rory had changed his tactics and was leaning gravely towards her across the desk.

"Tell me, Meriel," he said. "You're not on a *diet* are you?"

He made it sound like a fatal illness and, again, Meriel smiled in spite of herself.

"No, nothing like that," she replied, and suddenly she found the confidence to say exactly what she wanted. "The fact is that you have a reputation among the staff here as far as new women employees are concerned."

"I do?" Rory could not have looked more amazed.

"And I simply want to make it perfectly clear that if I accept the offer of dinner with you, I am doing just that. Nothing more."

Rory's eyes had narrowed during this last bit, and she thought she had probably annoyed him. His elbows resting on the desk, he was tapping his fingers together at the level of his upper lip, and eyeing her thoughtfully. After a moment, he flung his arms wide and smiled broadly.

"You know," he said, "you really shouldn't listen to all this gossip about me! Most of it is quite unfounded!"

"I mean it," said Meriel firmly. "I want you to promise that we're only going to dinner."

"Of course I promise, you silly girl!" Rory now appeared to be enjoying himself hugely. "So you see, you have absolutely nothing to worry about."

Meriel arrived at Roper's rather earlier than she had intended, and for a while she walked up and down the

113

pavement, too shy to enter the restaurant on her own. It was bound to be far more intimidating a venue than the places Andrew, her current boyfriend, took her to. But when it came on to rain she was driven indoors, only to find to her surprise that Rory was already there, and had been waiting for her all along.

Throughout the meal, Rory remained true to his word, and treated Meriel as he would have treated any respected employee. They talked mainly about the bank, and what role Meriel saw herself playing in its future development. As she relaxed under the influence of good food and drink, all of which she encouraged Rory to choose for her, she warmed to the prospects before her.

"You've no idea how grateful I am to you for giving me the job," she said as they waited for their coats to be fetched. "I only hope I don't ever let you down."

They had moved away from their table, in the direction of the door. Rory helped Meriel into her coat, then said softly, into her ear:

"That's rather my hope too, Meriel. Can I take it that means you'll spend the night with me?"

"Certainly not!" said Meriel, pulling away and uttering a giggle far louder than she meant to. At least, she supposed she must have done, given the way the other diners suddenly looked up and turned their heads in her direction. She had not, until now, realised that she had drunk more than was good for her.

Rory smiled into her eyes. "Oh, come on, Meriel! Don't waste time playing games with me!"

"No, I . . . I mustn't be late," she replied, beginning to flounder a little. "I have to be up early tomorrow."

"I think my profits would stand a couple of hours' lateness on your part tomorrow morning," said Rory.

"It's not that . . . it's just not really fair on Giles," said Meriel. "I mean, he's expecting me to be here . . ."

"Of course he is. And you're quite right about not being in late. But I promise you'll be home in good time." He

114

placed an arm around her shoulders and added: "We'll only be a couple of hours, and then I'll get my chauffeur to drive you home."

"No!" Meriel pulled away from him with such force that she knocked into the table behind her, causing wine to spill onto the rose-patterned tablecloth.

"Kindly bring these people a new bottle of wine," demanded Rory quietly of the wine waiter, slipping him a note of an unnecessarily high denomination. Then, with anger beginning to sound in his voice, he added: Meriel, will you please stop behaving so ridiculously? At least until we have left the restaurant. This really is no big deal, you know."

"There is no way I am going to leave this restaurant with you," said Meriel, her eyes and cheeks blazing. "You promised me – " she began, pushing away Rory's arm as he tried to take hold of her elbow, "you *promised* me," she added more loudly, "that you would take me for dinner only, and that, Rory Lassiter, is all you are getting!"

By now the other diners were unable to hide their amusement at this unexpected scene, and at Meriel's final pronouncement, a light ripple of applause sounded around the room. The diners now turned their attention to Rory, eager to see how he would respond. For some moments he eyed Meriel impassively, while he deliberated what to do. Then, his face breaking into a seemingly easy and unforced smile, he said:

"Perhaps you're right." He fetched a chair and seated Meriel by the restaurant door. Then, calling a waiter over, he said: "I'm leaving now. Would you be so kind as to call this lady a taxi? And could you make absolutely sure she remembers her home address?"

Neither of them had ever referred to this evening again. Early the following week, Rory announced a particularly lucrative deal with a Japanese bank, and celebrated the event by personally distributing glasses of champagne among the staff. When he came to Meriel, he smiled and asked how she was, and that was all. It was as though the incident had never taken place, the more so as Meriel was duly promoted along the lines Rory had indicated.

Sometimes, in the months that followed, she asked herself whether perhaps she had not overreacted to his proposition, if indeed it was seriously meant. She really had been so immature, so inexperienced in those days!

Today, she had enjoyed his company enormously, and had been genuinely pleased to see him again. Only the fact that he had taken her to Roper's, of all the restaurants in London, caused a flash of doubt as to his motives, and even this was quickly dispelled. If he telephoned her, she decided, she would see him again. There seemed no reason not to.

Jonathan drove home at lunchtime in the vain hope that Bella might be there. He knew she was out the moment he opened the remotely operated double garage doors and saw that his wife's little Mercedes was missing. He was irritated, but not particularly surprised. Later, he would ask her where she had been, and she would say she was out shopping, or lunching with a friend, and, as usual, he would have no idea whether she was telling the truth.

A feeling of resentment niggled at him as he turned off the Jaguar's engine and made his way into the house. What was the point of having a wife if she was never going to be there when he needed her? If all she ever did was spend, and then spend some more . . . The trouble was that Bella had no idea of the value of money. Jonathan sometimes thought that her spending on clothes would feed a medium-sized third-world country for a year. Nor did she begin to understand how little a small-town solicitor earned in the average year – at least, compared with the sort of income enjoyed by her father and other US attorneys of her acquaintance.

Jonathan first set eyes on Bella during a skiing holiday in Aspen, Colorado. She was one of a number of guests invited for dinner at the weekend cabin of a mutual friend, and when Jonathan was introduced to her, she was lying on a rug by the fireside, surrounded by other people's boyfriends. Dressed plainly in smart black ski pants and a tight red sweater, she none the less oozed class and money. Everything about her, from her straight, shoulder-length dark-brown hair to her slim legs pushed into soft suede ankle-boots, seemed designed to make the other women in the room look fussy and overdressed.

When, ignoring his protests, Bella rose to shake hands with him, Jonathan was only able to manage a couple of stilted phrases before moving on. Women like that seemed so far out of his reach that he saw little point in wasting time on her. But apparently Bella thought differently. She made a point of seeking him out after dinner, sitting down with him in a quiet corner of the lounge and getting him to tell her all about himself. Jonathan was both moved and flattered by Bella's interest and in no time at all found himself falling hopelessly in love.

For reasons he could never quite fathom – though he had enjoyed more than his share of success with women in the past – Bella was equally smitten by him. They were two of a kind, she told him, and even though he had a sneaking suspicion she was not being wholly complimentary, he believed her. By the time his holiday ended, he and Bella were deep into a love affair and she had asked him home to Boston to meet his parents.

The meeting with James Angus Cameron and his wife Cybill, which Jonathan had dreaded since the day it was first mooted, turned out to be an unexpected success. As Bella's father put it, there was always room in his house for a fellow-Scot, even though his own claim to Scottishness was perhaps a little tenuous, his great-grandfather having emigrated to the States from Inverness in the 1890s.

For some time after Jonathan might reasonably have been expected to propose marriage to Bella, he hesitated, terrified that she would turn him down. But when he finally plucked up the necessary courage, she accepted immediately – on condition that she chose their new home. Unlike the houses bought by most of their acquaintances in this part of Kent, No 6 Lauriston Drive was modern. Spacious, comfortable, well-heated – Bella had made this a condition of settling somewhere as northerly and barbarous as England – the property boasted six bed-rooms, three bathrooms, four reception rooms, a sauna and Jacuzzi, and a heated swimming-pool. It was miles too big for a couple with no children, but Bella seemed unable to contemplate living somewhere more in keeping with their requirements – or with their financial status, come to that, thought Jonathan ruefully.

He entered the large kitchen with its hand-made, indi-vidually painted units – each of which had cost nearly a thousand pounds – and looked about him. Already, Bella was beginning to make noises about not being sure pale yellow was the right choice, and Jonathan reminded himself that, this time, he really must be firm with her.

For a moment, he toyed with the idea of pouring himself a decent-sized Scotch – God knew he needed it – but then, remembering he had an important meeting with a client later on, he changed his mind. Instead, he drew himself a glass of iced water from the special compartment in the American refrigerator he had been forced to buy from Harrods (just under two thousand pounds' worth, in the *sale*!), and sat down at the kitchen table.

He needed to ponder the implications of a phone call he had received earlier that morning, which had caused him to return home at this unusual hour of the day. The call was from Bert Hollyfield – local property developer and self-made millionaire – and in itself it had been innocuous enough. Bert simply wanted to know what progress was being made with regard to a certain piece of land which he was interested in buying: as he had already informed Adam (so he explained to Jonathan), his architects' plans were at an advanced stage and most of the money was now

118

in place. What he wanted from Jonathan was an assurance that things were proceeding equally swiftly on other fronts. Had the necessary land searches been carried out? How soon could work begin? He was sure Jonathan would appreciate that, after such a long delay, he was anxious to proceed.

What Jonathan Fox found particularly galling about this information was that Adam had said not so much as a word to him about it, despite the fact that there had been ample opportunity and, moreover, that it had all been Jonathan's idea in the first place.

It all began some months after Edward and Vivienne Barton decided to retain Jonathan Fox's services on a part-time basis within Amberfield Wines. Previously, he had acted as family solicitor for a number of years, and had overseen the setting up of the company to the directors' acknowledged satisfaction. It made sense, therefore, to ask him to sit in on board meetings and offer advice when necessary. The Bartons had not, however, seen fit to offer him a seat on the board and this was an omission that rankled. There was certainly no great prestige to be had from adding Amberfield Wines to his other directorships, and the money would probably have been even less than the pathetic retainer he now received, but that was not the point. The point was that he felt he deserved some recognition for the work he had put in on the Bartons' behalf.

Perhaps it was a growing sense of resentment that gave his mental antennae the necessary sensitivity to winkle out the fact that, alone among the Bartons, Adam was less than ecstatic about growing vines at Amberfield. This was something Jonathan had not initially been aware of, and the moment he realised how the land lay, a plan began forming in his mind. When the time seemed right, he cautiously allowed himself to wonder aloud whether perhaps the land might not be put to better use. He had been surprised by Adam's swift, emphatic response.

"I couldn't agree with you more," said Adam. "If you want my opinion, these bloody vines are going to eat up every last penny we've got. And if that doesn't work they're going to reach out their lethal little tendrils and choke us all to death."

"In that case," suggested Jonathan, "why not sell off a choice piece of the land and get someone like Bert Hollyfield to build some expensive houses on it?"

Adam shook his head. "You don't understand, Jonathan. Mother and Father would never agree to that. Not in a million years! And as for Simon. . .!"

"But the company is losing money hand over fist! We've never fully recouped the initial investment, and now that we've had to add the cost of the winery to our outgoings it'll be years before we see a penny in profit! Your parents must be aware they can't go on like this for ever. Why don't I mention the idea to Bert? I'm certain he'd be interested! He never builds anything that sells for less than half a million, so he'd pay a good price for the land."

"Perhaps it wouldn't be a bad idea to talk to him . . ."

"Splendid!" said Jon. "I'll fix up a meeting. Next week some time?"

"Why don't you just give me his number?" asked Adam. "There's no need for you to be involved."

Was it obtuseness on Adam's part, Jonathan had wondered, or did he really think there was some way he could prevent the lawyer from being included in such a potentially lucrative deal?

"I would prefer to be involved, if it's all the same with you," Jonathan replied quietly. "There would be a need for a legal presence in the event of a sale, as I'm sure you are aware."

"What you mean is that you stand to make a very tidy sum out of the conveyancing on the new properties," murmured Adam, seeing that Jonathan had no intention of letting go. "Plus a bit more from the sale of the land."

"I wouldn't be the only one to see a profit," replied Jonathan. "You'd all stand to gain. You, Simon, your parents – all of you."

"I still don't think they'll sell," said Adam. "However, I can't see what harm it would do to have a chat with Bert. Fix something up, will you?"

Jonathan had been despatched like a messenger boy to sound out Bert Hollyfield who, in turn, had sent a surveyor to Amberfield. His report having proved more than satisfactory, Jonathan was just beginning to hear the sound of cash registers when Edward suffered his first stroke. The very next day, Jonathan received a phone call from Adam. He came straight to the point:

"Our little bit of business with Bert Hollyfield," he said.

"Yes?"

"This isn't a good time to proceed. I'd be grateful if you could keep all our conversations relating to this transaction to yourself."

"But – "

"Father may not survive. And if he does there's no telling what his mental state will be like. So leave it, Jon, there's a good chap."

Adam, reflected Jonathan as he slowly, very slowly, replaced the receiver in its cradle, was a good six years younger than he was. He had left school with one A level. Unlike his brother, he had not attended agricultural college and had acquired no professional qualifications. He had not trained to do any particular job. The only reason that Jonathan was prepared to be spoken to in this way was that Adam Barton was the son of one of his clients. Adam – as well as the other members of the family, for that matter – should realise that he had put a great deal of time and effort into Amberfield Wines, with very little to show for it. They should accept that someone of Jonathan Fox's abilities did not work for nothing.

The American icebox gurgled and thrummed gently into life, bringing Jonathan back to the present with a start. During the course of the past year, a year which had seen Amberfield reel beneath the shock of two major tragedies – Edward's second, far more serious stroke, and Simon's death – Jonathan had largely put the idea of profiting from the sale of Amberfield land out of his mind. The discovery that the scheme had been brought back to life should have been welcome: this was after all what he had wanted all along. But his pleasure was marred by the way Adam had gone behind his back to Bert. One day soon, he told himself angrily, Adam would have to be taught a lesson.

If it weren't for Bella, thought Jonathan, things would be a lot easier. The trouble was that he wanted to keep her, and the only way he knew how was by providing her with as much money as she wanted. For all his wife's faults, it seemed to Jonathan that Bella knocked spots off any other woman he had ever met. None of them could touch her so far as looks, style and sheer charisma were concerned, and he was frankly incapable of imagining that any normal man would think differently. Such an attitude was bound to lead to jealousy, and when Bella freely admitted, as she sometimes did, that she had had lunch with a male friend, or that she had "bumped into so-and-so" in London, Jonathan could only suspect the worst. Sometimes, he almost wondered whether Bella enjoyed his jealousy, relished the thrill of almost – but never quite – provoking her husband into hitting her.

She always seemed to know just when to stop, when to turn his rage into physical excitement, when to lower her voice to a sexy, husky plea to let her prove that it was him she loved, and no one else. It was a trick that always worked, at least at the time, although afterwards Jonathan would wonder at his stupidity at always being taken in by the same wiles. Then he would ask himself whether it really mattered if she had in fact slept with (to give but one example) Theo Presland, the fiftyish, overweight friend of Bella's father who had squired her around London's theatreland during his last visit to the capital, and he would try to persuade himself that it did not.

The only problem was that this approach did not work in all cases. Take Dan Courtney, for example, thought Jonathan, his hand tightening around the glass, his other fist hitting the table with light, rapid, nervous movements. He felt sure, as sure as he could be, that Dan and Bella sometimes spent time together. On one occasion he had observed Dan showing Bella to her car outside the Hare and Hounds, and kissing her hand as she climbed in; the way Bella had smiled up at him as she blew him a goodbye kiss haunted Jonathan to this day. Of course, Bella had denied there was anything out of the ordinary in her behaviour, and had reminded him – rather more impatiently than usual, he felt – that she was free to share a lunchtime drink with whomsoever she saw fit.

A familiar, gnawing jealousy began to spread through him. Pushing his chair back with a sudden, barely controlled violence, Jonathan rose abruptly and, taking the stairs three at a time, marched into Bella's dressing-room and began rummaging feverishly through clothes and pockets, shelves and drawers, handbags, everything he could lay his hands on. The time had come when he could bear the suspicion no longer. He simply had to find proof of her inconstancy.

When he had finished in the dressing-room, and found nothing, he turned his attention to the pretty little writing-desk she had placed by the landing window, overlooking the pool and the garden and the hills beyond. Still nothing. No letters, no incriminating address book, nothing. Then, almost as an afterthought, he opened an envelope of newly-developed photographs, recently collected from Boots. Inside were pictures taken by Bella in Bermuda: there was her mother, Cybill; there the hotel where they stayed; and here were a number of shots of birds and flowers – good pictures, well composed, taken with a first-rate camera.

But there was something else, too. His pale eyes almost glittering with triumph at the discovery, Jonathan pulled out a postcard from among the photographs. It was not recent. It had not been purchased in Bermuda. And it had been neither addressed to nor sent by Bella Fox. For some moments Jonathan stood and stared at the card, reading it over and over. It was perhaps not quite what he had anticipated, but he was sure none the less that this was the proof he had been looking for: the proof that Bella had lied to him about Dan Courtney. After a time, he replaced the card among the photographs. Some day, he knew, he would be able to use that postcard to his definite advantage.

Meanwhile, he would behave in his customary controlled way and carry on as before, and this applied to his position at Amberfield as much as to his relationship with Bella. The two things were interlinked; in order to keep Bella he needed a steady supply of cash, and that meant clinging on to all available sources. Amberfield might not be providing much of the stuff yet, but one day . . . one day! Of course, it was in some ways a shame to build on countryside of such beauty, but homes were urgently needed in this corner of Kent, everyone said so. And the site Bert had in mind – the area now covered by the vineyards at Amberfield – was perfect in every way . . . they had found nowhere else half as attractive, and not for want of looking.

All that remained was to find a suitable way of broaching the subject at the next board meeting. Vivienne might be a little tricky, but could surely be persuaded, eventually. And once she had agreed to the sale, there would no longer be any reason for Dan Courtney to remain at Amberfield. As for Simon's widow . . . what could Meriel Barton possibly do that would alter events one way or the other?

124

PART TWO

8

The new year, which had started promisingly enough as far as the weather was concerned, soon degenerated into storms and floods, with blustery winds making work in the vineyards impossible and inducing a constant fear that the stream at the foot of the main field would overflow its banks and drown some of the lower-lying grapevines.

Running across the courtyard one wet and wintry morning, Meriel was halted at the entrance to Michelle's office by the sound of raised voices.

"What's going on?" she asked the girl.

Michelle was looking mutinous. "Whatever it is, I don't see why I should have to sit here and listen to that bleedin' racket," she said sulkily.

"Look, Michelle, why don't you go and take a break? Come back when things have quietened down."

When the girl had gone, Meriel debated interrupting the continuing argument, then decided against it. She would just have to hope that no unexpected customers turned up. As she busied herself with the display of wines for sale, she listened shamelessly to the conversation next door. Whatever was going on, it was her business too.

"I can only repeat what I've already told you," said Adam. "I am on my way out, and I do not have time for this discussion right now."

"I'm sorry," Dan replied in the tone of voice people adopt when they are clearly not sorry at all, "but you're just going to have to be late for your meeting. I simply refuse to be fobbed off yet again. For God's sake, Adam, where have my bottles got to?"

"As I have already told you," replied Adam wearily, "everything is under control. Now, *please* – "

"You know damn well that isn't the case! Those bottles should have been here a fortnight ago, yet when I phone the manufacturers all I get is a load of waffle about them not being sure whether we want them or not. *Of course* we need the bottles! And the corks, for that matter! And the sooner the better!"

"Ah!" was all Adam said, and Meriel could imagine him leaning back calmly in his chair and tapping his fingertips together. "Yes, well, of course, there has been a slight problem."

"Problem? You're telling me *you've* got a problem? Believe me, it's nothing to the problem we're all going to have if I don't start bottling soon! I've got a couple of tanks just ready and waiting to be filtered, not to mention orders for scores of cases which won't be ready for delivery if I don't get to work immediately!"

"The problem is that, at this precise moment, we don't have the money to pay for the bottles. In fact, we don't even have the money to pay for the corks."

Dan's voice went suddenly quiet. "For God's sake," he said, "tell me you're joking."

"I'm afraid not, old chap. I'm in deadly earnest."

Meriel heard a movement from the inner office, then saw Dan walk past the door in one direction, then back again in the other. He was evidently having trouble controlling himself.

"Let's get this straight. I told you back in – when, October? November? – what my requirements were likely to be. When I mentioned the matter again before Christmas, you assured me that you were negotiating an extension to our overdraft so as to pay for our order. Are you telling me you forgot? Is that it?"

"Oh, no, I most certainly didn't forget," replied Adam smoothly. "And indeed I approached Hammond at once. I suppose you know he's moved on? Been replaced by a younger chap – Beagley. Which means that the overdraft process has had to be started all over again. You know how these things are. Mother and I have arranged to see him one day next week."

"Not till next week! And *then* how long is he going to take to make up his mind? Adam, don't you understand how urgent this is? Anybody would think you don't realise what all this means! We – "

Coldly, Adam interrupted him.

"On the contrary, I understand only too clearly. Because of your insistence on planting low-yielding vines, we've all but run out of wine to sell, and the result – "

It was Dan's turn to interrupt.

"My vines are not low-yielding, as it happens. There is simply no way they can be forced to produce grapes before they're ready. We've known this all along, Adam!"

"If you hadn't insisted on replanting, on grubbing up some perfectly adequate stock, we'd have had plenty of wine left to sell right through the winter, which would have given us the regular income we now so desperately need. And which we are very much without."

"That's just the sort of rubbish I'd expect to hear from you. You know very well that we had a lot of problems with the old stock. If we'd left them in the ground they'd have stopped yielding altogether by now. Either that or they'd have been carried off by disease. You also know – " on his latest turn past the open doorway he spotted Meriel and checked himself. "What the hell! The problem now is my bottles, and what's happened to them."

"As I am at some pains to put over to you, I will endeavour to sort the money out next week. I will try and explain to Beagley – "

"For pity's sake, what is there to explain? Simply tell him that I am ready to start bottling last year's wines. For which I need bottles, b-o-t-t-l-e-s. Without bottles we can't sell any wine, and if we don't sell any wine, we don't make any money. Is that so very difficult for a bank manager to comprehend?"

"All Beagley will want to know is whether we are ever likely to be in a position to repay a loan of eight thousand pounds."

"This is getting us nowhere," Dan said at last. "All I would say to you is that if that money doesn't come through fast, it's going to cost us an absolute fortune in lost sales. And you try explaining that to your mother and the other board members!"

"I'll see what I can do to speed things up," agreed Adam at last, clearly not relishing a major row with Vivienne.

Dan, his hands stuffed in his pocket, walked past Meriel with scarcely a glance. Reaching the door, he turned suddenly on his heel and called back to Adam:

"And while I'm about it, I suggest you round up a few unpaid helpers to give us a hand with the pruning. We're behind with that, too."

"Phew!" remarked Meriel, slipping into the inner office and closing the door.

"I assume you heard all that," said Adam. He sounded accusing.

"Not through choice."

"Well, it's probably no bad thing for you to see what I have to put up with from that man."

"Yes . . ." agreed Meriel thoughtfully. "On the other hand, doesn't he have a point? I mean, what can he do with no bottles?"

"I can't believe I'm hearing this! Are you seriously taking Dan Courtney's side against mine?"

She had not intended to annoy him, but his inability to control his anger made her want to retaliate.

"It's not a question of taking sides! All I want is to see the company in profit and to do my job to the best of my ability."

130

"Your job?" It was almost as though he did not know what she was talking about.

"Organising the shop, Adam! My job! How can I run a shop if there's nothing to sell?"

"Oh, that. I wouldn't worry too much about that, Meriel. Just do what you can. Now I really must be off. I'm frightfully late as it is."

Adam left. Michelle returned and sat sulking in the outer office. Meriel, more deeply wounded by Adam's dismissive attitude than she cared to admit, did what she always did when she needed to simmer down. She put on her track suit and went for a run.

Later the same week, quite by chance, Meriel happened on some further pages of Edward Barton's memoir. They had been folded lengthwise and used to mark a place in an anthology of travel writing that Simon had been reading before his last fatal trip to America. By now, Meriel had largely completed the task of sorting through her husband's papers, but one or two small jobs remained: disposing of Simon's books was one of them. This particular volume carried the Barton plate on its flyleaf, and had clearly been loaned to Simon by his father. Complete, presumably, with bookmark, though there was no way of knowing whether Simon had been aware of what the pages contained. Meriel was on the point of returning the book to Edward's library when its unexpected enclosure caught her eye.

Among the many interesting facts which came to my attention on the subject of growing vines in England are the following: firstly, in 1152, Henry II's marriage to Eleanor of Aquitaine brought the vineyards of Bordeaux under English rule, thus affording a plentiful supply of good cheap wine; secondly, some time during the fourteenth century, the Gulf Stream altered its course, bringing a period of cooler weather to the

131

British Isles under which our vines ceased to thrive. Add to this the decimation of the population caused by the Black Death, and it is perhaps not surprising that the number of vines grown on our soil was drastically reduced.

At first, I found this information rather depressing. Although the plague is no longer with us, the Gulf Stream, as far as I am aware, has not obligingly moved back to its original position and we still have easy access to cheap wine from France – in particular, red wines, which I am not convinced we shall ever successfully grow in this country. But a chat with Guy Hutchins of the Meteorological Office cheered me up no end. He assured me that the "mini ice-age" which Britain underwent between, say, the fifteenth and nineteenth centuries, has been followed by a long period of warmer weather, a period which is likely to last some time yet.

And there was more. According to the English Vineyards Association, whom I approached for help and information in connection with my plans, there was apparently a spate of planting at that time. All over Kent and Sussex and Norfolk and Wiltshire, and elsewhere too, sites were being cleared, couch grass killed off, wire netting erected, wooden stakes driven in, bamboo canes inserted, trellises installed and new vines planted. It was really rather exciting. I began to feel I was part of some glamorous coterie which mere money could never buy me: all I could hope was that the quality of our wines lived up to expectations!

Edward now turned to the day when he, Simon and Adam made the two-hour journey to the nursery to collect their stocks of new vines. To their surprise, these turned out to be rooted cuttings still growing in the soil in the propagating house. Previously, Edward had assumed everything would be ready and waiting for them, but in the event he and his sons were told to dig up the vines

132

themselves and replant them in little black plastic bags for transportation to Amberfield.

Given the need to collect several thousand cuttings, it was some hours before the work was completed, and Edward found to his dismay that Adam was more of a hindrance than a help. In his words, "the lad seemed unable to judge between a vine with a root system adequate for planting out, and one without." Although he tried to make allowances, it was clear to Meriel that Edward was disappointed at his younger son's lack of "feel" for the task in hand, whereas he was full of praise for Simon's efforts.

> The next few days were spent planting out the new vines, each of which already sprouted a number of pale, bud-like leaves which were just on the point of unfolding. The cuttings measured between ten and twelve inches in length, and getting them into the ground meant working bent over almost double for long periods. I remember being pleased to think this was one job that would not need doing again in a hurry. Little did I know then what lay in store for us! But despite our aching backs, it felt good to be handling the living vines at long last and I shall never forget how impatient I felt at the realisation that it would be a full three years before we were able to pick our first harvest.

Not for the first time, Meriel was left with the feeling that there must be more. Edward, she suspected, had composed his notebooks over a long period – all she needed to do was find them. On an impulse, she ran downstairs with the pages still clutched in her hand, with the intention of asking Vivienne what light she could throw on the matter. But Vivienne was nowhere to be found, and even Jacinta seemed not entirely sure of her whereabouts. Meriel was about to return, disappointed, to her room, when it occurred to her that she could always ask Edward himself.

133

Like the other members of the household, Meriel paid frequent visits to the old man when he was not well enough to be up and among them, as was increasingly the case. In the holidays, Hatta played the cello to her father most afternoons, but Meriel simply sat and told him what she had been doing, enjoying the occasional flash of pleasure in his eyes when she described something he particularly approved of. She had not previously attempted to ask him questions, although Miss Digby had sometimes urged her to do so, insisting that she would be able to understand what Edward wished to say in reply.

This time, just when Meriel needed her, Miss Digby was out of the room, but she sat down as usual and started chatting and before long was telling him how fascinated she had been to read about the digging up of the hops, and the planting of the vines, and the long wait before their first harvest. More than anything, she told him, she enjoyed learning what Simon's part had been in the bringing of the vines to Amberfield.

"You must have been so proud of him, you and Vivienne," she said, gently catching hold of his hand in her own and smiling into his eyes.

What she saw there made her let go of Edward's hand and stand up so suddenly that she knocked over her chair with a thump that shook her almost as much as what she had just seen. Quite simply, the man looked terrified. A violent trembling took hold of him, the twisted face became suffused with colour and his head began jerking spasmodically from side to side. At the same time, a series of choking, strangled sounds emerged from his throat, so that for a few horrible moments, Meriel believed she was about to witness Edward's death.

"Miss Digby!" she called frantically, but the nurse was already beside her, pushing her out of the way.

"If you don't mind," she was saying, "I think I'd better deal with this on my own. Don't worry, now. I – "

134

At the sight of the pieces of paper in Meriel's hand, she broke off abruptly and her hand flew to her mouth.

"Are you sure there's nothing I can do to help?" asked Meriel, in even greater alarm in the face of this unexpected behaviour. "Should I call Dr Dinwiddy?"

"No, no, that won't be necessary. He just needs to calm down, that's all." She was showing Meriel to the door now, almost pushing her out.

The whole episode had lasted no more than a few minutes. Meriel, returning to her room, deeply shaken, was haunted by two vivid images. One was of the fear in Edward's eyes. The other was of the way in which Miss Digby had reacted to the sight of the pages of Edward's memoir. There could be no doubt about it: she had known exactly what they were.

At first, when Adam told her Maurice Beagley was refusing to increase the overdraft to fund the purchase of urgently needed materials, Vivienne refused to take the news seriously.

"Oh, don't be silly, darling!" she had exclaimed. "Of course he'll let us have the money! I'll have a word with him myself. Drive me to the bank. Now."

Brushing aside her son's suggestion that she should telephone first to make sure the manager was able to see her, she swept into the bank's premises in resolute mood.

It was plain from the expression on her face when she eventually emerged and climbed into the waiting car that the meeting had not gone well. Vivienne said little during the drive home but once back at Amberfield she led the way to the drinks cabinet in the drawing-room and poured them both a large Scotch.

"How *dare* that awful man speak to me like that?" she demanded, taking a decorous sip from her glass and then, immediately after, a much larger one.

"I take it you had no more luck with him than I did?" asked Adam.

He seemed curiously untroubled by Beagley's refusal to help them, a fact which did nothing to improve Vivienne's temper.

"He wants us to reduce our outgoings, for pity's sake! How does he expect us to do that, I'd like to know? It's not as though we occupy expensive office space, or employ a staff of thousands." She was pacing to and fro in front of the fireplace, unable to keep still. "I suppose we could always sack Michelle," she offered after a moment. "It's not as though she does much for her money."

"She doesn't earn enough to make it worth the while," murmured Adam. "On the other hand, if we let Dan go – "

Vivienne stopped pacing and whirled round to where Adam sat sprawled on one of the pale blue sofas. "*What*?" she exclaimed. "Oh, Adam, I cannot believe you are being serious! That is simply the most ridiculous thing I've ever heard . . ." but her voice was tailing away uncertainly towards the end.

"Is it?" asked Adam in the same quiet voice as before. "Is it really, Mother? Think of the saving we'd make if we didn't have to pay Dan's salary. Beside which we could let the cottage to some University people – the rent would pay for Michelle. That's two lots of wages saved."

"But . . . oh, no, Adam, it's out of the question. Dan is family. I couldn't possibly do that to him."

"If Dan were here simply as part of the family, you wouldn't be paying him a salary. The fact is he's here as an employee, and we can't afford him."

"But how would we manage without a winemaker?" Vivienne seemed to Adam to be wavering.

"Very well, in my opinion."

"No," said Vivienne vehemently, making her mind up. "That's enough, Adam. I won't listen to any more. Besides, your father wouldn't agree to it, not for a moment. I shall simply have to find another way of getting hold of the money. Then, when we've actually got some income from sales coming in I'll approach Beagley again."

136

When Adam had left her, Vivienne finished her Scotch, and turned to pour herself another before deciding, reluctantly, that she had better not. She was going to need all her wits about her this afternoon, and a slurred voice coupled with a woolly line of reasoning would not go down well with the people she had decided she must speak to. Calling to Jacinta to bring a large pot of black coffee to her study, she made her way to her desk and sat down, willing herself to pick up the receiver. How repugnant it was, she thought, to have to telephone complete strangers asking to borrow money. To be strictly accurate, the people whose names she had before her were not complete strangers. They were men with whom Edward had done business in the past; men who in some cases might feel they owed the Barton family a favour. Even so, she could scarcely bear to demean herself in this way. Quite apart from anything else they were bound to think that it was she, a mere woman, who had brought about the company's present predicament. But there was no alternative. It had to be done.

With a sigh, she reached out towards the telephone, then withdrew her hand. Before she spoke to anybody she must address a particular thought that had been waiting, lurking, in the back of her mind, but which was now pushing forward insistently, refusing to be ignored any longer. What the thought amounted to was this: *Had she and Edward been right to follow Dan's advice and replant the vineyards at Amberfield? Would they not now be in a healthier financial position if they had left things as they were?* Although Vivienne had debated the question a dozen times in the past – with Edward and Dan, with Simon and Adam, with Hammond at the bank – she felt it necessary to rehearse the reasons once more, to reassure herself that, whatever everyone else's misgivings, they were indeed on the right track.

*   *   *

137

They had started off so optimistically, brushing aside any suggestions that they might be rushing into things too quickly, without sufficient preparation. Then, somewhere along the line, it all began to go wrong. When had the doubts first set in? she asked herself, casting her mind back to try and pinpoint the exact moment. Not until after their first, unforgettable harvest, that much was certain. As she remembered, Amberfield's first grapes were picked, on schedule, three years after the planting of the vines, and the occasion of that first *vendange* was quite simply one of the most exciting experiences of their lives.

That first harvest was a good one, easily fulfilling all their high hopes. They did not, in those early days, possess their own winery, so the grapes she and Edward and the others picked were collected by lorry, at around tea-time, by the firm they had selected to transform their magic berries into wine. Vivienne smiled as she recalled Edward's reluctance to part with his precious grapes, his sense of disappointment, almost of loss, as the boxes of grapes were loaded aboard and driven away.

Less than an hour after the lorry had left, Vivienne found her husband anxiously phoning the winery.

"Edward!" she admonished him gently. "It's forty miles to Furzedown! And across country! It's simply not possible for the lorry to have arrived already!"

It seemed that this same message was being relayed to Edward by the winemakers. Disconsolately, he put the receiver down, and ran a hand through his hair.

"All the same . . ." he muttered. "You know how essential it is for the grapes to be pressed as soon as possible after picking. Ideally, it should be done immediately. What if the driver loses his way? Supposing he were to crash and lose the entire crop? Oh, if only we had our own winery!"

"Relax, darling!" she said. "There's nothing to worry about, I'm sure of it. Now, come and sit down and have a nice cup of tea. Believe me, you've earned it."

But Edward would not rest until he had telephoned the winery to make sure his irreplaceable crop had arrived safely. Moments after she heard the receiver crashing back into place, Vivienne was enveloped in a massive bear-hug by her beaming husband.

"Thank God for that!" he exclaimed with heartfelt gratitude.

"I take it that means the grapes have arrived at Furzedown?" asked Vivienne, who was secretly every bit as relieved as her husband.

"What? Oh, yes, of course," said Edward as if this was the very last thing on his mind. "What really matters is that the people there reckon that Amberfield's grapes are among the best they've seen this season. Isn't that wonderful?"

She had to admit that it was almost the best news they could have hoped for, to be eclipsed only by the joy they experienced six months later, when their consignment of well over two thousand bottles of Amberfield Wine was finally delivered, sampled and pronounced good.

It must have been later that same year – though she could not pinpoint the exact moment – that the shadow which now hung menacingly above Amberfield began creeping slowly, insidiously towards them.

"Is something the matter, Edward?" Vivienne asked him one day, knowing full well from her husband's behaviour that something was seriously troubling him.

"Not that I am aware of," he replied, refusing to meet her eye.

"That tone of voice and that shifty look of yours always spell problems, Edward Barton!" she insisted. "Now, tell me what's worrying you. I know you sent some cuttings away for analysis. What did your expert have to say about them?"

Edward's mulish refusal to confide in his wife melted

139

away in the face of her direct, forthright approach. More, he was thankful to be able to share his burden with her.

"The long and short of it," he began, "is that I am worried about our Müller-Thurgaus."

"Oh, Edward!" said Vivienne, aghast. "It's not – "

Edward cut her short. "No. Our vines haven't been attacked by the dreaded Phylloxera. Nor by *coulure* and *millerandage* – "

"I always think these things sound more like French racehorses than diseases," put in Vivienne, in an effort at levity.

But Edward was not to be sidetracked. For some time now, he told her, he had been receiving disturbing reports about the Müller-Thurgau vine, that well-established, apparently reliable old standby, which covered almost half Amberfield's vine-fields. These reports would have gone straight into the waste-paper basket were it not for the fact that their contents echoed Edward's own observations.

Despite its popularity in Germany and Alsace, and the fact that it had been grown in England for nearly a hundred years, it seemed that the vine was not without its problems: in particular, it frequently fell victim to the mould Botrytis. And as Edward now confessed, despite that first, wonderful harvest, he was beginning to suspect that this was by no means the ideal vine for their particular site.

"Have you said anything to Simon about this?" asked Vivienne. "After all, he was the one who suggested we should plant this variety."

"Therein lies the rub," said Edward. "Simon refuses to believe there is anything to worry about. When I told him I was concerned about the state of the vines, he simply pointed out that the vast majority of English growers are perfectly satisfied with their Müller-Thurgaus."

"Which presumably they are?" questioned Vivienne.

"Yes, I suppose so. But the fact remains that our vines are not making the kind of growth they should

140

be by this stage. Simon says they'll catch up, but I'm not so sure."

"Then, what do you propose doing?"

"For the moment, nothing except waiting and worrying," replied Edward. "Who knows? Maybe Simon will turn out to be right after all."

But by the following January, when as normal Edward, Simon, Adam and their helpers began the job of pruning the vines, they found that well over half the plants had failed to ripen sufficient replacement wood on which to develop the following year's crop. There was new growth, to be sure, but of a weak and spindly kind, which Edward guessed would support only half the quantity of grapes they had picked at their first harvest.

"It's obvious what's gone wrong," Simon announced at this stage. "It's our programme of feeding and spraying that's at fault. We'll just have to devise a better one."

Edward on the other hand inclined to the opinion of one particularly learned West Country *vigneron* that the Müller-Thurgau grape requires a long, warm autumn before it will produce the next year's fruiting canes. And this, he felt – and Vivienne found herself in full agreement with her husband – was something they could not guarantee at Amberfield.

"It occurs to me," she said to him one day, "that if it were simply a question of inadequate feeding and spraying, we'd be having problems with the Seyval Blanc too, wouldn't we?"

"I would have thought so." Edward by now seemed exhausted, almost crushed by the problems besetting him.

"Come now, darling!" she chivvied him. "It's not like you to take such a defeatist view!"

"If you want my honest opinion," he said finally, "I believe that we have planted a vine that needs a warm, early spring, and a warm late autumn if it is to come up to expectations. Unfortunately, the trend in this country over

141

the past few years has been towards cold wet springs and cool, wet autumns. That's an established fact. The records are there for anyone to see. And if this trend continues, we haven't a hope in hell of achieving the returns we've planned for."

Then one morning, intending to pay a quick visit to the vine-fields before lunch, Edward went striding out across the courtyard. As he later recounted to Vivienne, he had taken only a few steps when the strangest sensation came over him: he felt lightheaded, he said, unreal, as though he were somehow walled in by thick glass through which both sights and sounds were blurred. He then blacked out, and fell to the ground with a thump loud enough to be heard by Jacinta. Later, when he regained consciousness in hospital, it was to learn that the stresses and worries of the past months had taken their toll. He had had a stroke.

When, to Vivienne's profound relief, it became apparent that Edward's mental faculties were unaffected by his stroke, she had asked him whether this event had caused him to change his mind about the vines currently growing at Amberfield. On the contrary, he had told her. Lying in a hospital bed had given him the perfect opportunity to think things through in detail. Now, more than ever, he was convinced that their only hope lay in certain radical changes, and he was looking to her to begin implementing them.

Vivienne picked up the receiver and began to dial a London number. Remembering the events that led to the replanting of the vineyards at Amberfield had banished any doubts from her mind. They *had* been right to bring in Dan Courtney. The decision to replant *was* the right one. But she still could not bring herself to go begging. Before she had even dialled 071 she had replaced the receiver.

9

Sometimes you get a February day that leaves you in no doubt that spring is only weeks away. For just a few hours, the wind loses its sharp cutting edge, the sky seems to lift and the world is filled with new sounds and smells. Yesterday had been just such a day, and Meriel, who had seen snowdrops and aconites in bloom as she ran through the woods, rashly let herself believe that winter was over. How silly to be so optimistic, she thought as she shivered in the icy wind that blew across the ridgeway. How could she have forgotten that only the previous week the first snows of the year had fallen on Amberfield?

It seemed like a contradiction in terms, really – grapevines under snow. But there they were, row upon row, the canes bowed under the weight of the thick white blanket which balanced, precariously in places, on every available surface. Everything looked as if an over-enthusiastic cook had run amok with the instant frosting, and as if that weren't enough, icicles had formed on the undersides of the rods and hung down, glinting in the weak light and beginning to drip gently as the day warmed up.

In Meriel's eyes, that snow-filled day had been beautiful, magical, as, in their very different way, the spring-scented woods had been yesterday. But now, everything had changed again, and definitely for the worse. As she stood stamping her feet and clapping her gloved hands, waiting for Dan to arrive, she was forced to admit to herself that, had she known what the elements were going to throw her way, she might not have been so keen to volunteer to help with pruning the vines. Then again,

143

she thought, how could she have refused? Every pair of hands was needed, Adam had told her. Dan was already considerably behind with the pruning, and the job needed to be completed within the next few days, the more so as new snowfalls were forecast.

Blowing on her hands to keep them warm, she gazed around her at the vineyard which, without its soft eiderdown of snow, looked dreary in the extreme, nothing but a forest of untidy canes sporting the odd leaf which refused to fall, and the occasional black, shrivelled bunch of grapes still clinging to its stem. Ahead of her, in the direction of the woods, rooks cawed and circled as they set off in search of the day's food. Despite the earliness of the hour, the sky was darkening again. Meriel could only hope that the clouds now moving in heavily from the north were not filled with snow.

She was not alone on the ridgeway. Adam had just driven over from The Lodge, and was introducing her to the other workers.

"You already know Jethro, Dan's assistant, I presume?" he asked. Meriel smiled at the old man, who nodded in return. "And this is Jethro's son, Kit . . . and Kit has kindly roped in a couple of his chums, er . . ."

"Robbie and Nick," put in Kit, helpfully.

"Robbie and Nick. Right. And here comes Dan. So. All present and correct, by the looks of things."

"My, what a turn-out," remarked Dan as he approached the little group. His eyes took in Meriel and the two new boys, with varying degrees of satisfaction. Meriel might look very decorative, but what was needed for the next few days was someone who worked hard, and fast, and accurately. He hoped, too, that she was not going to keep on complaining about the cold.

Impatient as he was to be getting on with the job, Dan knew how important it was to make sure everyone knew what they were doing. Incorrect pruning at this stage could spell disaster for Amberfield.

"Jethro," began Dan, "you and I will tackle the experimental vines and the older plants, as they're more complicated . . ."

"Might as well be getting on with that, then," said Jethro. "Seeing as how I've done this job once or twice before."

"Fair enough, Jethro. You go on ahead. But the rest of you come with me," continued Dan, "and I'll show you exactly what needs doing. And why." He led the way into the field and selected a suitable vine. "Now. The vines in this field were planted a little over two years ago. That means that next autumn, for the first time, they will be allowed to bear a crop of grapes, so correct pruning at this time is absolutely vital. Understand?"

Heads nodded and voices murmured in assent.

"OK. The vines you will be tackling today are trained on the Double Guyot system, named after Doctor Jules Guyot, its inventor. With me so far?"

They were of course, so he continued:

"At present, each vine consists of two canes. In future years the vines will be expected to crop on both canes, but for the time being they are too young. So what we have to do is this. First, choose the stronger, firmer rod – whichever looks thicker and healthier, I'm sure you're all quite sensible enough to decide which is the better one – and cut it back to seven or eight buds, or thereabouts. Then bend it down, like this, onto the bottom wire of the trellis. See? You then attach it to the wire with one of these – " he held up a small fastener " – like so. Having done that, you take the other cane – the weaker, spindlier one, remember? – and cut it back so that you leave just two or possibly three buds on it. Does that make sense?"

"Yes," replied Meriel for all of them, "but why keep any buds at all on the shorter cane? I mean, if you're only allowing one cane to bear fruit . . . ?"

"Good question. The point is that the spur that remains

145

when the thinner, weaker rod has been cut back carries the buds that produce the next year's fruiting crop. Which is why it is so vitally important to get this process right. With vines, you have to remember that you're always looking to the future. If you cut away too much of the material you need for the following year, you won't get half the grapes you would otherwise. Cut away too little, and you'll exhaust the plant before its time – which, given the enormous cost of planting vines, would be something of a tragedy. Any more questions? Kit?"

"Yeah, why *double* Guyot if – "

Dan laughed, interrupting him.

"Well spotted, young Kit. In fact, as we are keeping only one cane for the time being, this method should really be referred to as single Guyot. Next year, when we'll be keeping both rods, is when it officially becomes the double Guyot system."

Dan then allocated the workers their various rows and handed out secateurs and fasteners.

"Meriel, you'd better take the row next to Adam," he suggested. "That way if you have any problems you can ask him to help you out."

Adam was making his way steadily down the first of the long rows. Meriel, doing as she was told, began on the neighbouring line. Dan spent a few minutes checking that Kit's friends had fully understood his instructions before moving on to another part of the vineyard.

"Don't worry if your hands get cold," he called back to them as he went. "Jethro will be lighting a bonfire with the clippings as soon as we've got enough!"

"I can't wait!" murmured Meriel. After only half an hour's work, and despite the thickness of her woollen gloves, her fingers were already turning numb. The air was cold and damp, with an insidious clamminess that seemed to work its way slowly but inexorably through her layers of thick clothes, past her skin and in towards her very bones. Somewhat to her surprise, Meriel found that she could almost keep pace with Adam. Or was it simply that he was slowing his rate of work so as to be able to keep a surreptitious eye on her? Certainly there were moments when she caught him watching her, then averting his eyes quickly the moment she looked his way.

The arrival of Jacinta with mugs of hot coffee brought welcome relief, but afterwards it was back to work once more. By now, Meriel had fallen a long way behind Robbie, her neighbour on the other side. With the headphones of his Walkman clamped to his ears, the lad moved along the vines with a dreamy expression on his face, occasionally striking one of the supporting chestnut stakes with his cutters in time to the beat of the music. To look at him, you wouldn't think he was capable of doing anything as fiddly as pruning, yet there he was with quantities of clippings lying on the ground behind him and a considerable number of beautifully shaped vines to his credit.

With practice, Meriel found that her rate of progress was gradually speeding up, and as she grew used to the cold, she almost began to enjoy what she was doing. There was something curiously satisfying about actually being able to handle the vines, and helping them on their way to producing their first, eagerly awaited harvest. Meriel let herself imagine that, in earlier times, workers had felt the same satisfaction when they trod the grapes at pressing time . . . but maybe they had merely been hired hands whose interest stopped at their pay-packets.

When she finished her first row, she stood back to admire her handywork, unable to suppress a glow of achievement at the sight of the neatly trimmed canes, with their firm brown buds which needed only the warmth of spring to burst into leaf. She turned to find Kit waiting to rake up the clippings, and made her way towards her next allocated row.

By the time they stopped for lunch, a good-sized area of the vine-field had been pruned and cleared, though it

147

was evident to Meriel that this particular job would take several days to complete. Adam had already indicated that this one morning was as much time as he could spare from his other duties, but Meriel decided to carry on for as long as she was needed. This was, after all, what Simon would have done. And, not for the first time, she was surprised at how strongly she felt about the well-being of the vines: she felt proprietorial, somehow, responsible.

The workers straggled in to the kitchen where Jacinta began ladling out steaming bowls of vegetable soup so thick it was more of a stew than a broth, and handing round thick slices of warm bread.

"The beer, it is in the crate next the door," she said. "Everyone, he take what he wants."

Before long, the kitchen was filled with the sound of laughter and voices as the men relaxed and tucked in to their meal.

"Is that for us poor hard-done-by workers?" asked Kit, seeing Jacinta taking a huge apple crumble from the depths of the Aga.

"For you?" teased Jacinta. "You think this is for you? I only cook it for the family, for dinner . . ."

"Then why are you making custard?" demanded Kit. "It'll be nothing but skin by tonight!"

"So, you think I must give this food to you? First, I think I have to ask Mr Courtney if you work hard enough!" She looked around, but there was no sign of Dan. "Where is he, Mr Courtney?" she asked. "He not wanting his lunch today?"

"He'll be along in a minute," Jethro told her. "He was just having a word with Mr Adam."

"Having words with Adam, more like," opined Kit. "Something about bottles, wasn't it, Robbie?"

Robbie nodded, and shovelled away a few more spoonfuls of soup.

Jethro sighed. "Well, you've got to admit it's a worry, not being able to get on with the bottling . . . We could lose a lot of customers if we're not careful. Still. That's not our main concern right now. Come on, you lot. Eat up. We've got work to do."

Meriel, stopping by the office to check that nothing required her immediate attention, reached the vineyard a little later than the others. As she made her way to the next of "her" rows, Dan detached himself from the blazing fire Jethro had made on the ridgeway and came up to her.

"You can leave us to it, if you like," he said. "We shan't be needing you this afternoon."

"Don't be silly!" she laughed. "Of course you will! You're way behind – "

"All the same, I mean it. Thanks a lot, but we can manage."

It seemed to Meriel that she hadn't been dismissed so peremptorily since her school days.

"What is this?" she asked, puzzled and not a little put out. "You know very well you need every pair of hands you can get!"

"Not if they can't do the job properly," replied Dan, politely but firmly. "I'm sorry, but I would prefer it if you left."

"And I would prefer it if you could explain exactly what you're on about," retorted Meriel.

"Certainly."

He led her to the end of one of the rows she had pruned that morning and added. "You've cut the canes wrong. Why didn't you check if you weren't sure what to do? Have you any idea how much your morning's work is going to cost us?"

An icy trickle seemed to pour slowly from the top of Meriel's head, down her neck and across her back. So this was what people meant about your blood running cold, she thought as she moved, almost crept, towards the vines. *Her* vines. On all of them, the shorter cane, the spur carrying the precious buds which would in due course grow into the rods that carried the crops of future years, had been roughly cut off at the base.

"I thought I'd explained," Dan went on. "Those buds are our future – I know I said they won't bear fruit this year, but they will give us our next year's crop. Or at least they would have done if – "

"I understand all that perfectly," said Meriel, too shocked to think straight. "And I can promise you I pruned those vines correctly."

"Come off it, Meriel! You can't deny the evidence of your own eyes!"

"I am not responsible for the damage to those vines," she insisted, beginning now to feel anger. "I don't know how it happened, but I didn't do it. Ask Adam! He was watching to make sure I didn't make any mistakes!"

"Adam's had to leave. He said something about a meeting."

"Then, ask Robbie! He'll tell you!"

"OK, OK," said Dan, clearly not believing a word she said. "I don't have time to stand here arguing all afternoon, so let's just leave it, shall we? I accept that it was a genuine mistake on your part, and luckily only a couple of dozen plants are affected. But please. Don't do any more pruning."

When he had gone, Meriel, dazed and disbelieving, took a further look at her vines. The cuts she had made – angled, neat – contrasted strongly with the rough tearing Dan had accused her of. It was inconceivable that he should think her capable of such butchery. She felt belittled, slighted, and suddenly felt she could bear being here no longer.

Almost without being aware of what she was doing, she bent swiftly, picked a few stray twigs off the ground and stuffed them into the pocket of her jacket. Minutes later, Vivienne was puzzled to see the black MG tearing down the drive at high speed. She shrugged, and continued her perusal of the account books. It seemed to her that there

150

were more serious matters to concern herself with than her daughter-in-law's erratic behaviour.

Anger, and a burning sense of injustice, tore at Meriel as she roared off down the drive, sending pieces of gravel spitting into the grassy verges and causing the sheep in the neighbouring fields to look up in amazement. Now, her foot down hard on the accelerator, she no longer knew in which direction she was travelling. It was all a matter of following the line of least resistance: if turning right meant waiting for approaching traffic, she turned left instead. If going straight on left her following a slow-moving tractor, she turned in a gateway and retraced her route. What mattered was to keep moving, and fast.

Leafless trees, hedges, the occasional house, all flashed past her, not that she noticed anything much. At one stage she was aware that she was crossing a dual carriageway, and assumed this was the main road from Dover to London, but as she did not recognise this particular section she could not be sure. Eventually, the ploughed fields and deserted orchards gave way to uniform suburban development, and Meriel, unable now to take the car wherever she wanted, found herself at the mercy of one-way streets and other road signs.

She was in a small town, but she did not know its name. When traffic lights forced her to stop, she revved impatiently at the MG's engine, occasioning some appreciative wolf-whistles from two youths in a Mini which had drawn up alongside her. Meriel ignored them, and tapped irritably on the steering-wheel with her finger-nails.

The moment the lights changed, she was off, snaking through the cars and delivery vans as fast as possible, screeching reluctantly to a halt at zebra crossings, then on again until she was once more out of the centre of the town. All of a sudden, the buildings to her left petered out and Meriel discovered she was driving along the town's promenade. She had not even realised she was anywhere near the sea, but there it was, complete with angry grey breakers and flying spray.

At least she was heading in the right direction, out of town, she thought. As she left the last of the buildings behind her, and began picking up some real speed, the promenade gave way to low dunes, from which the sand blew in gusts onto the road ahead. Her right foot was now down on the floor. With the engine starting to complain that it was being overworked, Meriel shot along the road and into a small mountain of blown sand. Unable to maintain their purchase, the wheels skidded and spun, while Meriel wrestled helplessly with the steering-wheel, vainly trying to bring the car under control.

It was with a sense of something resembling disbelief that she found herself spinning and spinning, four or five times, maybe more – how could anyone be expected to keep count in such a situation? – before the car suddenly left the road and ploughed into the side of a dune. The engine ran on for a moment longer, then, choking on sand, shuddered and fell silent.

Muttering under her breath, willing the car into life, Meriel tried to switch on the engine, but, apart from one pathetic cough, nothing happened. She supposed she ought to feel relieved that the car remained upright, and that she was not hurt, but gratitude was the last thing on her mind right now. Forcing open the driver's door, she climbed out of the car and walked calmly away in the direction of the town.

After only a few yards, she suddenly felt faint. Her legs threatening to give way beneath her, she made for a gap in the dunes and sank to the ground at a spot facing the sea. Though the wind was bleak and blustery, and occasional flurries of sand scalded her face and hands, the air gradually revived her, to the extent where she could have continued her walk back into town.

But she did not want to return just yet. She needed to be alone with her thoughts for a time – and there couldn't be many places lonelier than an English beach in February. Hot, salty tears were running down her cheeks and over her lips. She licked them away, sniffing loudly, overcome by self-pity. *So what*, she thought: didn't she have a right to feel sorry for herself?

As if losing Simon wasn't bad enough, she had had to contend with his family's less than whole-hearted welcome of her, and now she was being accused of trying to wreck the very business she had set her heart on building up. Groping in her jacket pocket for a handkerchief, she found the twigs she had picked up in the vineyard.

She had picked them up, she now realised, because she had instinctively sensed that something about them was not right. At the time – only a couple of hours ago, yet it felt like days – she had been too upset to think clearly, and even now, with the twigs laid out neatly on the sand beside her, she was puzzled as to what might be bothering her. She closed her eyes and thought back to the scene in the vineyard when she left: there were Kit and his friends, already hard at work after the lunch break; and there was Jethro heaping vine cuttings onto the fire – and then, quite suddenly, she knew what was wrong.

"You," she said blowing the sand from the cuttings and replacing them in her pocket, "are my evidence. Come with me."

Feeling stronger now, she rose and walked slowly towards the sea, half-frightened, half-thrilled by the size of the massive waves that reared up and crashed before her, clawing at the shingle and dragging it back like angry animals attacking their prey. As she stood there, not even noticing that she was drenched with spray, she found herself wondering why Dan's behaviour this morning had hurt her so much. What did it matter what he thought of her? This feeling, this sadness, made no sense at all.

She picked up a stone and flung it at a breaker with all her might. When you were down, there was no place to go but up. First, she would return to Amberfield and force Dan Courtney to admit that he had made a mistake in accusing her of damaging the vines. It shouldn't be difficult, now she had the proof she needed. And then she would – but then she stopped, as an idea came to her. Dan Courtney could wait, she decided. There was something more urgent to be done first.

Minutes later, when she was back on the road, heading towards the town, a police car drew up alongside her.

"Are you the owner of a black MG, registration GMX 366 P?"

"Yes, I am. I was just on my way to find someone to rescue me. It's lucky you came along."

"Some lads reported seeing the vehicle in question. They said it looked as though there had been an accident, but that there was no sign of a driver."

"That's right – I skidded on some sand. But I'm perfectly all right. Really I am."

With the car safely towed to a garage, and after hearing the welcome news that no permanent damage had been caused, but that it would be a day or two before the engine could be cleaned of sand, Meriel gratefully accepted a lift to the railway station. There, ignoring the puzzled looks that her dishevelled appearance occasioned, she caught the first available train to London.

Rory opened the door and looked her up and down in surprise.

"Meriel!" he exclaimed. "Can I take it you did not bring your camel with you?"

She gave a small, embarrassed laugh, aware for the first time of what she must look like. Her jeans, jacket and sneakers were still covered with sand, and her hair was matted and stiff with salt.

"I drove my car into a sand dune," she explained. "But I'm all right now."

154

"A sand dune," he repeated as he ushered her into the flat. "Would you care to elucidate?"

"One day I'll tell you all about it," she promised. "In the meantime – "

"In the meantime you'd better have a long hot bath and a change of clothes," suggested Rory. "We can talk afterwards."

Hot bath . . . clean clothes . . . She thought, as she swished the scented water into a froth, that these must be among the most beautiful words in the English language. She sank down into the water until her chin was hidden by bubbles, and let the soothing warmth do its work.

"I've made us smoked salmon omelettes and fried potatoes," Rory informed her when she emerged from the bathroom in borrowed tracksuit bottoms and a cashmere rollneck sweater. "OK with you?"

"Mmmmm. Sounds wonderful. Far more than I deserve."

Rory regarded her quizzically for a moment, before turning his attention back to the potatoes. It seemed he had decided not to pester her with questions and Meriel was grateful to him for that.

"Why don't you pour yourself a drink?" he suggested. "There's white wine in the fridge . . ."

Seated in chrome and black leather chairs, they ate at a glass-topped table next to the deep window with its fabulous view of the lights of London.

"You're so high up here," she remarked at one point. "Doesn't it ever feel isolated?"

"You mean, when I'm not busy making one of my famous conquests?" he enquired.

So he did remember, she thought, and just for a moment she wondered whether she had been right to come here. Then she put her doubts aside.

"I think maybe I'd better tell you why I'm here," she said.

"Sure, if that's what you want to do. Go ahead."

"I need money," she said simply.

155

"You've got money," Rory replied. "At this moment I should say you've got something in the region of – "

"No, I mean now."

"As in now this minute?"

"Yes. Eight – no, better make it ten thousand pounds."

The eyebrows rose, and now Rory broke his self-imposed rule not to ask questions.

"I probably don't have the right to ask, but are you going to tell me what this money is for?"

"Whose money are we talking about, I'd like to know!"

"Yours, of course, but . . . all the same, you did ask me to invest it for you. And I therefore feel responsible for what happens to it."

She was defensive at first, talking too fast and telling him in too much detail about the bottles, and how desperately they were needed, but when she saw him listening seriously to her, she relaxed.

"Just a couple of things," he said when she had finished. "First, I want to be sure you understand that you are unlikely to get this money back. Reading between the lines, I'd say that Amberfield's troubles won't be solved by a mere ten thousand pounds."

"Yes, I realise that. I'm not interested in getting my money back. But I do think that, with the income from sales and, hopefully, a really good harvest this autumn, we should be able to turn the corner."

"That brings me to my other point," continued Rory. "This year's harvest. What happens if that fails? Where do you stand then?"

"I refuse even to think of that possibility," she replied. "And anyway, what difference does it make? I've already told you I don't want my money back."

After a pause, Rory drew a sudden breath and stood up.

"I'll give you my own personal cheque right away," he said. "And I'll sell a tranche of your shares at the next favourable opportunity to cover the amount I'm lending you. All right with you?"

"Thank you, Rory," she said simply. He would never know how grateful she felt at that moment.

"As you said, it's your money."

"All the same . . . Rory, I just want to say how sorry I am to burst in on you like this. Unasked, and wanting a favour . . ."

"My dear Meriel, I was delighted to see you dripping on my doorstep. More delighted than I can say, particularly as it's sheer luck that you caught me in. I'm not here all that much. More often than not I work late at the bank, or else I'm at the theatre or the opera. And I spend the weekends in Wiltshire . . . you know about Melbury, I suppose?"

"Your country house? I heard you bought it just before the stock market crashed."

"No prior knowledge, I promise you. Rather the contrary, in fact. Everyone I consulted told me I should leave my money where it was and not spend it on some vast pile that was going to cost a fortune to restore."

"But your instinct told you otherwise?" prompted Meriel. There had been gossip among her former colleagues regarding Rory and his almost stately home. It was said that Melbury's former owner, an elderly, unmarried peer given to idiosyncratic ideas as to what constituted a good investment, had lost so much money that in the end he had almost begged Rory to take the house off his hands. Even allowing for the amount of restoration that was required, Rory was said to have snapped up a bargain.

"I suppose you could say it was partly an instinctive move," agreed Rory. "Ever since I joined Vere Chalmers, as they were then, I've put every penny I've earned into buying stocks and shares. As soon as I sold one lot, I bought another. It never occurred to me that money had any other purpose. Not, that is, until I saw Melbury. Tell me," he said leaning forward with sudden enthusiasm, "what would you say if I asked

157

you to come down one weekend and look the place over?"

"Well, I don't know . . ."

"The fact is, Melbury needs a woman's touch. I mean, as far as the redecorating is concerned. I don't want one of these professional designers who charge the earth and insist on having everything matching. Nor do I want my sister's Laura Ashley approach. For such a big girl Patsy has astonishingly twee taste. Don't get me wrong. I am of course devoted to my darling sister. I just don't want her decorating my home."

"Honestly, Rory, I'm very flattered that you should ask, but the last thing I want is to upset your sister . . ."

"Nonsense! Patsy will adore you. And you will like her, too. Right, then. That's settled. You're coming to Melbury."

10

"Vivienne tells me we have you to thank for the bottles."

Dan stood in the doorway of her office, eyeing Meriel cautiously.

"Ah, Dan. I wanted a word with you."

If he objected to being spoken to so bossily he gave no sign of it. Instead, he perched himself on the edge of Adam's desk and said:

"I think I probably owe you an apology for what I said to you the other day."

"That's what I wanted to talk to you about," she said, placing her carefully preserved vine-twigs on the desk. "These cuttings – "

But Dan interrupted her:

"I know. Kit had already been round raking up all the clippings before you went indoors. So it couldn't have been you who mauled my vines. Is that what you wanted to tell me?"

His words were conciliatory and sympathetic, and even though she detected a hint of amusement in his eyes, she was thoroughly disarmed.

"Do you mean to say I've been carrying these bits of dead wood around for no good reason?" she laughed.

"I realised what must have happened almost at once," continued Dan, "but when I came to find you, you'd gone."

"Have you any idea how it happened?"

Dan shrugged. "Not really. Most probably it was one of Kit's friends. The one with the headphones gets my vote. Brain-damaged from too much pop music, I expect."

159

She thought: But he seemed so able and nimble-fingered! How could he have made such a dreadful blunder? But she saw no point in prolonging the inquest.

"Maybe you're right. Well . . . is that it?"

"I can apologise some more, if you like. And of course I take back what I said about your pruning abilities. Any time you want to help out you'll be more than welcome." He stood up to leave. "Well, I'm glad we've sorted that one out. Time now for a spot more bottling, I think."

Meriel didn't know whether to feel relieved or resentful. It was good to know he no longer blamed her for something that was not her fault. On the other hand, he clearly had no idea how much he had upset her. Then she thought: what did it matter? He had apologised, hadn't he? And she couldn't keep up that headmistressy attitude for much longer.

Running after him across the courtyard, she said:

"Did you say you've started bottling?"

"Yes . . . It's not one of our own wines. It's some Huxelrebe for one of our clients."

"I'd like to watch, if I may."

"Be my guest," replied Dan, "particularly as it's your bottles we'll be using."

"Our bottles," Meriel corrected him.

"Either way," said Dan, "I can't tell you how grateful I am to you for getting hold of them. I was beginning to think Adam was deliberately trying to hold things up. Heaven alone knows why."

Inside the winery, Jethro and Kit were already at work sterilising the bottles, hoses and other equipment, and the air was cloudy with steam.

"The wine is pumped from the vats into a filler tank via these filter sheets," Dan explained, pointing out the various components. "In an ideal world," he added, "I wouldn't filter at all at this stage. My own preference would be for a wine that's left 'whole', as they term it.

160

The only problem then is that if you have any yeast cells left in the bottled product, they might start fermenting again, in which case you would probably find yourself with an exploding cellar. So, on balance, it seems best to play safe."

"How do you decide when a wine is ready for bottling?" Meriel asked.

"Taste it and hope for the best," replied Dan.

"Don't you believe him!" exclaimed Jethro. "It takes a lot of experience to judge when the wine's developed to the right degree. And there's not many winemakers as good as Dan at knowing just when enough's enough."

Dan's smile at this vote of confidence was almost shy. Not for the first time, Meriel was aware of being won over by the man's sheer enthusiasm for his job.

"There are various factors involved," he conceded. "Taste is obviously the most important thing. With English wines in particular you want to keep as much of that wonderful freshness as possible, and that means bottling early. But the look of the wine is important too. It must be clear as a bell. It must fall 'star bright', as the experts say."

As each batch of bottles was steam-cleaned, Jethro lined them up on the bottling machine's conveyor belt. Meanwhile, at the far side of the room, Kit was unpacking and checking corks and unfamiliar-looking labels.

"Deerhurst Wine Huxelrebe," he read out. "Is that the right one, Dad?"

"That's the one," nodded Jethro. "And don't forget to check the neck labels while you're about it."

"What about the corks?" Meriel asked. "Are they from Deerhurst too?"

Without answering, Kit tossed her a cork from the box in front of him. Meriel caught it deftly and saw that it bore a letter W and the figures 8181, as well as the words "Amberfield, Kent".

"As you see, we use our own corks," Dan said. "The letter and the number have been imposed on us by the

161

Wine Standards Board. They're our official bottling code, their purpose being to identify the bottler."

"But doesn't 'Amberfield, Kent' identify the bottler when it's printed on the cork?" asked Meriel.

She heard Kit and Jethro chuckle before Dan replied. "That might make sense to you and me," he said, "but we're dealing with the EEC here . . ."

There was no need for further explanation. Meriel watched as the hoses were connected up and tested for leaks. "So now you pump the wine through – ?"

"Just about. Any problems, anybody?"

Jethro shook his head. "None that I can see."

"I think we're about ready to roll," Dan now informed them. "OK, Kit. You can switch on now."

Meriel was quite unprepared for the din that filled the winery as the motor clattered into gear and the moving belt of bottles began rumbling and shuddering forward. She took an involuntary step backwards and clamped her hands over her ears, aware of the men's amusement at her reaction.

"You might have warned me!" she shouted to Dan, but her words were lost in the noise of the machinery and the rattling of many bottles on the metal belt. In any case, Dan's attention was with the bottles as they passed under the hose nozzles and were filled with wine before passing on to the automatic corking machine. Once corked, the bottles were taken off the belt for labelling.

"You could give us a hand, if you like," Kit shouted into her ear, and Meriel dutifully followed him over to the table where the young man began laboriously spreading paste onto the labels and fixing them to the bottles. But after watching his struggles for a moment or two she shook her head.

"Why not try spreading the paste directly onto the table?" she suggested. "Then if we place the labels on top of the paste we can simply lift them off and pop them onto the bottles."

162

A broad beam spread across Kit's face as Meriel demonstrated how much easier and faster was her way of doing things. In particular he found his own pet hate – the process of attaching the small, fiddly labels that went round the necks of the bottles – greatly simplified.

"Now what?" asked Meriel when the machines were switched off and a blessed silence returned to the winery.

"Now we wait for the labels to dry, then we package the bottles and wait for the proud owners to claim their new wine," responded Dan.

"Shouldn't we taste it first?" demanded Kit, innocently. "Just to make sure it's all right?"

"Cheeky monkey!" Jethro looked aghast, but Dan merely nodded and sent Kit off to find some glasses.

"But it's good!" exclaimed Meriel after she had taken her first sip. "It's like Muscadet," she pronounced confidently. "At least, I think so."

"I'd agree with you there," said Dan, sniffing and swirling the pale liquid around the glass. "The pity is we can't grow Huxelrebe ourselves. The land here's too chalky."

"Do you think the growers will be pleased with their new wine?" asked Meriel.

"If they don't drink it too quickly, they will," replied Dan. "Improves with age, does the Huxelrebe."

"Unlike some I could name," muttered Kit, with a mischievous glance at his father. The shower of corks aimed at his head only just missed.

In the saloon bar of the Hop Pickers' Arms, over chilli con carne and treacle pudding, washed down with rather more Kentish ale than either of them should have consumed on a working weekday, Adam was having trouble keeping his temper.

"I assure you, Jonathan," he said, "there was no question of trying to cut you out of this deal."

"I'm delighted to hear that," replied Jonathan. "Because believe me, Adam, if that were the case I'd have no

163

compunction about going to Vivienne and telling her what you're up to."

Adam glanced at the lawyer sharply. Did he mean what he said, he wondered?

"You do that," he warned, "and we can kiss goodbye to the whole idea for ever. If Mother suspected, even for a moment, that I wanted to get rid of the vineyards she would make sure I never gained control of the company. And where would that leave you, I'd like to know?"

"Be that as it may," said Jonathan, "we do seem to have rather a lot of problems on our hands. We're agreed, I take it, that since Vivienne will never willingly agree to the sale of the land, we need to ensure that the vineyards lose so much money that she has no option?"

"Given time, that won't be a problem," replied Adam.

"There's the rub," said Jonathan. "The fact is that Bert Hollyfield wants to go ahead *now*. If there's a delay, he'll pull out."

"I'm well aware of that," retorted Adam. "Believe me, I'm every bit as anxious as you are to be getting ahead with all this. Of course, I had hoped to prevent any wine being bottled this spring – that way we'd have had no money coming in and there was a chance the bank would call in the loan. In which case Mother would have had to sell right away."

"But Meriel put paid to that," observed Jonathan. "You know, she bothers me, does Meriel. I have a feeling she could spell trouble."

"I don't see how. She'll be off soon enough. So long as she's not encouraged to put down roots."

"I hope you're right."

"In my opinion, it's Cousin Dan who's the problem, not Meriel. I tried suggesting to Mother that we couldn't afford him, but . . ." he shrugged.

"But?"

"No dice, I'm afraid. She won't hear a word against her beloved nephew. I tell you, Jon, I'd give a lot to get rid of that man. My gratitude would know no bounds."

"Is that so?" murmured Jonathan. "No bounds, eh?"

"Well, you know what I mean. But anyone who could persuade Mother to fire Dan would be handsomely rewarded, that much I can promise you."

"I see . . ." said Jonathan slowly, watching Adam through narrowed eyes. "I hope you mean what you're saying, Adam," he said at last. "Because I may just hold you to that."

Afterwards, Meriel realised that Miss Digby had been acting strangely throughout breakfast, but at the time she paid it little heed. She was aware, once or twice, of Miss Digby's eyes on her, and of a lot of throat-clearing, but as the nurse only replied to Meriel's polite attempts at conversation with monosyllables, it had to be assumed she was not in the mood for chit-chat. So when Miss Digby stood up suddenly, rummaged in her bag and slapped some sheets of paper down on the table before her, Meriel was taken completely by surprise.

"You'd better have these, I suppose," said Miss Digby. "Seeing as how you've got the rest."

Meriel stared at the notebook pages covered with the now familiar handwriting, then slowly raised her head.

"I thought maybe you knew something . . ." she began.

"I didn't want you thinking I was holding anything back," said the nurse, a little stiffly.

"Where did you find these?"

"They were in the chest of drawers that was brought down to the sickroom when Mr Barton was taken ill," she replied. "I remembered about them that time . . . you know."

Had the nurse really "remembered" the notebooks the day that Edward became so upset, wondered Meriel, or had she deliberately been keeping the pages hidden?

"What I don't understand is why you're giving these to me," she ventured. "Why not to Mrs Barton?"

"Oh, no," replied Miss Digby quickly. "Well, that is . . . seeing as how Mr Barton was so upset, I thought perhaps . . ."

Miss Digby's reluctance to discuss the matter further was evident. It also struck Meriel as incomprehensible.

"I don't know whether you've read the notebooks – " she began.

"It's not my place to go nosing into Mr Barton's private papers," replied Miss Digby.

"But . . . the fact is that they are simply Edward's account of the story of Amberfield Wines. I can't think why anyone should be upset by them."

"I'm sure I don't know the answer to that," insisted Miss Digby, clearly eager to leave. "But I think it might be best not to go showing them to Mrs Barton. At least, not for a while."

Puzzled, and not without a niggling sense of foreboding, Meriel took them to her room and began reading.

When I returned home after several weeks in hospital – where, if I may take this opportunity to say so, I was treated with the utmost kindness and skill – I found that the situation at Amberfield had changed in the subtlest and most unexpected of ways.

By this time I was beginning to make a good recovery. There were some physical limitations, to be sure, but mentally I felt I was functioning as well as ever. It was this fact, coupled with the added perspective that absence often brings, that allowed me to see the situation so clearly.

To my surprise, I found that Vivienne had taken over the running of Amberfield Wines. I had taken it for granted that Simon would be the one to assume control, but it seemed that his attentions were engaged elsewhere. He had recently met and fallen in love

166

with a young woman named Nikki, who worked as a management trainee in a hotel near Chilham, and had begun spending increasing amounts of time away from home.

Meriel paused while she took in the news of Simon's involvement with Nikki. If she was honest with herself, the discovery came as only a minor surprise. Hadn't Simon hinted at it when he gave her his reasons for wanting to keep her and Vivienne apart until after the wedding? Besides, he had told Meriel over and over that *she* was the love of his life, and he had proved it by marrying her. She read on:

Soon after, Simon brought Nikki, to whom he was now engaged, to be introduced to us. I was surprised to discover that she was four or five years older than Simon. Far from being fresh out of school, Nikki was actually a divorcée embarking on a new career. Anyway, she seemed a nice enough young woman to me, and as Simon appeared happy at the prospect of spending the rest of his life with her, I made no objections.

Vivienne, on the other hand, decided not to like Nikki. Though she was always scrupulously polite towards Nikki to her face, she described her as "a heartless little fortune-hunter" behind her back.

At this, Meriel was unable to suppress a smile. Was this not exactly what Simon had warned that Vivienne would say about her also? Then, she continued reading:

Meanwhile, Simon accepted that he had been neglecting his duties with regard to the business, after which Nikki began to spend as much time at Amberfield as Simon previously had at Chilham. It was during one such visit that Nikki made the fateful mistake of remarking, in

167

Vivienne's hearing, that Amberfield would make "a lovely hotel".

This remark, made in all innocence, confirmed Vivienne in her belief that Nikki was only after Simon for the house he would one day inherit. From that time on, Vivienne saw to it that the attachment between the two young people grew weaker and weaker. Faced with opposition of that calibre, Simon and Nikki simply didn't stand a chance. I felt sorry for Simon, who was clearly upset by the break-up of his relationship. For a while I thought he would never forgive his mother for her interference, but as we all know, the passage of time does strange things to the human heart.

Poor Simon! thought Meriel. Or was it Nikki who should be pitied? She did not sound like the sort of person who could ever have hoped to stand up to Vivienne.

Edward now returned to the subject of the vineyards, and to the arrival of Daniel Courtney from Australia. On leaving hospital, Edward was surprised to learn that Vivienne had heard from her nephew for the first time in many years.

Vivienne had lost touch with her brother's family after Philip died in a sailing accident within months of arriving in the Antipodes, and was amazed to discover that Dan was now a qualified winemaker. When he told her that he was coming to England and needed somewhere to stay, she instantly invited him to Amberfield.

According to Edward, Vivienne had made up her mind to persuade Dan to stay and work for her even before he arrived. It took Edward a little longer to reach the same conclusion, but he too was impressed by Dan's knowledge and experience. Only Simon and Adam resented their cousin's presence.

The main bone of contention was Dan's strongly voiced

opinion in favour of grubbing out our Müller-Thurgaus and replanting them with nobler varieties.

While admitting that there was nothing wrong with the Müller-Thurgau *per se*, Dan felt that in our case, because of our inexperience and impatience to plant our crop, we had purchased poor-quality rootstock. In his opinion, nothing we did now or in the future could make up for the plants' inbuilt deficiencies.

As he saw it, we now had the chance to grow good wines; or we could grow great ones. Rather than looking on the loss of our earlier planting as a catastrophe, why not grab this unexpected opportunity with both hands and turn it to our long-term advantage? Simon, when he was eventually forced to agree that the old vines would have to go, was none the less opposed to Dan's suggestion, in which he saw only financial risk and another potential disaster.

But to Vivienne and myself, the attraction of growing vines of the quality that Dan spoke of was overwhelming. To prove his point, he had brought with him a selection of some of the best wines grown in other English vineyards. In particular, I remember a rosé from . . . ? where was it now? Not far from here, as I recall. Whatever its provenance, this was a quite outstanding wine which, when entered anonymously at a French wine fair, had walked off with first prize, leaving behind a lot of very red Gallic faces. The very idea of beating the French at their own game, and on the basis of a totally unbiased blind tasting, had Vivienne and myself chortling with glee, though we are both, I hasten to add, ardent francophiles.

Simon eventually gave way, but only because he was defeated by the sheer force of numbers, not through any sympathy with our ideals. To this day, I am not sure that he has ever quite forgiven us.

This is all the more painful to me as I cannot but look ahead to the time when Simon is master of Amberfield.

169

When that day comes, will he then dispense with Dan's services and take over the reins himself? My guess is that he will, after which I fear that the high standards my wife and I have worked so hard to achieve could be seriously undermined. And I have no doubt that, unless we follow Dan's advice and aim to produce quality wines, the company will eventually fail.

My worry, then, is for the future. Neither Vivienne nor I can go on for ever. Though it breaks my heart to say so, Simon's abilities are, in the long run, suspect. Adam meanwhile is so half-hearted in his commitment to the company that I have no doubt he will one day leave us in favour of some other employment. Whether we like it or not, we need a winemaker of the class of Dan Courtney to help us in our endeavours. And this being the case I have no choice but to put up with the continuing coolness between Simon and myself that Dan's appointment has occasioned. Sometimes I wonder how long my health will stand it.

Reading these pages, Meriel was left with the feeling that it was she, rather than Vivienne, who might have been hurt by their contents. What troubled her particularly was this latest evidence of disagreement between Simon and his father. It seemed that Jonathan Fox might be right after all. She tried to remember what he had said to her the day she visited him in his office: *Edward sometimes felt his sons were not to be trusted . . . and that goes for Simon as well as for Adam.* At the time, she had dismissed these seemingly incomprehensible remarks as a figment of Jonathan's imagination, but now Edward's own words gave her pause for thought.

Up until now, she realised, she had been clinging to the idea that everything Simon had said and done was right. That he had acted from the best of motives was not in doubt, but now at last Meriel found she could begin to make her own judgements without worrying that she was being disloyal to Simon, and she was able to admit that Edward and Vivienne had had little choice in the matter of replanting.

Meriel could well understand how betrayed Simon must have felt when Dan Courtney was employed and yet, if the original rootstock was indeed faulty, as seemed likely, would it not have been madness to risk the same variety all over again? Did not Dan's arguments for replanting make a great deal of sense? If Simon were still here, Meriel would have convinced him of this fact, she decided. They would have built upon that.

And then it came to her that she could make amends to Edward for Simon's reluctance to learn from Dan Courtney. She would do it instead. She would get him to teach her how to make the wines of Amberfield.

As usual, it was impossible to get Bella to answer seriously.

"I thought your class finished at nine," Jonathan said.

"Jonathan, don't be such a pain!" exclaimed Bella, flopping into a chair and extracting a leotard and leggings from her bag. "You know very well what time my class finishes."

"Which is?"

"At nine, like you said."

"So. It is now ten fifty-five."

"Ten fifty-seven by mine," said Bella.

"The drive from Canterbury takes approximately ten minutes," said Jonathan. "Are you going to tell me what you've been doing for the missing hour and three-quarters?"

"Nope." She sprang to her feet and started towards the door. There was no reasoning with Jonathan when he was in one of these moods.

"Then perhaps you'd care to explain why you're no longer wearing the clothes you went out in," continued Jonathan.

171

Perhaps it was the slight but ominous tremor in his voice that warned her to be more careful. At any rate, she now wandered over to where her husband sat, stiff-backed in the other armchair, knelt down before him and placed her arms round his knees.

"Jonathan, Jonathan," she sighed. "What am I to do with you? Look, I'm sorry, OK? Rosie – you know Rosie from my aerobics class – well, it was her birthday and we all went out for a drink afterwards. But first we changed out of our leotards – you've no idea how complicated it is going to the john in one of those things. I should have phoned you. It was mean of me."

"Is that so?" asked Jonathan, pushing her away.

"Truly, Jon, that is so. You can check with the staff at the Hare and Hounds. They'll certainly remember our little gang. We made enough noise." She attempted to re-establish contact with Jon's knees but he stood up so suddenly he knocked her sideways and she all but fell onto the thick carpet. "Jonathan!" she exclaimed.

"Quite one of your regular haunts, the Hare and Hounds, isn't it?"

She tried to laugh. "It's Amberfield's only pub . . ." she reminded him.

"And did anyone else just happen to be at the Hare and Hounds this evening?"

"Anyone else? Well, of course. There was Susie, and Jane, and . . . Eileen I think her name is, and – "

"I'm not talking about the women in your class." He caught hold of her under the chin in a painful, twisting grip that made it difficult for her to breathe. "What about your friend Dan Courtney, for example. Was he there?"

"Dan? No, I don't think so . . ."

"You don't think so? Well, think again, Bella. Was he there, or wasn't he?"

"No, he wasn't. He definitely wasn't there."

"And you'd have noticed if he was there, would you?"

"Jonathan, what is this!" She tried to make light of his

172

questions but this time he had her worried. This time, his anger was for real. "Sure I'd have noticed if anyone I knew was there."

"Always assuming you were there yourself, of course."

"*What?*"

"For all I know, you and Dan might both have been elsewhere. Back at his cosy little cottage, for instance."

"Now you're being ridiculous," she muttered, but the frightened glance she flung at Jonathan only confirmed his suspicions.

"Bella," he said. "I *know* about you and Dan."

"There's nothing to know about me and Dan," she said. "Jonathan, you've got to believe that!"

The look of contempt on Jonathan's face as he turned away clearly showed that he did not believe her. For a while he said nothing, but simply stood with his back to her by the uncurtained window. She could see him, reflected in the glass, biting his thin lips in an effort to control himself: the effort was presumably successful because when he finally spoke, it was in a calmer voice.

"Bella," he said, "would you do something for me?"

"Of course, Jonathan," she agreed quickly. Too quickly, perhaps.

"Would you fetch those photographs you took in Bermuda? I haven't had a chance to look at them yet."

"The . . . photographs . . .? Yes, sure."

Weird, she thought as she ran upstairs to her desk on the landing. Then she remembered where she had put the postcard she had taken from Dan's cottage on the occasion of her last visit to him. Her first instinct was to take the card out and hide it somewhere else, but something warned her that Jonathan already knew it was there. If she attempted to conceal it he would become even more suspicious than he was already.

It also occurred to her that Jonathan must have seen her that time Dan kissed her outside the pub the day after they first slept together. For a second, the realisation that her

173

husband knew so much about her movements struck fear into her. Then she pulled herself together. By sending her to fetch the pictures, Jonathan had unintentionally provided her with a breathing space. While she made a show of looking for the snaps she had time to think. Time to decide what to say.

By the time she had come back downstairs, and handed Jonathan the envelope containing the photographs and the postcard, she was almost relaxed.

"Why don't we sit down and look at them together?" she suggested, seating herself on the long, curved settee and patting the space next to her.

Jonathan ignored her. Instead, after pretending to look through the pictures, he came, inevitably, to the item he had been searching for all along.

"Well, well," he remarked. "What have we here? A postcard of Venice addressed to Dan Courtney from someone called . . . Laura, would that be? Tell me, Bella. What is this doing among your newly developed snapshots of Bermuda?"

"Is that where it got to!" exclaimed Bella with considerably more enthusiasm than she felt. "I meant to show you that ages and ages ago."

"Oh, yes?"

"Sure, yes! One day . . . I can't remember when exactly it was . . . I was lunching at the Hare and Hounds with some of the girls, and I happened to leave at the same time as Dan Courtney – "

"Whom you just happened to bump into, I suppose."

"Why, yes! Well, to be honest, he'd had just a little too much to drink, and he insisted on walking me to my car, and kissing my hand, or maybe it was my cheek, I really can't remember, but as I got into my car I saw he'd dropped this card."

"And so you picked it up. And kept it." Jonathan's scepticism was total.

"*Yes!*" By now she was well into her stride, to the extent

174

that she almost believed what she was saying. "Jonathan, didn't you notice the address on that card?"

Jonathan sighed. "Some quaintly named Australian out-post. Nowhere I've ever heard of."

"But Jonathan! That's just the point! You've so often said you felt Dan acted touchy whenever the subject of his previous vineyard came up. I just thought you might be interested to know where exactly it was, that's all."

Jonathan looked again at the written side of the card, more closely this time. Then, sliding it into his pocket, he said:

"By the way, Rosie rang just before you got back. She says she left her leotard in your car, and could you please bring it to the class next week."

So, thought Bella, leaning back into the squashy depths of the settee. Jonathan knew all along that she had spent a perfectly innocent evening with her girlfriends. Whether he really knew about her and Dan, or whether he was merely bluffing, she was not so certain, but given the fact that he now appeared willing to drop the subject, she let herself hope for the best. Besides, she and Dan were through. She had decided as much the night she took the card from his desk.

Partly it was because she sensed that Dan was really beginning to lose interest and she had no intention of suffering the ignominy of being jilted. But the main reason lay with Jonathan. She was well aware that, to a certain extent, he was turned on by the fact that other men were attracted to her: but only to a certain extent. Whenever she began to overstep a particular, undefined line, he made his displeasure clear. Sometimes, she felt he was only inches away from hitting her, and the knowledge of this contained violence excited her. In the end, it was what made her turn away from whichever man she had been seeing and devote herself to Jonathan once more.

All the same, he had no right to go treating her as he had done this evening. No right at all. She had been

175

frightened rather than excited, earlier, and she would see to it that Jonathan paid the price for upsetting her so. The payment, she decided as she congratulated herself on some extremely quick thinking, would probably take the form of a new coat. A very expensive new coat.

11

Once the previous season's wines were released for sale, a steady stream of visitors began making their way to Amberfield. Since Adam made it plain that he was not interested in dealing with this side of the business, Meriel had her hands full. Arranging tastings, processing orders and answering queries proved to be surprisingly time-consuming work, made all the more so by the lack of adequate facilities for receiving so many people.

Visitors ranged from those who just happened to be driving past and decided to see what an English vineyard looked like, to others who had travelled great distances to be there. Among the latter was an Australian, Bob Crace, who spent the better part of two hours tasting Amberfield's products before going away without making a single purchase.

"Typical bloody Australian!" exclaimed Adam, though Meriel failed to see what was so typical about the man's behaviour. Besides, he had said he would return the next day, and something told her he meant what he said.

But when he came back, not the next day but later that same week, and after he had placed a healthy order with Meriel, he asked to speak to Dan. It turned out that Bob Crace was the owner of a large vineyard in South Australia. More to the point, he was the man who had given Dan his first job as a trainee winemaker, and he seemed to have gone to considerable lengths to track down his former employee.

"You're not an easy man to find, Dan Courtney!" Bob told him, shaking him warmly by the hand. "I knew you went to Coonawarra after you left me. But after that, all anyone could tell me was that you were setting up in business on your own. Change your mind, did you?"

"Not exactly," replied Dan, non-committally. "But things didn't work out for me, so I decided to come and learn something about cold-climate wines."

"I knew it!" he exclaimed. "Didn't I just know it? That's precisely why I came in search of you once someone let slip you'd come to the old UK! Funny thing is, I just happen to be looking for an expert in cold fermentation."

"Are you saying what I think you're saying?" asked Dan.

"Too right I am! I need you, Dan. I must have visited nearly every vineyard in England and there's only about two others that make wines as good as yours. So how about it?"

"This is very sudden!" laughed Dan.

"Think about it, Dan!" Bob urged him. "I don't for a minute imagine I'm the first to put a proposition of this sort to you. I won't be the last either, if you carry on making wines this good. But I'm offering good money and smashing living conditions."

"And I appreciate the offer," replied Dan, "but I'm happy here, as it happens. Besides, I wouldn't want to let Aunt Viv down."

"Listen, Dan. Just do me one favour. Think about what I've said at your leisure, and be sure to call me if anything ever happens to change your mind. We don't start picking for another couple of months, so you've got time to weigh up the pros and cons. Right now I guess you're pretty busy?"

"Don't remind me!" said Dan. "April's always a nightmare time for English wine-growers. You never know when there's going to be a sudden frost."

When Bob Crace had gone, Meriel asked Dan whether he was seriously worried about the weather.

"It's been so warm these last few weeks," she reminded

178

him. "And some of the vines are just smothered in buds."

"That's what worries me," said Dan. "It's the buds that are vulnerable to frost. Ideally, they wouldn't have broken for another week or two. Still, we may be lucky. Who knows?"

Another category of visitor included vine-growers who sent their grapes to Amberfield for vinifying, and who occasionally felt the need to check on the progress of their developing wines. Generally, these people telephoned in advance to ascertain whether or not a visit would be convenient, but Malcolm and Yvonne Walden simply turned up one morning unannounced.

They'd come all the way from Norfolk, they told Meriel, because they felt they had to see how their Ortega was getting on. But when Meriel sought Dan out and told him the Waldens wished to see him, he groaned.

"Oh, no! Not the Waldens! Anyone rather than the Waldens! Meriel, couldn't you possibly deal with them yourself? I can't tell you how busy I am – "

"The same goes for me," replied Meriel. "On the other hand, if you were to teach me about winemaking, in future I could take people like the Waldens off your hands."

"I see," said Dan equably. "We're back with that one, are we?"

Twice before she had asked him the same question, and twice before he had wriggled his way out of giving her a straight answer. She could ask Jethro, he suggested; or read books on the subject. But she was adamant. If she was going to learn about wines, she wanted the best teacher available. And that teacher was Dan.

He gave a large, exaggerated sigh and stood looking at her for a moment with his arms folded. To Meriel, it was almost as if Dan were seeing her properly for the first time and the sensation this awareness occasioned in her was definitely not unpleasurable.

"So that's where you've been hiding yourself!" exclaimed

179

Yvonne Walden who, unknown to Meriel, had followed her to the winery. "We were so hoping you could spare us just a few minutes," she went on, "even if we are one of your smallest customers!"

"All our customers are equally valuable," murmured Dan smoothly, casting a wryly resigned glance in Meriel's direction.

She returned to the office, leaving Dan to see to his unwanted visitors. As he led the way down to the lower floor of the winery, Dan reflected that all in all he had done the best he could with the less-than-wonderful ingredients to hand, but inevitably the resulting wine was thin and tasteless. It was such a shame, he thought, as the Waldens tasted their new wine and beamed with uncritical delight, that so little good advice was available to English wine-growers when it came to planting new vineyards. No doubt Malcolm and Yvonne had read that Ortega grapes ripened early, and had deduced from this that it would be the right variety to grow in their part of the world. Alas, this was not the case. There was, in this instance as in so many others, nothing intrinsically wrong with the grapes themselves: they were simply not happy with the soil on the Waldens' land.

"I sometimes wonder," Dan suggested, "whether you have ever considered blending your Ortega with another variety – perhaps with a higher quality grape – ?"

"Oh, no!" exclaimed Yvonne sweetly. "We wouldn't want to produce a *blend*, would we, Malcolm?"

"*'Thou shalt not sow thy vineyard with divers seeds: lest the fruit of thy seed which thou hast sown, and the fruit of thy vineyard, be defiled,'*" quoted Malcolm unctuously.

"Come again?" said Dan.

"Deuteronomy 22:9," explained Malcolm.

"Oh, I see!" laughed Dan. "Well, maybe you shouldn't base your methods too closely on those of biblical times . . . in any case, I can assure you that some of the world's finest wines are blends. Claret, for a start."

180

"Well, we're very happy with what we've got," said Malcolm.

"Thanks to you!" added Yvonne.

There was no point in pursuing the subject. All that mattered to people like the Waldens was that they were able to grow their own grapes, and then drink the wine that was made from them. If Dan had turned the grapes into neat vinegar, Malcolm and Yvonne would have been just as happy. Like so many other people, they were caught up in the mystique of viticulture, and no one was going to spoil their fun.

When they had gone, Dan made his way over to the office where Meriel was finishing a phone call.

"OK, you're on," he informed her.

"You mean – you'll teach me about winemaking?"

"You've twisted my arm," he replied. "You and the Waldens between you. First lesson on Wednesday at nine o'clock sharp. All right?"

"Great! That's wonderful, Dan. Thanks a lot!"

"You'd better fetch the keys and unlock the doors," said Dan. "As you can see, I've been raiding the kitchen."

To Meriel's surprise, she saw that Dan was carrying an assortment of unlikely food items which he proceeded to spread out before her.

"Right! First things first. Let's start with this." He pointed to a packet of sugar. "Taste that."

"Dan!" Meriel exclaimed laughingly. "I do know what sugar tastes like!"

"Oh, you do, do you? OK. Tell me, where exactly on your tongue do you experience sweetness best?"

"Does it really matter? Dan, I thought you were going to teach me how to *make* wines!"

"And so I shall, once you've convinced me of the adequacy of your palate. If you don't have that, there's no point in teaching you anything. The exercise would simply be a complete waste for both of us."

"Oh, all right." More out of natural curiosity than a desire to please Dan, she had tasted and tested first the sugar, then the other items that Dan had fetched, liquids as well as solids, dutifully describing to him in exact detail the sensations her taste buds experienced.

His manner with her was friendly, but brisk and authoritative, and instinctively she felt that they would work together very well.

"Now," continued Dan. "How about letting you try a few wines? Just from the point of view of sweetness on the tongue, remember? Shut out all other taste sensations. Concentrate only on that one thing, then tell me which, in your opinion, is the sweetest, then the next sweetest, and so on, until you've tasted them all."

"Good," said Dan after she had completed that particular exercise to his satisfaction. "There's obviously nothing wrong with your sense of taste. Sweetness is probably the most obvious of the four basic tastes to a learner like you. Next time we'll go on to acidity."

"Is that it?" asked Meriel when she realised Dan was winding up the lesson.

"That's enough for one day," Dan said. "There's a limit to how much the human palate can stand, you know. Besides which, I have other things to see to."

"When can I come again? Tomorrow?"

Her enthusiasm was both flattering and infectious. "Oh, very well," agreed Dan, the grudging tone belied by the smile in his eyes. "Tomorrow, same time."

The following day Meriel learned that "acidity" was what she had always thought of as sharpness, or tartness. On this occasion, however, before allowing her to taste the selection of drinks he had assembled for her, Dan made her sniff each one first.

"What do you notice?" he asked.

"I feel – " Meriel drew her face away from the glass of plain lemon juice she was holding "– it feels as though my tongue is curling up at the edges."

182

"That's precisely what *is* happening. Acidity has such a powerful effect on the tongue you don't actually need to sip your drink to experience it."

"So that's why you sniff your wine before tasting?"

"Absolutely correct. Very, very important, your sense of smell, when you're tasting wines. Tasting anything, really. Think of the effect that freshly roasted coffee . . . or frying onions . . . can have. Your nose is a very vital organ, I'll have you know."

Saltiness, bitterness, then the tannic properties of certain drinks were discussed and demonstrated, and always Dan made Meriel compare and contrast, and remember what it was she had tasted. She was astonished to discover how little she had bothered to think about what she was tasting hitherto. When you set your mind to it, it was not difficult to differentiate between the various components, if that was the right word, of a particular flavour, and the more you tasted, the more components you discovered.

Dan encouraged Meriel to use her own words to described the sensations she experienced.

"If a wine tastes like cardboard to you, or diesel fuel, then say so. At least that way you'll recognise a flavour when you come across it again. Flavours mean different things to different people, so there's no point in accepting someone else's definition when it means nothing to you. The object is to program flavours into your memory so that you can refer back to them in future. Try this, for example. Tell me what this reminds you of."

The wine he handed her was pale, almost straw-coloured. "Nosing" the liquid as she had been shown, she pulled a face, started to speak, then stopped and laughed.

"Go on," Dan urged her.

"Well . . . I don't quite know how to say this, but to me it smells exactly like cat's pee."

She expected a look of impatience mixed with irritation to appear on Dan's face, as sometimes happened with

183

Giles Atkinson, her teacher at Vere Lassiter, when she was slow to grasp a point, or when she disagreed with him. Instead, Dan merely nodded in agreement.

"It does to me too. And to a lot of other people, as it happens. It's Sancerre, by the way. From the Sauvignon Blanc grape. Now taste it."

Dan encouraged her to take a generous mouthful rather than a tiny sip, and to hold it in her mouth for a little while before either swallowing it or spitting it out.

"Try if you can to take in some air along with your mouthful of wine," he suggested. "That way you give the wine's volatile elements a chance to come into play. Go on, try."

She did as she was bidden, her palate ready for a flavour as distinctive as the wine's aroma had hinted, but in fact the taste was, in her opinion, on the ordinary side. Again, she expected Dan to contradict her, but again he shared her view.

"Easily confused with a dozen other similar wines, wouldn't you say?" Dan asked her. "But the aroma gives it away every time. *That*'s why you have to develop your sense of smell."

Dan was a good teacher when he set his mind to it, particularly when his pupil was as keen to learn as this one. He tended to keep praise to a minimum, but Meriel soon learned that when she was in the wrong, or when she said something he did not agree with, he would look at her sharply. When, on the other hand, she came up with a correct reply, or some insight that had previously escaped him, he tended to lower his eyes, as though trying not to let her see he was pleased.

What she did not realise was that Dan was frequently astonished by her progress. By the end of the third or fourth lesson he had concluded that Meriel was gifted with a simply amazing palate, though he did not tell her so. What was more, she had a good enough memory to

184

retain what she had learned, and this store of knowledge would surely stand her in good stead.

Their sessions together were necessarily short, neither having much spare time during the day, but the more she learned, the more Meriel looked forward to the next lesson. One morning, as she sat on the winery steps waiting for Dan to appear, Jacinta called across the courtyard to her:

"You not working this morning?" she asked.

"Oh, yes! I'm just waiting for my next lesson in wine-tasting."

Jacinta made her way across the yard, laughing loudly. "You take lessons in drinking the wine?" she asked, disbelievingly. "I think, that is something I can teach you!"

"Not drinking, Jacinta! Tasting! You know?" She mimed the action of raising the glass to her mouth, swirling the liquid around her tongue, then spitting it out.

"Why they always do that spitting?" Jacinta wanted to know. "Why they always waste so much wine?"

"Two reasons," Meriel told her. "First to stop all the wine-tasters ending up blind drunk, and secondly because you can only taste wine on your tongue, not in your throat."

"How you mean, you cannot taste wine in your throat?" asked Jacinta.

"There are no taste buds there. It's as simple as that."

"So . . . but it is terrible, what you are saying. If you like the taste of wine, you do not ever have to drink it. Just taste it and spit it away and that is the same thing as drinking it?"

"So Dan Courtney tells me," laughed Meriel. "If it's just the taste you're after."

"That is the most sad thing I ever hear," said Jacinta, shaking her head sorrowfully as she returned to the kitchen.

"Ready?"

It was Dan, who had approached unheard and stood looking down at her.

She smiled a welcome, holding out her hand so that he could help her to her feet, then took the keys from him and unlocked the winery door.

"Today, I thought we might talk about making red and rosé wines. That OK with you?"

Whatever he suggested, she was always eager to learn. Sometimes she worried he must think the enthusiasm she displayed during their sessions together was almost unseemly, but she could not disguise the pleasure she derived from them.

"I've got a sparkling pink on the go, using only Pinot Noir grapes which we left to ferment for several days on the skins to extract the colour. What I haven't got around to yet is making a still rosé."

"Using the Pinot Noir again?" asked Meriel.

"Yes, but I was thinking of blending it with the Seibel, and maybe another white variety. Anyway, that's for the future. What I *have* done is to make a few bottles of red wine from our Léon Millot and Triomphe d'Alsace grapes."

"I thought they weren't ready for picking yet," said Meriel.

"On the whole they're not, though I did manage to squeeze a few bottles from last year's crop. To be honest I'm not too thrilled by the quality." He gave her a glass to taste. "It could be because the vines weren't sufficiently mature – or maybe it's because we need to find more suitable red-wine varieties to grow in the UK." He tasted the wine and pulled a face. "In my opinion, it would be undrinkable without chaptalisation – "

She interrupted him immediately to ask what that meant.

"Chaptalisation," he replied with a show of mock exasperation at these endless questions, "is the process

186

whereby sugar is added to the wine to bring up its alcohol level."

"Isn't that cheating?" she had asked.

"If it were," he replied, "we wouldn't do it. All the same, I know what you mean. I always feel the best wines come from grapes with a high enough sugar content – "

Just at that moment, the telephone extension on the upper floor of the winery started ringing.

"I'm going to ignore that," decided Dan. "Whatever it is can wait."

But Michelle, who was trying to put the call through, evidently disagreed and when the telephone remained unanswered· she came across to the winery to find out why.

That was when it happened. Dan, placing a finger to his lips, gently drew Meriel into the shadow of one of the tall steel tanks. For the time it took Michelle to come to the top of the stairs, start down them, change her mind and go away again, they stood side by side in silence like naughty children trying not to giggle. And then, when Michelle had gone, Dan, before resuming his explanation, bent swiftly to place the briefest of kisses on Meriel's lips.

He meant nothing by it, she felt certain. He was teasing her a little, that was all. Whereas she . . . she must be crazy to let herself react so powerfully to such a little thing, she told herself as Dan resumed his explanation. She tried to tell herself that she couldn't possibly be falling for Dan Courtney. But she knew she was.

The customary, comforting smell of shampoo, perm solution and hairspray greeted Vivienne as she stepped out of the morning sunshine and into Hairway to Heaven.

She was almost ten minutes early for her appointment, but they were ready for her, and moments later she was seated in the hard plastic chair while Betty combed through her hair and checked it for length.

"Should I trim just a little bit round the back, Mrs Barton?" she asked.

"What do you think, Betty? Does it need it?"

"Well, a quarter of an inch, maybe. Just to neaten it up. And then we'll do your roots, as usual."

At the word roots, with its inescapable connotations of greyness, Vivienne shuddered slightly. *I will not permit a grey hair!* Vivienne had said to Betty some while back. *Not a single one!* Betty, who for some time now had been wondering whether she dared suggest that Vivienne might like to start letting some of the natural colour show through, correctly interpreted her customer's reaction to mean that this was not the time to advance such a proposition. Wisely, she said nothing.

"Cup of coffee, Mrs Barton?" she asked instead when she had finished applying the blonde dye.

"Thank you, Betty. Black, no sugar."

Left alone at last, Vivienne opened a magazine and attempted to become deeply engrossed in a gardening article, but her thoughts were in too much disarray to allow her to concentrate. How was it possible, she kept asking herself, that fate, which had already dealt her enough blows for a lifetime, had been keeping yet another trick up its sleeve? And yet, and yet . . .

The coffee Betty brought her was scalding hot and bitter tasting. None the less, she gripped the cup gratefully in both hands, and abandoning all pretence at reading, closed her eyes and tried to put what had happened into perspective.

Last night, she had dined with Adam at The Lodge. Some days earlier, Sophie had returned to France to attend the christening of her new nephew, so Vivienne and her son were alone. The food they ate had been secretly prepared by Jacinta earlier in the day. Adam had managed to assemble the melon and prosciutto for

188

their first course, but that, apart from the salad they were now enjoying, represented the limit of his endeavours.

"Those beef olives were delicious, darling," said Vivienne. If she recognised them as the product of her own kitchen, she was not giving the game away.

"We aim to please," murmured Adam.

"I do just wonder," said Vivienne, "whether perhaps we shouldn't have included Meriel?"

"No," said Adam quickly. "I don't think that would have been a good idea. Besides, I've invited Jonathan to join us for coffee."

"Jonathan? But why . . .?"

"I'm afraid to say," replied Adam, "that Jonathan has some bad news about Dan. Some very bad news, as a matter of fact."

Her immediate thought was that he had met with some accident, though why it needed Jonathan to tell her about it . . . and then the lawyer arrived and, within minutes, had cast her into her present confusion.

"You are quite, quite certain about all this, are you?" she asked when he had finished.

"I'm sorry, Vivienne, but yes," he replied. "As I explained, I stumbled on the information quite by chance. I've always had the greatest respect for Dan, myself. And I know how fond of him you must be."

"Tell me again. How did your client come to know Dan?"

"He has relatives in Australia whose land adjoins Dan's former vineyard. Quite frankly, he seemed astonished that anyone with Dan's history should have been taken on at Amberfield."

"I don't doubt that what you say is true," said Vivienne after a while, "but don't you think what happened was an accident? At worst, an oversight?"

"Maybe, maybe not," said Adam. "The point is, if Dan had told you the truth – that he lost his previous vineyard

189

because of recklessly irresponsible behaviour – would you and Father still have taken him on?"

Vivienne hesitated. "Surely what matters is that Dan has performed to our satisfaction here at Amberfield? Shouldn't we judge him by his record here?"

"As to that . . ." Adam put in.

"Yes, I know, we see things in a different light, you and I."

"Look, Mother, I wouldn't have come to you with this information if I didn't feel some action should be taken. In my view, Dan has shown himself to be utterly unsuited to the post he now occupies, and I think you should let him go."

"How I hate that kind of euphemism!" said Vivienne.

"Then sack him, if you prefer to put it that way."

"You've got more than enough grounds," put in Jonathan when Vivienne did not answer immediately. "There'd be no question of his suing you for wrongful dismissal."

"Adam, Jonathan, please!" said Vivienne. "You seem to be forgetting that Dan is my brother's son! I'm sure he wouldn't dream of going to law against me! In the meantime I insist that I be given a chance to think about what you've told me. For the moment, can we just leave things as they are?"

"No doubt you will do as you see fit," responded Adam curtly, "but I can't help regretting the fact that you and Father didn't look a little more closely into Dan's background. It always hurt me – and Simon too, for that matter – that you appointed Dan Courtney over our heads, and without taking our feelings into consideration."

Vivienne put down the remains of her coffee with a sigh. She supposed she would have to confront Dan with what she had been told, but she did not relish the prospect one little bit. There was always, of course, the possibility that he would convince her that Jonathan's informant had got his facts all wrong, but something warned her the lawyer was telling the truth. Even so, the idea of sacking Dan – *sacking Dan!* – was surely out of the question!

It was all very well for Adam to say these things, but finding a new winemaker could take months, and then he might turn out to be no good, and what if he demanded a higher salary? Then there was always the worry that Edward might be upset. Vivienne shook her head. By the time Betty came hovering over, Vivienne had decided that, like it or not, Adam would have to be told that she would not dismiss her winemaker.

"How are we doing, then?" asked Betty, expertly checking the newly tinted roots. "Got rid of all those naughty little grey bits, have we?"

Vivienne smiled up at her. "I sincerely hope so!" she said.

"Paula!" Betty called to the salon's latest trainee. "Mrs Barton's hair is ready for shampooing. Right, Mrs Barton. Would you come across to the basin, now?"

As she leaned back and felt the comforting warmth of the water enveloping her head, and as the girl's fingers began deftly massaging her scalp, Vivienne felt suddenly better. Her decision was made. Dan would stay. But it might be politic to make some kind of concession to Adam. She would have to see what could be done.

"Take the M3 until the junction with the A303, then turn left towards the Woodfords once you're past Amesbury."

That much Meriel could remember, but after she had passed through Woodford Parva and Woodford Magna and had left the B roads behind she had to have recourse to the map Rory had sent her. She drove through a couple of villages with a hint of the West Country about them, then down a hill and past a long thatched house bordered by a wide, shallow stream. "Turn sharp right at the thatched house," said the instructions, and Meriel obeyed them, briefly envying the house's owners for their perennial view of ducks and weeping willows.

191

"House," was all it said on the map next to the blob marked at the far end of this road, but "stately home" would have been a more accurate description. Not that Meriel was unprepared. For some moments before she reached the wrought-iron entrance gates she had been driving past an imposingly ancient brick wall some ten feet high which effectively concealed whatever lay behind it. Tall trees further contributed to the air of privacy, but the gates between the lodge-houses stood open; indeed, they looked as if they were never closed and the lodges on either side appeared uninhabited. So Rory wasn't over-neurotic about security, thought Meriel. All in all, that was probably a good sign.

She had thought Amberfield was impressive enough when she first saw the long drive leading up to the house between fields, but this was in a different league altogether. On turning in through the gates and crossing a cattle-grid, Meriel found herself in what she could only describe as a park, a vast area of closely cropped grass with, here and there, a centuries-old cedar or a massive oak tree whose giant size only served to accentuate the grandeur of her surroundings. All the place lacked was a herd of deer, she decided, but she could not see any: only a handful of sheep who were presumably employed as lawn-mowers.

The house itself was invisible from the gates, and it was not until the drive bore round to the left and under an avenue of beech trees that she found herself before Rory's home. Where Amberfield was all red bricks and tall and square in shape, Melbury was long, greyish-beige in colour and with a square castellated turret at either end. Meriel, who had never entered a building of this quality without paying, was relieved to see that Rory had heard the sound of her car pulling up and was at this very moment bounding down the wide stone steps that led to the main door, arms outstretched.

"Meriel!" he said, kissing her warmly and holding her

192

for some moments in his embrace. "How very good to see you here. I always knew how wonderful you would look at Melbury!"

"I was expecting your house to be special," she said, "but this!" She shook her head. "I never imagined anything quite this grand!"

Rory's laugh showed how pleased he was by her reaction. Placing an arm around her shoulders, he said: "Come. There's so much to show you. Are you tired, or would you like to see some of the house before tea?"

It was hard not be swept along by Rory's enthusiasm, and in any case Meriel was not tired. She had always found driving to be far more of a pleasure than a chore.

"I'd love to see some of the house. But could I freshen up, first?"

"Of course!"

With Rory's arm still around her, she walked up the steps between urns planted with tumbling shiny green ivy and early white tulips. A butler held the door open for them:

"This is Willcox," Rory informed her. "Willcox, would you have Mrs Barton's luggage sent up to the yellow room? And we'll have tea in the drawing-room in about half an hour."

"Very good, sir," murmured Willcox.

Meriel, who at Amberfield had needed a little while to get used to the fact that Jacinta not only cooked her meals but saw to her laundry and the cleaning of her room, decided then and there that the only way to cope with Melbury Hall was to treat the place as a hotel. Butler, uniformed maid, a cook too, she supposed – it was all very daunting for someone who only a year ago survived perfectly happily in a small flat in Battersea, cooking her own food and doing her own ironing. Then it occurred to her that Rory was no more born to this style of living than she was, and she drew comfort from the thought.

"I'll see you shortly, then?" enquired Rory, letting go

of her at last and watching with a smile as she ran up the stairs after Lucy, one of the maids.

"Just give me a couple of minutes!"

One small worry had nagged at Meriel during her journey to Melbury, but this was dispelled when Lucy explained that she would be staying in the guest wing, some distance away from the house's main bedrooms. When he rang to invite her to Melbury, Rory had insisted that her visit would carry no strings, but she had been unable to suppress the occasional doubt. The fact that he had not placed her in a room close to his, however, seemed to indicate that he meant what he said, and it was with some relief that she returned downstairs to join him.

"Let's start with the dining-room," Rory was saying, leading Meriel across a stone-flagged, galleried hall, into a room whose walls bristled with oil paintings of racehorses. "I bought these along with the house," he told her, quite without embarrassment. "This one here is Dorabella," he said, pointing to a haughty-looking grey mare, with flaring nostrils and startled eyes. "She was one of the country's most successful fillies. Won all sorts of things, then went on to breed."

"Do you keep horses?" asked Meriel.

"Horses yes, racehorses no. My sister, Patsy, keeps her horse here. She'll probably be down for a ride this weekend. And I have a couple of my own."

"I suppose you play polo," said Meriel.

"Actually, no. Though I must be about the only man in Wiltshire who doesn't. What about you, Meriel. Do you ride?"

"I'm afraid not, no."

Rory clapped his hands in delight. "Then I'll teach you!" he announced.

"I'm not sure . . ." began Meriel, not too happy at the thought.

"Oh, don't worry, you'll love it!" Rory assured her.

"And anyway, I didn't bring any jeans – "

"You can borrow some of Patsy's gear. She won't mind."

She was obviously going to be given no choice in the matter. All she could do was hope for rain. Rory led her through library and study and gun-room and music-room and, unbelievably, ballroom until she was almost dizzy with the effort of trying to take in all that Rory was telling her.

Eventually, they came to the drawing-room just as Willcox arrived with the tea.

"I think we've earned this, don't you?" said Rory, motioning her to sit down in one of the chintz-covered sofas.

Meriel looked about her. Most of the rooms she had seen so far had been little more than a blur of highly polished antique furniture and large, dark paintings. Despite its size and the undoubted value of most of its contents, the house had an agreeably lived-in feeling, and it was clear to Meriel that Rory had not simply purchased the oil paintings in the dining-room when he bought the house. Virtually everything she had seen had probably been at Melbury for generations.

In some rooms the lived-in feeling threatened to give way to plain clutter, of a kind Meriel found hard to associate with Rory and his pristine, ultra-modern Barbican flat, let alone his immense fastidiousness with regard to his personal appearance. She began to understand why he felt the need for change at Melbury, and why he might feel a little uncomfortable in his surroundings.

Here in the drawing-room, for example, a rosewood writing-desk stood against a dark-red papered wall flanked by a mahogany tallboy on one side and a dark oak bookcase on the other. A couple of paintings on unrelated themes and with non-matching frames hung above the desk, so that Meriel's inevitable impression was that each of these pieces had come into the previous

owner's possession at different times and had been positioned wherever there was room, with no regard as to its
suitability.

Shifting her position on the sofa, she heard the tell-tale
twang of a broken spring, and noticed that the chintz
covers, though freshly laundered, were faded and wearing
thin in places.

"You see what I mean?" said Rory. "The whole place
is in need of a total revamp. I've got some ideas about
what needs doing, but I would certainly welcome your
advice."

"I'll be glad to help," she replied, though it occurred to
her that Rory, who had never visited her Battersea flat,
could have no idea of her taste. As she poured the tea,
Rory, watching her, asked:

"So, did that ten thousand pounds have the desired
effect?"

She had already thanked him, more than once, for his
help, and was puzzled by this latest question.

"How do you mean, the desired effect? We've done a
lot of bottling if that's what you wanted to know. Thanks
to you."

"I had a feeling there was more to it than simply
getting Amberfield out of a hole," Rory said. "I wondered whether there wasn't someone you were trying to
impress."

"Impress? No, of course not. Who would I want to
impress?"

But Rory merely gave a slight shrug, and changed the
subject.

That night, after he had placed a perfectly proper kiss on
her cheek and had wished her a good night's sleep, Meriel
sat for a while on her bed, fingering the soft crispness of
Egyptian cotton sheets and wondering exactly why she
had accepted Rory's invitation to spend a weekend at
Melbury. Partly it had been out of gratitude for his
help; partly it was curiosity to see this house which

196

only a few of Rory's most favoured employees were ever invited to.

But there was also another reason, one that she was unwilling to admit to herself, yet which she found herself unable to banish altogether. The truth – the strange, disturbing truth – was that while she remained at Amberfield, her thoughts kept turning to Dan Courtney, and when they did she would experience an inner twist, a tug, which something told her she must resist.

Only now that she had put a safe distance between herself and Dan could she afford to think about him, to chide herself for responding in this way to a man who had been no friend of Simon's. By the time she had undressed and climbed into bed, she thought she had found the answer to her dilemma. It seemed to her that when something troubled or frightened you, there were two ways of handling it. Either you stayed and faced it head-on, or you ran away.

In this instance Meriel decided that both approaches were necessary. If she wanted Dan to continue teaching her about winemaking, which she definitely did, she would have to spend quite a lot of time in his company. Well, then, she would use these occasions to make herself impervious to the man's attractiveness. Once she became used to the effect he seemed to have on her, Meriel was quite certain she would tire of it, and the problem – if that was not too strong a word for it – would disappear.

As for running away, although this might not be a practical solution in the circumstances, she could at least ensure she put some distance between herself and Dan whenever possible. And this she intended doing by visiting Rory at Melbury on a regular basis. She liked it here, and she trusted Rory not to pressurise her into a relationship for which she was not ready.

Soon after reaching her decision, Meriel fell asleep. She was awakened next morning by the sound of the maid,

Lucy, wheeling in the breakfast trolley and drawing back the curtains to admit a burst of brilliant sunshine.

"Shall I close the window, miss?" she enquired, but Meriel told her no, to leave it open. Far from the rain she had hoped for, the day seemed to promise nothing but warmth and cloudless blue skies. Even so she hoped that Rory's remarks of the previous evening had not been seriously meant. Seconds later, her hopes were dashed.

"Mr Lassiter said to give you these to try," continued Lucy, lifting a pile of neatly folded clothes from the trolley's lower shelf. "Some of the things will be too big for you, but he says not to mind. Will that be all, miss?"

"Yes, thank you, Lucy," said Meriel with a sigh. There was, then, to be no escape. When she had drunk a cup of tea and munched her way through two slices of toast, she rose reluctantly, bathed and tried on the likeliest of the riding clothes. The fawn jodhpurs were indeed a good two sizes too large for her, but, being made of tough stretchy material they were not too uncomfortable. The off-white cable-knit sweater was probably Rory's own, Meriel decided as she slipped it over her head. As for Patsy's boots – old, supple, regularly oiled and in superb condition – they fitted perfectly.

"Mmm," was all Rory said when he caught sight of her descending the staircase towards him. "You'll do."

"I'm really not sure this is such a good idea," Meriel tried, one last time. "To be honest, I feel quite frightened."

This was putting it mildly, but Rory merely laughed.

"Nonsense! There's nothing to be afraid of! You'll take to riding like a duck to water. Come along, then, there's a good girl. Mustn't keep the horses waiting."

There was no getting out of it. No way of delaying the dreaded moment when she was expected to risk life and limb doing something that had never appealed to her in the least. With a brave attempt at a smile, Meriel followed Rory down to the stables.

What happened next counted among the biggest surprises in Meriel's life. As Rory predicted, Meriel took to horse-riding from the very first. More, she fell in love with the little toffee-coloured horse with the silver mane and tail the moment she saw her.

Paloma arched her graceful neck and pulled in her head in mock-wariness at the approach of the stranger, but Meriel could tell from the animal's expression – almost an amused smile – that she wasn't genuinely frightened, simply that she felt she ought to make a point. For the same reason she skittered sideways when Rory's groom Peter demonstrated to Meriel how to check the saddle-girth and mount correctly, but stood perfectly still when it was Meriel's turn. Anyone watching would have sworn Paloma considered it unfair to play up to a rank beginner. At heart, she was as gentle as a dove, as her name implied.

After half an hour of walking and trotting on the lunge-rein under Rory's expert tuition, Meriel felt so at home she did not want to get off, but Rory insisted. He was in fact itching to get a gallop before lunch, but he suggested that Meriel learn what she could about unsaddling and other equine matters from Peter before he returned. Meriel had watched Rory mounting his big bay gelding and vanishing into the distance with a pang of real envy. How long would it be, she wondered, before she was good enough to accompany him?

When the time came for her to return to Amberfield, she was aware of mixed feelings. She had come to love Simon's home dearly, and had over the past few months grown very fond of both Hatta and Sophie. Even Vivienne's attitude towards her had warmed and softened as the weeks went by, and as for Dan . . . but Meriel told herself she must not think about Dan. Only Adam remained aloof and uninterested, which was all the sadder given his fiancée's eagerness to be friends.

The disadvantage of Amberfield was that it represented

all that was worrying in her life at present. There was the crop, for a start, and anxiety about the weather. There was concern about the state of the company's finances, and whether the harvest would be good enough to lift the company out of trouble. There was also Dan – but again, Meriel checked herself.

By contrast, Melbury seemed a place of blissful ease, a place where worries seemed not to exist. Meriel had only been there a few hours before she found herself unwinding and falling in step with the house's leisurely pace. If Rory wanted to organise her and make decisions for her while she was in Wiltshire, so much the better, she decided. The freedom from worry and responsibility could only do her good.

12

Among the many things that Meriel learned that first
spring at Amberfield was that there is in wine-growing
circles a widely held belief that exactly one hundred days
should elapse between the flowering of the vines and the
harvesting of the grapes. Even Dan, who was not the kind
of man to take too much notice of old adages of any sort,
seemed to agree that too many days, or too few, either
side of that rough figure always spelled trouble.

"I don't like it," he told Meriel one day in late April.
"Everything's happening too fast. If this goes on we'll be
harvesting in August."

Given that the earliest harvest ever to be gathered at
Amberfield had been picked in mid-October, this seemed
something of an exaggeration and Meriel refused to take
Dan seriously. "I'm sure you've got nothing to worry
about," she told him.

This, at least, was how it seemed to her. After a long,
cold, but fairly dry winter, the weather had suddenly
changed. A period of rain lasting through much of March
eventually gave way to milder, drier conditions, and within
the space of a couple of weeks the buds – nut-brown in
colour, triangular in shape – began visibly swelling on
the vines.

Gradually, and with a disconcerting lack of logic as
to which vines ripened first, the buds began throwing
off their hard outer shell and revealing the velvety pink
skin beneath. Underneath that newly exposed layer, still
hidden from view, nestled a tiny cluster of embryo flowers,
genetically programmed to turn into grapes if the requisite

conditions of food, drink, fertilisation and decent weather were met. When Meriel thought about it, there did seem to be rather a lot of 'ifs' attached.

"My worry," said Dan in answer to her attempts at reassurance, "is that some of those buds are beginning to burst into leaf. That's the stage at which they are particularly vulnerable to a late frost. But then again, we've had years when bud-burst has been so late the grapes haven't had a long enough growing season . . . ." he shrugged. "In other words, there's no telling what might happen."

Hatta came barging in, her upper half almost completely obscured by an unusually large bunch of flowers. When she saw Dan she halted momentarily in her stride, and Meriel guessed that whatever had occurred between the two of them that night in the cottage was still proving an embarrassment to Hatta. Dan, however, had no such scruples.

"Hatta, fair coz!" he exclaimed, holding his arms wide at the sight of the lilies, alstroemerias and gypsophila capped by a shiny blond bob on top, and supported by long legs in black tights and Doc Marten boots underneath. "Are they for me?"

"Of course they're not, silly," replied Hatta, quickly regaining her composure. "Who'd send *you* flowers, I'd like to know? Actually, they're for Meriel."

She dumped the bouquet on the desk, revealing that she was dressed in her school uniform. "Don't look at me like that," she continued, seeing Dan's expression of surprise. "Term starts today, worse luck. And Meriel is driving me there. Well?" she demanded of Meriel. "Aren't you going to tell us who they're from, as if we couldn't guess they were from Roaring Lassie?"

"She means Rory Lassiter," explained Meriel. "My former boss. I rather think he's still hoping I'll go back and work for him."

"Go on, read the card!" urged Hatta. "I bet it says something like: '*To my darling Meriel, in memory of a mega-brill weekend . . .*' or something like that. Am I right or am I right?"

To her considerable relief, Meriel was spared the ordeal of having to read the card in the presence of Dan and Hatta for Vivienne appeared at that precise moment to bid her daughter farewell.

"It really is most kind of you to offer to take Hatta to school," she said to Meriel. "I do appreciate it."

"Hatta?" said Meriel once they had loaded the girl's school trunk, cello, ghetto-blaster and assorted plastic bags into the MG. "Why does your mother think I volunteered to take you back to school?"

"Ah," replied Hatta, looking just a little embarrassed. "I just thought . . ."

"Come on, what is all this about?"

"I just fancied turning up at school in a decent car, for a change," she revealed.

"And the family Rover isn't good enough?"

"I have to consider my image," said Hatta.

Meriel laughed. At some stage during these Easter holidays, the two of them had become friends. She couldn't quite pinpoint how or why it had happened, but it had. Perhaps Hatta had been won over by Meriel's genuine admiration for her musical talent.

They drove through the village of Amberfield, stopping at the traffic lights outside Jonathan Fox's office. As they waited, a man emerged from the door that led to Jonathan's office. He was short and stocky; and he was smoking a cigar. Meriel recognised him immediately as the man she had once seen talking to Adam at Amberfield House.

"Who is that man?" she asked Hatta.

"Oh, that's Bert," replied Hatta.

"Bert who?"

"Bert Hollywood. No. Hollyfield. He has a wife called

Davina who wears amazingly putrid clothes. You know. Blue velour with glittery bits. That kind of thing."

"And what does he do?"

"Bert? He builds houses, I think. The sort of places that have a drinks bar in the living-room. Sorry, the *lounge*. Why?"

"I saw him up at the house once," remarked Meriel.

"At Amberfield?" Hatta almost shrieked. "It can't have been him. Mum can't stand him. She always calls him 'that dreadful little man'." Hatta finished with a very fair imitation of Vivienne's tinkly laugh.

"You are *wicked*!" Meriel told her. But she was laughing too.

Although she had gone to bed, as usual, at around ten thirty, and had not joined Meriel in an after-dinner cup of coffee, Vivienne was finding it impossible to sleep. She could take a pill, of course; Dr Dinwiddy had prescribed some to help her through the terrible weeks following Simon's death, but she knew from experience that they did not suit her. She would fall into a heavy, dreamless sleep almost immediately, only to wake again at dawn, unrefreshed despite the oblivion of the past few hours. On the other hand, the knowledge that she could switch her mind off, that she could stop these worrying thoughts tormenting her hour after hour was very tempting.

For the moment, though, she decided against the sleeping pill. Instead, she got out of bed, pulled her dressing-gown around her shoulders and made her way to the small table by the window on which she kept the electric kettle and sachets of herbal teas which she found so useful on nights like this. As she stood by the window waiting for the water to boil, she became aware of just how chilly the night had become. Drawing her dressing-gown tighter about her she tried not to think about what would happen if there were to be a frost at this late stage. But there had been no forecast of frost.

Looking out of the window, she saw that the moon had risen, and was casting its colourless light over lawns and hedges, trees and flower-beds. In all probability, she reasoned, it was simply the cold quality of the light that made her think of frost. For all she knew, it might be quite warm outside. At least there was no wind . . .

And then, unable to stop herself, she was reliving that event, totally unexpected, utterly beyond human control, which had so very nearly spelt catastrophe for Amberfield and its wines.

The summer of 1987 had been a poor one, she recalled. Cool, grey and damp, with only the briefest glimpses of the sun, it was a wine-grower's nightmare. Then, just as they were beginning to despair, the weather improved and the crop which they had feared they might lose altogether began ripening beyond all expectations. To their astonishment, they found that by early October they were on target to produce twenty thousand bottles of wine for sale the following year. As the days wore on, so the Barton family became increasingly optimistic about the size of the crop. All they could do was wait, and hope that the weather held.

That night, she and Edward went to bed soon after eleven o'clock. This was a little later than usual, but otherwise everything was much as usual. Since none of the children was at home, Edward checked that Jacinta had retired to her room, then locked and bolted the downstairs doors before making his own way up to bed. Pausing for a moment at the kitchen door, he noticed that a section of the metal cowl on the old oasthouse across the courtyard was clanking in the quickening breeze. This was so much a normal part of life, however, that he paid it no heed.

True to his habit, Edward fell asleep almost immediately, but Vivienne was kept awake for some time by a rattling window which she eventually silenced by jamming a handkerchief between the catch and the frame.

The catch in question had long been suspect, and she was not unduly worried by this further evidence of a gathering storm.

The first genuine hint that something serious was afoot came some two hours later, when they were roughly woken by a loud crash and the sound of breaking glass as the same window was flung open and smashed against the wall. Even so, after attending to the damage, they returned to bed and lay listening to the wind while waiting to fall asleep once more.

"Quite a gust, that one, eh?" said Edward, beginning to sound drowsy. "Never mind. Things will quieten down soon, you'll see."

Vivienne wanted to believe him but as they lay side by side it soon became obvious that this was not to be the case. Far from dying down, the wind, which was blowing from the south-west, began to grow in intensity, and continued to do so hour by hour. By three o'clock, it was howling and screaming as if a thousand devils had been unleashed with the sole aim of wreaking havoc upon Amberfield and its environs. There were moments when it sounded almost as if this same wind, furious at finding the leaves still on the trees because of the late summer, was seeking to batter and smash them out of existence, determined at all costs to wipe out these areas of resistance to its progress. Sometimes a gust, travelling at such speed that it generated its own shrieking, whistling sound as it went, hit the house amidships, causing it to tremble to its foundations.

"Darling," Vivienne said to Edward at one point, "I think I'm frightened."

Edward gathered her in his arms so that she could feel his own fast-beating heart. "So am I," he admitted. "So am I."

At that, they rose once more and made a quick tour of inspection of the house. They did at least have the consolation of knowing they need not worry about the children. Hatta had recently begun her first term at boarding-school, Simon was in the States and Adam was spending that particular night up in London. To Edward and Vivienne, London signified safety, for at that time they assumed the storm was confined to their own corner of Kent. There was no damage, as yet, that they could see inside the house and, after yet again making fast all doors and windows, they made their way to the kitchen, where they found Jacinta in a state of near-total terror.

"Oh, Mrs Barton, Mr Barton!" she exclaimed, clutching a blanket about her and gabbling away in a mixture of English and Spanish. "It is the end of the world, no?" she asked, crossing herself repeatedly and muttering away at the rosary beads clutched in her shaking fingers.

Although Vivienne did her best to sound reassuring, she was secretly of the same opinion. Outside, the gale seemed to be gathering even greater strength, and there were moments when the house creaked so that she feared the entire roof would blow away. Suddenly, one of the cowls on the old oasthouse, now the winery, came loose and blew past the kitchen window like a scrap of paper, missing it by inches. It was later found hundreds of yards away where it had plunged into the hard dry ground, fortunately without causing any damage.

"Well," said Vivienne after a time, and with a greater show of confidence than she in fact felt, "the house has withstood the storm so far . . . I suppose we might as well go back to bed . . ."

"I no go back to bed," said Jacinta. "I stay here, in my kitchen, where is a good strong table."

Vivienne opened her mouth to remonstrate, to beg Jacinta to be sensible and return to her room, when two things happened, almost simultaneously. A tremendous creaking and groaning, as if a massive ship were breaking up on a storm-tossed sea, made itself heard through the roar of the gale, followed by an earth-shattering, pounding crash which rocked the three of them where they stood. Vivienne and Edward looked at one another in disbelief.

"Was that . . .? No! It couldn't have been!" said Edward. But they both knew it was. They knew, beyond any doubt, that they had just lost the fine oak planted over three centuries ago in the field that bordered the drive to Amberfield House. The oak that had suffered the weather of ages, that had survived being rammed by a tractor when Simon took it into his head to go berserk with the wretched machine during an adolescent prank with some inebriated friends, that had withstood drought and civil war and heaven knows what else during its long life, had been brought low by a mere wind.

And then, a second later, all the lights went out. Jacinta, with a scream, flung herself under the table and pulled her blanket over her head. Edward felt his way over to where Vivienne was standing and held her close.

"Darling," he said, "if you want to get under the table with Jacinta . . ."

"Never!" said Vivienne. "Never in a thousand years! I'll find some candles . . ."

A hammering at the back door announced the arrival of Dan Courtney. He too had heard the crash of the oak tree and, worried for his uncle and aunt's safety, had come over to the main house from the cottage where he lived. It appeared that it was not only their own power lines that had succumbed to the storm: as far as the eye could see, the countryside for miles around was in total blackness.

Then Vivienne forced herself to pose the question which, she could tell, Edward did not dare ask:

"What . . . what about the vineyards, Dan? Could you see anything on your way here?'

Dan told them that from the little he had been able to see, the new vines, which were not due to produce grapes for another few years, seemed to be in reasonably good shape. No doubt they had the advantages of youth and suppleness on their side. As for the others . . . he shrugged, saying they would have to wait until morning before the extent of the damage was known.

At first light, and in spite of the fact that the wind was still blowing strongly, Edward, Dan and Vivienne set out to see for themselves the effect of the storm. They walked in silence, for they knew what they would find. All around them lay the most awesome devastation. Trees, branches, sections of roofing, fences, even whole shrubs lay scattered about their path as though tossed there by an irritable giant venting his spleen on anything that happened to stand in his way.

The roots of the old oak tree had come clean out of the ground and reared up high above their heads. Horrified and amazed, they raised their eyes, unable to believe that this lofty, massive thing could have been lifted so effortlessly. The crater left by the roots was vast: ten or more feet deep and at least thirty across. The pattern of destruction was one they were to find repeated time and again: tree after tree had simply been ripped, whole and entire, from the ground. Seen from a distance, the chalk still adhering to their roots gave them the appearance of giant marble tombstones.

Vivienne, seeing how affected Edward was by the loss of his favourite oak tree, was struck by a sudden idea.

"We must leave it there," she said. "Right there where it fell. As a reminder of the storm, rather like the shells of churches that were bombed in the war."

"Dear God!" Dan, gazing in the direction of the woods beyond his cottage, was scarcely able to believe his eyes. For there, the giant who had destroyed the oak had ploughed a crooked and extraordinary path through the trees, flattening one after the other as he went until they looked like a row of fallen dominoes. Yet on either side of the carnage, it was as though nothing had happened. At this unimaginable sight, Vivienne allowed herself the faintest, the merest glimmer of hope that maybe the vineyards too had suffered only piecemeal damage.

209

That hope was soon dashed as they came to the area planted with the older vines and beheld the desolation before them. It looked, as Edward remarked later, as though the Day of Judgement had finally come. Most of the trellises and vines lay flattened and twisted on the ground, but even those that had not fallen had suffered serious damage. The top wires holding the vines had snapped, leaving the stems hanging loose with their foliage and precious berries drooping over towards the ground. When Dan attempted, with the utmost care, to lift the vine stems, he found that more often than not the bunches of grapes caught on the lower wires and simply snapped off. And this was supposed to be the current year's crop! The sight was enough to break a man's heart, and indeed Edward, his eyes brimming with tears, turned in despair to Dan when he beheld the night's work.

"What are we to do?" he asked, his voice breaking.

"Fetch Kit and Jethro and start harvesting," was Dan Courtney's brisk reply.

All that day and the next they laboured in their vine-yards, working under near-impossible conditions, in an attempt to salvage what little they could. Although the power lines were still down – and were to remain so for a further week – and the telephones were still out of order, an astonishing bush-telegraph promptly evolved. Within hours of setting to work, Dan, Kit and Jethro were joined in the vineyards by their neighbour Bryan Talbot, as well as a number of others who volunteered their services out of sheer generosity of heart.

The state of the plants meant that only a tiny proportion of the grapes could be picked, and even then Dan admitted he was worried that the skins might taint the juice. By the time their pitiful harvest had been gathered in, it was evident it would not be possible to make even one single varietal wine. Vivienne remembered how, rather than waste the grapes, he had decided to devote his considerable skills to producing a special blend in memory of the storm. Amberfield's "Hurricane Harvest" as he aptly named it, would not be remembered as his finest wine, but for those at Amberfield it always held a special, unique flavour.

That terrible year, they lost over four-fifths of their harvest along with most of their anticipated profits. None the less, they had escaped total financial disaster because much of their acreage was planted with younger vines which had not yet fruited.

This year virtually all Amberfield's vines were mature, and ready to fruit. A frost at this time of year would mean devastation on an unprecedented scale. It would mean the end of everything as far as Vivienne was concerned. The house, the business –

Then, angrily replacing her cup on the table, she made herself stop thinking these depressing thoughts. That white, hoary glimmer on the grass outside was not frost, it was simply moonlight. Moonlight always looked like that. And this chill in the air, the reason why she was shivering, suddenly – no, it was not cold, it was merely because she was tired. Too tired to sleep.

Very well. So be it, she decided. She would take one of Dinwiddy's sleeping pills. Possibly two. Lying awake all night worrying wasn't going to do anyone any good. Not long after, as she drifted off into that familiar heavy sleep, she had the oddest sensation of a ringing sound in her ears. It seemed to go on and on. Then, she heard nothing more.

Meriel, waking suddenly from the deep sleep she had only recently fallen into, thought she heard the phone ringing. But when she climbed out of bed, opened her bedroom door and listened, all was quiet. After a moment, she shrugged and closed the door. She must have been imagining it. All the same, some noise had awakened her, of that she was certain.

She was about to slide back under the duvet when the

ringing began again. But it was not the telephone, she now realised, it was the bell to the back door, and whoever was pressing it was clearly in no mood to take no for an answer. Running down the stairs, she drew back the bolts of the door and was almost knocked backwards by Dan Courtney.

"You took your time!" he said. "I've been trying to attract someone's attention for the past half-hour at least!"

"I'm sorry . . ." began Meriel, mildly. "I assume everyone is asleep. Is something the matter?"

"I need a word with Vivienne, urgently," said Dan. "Can you fetch her for me?"

"Dan, it's half-past one! Surely whatever it is can wait until the morning! Or is it something I can deal with?"

"No, it can't wait until the morning! And as for whether you can help, that depends on whether you know where the frost candles are."

"Frost candles?" Not only did she not know where the frost candles might be found, she did not even know what they were. A further glance at Dan's face convinced her that she had better risk waking Vivienne. This, however, proved more difficult than she might have imagined. She found her mother-in-law lying on her back, snoring lightly, and profoundly unwilling to be roused. When Meriel gently shook her by the shoulder, urging her to wake up, Vivienne simply turned onto her side and slid into an even deeper sleep.

Uncertain as to what to do for the best, Meriel pulled a tracksuit on over her pyjamas, slid her feet into a pair of boots and ran back down the stairs.

"I think she must have taken a sleeping pill," she said. "I can't wake her. Perhaps if you explain the problem to me I can help sort something out."

She was halfway out of the door before Dan grabbed hold of her arm.

"Coat," he said, abruptly.

212

"I'm OK like this – " she began.

"I said, get a coat!" repeated Dan, and, with another look at his face, she returned indoors. "Now," she said, emerging seconds later, slipping her arms into a sheepskin jacket, "you'd better tell me what's going on."

It did not take long for Dan to explain to her that at this time of the year, whenever the thermometer dropped to dangerously near freezing, frost candles were lit in the vineyards to help raise the ambient temperature.

"You may not have noticed," he continued, "but we're already down to three degrees Celsius. And it's getting colder by the minute."

Already, just walking across the cobbled yard, Meriel was beginning to feel grateful for the warmth of the jacket. "What do these candles look like?" she asked. "And where are they kept?"

"They're simply big fat candles which we light and put in tin cans. Some vineyards have special heaters to do the job, but we have to make do with candles. The secret is to place them in low-lying frost pockets so that the warm air rises and protects the higher ground as well. We usually keep them in here – " Dan pulled open the door to one of the store-rooms " – in cardboard boxes."

The store-room, as Meriel could immediately see, was empty.

"I wish Adam wasn't away!" she said. "I'm sure he could help!" Then another thought struck her. "What about Jethro? Surely he knows where they are?" she hazarded.

"I've just phoned him. He said they were here when he checked them a couple of weeks ago. And yes," he continued, seeing that she was about to speak. "I do trust Jethro's word."

"Then who – ?"

"Someone who presumably thought we wouldn't be needing the candles this late in the year. I just wish they'd thought to let me know they were moving them."

"Well, they can't have got far," said Meriel. "I propose that we each hunt through all the store-rooms and out-houses, the gardening sheds, the winery – anywhere the boxes might have been put. You say there are several of them? Well, then. They can't be difficult to find."

"Right," said Dan. "But let's get a move on. We don't have much time."

She turned and began walking swiftly across the yard in the direction of the winery, but she had not taken two steps before her boots slipped suddenly on the cobbles and she almost lost her balance.

Dan was beside her in a moment. "OK?" he asked.

She nodded as she slid first one foot then the other over the rounded cobbles. "Is that ice?"

But she did not wait for his answer. She did not need to. Instead, grabbing a set of keys from the office, she began a hectic, desperate tour of Amberfield's likely stor-age places, flinging open doors, hauling aside polythene sheeting, rummaging through containers of fertiliser and pesticides. Nowhere was there any sign of the candles. Meanwhile, it seemed to her that it was getting colder all the time. If the candles were not found soon . . . As she continued her frantic search, the picture in her mind's eye was of unimaginable destruction.

She heard Dan coming across the courtyard and knew, even before she turned and saw the dejected stoop of his shoulders, that the candles had not been found.

"There must be some other way!" she said, refusing to accept defeat, but Dan merely shrugged his shoulders.

"We can always hope for a sudden blast of hot air from the Sahara, I suppose. But apart from that, there's nothing more we can do. You might as well get back to bed."

"I wouldn't sleep if I did," she told him. "Dan!" she cried suddenly. "The garages! We didn't check the garages!"

They did find candles in one of the garages. Three of them, to be precise, along with half a dozen tin cans, all of which appeared to have been inadvertently dropped and left lying on the ground. Dan was at a loss to explain it.

"Maybe they've been there for years," hazarded Meriel. "Maybe . . ." but she could think of no other likely explanation, and in any case Dan shook his head, pointing out that cars were frequently parked here. The tins and candles would by now have been crushed, instead of which they were whole and unmarked .

Dan picked up the three candles and a tin each.

"Come on," he said to Meriel. "Let's see if we can save one vine, at least."

Under the icy pallor of the moonlight which all but eclipsed the sharp brilliance of the stars, Dan lit the candles and placed them around a vine, chosen because its leaves appeared further unfurled than its neighbours'.

"Would the candles really have made that much difference?" asked Meriel.

"Maybe, maybe not. It depends on the degree of frost and how long it lasts. It may sound a bit primitive but it's a trick I picked up on a visit to France, as it happens. If you're lucky, it works. The problem is that the vineyards here have never been so vulnerable. Virtually all the vines are mature. When we had the hurricane, we did at least manage to save our younger plants."

"But surely we're insured against this kind of thing?"

Dan shook his head with a wry smile. "Meriel, Meriel!" he said. "Have you any idea what it would cost to insure against the thousand natural shocks that vines are heir to? No vine-grower could possibly afford the premiums."

"So, what's going to happen?" asked Meriel. She felt almost sick with fear.

"If the temperature drops another degree or so, we could lose a few thousand bottles. If it goes down by three or more degrees – then we can say goodbye to the whole lot. It's as simple as that."

"When will we know?"

"*I'll* know within the next two or three hours. But we'll have to wait until morning to be sure."

"Then I'll wait with you," said Meriel. "I'm sure everything will be all right," she said in an effort to reassure him. "And even if we do lose a few vines, it won't be your fault."

"You don't understand what it would mean to me," said Dan softly. "Losing another vineyard."

"Tell me," said Meriel. "Tell me about it."

They pulled up two armchairs as close to the newly lit fire as safety would allow. The dogs, after an initial burst of excitement caused by Meriel's arrival at the cottage at this late hour, flopped down to sleep once more. Meriel, still huddled inside her sheepskin jacket, her cold hands extended towards the flames, watched Dan's face as he continued with his story. Talking about it, even after all this time, was clearly not easy for him.

"I was twenty-four," Dan told her. "And very immature for my age, I suppose, although I didn't think so at the time. Since leaving school I'd worked at various vineyards – Bob Crace's was the first – and the minute I'd got a bit of money put together I borrowed the money to buy a small vineyard from a guy who wanted to get back to the city.

"Well, the vines were good and the site was good – except for one thing. There wasn't much in the way of natural water, and the guy who sold me the place had spent a fortune developing an irrigation system. Still, it worked, and I knew from the quality of the grapes that I could make some first-rate wine.

"And then I went and fell in love. Her name was Laura . . . Later, I realised that she was cold, selfish, manipulative, cruel even. She also happened to be married, to a farmer, but that didn't deter me. And then, after a couple of months, when she left me – when she told me she no longer had any use for me – I decided that my heart was irrevocably broken, and set about proving it."

216

"How did you do that?"

Dan flashed Meriel a look of embarrassment tinged with amusement.

"I started drinking. That and . . . generally behaving as obnoxiously as I could, although that must have made Laura even more relieved to be shot of me. I used to turn up outside her house and make an exhibition of myself, or march into the local watering holes and start haranguing anyone who knew her . . . But basically, I drank. And then I drank some more. Until . . ."

"Until what?"

Now the amusement faded from Dan's face.

"Until I couldn't stop," he said. "Until I couldn't face getting up in the morning until I'd had a dose of the magic tincture. Until I seemed to be spending every hour of the day looking forward to the next intake of alcohol. As you might imagine, the idea of a drunken winemaker struck most of my friends and neighbours as highly amusing."

Meriel nodded slowly. "Yes, I imagine it might."

"Well, things went on getting worse, until it came to a stage when I got it into my head that I could simply go to Laura's house, grab her, and force her to come back to me. Don't ask me how I thought I was going to make her stay with me once I'd kidnapped the poor woman. I wasn't in a fit state to work things out in that much detail. To cut a long story short, I drove like a mad thing to her house, only to find that she and her husband had gone away. Probably to escape my attentions. Anyway. I'd got a bottle with me, and I assume I drank most of the contents and then, stupidly, I tried to drive home."

"What happened?"

"I crashed, of course."

"Were you hurt?"

"Not badly. And luckily I was alone on the road. It seems I took a corner far too fast and overturned. Somehow or other, I was unharmed apart from a blow

217

to the head, but I was unconscious in hospital for almost two weeks. By which time . . ."

Meriel thought she was beginning to understand. "Something had happened to the vineyard?" she asked. "Not a frost, surely?"

"No." Dan shook his head. "Not a frost, no. It was too late in the season for that."

"What, then?"

Dan hesitated. "Let me check the vineyard first," he said.

On his return, he seemed a fraction less anxious. "Fingers crossed," he told her. "The thermometer's still hovering around the zero mark, but it hasn't dropped any further."

"That's wonderful, Dan!" said Meriel. "So, when you came out of hospital?"

Dan sat with his head bowed for so long Meriel began to think he was not going to continue. Then, at last, he lifted his head again and began to speak. Once he regained consciousness, he told her, and realised that he was not seriously hurt, his only thought was to be allowed to get up and go – back to his home, and back to the bottle.

Before being allowed to leave, Dan was given a lecture by one of the doctors about the dangers of alcohol abuse, but the words simply washed over him. He had things under control, he assured the doctor. He knew what he was doing. OK, so he shouldn't have so much to drink when he knew he was going to be driving, but that was just a minor oversight.

And so he had driven home, full of confidence, not in the least way prepared for the sight which met his eyes when he set foot once more in his vineyard. In fact, what he saw so shocked him that at first he felt his mind must be playing tricks on him. That his head injury was more serious than he had been led to believe. But eventually he was forced to accept the evidence of his own eyes: the grapes which had been ripening to a juicy fullness at the time of his accident, and which needed only a few more weeks before picking, had shrunk and shrivelled to a stage where they were of interest only to the birds.

"But how – ?" queried Meriel.

Dan gave a harsh laugh. "The pump on the watering system jammed. Just at the crucial time. The irony was that it's a problem I could have fixed in five minutes, if only I'd been around. So there I was. Ten thousand bottles of wine down the drain, no income for the following year, no way of repaying the loans I'd taken out to buy the place. I had no option but to sell up and move on."

"And the drinking?" asked Meriel. "Did that stop?"

"Oh, yes! I came to my senses the minute I realised what had happened. But by then, of course, it was too late."

He fell silent, leaving Meriel to think about what he had told her. He must now be expecting her reaction, her judgement, even. The surprising thing was that she found it almost impossible to feel the disapproval he probably deserved. What Dan had done was dangerous, foolish, irresponsible; moreover, he could well have injured others when he crashed his car. But in the long run, no one had suffered but himself, the events he spoke of all happened years ago and what mattered, surely, was what he had achieved since.

"I can see why you feel so badly about it," she said at last. "But it's not as though this is recent history . . . and if Edward and Vivienne can accept you on your terms . . ."

"That's just it," said Dan curtly. "Edward and Vivienne don't know. I never told them. Look, I needed this job. Do you suppose for one minute that they would have taken me on if they knew I'd just destroyed my vineyard because of my addiction to alcohol?"

"No," replied Meriel. "I don't think they would. Tell me something," she added after a pause. "Why tell *me* about it? And why now?"

Dan's intense gaze was on her when he replied. "I haven't the least idea."

"Dan – " she began, but broke off as he sprang to his feet and crossed to the door in swift paces.

"Look!" he said.

She rose and crossed to where he stood outside the open door. It appeared Dan was right. The sky did seem to be clouding over. The moonlight was fading and the stars now shimmered rather than sparkled in the sky. With the clouds came the hope that the last of the earth's warmth would now be prevented from escaping, and that the vineyards would be saved.

For some moments they stood side by side, oblivious of everything except that the immediate danger was past. And then Meriel forgot even about the threat to the vines, for Dan's hands were tugging gently at the lapels on her jacket and he was lowering his head towards hers, and she was turning her cold face upwards as the heaviness of desire began to settle on her.

Cautiously at first, uncertain as to how she would respond, Dan let his fingers slide upwards, stroking her neck and collar-bone, until he was holding her head cradled in his palms, her hair springy to his touch. Even without the pressure of his hands to help her, Meriel would have had no choice but to let her head tilt back, her eyes close, as Dan's lips brushed against her eyelids, her forehead, her cheeks and deliciously, her own hungry mouth. For a few drunken moments, as Dan's tongue found its way between her eager lips, and pushed insistently at her teeth, she was shot through with such dreamy, swooning weakness that she thought her legs would fail her. Dan, sensing her sudden frailty, slid his hands under her jacket and round her back, pulling her tightly to him, shaping her body to his, supporting her while he continued to fill her with his kisses.

Dan, tearing himself away with a soft laugh, ran one hand down her back, over her buttocks and thighs until he reached the crook of her knees. Without saying a word, he lifted her swiftly into his arms and, kicking the door

220

closed behind him, carried her back into the cottage, deftly skirting the furniture and somehow contriving to free Meriel of her jacket on the way.

Setting her down before the now-blazing fire, and holding her at arms' length, he gazed at her, heavy-lidded, for some moments until her body began, in spite of itself, to sway towards him. With a gasp, she became aware of his hands, far smoother than she might have expected from someone of Dan's calling, on the bare skin of her waist, one hand sliding around her back, the other moving upwards along her ribs, an index finger brushing the rounded underside of her breast until it found the hardening nipple.

With a moan, Meriel let the upper half of her body twist until the full weight of her breast lay in Dan's hand, the straining nipple now grazing his palm, while she began to undo the buttons of his shirt. Running her hands over the lean hardness of his chest, the taut ribcage, the knot of muscle on his upper arms, she was both moved by and filled with longing for the tanned softness of his skin. Deftly unbuckling the belt of his jeans, unfastening the zip, she bent and placed a swift kiss at the spot where the line of curling hairs began, and heard Dan's sharp intake of breath at her touch.

Sliding and shrugging out of their clothes, their movements interrupted only by the contact of their lips as they drank in one another's kisses, unable to remain separated for more than a few seconds at a time, they stood naked before one another. Dan, oblivious of a sudden shower of sparks thrown out by a blazing log, drew Meriel closer to him, plunging his head into the warm hollow of her throat while she ran her fingers through his dark, wiry hair, and deposited kisses on his temples, his ears, his eyes.

Now she could feel the pressure of Dan's rough, naked thigh between her own, as well as the smoother, harder thrust of his erection and, momentarily, she experienced a slowing in the tide of passion that was overwhelming her. So often, in the past, she had been led to this degree of ecstasy, only to be entered abruptly, too soon, before she was ready to enjoy the moment to the full.

"No . . ." she started to say, but long before the word had been uttered it had turned into an exhalation of pleasure as Dan, far from forcing himself into her, dropped his head from her shoulders to her breasts and began kissing and licking the taut nipples, nibbling and teasing at them until her whole body was aflame once more. Then, his hands and his mouth moved downwards, intent, or so it seemed, on kissing every inch of her, while she moaned and arched at his touch, and the coil of longing in the pit of her stomach twisted ever tighter and tighter.

When the hands that explored and stroked her back, waist and buttocks finally slid around towards the moistness between her thighs, she knew the ache within her must be stilled. Dan knew it too. Gently, he lowered her onto the patterned Indian rug before the fireplace, where she took him into her, her body bucking at the sheer pleasure of it. As Dan began to move inside her, Meriel heard someone – not herself, surely! – cry out with delight. She let her body float away on an unstoppable, rhythmic tide, slowly at first, then faster, but still dreamily, langorously until, racked by a splintering explosion of pleasure, she felt Dan climax and she knew she would remember this moment for the rest of her life.

The warmth of total satisfaction, of utter fulfilment, enveloped her. Dan drew away from her and, shielding her body from the heat of the fire, gazed into her eyes with something approaching disbelief.

"Dan . . .?" she started to say.

But he was stopping her lips again with his kiss, and never in a million years could she have resisted him.

The moon had vanished by the time they returned to the vineyard for a further check. It was as though the stars had been switched off. There was, in fact, no sky to be seen as Dan and Meriel, arms tightly around one another, stumbled and felt their way through the dark.

The candles had burned out, but when Dan shone a torch on this and other vines, Meriel could see no sign of damage. The buds were either closed, plump and brown, or were sprouting pale green shiny leaves. All was as it should be.

She kissed Dan's neck in pleasure at the discovery, but when he turned to her there was despair in his eyes.

"Listen," was all he said.

And then she heard it. In the deep stillness of the night, across the vineyard from near and far, came a sound she had never heard before, but which was only too instantly recognisable. Those were not rainclouds they had seen building up, Meriel now realised. They were the first indicators of a murderous fog, which was now wrapping itself in freezing swathes around its unsuspecting victims. What they could hear was the slow, soft, irregular thud of vine buds hitting the ground. As the invisible scissorman snipped indiscriminately at the next season's crop, it seemed to Meriel she could hear the vines dying.

When the horror of what the frost was doing to the vineyards finally gripped her, she had turned to Dan and hugged him closely to her. Without speaking they returned to his cottage, to his bed. They made love again, this time with less urgency, which only made the experience all the sweeter.

Just before daylight, Dan walked her back to Amberfield House, burying his head in her hair as they passed the vineyards, refusing to look – yet – on what he knew he must see. They could not know that the effect of Vivienne's sleeping pills had worn off and that she was already awake. Staring anxiously out through her frost-rimed window, she watched in disbelief as the two figures stopped and kissed and, moments later, stopped and kissed again . . .

Meriel did not mean to, but when she finally wrenched

herself away from Dan and returned to her room, she fell fast asleep. It was late afternoon by the time she awoke, and when she went in search of Dan, Jacinta told her she thought he had gone out.

"You wouldn't know where he's gone, would you?" Meriel asked.

"I not know . . . but . . . I think Mrs Barton very angry with him!"

"Vivienne? Angry with Dan? But why? Surely she doesn't blame him for the frost! He did everything he could!"

But Jacinta merely shook her head. "I sorry. I not know."

That night, Meriel visited Dan's cottage, only to find the door locked. There were no lights burning, and when, later still, she tried to telephone, there was no reply.

The following morning, Dan failed to appear at the winery as usual, and when Jethro evaded Meriel's questions, it became clear that something was badly wrong.

Dan finally came into the office shortly before lunch, swiftly cutting short Meriel's relieved, welcoming smile.

"I promised Jethro I'd have a word with you before I left," he said without preamble, "otherwise I wouldn't be here now."

"Before you left . . .?" she stammered, uncomprehendingly. "Why . . .what's . . ."

"Vivienne's fired me," he told her. "As you must surely have known she would do once she found out about my other vineyard."

"But . . . how did she find out?"

Dan's voice remained calm, almost friendly. "Oh, come, Meriel! You were the only one who knew. You are the only person I have ever told. I can imagine you thought there was no harm in saying something – "

"I promise you, I swear to you, I have said nothing to Vivienne. I haven't seen her since I was with you!"

"I wish you hadn't said that," Dan went on, more quietly

224

now. "Because now I know you're lying. It's not only the vineyard. Vivienne knew about us! By the time I went to fetch her to show her the frost damage she knew we'd been together! So how can I believe you when you say you didn't see her? For heaven's sake, Meriel, what made you tell her? Why did you do it?"

But she found she could not answer. The words that came to her were inadequate, unconvincing, mainly because she could offer no explanation as to how Vivienne might have found out. All she knew was that she had said nothing.

Dan left Amberfield later that same day, despite Meriel's last-ditch attempt to intercede on his behalf. Unable to believe that Vivienne really meant to get rid of him, she approached Adam with the aim of getting him to persuade his mother to change her mind. But she found Adam even more intractable than Vivienne. Dan was a liability, he informed her. He had brought about many of their present problems. He should have gone a long time ago.

"As far as Dan Courtney is concerned," finished Adam, "I have to say that in my opinion your judgement is suspect. If it's all the same with you, I'd prefer not to discuss the matter further. Mother and I have made our decision. Let's leave it at that, shall we?"

Meriel, still reeling from the accusation Dan had levelled at her, was silenced by Adam's words. She would have liked to tell him that there was a side of Dan of which he was unaware – that he could be patient and concerned and more than generous when it came to sharing his knowledge. But she feared that if she spoke, Adam would simply laugh at her, and then all her distress at Dan's going and the loss of the harvest would come tumbling out.

She felt she would die rather than show weakness before Adam, but when he had gone she slumped down at her desk and buried her face in her hands, trying to make sense of what had happened. When she first came to

Amberfield, she had hoped she and Adam might be friends. Now he was behaving almost as if he wished her to leave and never return. Was this Vivienne's wish also? On balance, she thought not, but maybe she was simply too confused to understand what was required of her.

A discreet cough caused her to raise her head. "Oh, Jethro!" she exclaimed, almost pathetically pleased to see the old man.

"Now then, now then," he said, aware of her misery and patting her awkwardly on the shoulder.

"I just don't know what to do, Jethro," she said simply.

"So long as *you* don't even think of leaving," he said, reading her thoughts. "Now that Dan's gone I'm going to need you around the place."

"Do you really mean that?"

"I certainly do."

"But couldn't Adam – ?"

"I know I shouldn't be saying this," replied Jethro, "but if you ask me, we're better off without Adam throwing his weight about in the winery. You know what he's like. So long as it's liquid and it's inside a bottle labelled 'wine', then it's all right. Well, that's not the way Dan taught me to see things."

"Where did he go, Jethro?" she asked at last.

"South Australia. He'll be working for Bob Crace – remember?"

Meriel nodded.

"Well," said Jethro with a sigh. "Work to be done. And if you want to make yourself useful you can order some more frost candles. Not that we'll be needing them before next year, but best be safe than sorry."

Michelle was unable to lay her hands on a previous order for candles, or to remember where they had come from.

"Maybe one of the boxes has got the maker's name on it," she hazarded.

Coming from Michelle this was an unusually sensible

226

suggestion, and although Meriel was certain the store-room had been stripped bare, she decided it was worth having one last look.

It proved almost impossible to open the door, so high were the boxes piled behind it. For a while, she could only stand and stare, unable to take in what she was seeing. Yet the evidence of her own eyes was clear enough. The boxes of candles which had been removed at some earlier stage were now back where they belonged. They had been taken away some time after Jethro had last checked on them and they had been returned during the past few hours. It was enough to make Meriel wonder whether she had really seen the store-room empty. But she knew she had.

PART THREE

13

"You mustn't worry about Daddy," Hatta said to Vivienne. "He'll be all right, really he will! He's got Diggers, and the doctor said he'd drop by every day. Anyway, Meriel's there. So relax, and enjoy yourself like I'm going to."

Meriel, yes, thought Vivienne, with a pang of unease. Her daughter-in-law had of course been invited to the wedding. More, she had accepted with pleasure and was on the point of buying her ticket when she sensed that Vivienne was on the point of crying off.

Vivienne had tried to explain. "It's simply . . . oh, I know I'm probably being silly, but I do wish someone from the family were staying with Edward. Do you see?"

Meriel did see. Over the past weeks Edward's condition had deteriorated further. Dr Dinwiddy had strongly advised against taking Edward to France, while insisting that there was no immediate danger to his life.

There had been a time when Meriel would have hesitated before saying what she said next. Following the occasion when Edward had reacted so violently to the sight of her, she had kept away for a while. But soon Miss Digby persuaded her to start seeing him again. *Don't go worrying yourself*, she had said, mysteriously. *It wasn't you that upset him so.* And Meriel, though not understanding, had done as she was bidden, and was hugely relieved to find that Miss Digby was right. Edward did not grow disturbed when she entered the room. On the contrary, she was certain he looked forward to seeing her, and it was for this reason she had no difficulty in offering to remain at Amberfield.

231

"I'm family now," she stated matter-of-factly. "I'll stay with him."

And Vivienne, accepting the offer with relief, had experienced an unexpected and uncharacteristic rush of gratitude towards the girl. It was at that moment that she realised for the first time that what Meriel said was true. Her daughter-in-law *was* part of the family, and she had been accepted as such, which only made Vivienne feel all the more unhappy about what she had done that day almost five months ago, after the frost. But what other course of action was open to her, she asked herself as the plane skimmed low over the bay at Nice and turned towards the runway? She had had no choice; she did what she had to do.

Adam was there to meet them at the airport. He drove them to the Meyreuils' house where they were greeted by the entire family with a typically Gallic mixture of handshakes, hugs and kisses on both cheeks plus an extra kiss which Vivienne kept forgetting about. The excitement generated by the approaching wedding was tangible, not only in the Meyreuil household, but throughout the village, as Vivienne discovered when she took a quiet walk later that afternoon.

Stopping by the baker's to admire an assortment of glazed croissants and fruit tarts, she was accosted by an elderly man who spoke to her in peculiarly accented French at full speed and then waxed ecstatic when she replied to him in his own language.

Within seconds, this self-proclaimed best friend of Monsieur Meyreuil senior (Vivienne assumed he was referring to Sophie's grandfather, whom she had not yet met) had summoned half the population to meet the mother-in-law of Sophie Meyreuil and Vivienne found herself surrounded by smiling, chattering faces, while she smiled back and nodded and did her best to understand what was being said. Eventually, to her relief, they let her go, and she made her way back to the house.

The house was large, modern, surrounded by a dry garden in which viciously coloured marigolds held pride of place.

"Before this was built," Adam informed her when he came to fetch her down for dinner, "they all lived in the old man's house, just outside the village. Now *that's* what I call a house. A sixteenth-century stone farmhouse, somewhat in need of modernisation, I grant you, but rather wonderful all the same. The trouble is, all these families are alike. They don't feel they've made it until they've abandoned their beautiful ancestral homes and moved into boxes like this. Oh. There's a pool, by the way. Last time I looked, Hatta was in it being heavily chatted up by . . . let me see . . . five young men, I think I counted. They're all more or less related to Sophie, so there's no need to worry."

"Adam – wait," she said as he opened the door for her. "There's something I want to say. It's about your wedding present . . ."

"We're thrilled with it, Mother, I promise! It's going to look great in the dining-room."

Vivienne had commissioned a painting of Amberfield House from a local artist of increasing reputation. When the work was finished, she liked it so much she was at first loath to part with it, and wished she could afford to commission a further work for herself. However, this was not what she wished to discuss with her son.

"I'm glad you like it, of course, but there's something else I'd like to give you for your wedding. Adam. I'd like to offer you joint managing directorship of the company on your return from honeymoon."

"This is . . . unexpected." Adam seemed nonplussed.

"I was thinking in terms of us working concurrently for a year, before you eventually take over from me altogether. I'm not getting any younger, you know . . ."

"Really, Mother, I don't know what to say . . . except, yes, I accept. Of course. And thank you."

233

He dropped a quick kiss onto her forehead. "Tell you what. If there's time tomorrow I'll take you to see the old man's house. OK?"

But in the event there wasn't time. Vivienne scarcely set eyes on her son, or Sophie, or even Hatta for that matter, during the following day. When, in the late morning, she risked another walk, she was greeted like an old friend. In the streets and squares, white-trunked trees spread a welcome shade; fountains splashed and trickled; metal chairs and tables stood outside the village's two cafés and Vivienne would have stopped for a coffee had there been any other single women doing likewise. At the end of one narrow street she came upon the public *lavoir*, the centuries-old stone trough where some of the village women still chose to wash their laundry: indeed, there was one old crone there now, too intent and absorbed in her task to notice Vivienne's passing.

The following day, the religious ceremony over, Vivienne emerged from the cool darkness of the church into the blinding sunshine of the square. Mme Meyreuil, laughing and crying by turns, emerged to ask whether Vivienne had ever seen such a beautiful couple. Vivienne had no difficulty assuring her that she had not.

Even the fact that Adam's wedding had been conducted according to Roman Catholic rites failed to dampen her delight in all she saw and heard. Above her, the church's cracked and tinny bell rang out in celebration as Adam and Sophie, looking as happy as anyone could wish, proceeded to the *mairie* for the civil ceremony which finally, legally, declared them man and wife.

Then Adam and Sophie rode hand in hand to the wedding lunch, blowing kisses to the children running along beside them. Behind the newlyweds came a procession of guests in their cars. With white ribbons fluttering from their aerials and horns blaring, they made a cheerful, noisy motorcade – all very un-English, in Vivienne's delighted opinion.

"Is the whole village invited?" she asked, noting with amazement the vast number of tables arranged in a long oblong under the trees, rapidly losing count as the tables filled up and the wine began to flow.

"But of course!" replied Madame Meyreuil. "Only they do not all come at once. Some come now, for lunch, others later in the night . . . you understand?"

They ate and drank, then drank a toast or two, then drank and ate some more. After a time the band struck up and couples, led by Adam and Sophie, took to the space between the tables and began dancing. Vivienne danced too, though she had little idea who half her partners might be. Only Mr Meyreuil remained clearly in her memory when she attempted to recall some of the detail of that beautiful day.

"You must not think you lose a son . . ." he began, in a worthy attempt at speaking English, an effort no doubt facilitated by a steady ingestion of alcohol. "You must think more . . . think more that . . ." he stopped, and shrugged his shoulders helplessly.

Vivienne giggled. "I must think more in terms of gaining a daughter, is that it?" She was vastly amused to think that this cliché had crossed the Channel. But Monsieur Meyreuil merely looked puzzled.

"Ah, yes, perhaps . . ." he said, doubtfully. "I simply wish to say you must come here many, many times, especially if there are grandchildren. We want you to see them very often."

"You mean, *you* want to see *them* very often!" Vivienne corrected him, but he looked so bewildered she gave up trying to explain that he had got his pronouns mixed up, since the young couple and any children they might have would be living in England, not France. Later, she returned to the house for a rest before rejoining the festivities. In the meantime, Adam and Sophie had left to catch a plane, but their absence deterred the revellers not one whit. From time to time, Vivienne would catch sight of Hatta whirling past her, eyes shining, having, in the girl's own words, a truly mega-brill time. It must have been well into the early hours before the party came to an end, but when it did, Vivienne could not remember having enjoyed herself so much in years. If only Edward could have shared with her!

Then, all too soon, they were back in England, Hatta had gone back to school, and Vivienne found herself in this strange, restless state, unable to concentrate on anything much. She would feel like this, she suspected, until Adam and Sophie returned from their honeymoon, and some semblance of normality was resumed.

She was half-sorry, half-relieved to learn from Miss Digby that Edward appeared to have been unaware of her absence. But she was not surprised. It was some time since he had given clear signs of recognising her, though Diggers insisted that he was still capable of responding to Hatta's music. That was as may be, she thought, as she relayed the details of Adam's wedding, and showed Diggers the many photographs of the event. She hoped Edward was listening, and understanding. But most of all she was relieved he could not know that five months ago, after the loss of the harvest, she had sent Dan away.

"What do you think, Jethro?" asked Meriel, "Should we go ahead?"

She could tell he was worried and uncertain what to do, for the responsibility for ordering the start of the harvest had never before been his alone. In the old days, when hops had been grown at Amberfield, the decision to pick had been based on instinct coupled with long experience.

"No need then for all this fancy technology," he said, gloomily inserting the refractometer into a grape to measure the sugar level. The previous morning he had used a hydrometer to test the specific gravity of the grapes, but Meriel could see he did not know whether to trust the readings he obtained.

236

It was the last week of October and the forecast for the next few days was good. Although Adam was all for delaying the harvest by another week or two, Meriel was uneasy. Too much sugar in the crop would lead to a decrease in acidity and a correspondingly overripe taste – what Dan had described to her as "flabbiness". On the other hand, if the forecast was wrong and it started to rain heavily, the sugar content would be diluted and the flavour ruined. Eventually, she sought Vivienne's opinion.

"What does Jethro think Dan would have done?" she asked at last.

"On balance, he thinks we'd have picked."

"Then go ahead," she decided, ignoring Adam's protests. "Pick."

With only a few extra helpers, they began picking the small quantities of grapes spared by the frost. The Seyval Blanc vines appeared to have come off best, though the yield was well down. Virtually all the Schönburger and Chardonnay had gone, and there were varying quantities of Siegerrebe, Seibel, Pinot Noir, Triomphe d'Alsace and Léon Millot grapes.

Meriel, snipping carefully at the bunches of Seyval Blanc before laying them in a plastic bucket, could only be grateful that virtually none of the vines had actually died. That terrible night, when she heard the sound of buds dropping to the ground, she thought it signified the end of the vineyards, but she was wrong. The crop was largely lost, certainly, but the plants were made of tougher stuff. They would recover. They *must* recover.

Even so it was depressingly obvious that only about a quarter of the vines had survived the frost unscathed. Of the others, some had suffered piecemeal damage only, but many had been stripped of all their fruit. Since then, secondary growth had produced reasonable quantities of new grapes, but these were useless: bright green and hard as bullets, they were fit for nothing.

When they came to harvest the Pinot Noir grapes Jethro

balanced one of the tight black bunches in his hand and shook his head.

"Pity," he said. "No mould at all, this year. But without the Chardonnay, Pinot Noir isn't much use to us."

These were the varieties used to make Amberfield's traditional method sparkling wine, and Meriel, while agreeing in principle, was unhappy at the thought of so much waste.

"Couldn't we use the Pinot Noir for something else?" she asked. "Rather than simply throwing it all away?"

She glanced across at Jethro and when she saw him studiedly avoiding her eyes, she knew he was thinking what she was thinking. At times like this there was no doubt about it: they needed an expert winemaker to advise them.

"Is there someone we could ask?" she suggested, but Jethro shook his head.

"When Adam told me I was to take charge of the winemaking I warned him there'd be problems, questions I couldn't answer. But he said I was just to do the best I could." He shrugged. "I suppose we can make a blend of some sort, but I wouldn't be happy with that. I prefer to stay with what I know."

"Jethro . . ." said Meriel, very slowly, because the idea was only just beginning to come to her.

"When my missis says my name like that it always spells trouble," the old man grinned.

But Meriel scarcely heard him. "Jethro . . ." she said again, a look of pure excitement beginning to spread over her features. "We've got the Pinot Noir, and some Seibel . . . and small amounts of one or two other varieties . . ."

"Yes," said Jethro, patiently.

"We could make a rosé. Dan said he'd always meant to make a still rosé from the Pinot Noir grapes. He was going to blend it with Seibel. He explained exactly how he would do it!"

Jethro was shaking his head. "Like I said, I prefer to

stick to what I know. We've never made a rosé here. Apart from the sparkling wine, that is, and I had nothing to do with that. I wouldn't be happy to try anything like that."

"Fair enough," said Meriel happily. For a moment, Jethro thought he had convinced her. Then she added: "Perhaps what I should have said was that *I* could make a rosé."

Jethro, who in every other respect had been a hundred per cent supportive, drew the line at venturing into unknown territory.

"What worries me is that you have to process grapes differently depending on whether you're making a white or a coloured wine. Take these Pinot Noirs, for example. If we're making our sparkling wine, we mill the grapes very, very gently, then get the juice off those skins as fast as possible. Whereas – "

"I know what you're going to say!" she interrupted him impatiently. "That it's the skins of black grapes that give wine its colour, not the juice. Jethro, I know that! I know I've got to leave the must on the skins until the colour has been extracted!"

If Jethro was taken aback by Meriel's insistence he did not show it, but continued in the same patient manner:

"It's not that simple. Don't forget that all the time the juice is on the skins you're extracting tannin, so it's a matter of taste as well as colour."

Meriel was shame-faced. "I'm sorry, Jethro. I didn't mean to snap at you. And of course you're right. But I'm sure Dan told me he left the grapes for at least a week before pressing them, so that's what I'll do too."

"A *week*?" queried Jethro, clearly not convinced. "Are you sure?"

Meriel decided to go ahead in defiance of Jethro's objections, but right from the start she was made to doubt the wisdom of her actions.

After milling, the pulp from the Pinot Noir was transferred to a vat, to which yeast was added to assist fermentation. If Meriel had harboured the least doubt about the efficacy of the yeast starter, that was dispelled the following morning when she lifted the lid off the container and saw the violent activity raging beneath.

"Jethro!" she called in alarm. "Do you think it's supposed to be reacting this strongly?"

Although she could tell he was anxious too, he did his best to reassure her.

"I imagine so. Now, don't worry. It'll probably start calming down soon."

Later that day however, when she next inspected the ferment, she became even more worried. The level had risen so high that she feared it would overflow the vat, and that much of her wine would be lost.

In the event, the brew did calm down, just as Jethro had predicted, and for some days afterwards Meriel inspected it at regular invervals, making sure the pulp was pushed down below the surface of the liquid, wishing she could be certain that she doing the right thing. Not until a full week had passed did she made the crucial decision.

"I'm going to take the plunge, Jethro," she said, trying to conceal her anxiety. "I'm going to extract the juice."

The liquid yielded by the final pressing was a dirty, deep reddish-purple in colour.

"It's going to be too dark, isn't it?" asked Meriel despondently, handing Jethro a sample of juice.

After several minutes of deliberation, during which Jethro swirled the liquid to and fro, and poured it from one container to another – more, Meriel sensed, to give himself time to find a helpful answer than for any other reason – he finally gave his verdict.

"Yes. I think maybe it will be on the dark side. The important thing is, have you tasted it?"

"Not yet." She lifted a glass to her lips, but Jethro halted her.

"Remember," he said, "It's going to taste pretty rough at this stage. Don't get too much of a shock."

None the less, she *was* shocked. Her newborn wine was not simply rough, it was burningly raw and tannic to the palate. Meriel knew, immediately and beyond doubt, that even if it were allowed to mature for a hundred years it would never mellow into anything remotely drinkable.

Jethro, correctly interpreting the look on her face, said kindly:

"That bad, eh? Here, let me try it." He took a small, wary sip. "Reminds me of some of Edward's earlier efforts," was all he said. "Now, don't go upsetting yourself! There are far worse disasters in this world than leaving some grapes too long on their skins."

Meriel brushed away the tears from her eyes and reached up to give Jethro a kiss.

"Thanks," she said. "I should have listened to you all along."

As soon as Friday came round again, she packed a small suitcase and left for Wiltshire. After her first, unexpectedly enjoyable weekend at Melbury, she came to the conclusion that Rory's home would provide a convenient bolthole for moments when, for whatever reason, life became uncomfortable at Amberfield.

Her lack of success at making her own wine seemed to her a very good reason for seeking the sanctuary Rory was able to offer, and in any case she always found it impossible to be sad when she was riding Paloma. Rory's sister turned out to be another of Melbury's assets. She was a sporty, forthright young woman, with a job as a glorified secretary to a firm of china importers. She did not bat an eyelid when she arrived at Melbury one weekend, with a young stockbroker named Jarvis in tow, to find her brother teaching a total stranger how to ride. On the contrary, she went out of her way to put Meriel at ease.

"I say," she said conspiratorially, as though she and Meriel had known each other for years, "what do you

241

think of Jarvis? Isn't he scrumptious? Should I marry him, do you think?"

The man was stocky, florid, dark-haired and given to yellow waistcoats. "Scrumptious" was not the first adjective that had come into Meriel's mind on sight of him, but who was she to judge the workings of Patsy's heart?

"When did you meet?" she asked.

"Two weeks ago," came the reply. "To be exact, twelve days and about seventeen hours ago. We simply adore each other."

"Well . . . maybe you should wait just a little while longer," suggested Meriel. "By the way, I've been meaning to ask you . . ."

"Yes?"

"I hope you don't mind me helping Rory with this decorating business."

Patsy looked puzzled. "I didn't know you were," she countered.

"I mean, this was your home, wasn't it? Before you moved to London? I wouldn't want to come up with anything you didn't like."

"Oh, but I thought . . ." Patsy broke off. "Never mind. I've probably got the wrong end of the stick. Anyway, no. Melbury has never been my home. It's true I lived with Rory for a few months between jobs, but what he wants to do with the place is his business. So, please feel free to choose whatever you like, if that's what Rory has now decided."

She was gone before Meriel could pursue the matter, but Patsy's response gave her pause for thought. Whenever she came to Melbury she brought with her swatches of material and samples of wallpaper and spent a considerable part of her time trying to decide how best to refurbish this wonderful house without altering its character utterly. Whenever she decided upon a particular item, Rory would commend her on her good taste and, as often as not, change the subject.

242

"Rory," she asked him that night, as they began climbing the staircase to their separate bedrooms. "Are you sure you want my opinion about the redecorating? Only you never seem to take much notice of what I'm saying."

Rory placed his arms on either side of her, gently pinning her against the wall.

"Of course I take notice of what you say!" He bent his head to kiss her on the lips, slowly, taking his time. "You mean a lot to me, Meriel. You must know that."

Slowly, gradually, their relationship had become more physical. The quick kisses on the cheek had given way to deeper, closer embraces, and Meriel, seeing the pulsing vein in Rory's neck, and hearing his breath come faster as their bodies inched closer together, was left in little doubt as to his desire for her.

She slid the backs of her hands up the wall until she found Rory's and linked her fingers with his. For some moments they gazed at one another, saying nothing. She was almost, but not quite, ready for him and, feeling her tense as he bent his head towards her again, Rory stopped and drew back. He knew that to force her would be to drive her away for good.

"Will you spend Christmas with me?" he asked instead.

"Not Christmas," she answered. "I'd rather be at Amberfield for Christmas."

"Fair enough. How about New Year, then? But come for longer this time. For a week, maybe?"

She hesitated before replying, knowing that this time his invitation carried a different meaning. But she said yes all the same.

Two days after her return to Kent, Meriel wandered among the few remaining unharvested vines under what was surely the last of the autumn sunshine. Any day now the weather would change and winter would be upon them, but for the moment the grapes were still ripening and it was still pleasant to be out of doors.

243

Only a few dozen Léon Millot and Triomphe d'Alsace vines still bore their fruit, and that simply because Jethro saw no point in picking them. These were five-year-old specimens which Meriel knew Dan had planted with the idea of making a blended red wine. The previous year he had allowed a few of the plants to fruit, despite knowing that they were not ready, and had made a small quantity of wine. As he had demonstrated to Meriel, the results were disappointing, but Meriel was certain that this year, had the bulk of the crop not been lost, and had Dan been there to oversee the process, Amberfield would have produced its first commercially viable red wine.

She picked a couple of Léon Millot grapes and began idly peeling the skin off one of them. Interestingly, and unlike any of the varieties she had previously handled, the interior of the grape was reddish in colour. Out of curiosity she subjected a Triomphe d'Alsace grape to the same treatment, and found that it too had red-coloured juice.

On an impulse, she selected a bunch of each variety and went in search of Jethro.

"No," he said flatly, recognising the eager look in her eye and guessing what she was about to say. "Absolutely not!"

"Jethro, listen to me!" she urged. "How would it be if we were to pick the remaining grapes and treat them exactly as if we were making a white wine?"

Jethro was taken aback. "Can't be done, Meriel," he told her. "These varieties are red right the way through. There's no way you can make a white wine out of them."

"But I don't want to make a white wine! I want to make a rosé!"

One by one Jethro listed his objections, and one by one Meriel countered them. At first, he worried that the grapes had already been too long on the vine, but following tests for acidity and sugar levels he was forced to admit that the fruit was still usable. Meriel went further, claiming that

244

they could not have chosen a better moment to harvest this particular crop.

"This late run of fine weather is just what the grapes needed. Believe me, they're perfect for what I have in mind!"

Once picked, the grapes were stripped of all extraneous matter and then crushed, or milled with the utmost gentleness. This time, instead of leaving the pulp to ferment on the skins, Meriel insisted that the pressing be carried out immediately, and this brought a further objection from Jethro.

"Even assuming the colour is good, won't it be lacking in flavour if you do away with the tannin content altogether?"

"What I'm aiming for," she explained, "is a light, fresh wine – the very opposite of tannic. This is a wine to be drunk very, very young. Like next year, for instance."

"*Next year!*" exclaimed Jethro. "That would be fine for a white wine, but I'm really not sure about a rosé!"

But when, just a few days later, Meriel racked off the fermented must and transferred it to a clean tank, Jethro's attitude changed.

"This isn't half bad," he admitted after tasting the new wine. "In fact, given a couple of good frosts and a following wind, it could very well be drinkable by next spring. I'd say you've got the makings of a nice, fruity little number here. Maybe you're not just a pretty face after all!"

14

If this Christmas was no more than a pale imitation of former Christmases at Amberfield, Vivienne seemed determined to ignore the fact. She was wearing a slim-fitting
dress in a deep purple that vividly set off her most precious
jewellery – wide diamond bracelet, necklace and ear clips
– that Edward had given her to celebrate the births of
their three children. She always wore her diamonds on
Christmas Day: it was part of a ritual that had grown up
over the years, and which she was anxious to re-establish
after the previous year's period of mourning.

She glanced approvingly at the decorations put up by
Hatta and Meriel, pleased with the way they shimmered
and sparkled in the soft light, swaying gently in the draught
from the roaring fire. And there was more: a Christmas
tree every bit as high as those they had had in previous years stood by the doors to the conservatory, its
branches festive with lametta, tartan ribbons and assorted
red wooden fruits and toys that had been in the family
since Victorian times. Standing back to admire the tree,
then stooping to rearrange the growing stack of presents
beneath it, Vivienne reflected that with the exception of
the candles which had now given way to electric lights,
what she saw was what she might have seen a hundred
years ago. She found this fact curiously comforting.

After breakfasting with Hatta and Meriel, she had spent
the morning in the kitchen with Jacinta, supervising the
cooking of the Christmas lunch. Then, before returning
to her room to bathe and change, she had looked in on
Edward only to find that he was asleep.

"I'm sorry, Mrs Barton," apologised the relief nurse, Emily, whose presence meant that Miss Digby was as usual able to spend Christmas week with her sister. "I propped Mr Barton up on his pillows, like you said, but he was so tired, he kept slipping down."

"Don't worry, Emily, you did the right thing. Of course Edward must sleep if that is what he needs. But how disappointing that he won't be able to join us for lunch! I had so looked forward to it!"

Meriel was the first to join Vivienne, followed soon after by Adam and Sophie.

"Mother! Meriel! You both look absolutely stunning!" announced Adam, enfolding first Vivienne then his sister-in-law in his usual bear-hug. Not for the first time, Meriel was aware that Adam rarely looked her directly in the eyes, though the wide, easy smile was in place.

"Let me bring in the presents," he said, and vanished into the hall only to reappear moments later balancing a teetering stack of wrapped boxes which he gingerly carried across to the Christmas tree. Watching him, she could not but be struck by how similar in appearance he was to his brother. She was instantly, painfully reminded of the first time she saw Simon, clasping that box of wine as he crossed Southwark Bridge, moving in just the same way as Adam was now doing.

Then it was Hatta's turn to slide self-consciously into the room, peering bright-eyed from under her newly bobbed thatch of blond hair. She was dressed in a tube of bright red clingy material that stopped some way short of her knees, exposing her long slim legs to considerable effect. She had embellished some plain hoop earrings with holly leaves and berries, and if these now scratched her face each time she moved her head, she was not going to admit it.

"You look lovely, darling!" said Vivienne. As it was Christmas, she decided not to comment on the fact that for once, Hatta was not wearing her Doc Marten boots. Last

247

of all came Emily, still apologising for allowing Edward to sleep.

"Come on in and have a glass of champagne," Vivienne urged. "I'm sure you've earned it."

By the time they were ready to move on to the dining-room, Dan's *méthode champenoise* had done its work. Relaxed and mellowed, they took their places at a table festooned with strips of variegated ivy interspersed with red candles and poinsettia flowers.

"Ah-ha!" exclaimed Vivienne after the soup bowls had been cleared away and Jacinta was pushing in the trolley laden with covered dishes. "Our *tour de force*! Now then. Who is going to explain this dish to Meriel and Emily?"

"Explain it to me?" asked Meriel, confused.

"Why yes!" Adam put in as he helped lift the large salver with its domed cover onto the table. "This isn't your ordinary roast turkey, I'll have you know! This is . . . this is . . . oh, go on, Mother! You describe it!"

"Very well. What you see before you, Meriel, is a dish which as far as I know is peculiar to Amberfield. With the exception of last year, it's been served every Christmas Day for as long as anyone cares to remember. It's a dish we're very proud of, and one which Jacinta invariably cooks to perfection – "

She paused to allow the shout of approval which greeted her words to die down, then, smiling at the bobbing, broadly grinning Jacinta, continued:

"We simply call this Amberfield Goose, but if I cut into this delicious-looking bird, like so . . ."

Picking up the carving knife and fork she began slicing carefully before changing her mind:

"Simon . . . er, Adam: I think maybe you should take over."

Adam did just that, cutting through the crisp skin as gently as he could until he was able to reveal the surprise beneath.

"As I say, we call it Amberfield Goose," continued

Vivienne, "but it is in fact much more than that. It's a plump, locally bred goose, stuffed with no fewer than three local rabbits, which in their turn are stuffed with our own special forcemeat. The stuffing is made of sausagemeat in the traditional way, but what makes it special to Amberfield is the fact that in recent years we have taken to adding our very own raisins, from Muscatel grapes grown in one of our greenhouses. Ladies and gentlemen," she said, as Adam held aloft the first cut slice, "I give you . . . Amberfield Goose!"

Exactly six days later, in the taxi taking them home after a neighbour's New Year's Eve party, Meriel slid into Rory's arms as if it were the most natural thing in the world. They were tipsy, both of them, but by no means drunk. For the length of the journey, Meriel rested sleepily against Rory's chest; from time to time he caressed her hair with his lips, but other than that he remained still, holding her in his arms in the back of the car.

"Penny for them?" he enquired at one point, but she shook her head with a smile, and he did not pursue the matter.

It was just as well. She was, for reasons which she understood only too well, remembering the last time when she had been this close to a man, and although the memory was painful, it refused to go away.

The taxi stopped with a crunch of gravel, jolting Meriel out of her reverie. Rory withdrew his arms from around her. When the driver had been paid off, and the front door closed, he walked up the stairs beside Meriel, saying nothing until he reached the top.

"My place?" he asked.

"Yes," she said. "Yes."

That January seemed to pass more slowly than any month Meriel could remember. The problem did not lie with Rory, who gave every sign of delighting in their closer

249

relationship and who now suggested that she spend all her weekends with him at Melbury. On the contrary, when she was in Wiltshire, either riding Paloma or meeting Rory's friends and neighbours or engaging in endless searches for household furnishings, the time flew by.

By contrast, at Amberfield the days seemed to follow one another with unbearable slowness as Meriel waited for the moment when she could bottle her new rosé. On the one hand she was terrified to leave it too late and risk losing the fresh-picked quality that was a feature of some of the very best English wines. On the other, she was aware that an under-developed wine would be tasteless and lacking in character. The last thing she wanted was to have to pour this wine away, as she had done with her previous effort.

By the middle of the month, she began to think she could bear the suspense no longer, yet every instinct told her that to bottle this early would be a mistake. Had Rory not been abroad on business, she would have joined him in London so as not to have to make the daily pilgrimage to the winery and to suffer the same agonising doubts at every visit.

It was at this point that Peter Simmonds, the owner of a vineyard in nearby Maidstone, telephoned the office "for a chat with whoever runs the place these days". As Meriel was alone at the time, she took the call and discovered that Simmonds knew Amberfield well. Until the building of his own winery, he had regularly brought his grapes to Dan for vinification, and he was ringing now, he informed Meriel, to swap sob stories about the sad state of the previous year's crop.

She was only too happy to oblige. Within minutes, she had arranged to pay a visit to Peter Simmonds' vineyard, and no sooner had she put the phone down than she started ringing round other vineyards within easy driving distance of Amberfield. She decided it was high time she saw how other wine-growers made ends meet. Besides, the outings would keep her mind off her wine.

250

Amberfield's first rosé was eventually bottled early in February. By now it had lost the faintly unappetising tinge of purple that characterised the must, and the winter frosts had ensured that no suspended particles or other unwanted bodies remained to cloud the finished product.

Meriel helped label the bottles – there were exactly five hundred and thirty – and lay them down to mature further. She calculated that by the time the wine was ready to drink, a full year would have passed since she had last seen Dan. Already it seemed like for ever.

The silence that followed Meriel's suggestion seemed to go on and on.

"You'll obviously need time to think about what I've just said," she added, as if that weren't already clear enough. "I realise there may be snags I haven't thought of, and of course there are a lot of details to sort out. But . . . basically, that's it, really."

She sat back in her chair, waiting for the response. Although they were now well into February, this was the first board meeting of the new year. Both Adam and Vivienne had been ill with flu at the end of January and the meeting had been postponed, giving Meriel the time to visit a score of other vineyards. Still no one spoke, and Meriel was on the point of offering to leave the room so that the other board members could discuss the matter among themselves when Vivienne cleared her throat.

"Can we just get this quite straight?" she asked. "You, Meriel, are offering to use your own money to fund the redevelopment of this building – " she gestured about her to take in the area of the barn " – so that it can be used to accommodate visitors?"

"That's right, yes. I'm well aware that conversion work doesn't come cheap, but the money from the sale of my flat is just sitting around doing nothing, and I'd like to put it to some use."

Jonathan leaned forward. "Forgive me . . . but is that

251

strictly accurate? Your money is invested, I assume? In which case it most certainly is not 'doing nothing': on the contrary, it's working very hard for you."

"You know what I mean," said Meriel. Her enthusiasm, which had started to flag, now began to return. "Look," she said, "I've spent most of the past two weeks visiting other vineyards locally and in Hampshire and Sussex. None of them live by selling wine alone. They have shops, restaurants, conducted tours, vineyard trails . . . you name it, they've got it."

"I'm aware that sort of thing goes on elsewhere," said Vivienne. "In fact, I seem to remember that Simon once tried to persuade us along those lines. Am I right, Adam?"

Adam nodded. "That's correct, yes. I went as far as looking into the development possibilities at Amberfield, but unfortunately the costs were prohibitive."

"You see?" said Vivienne, turning to Meriel. "We did consider the matter, but we ruled it out. Besides, I'm not at all sure that what is suitable for other growers is suitable for ourselves. And we also have to bear in mind the fact that we're already in your debt. You've been more than generous as it is."

She was referring to the money for two years' worth of bottles – money which Amberfield Wines could still not afford to repay, even if Meriel had wanted to accept it.

"Hear, hear," murmured Adam.

"I don't regard myself as being at all generous," replied Meriel. "On the contrary. I am involved in this company, and I don't want it to fail. I happen to be in a position to help out, so it's in my interest to do so, every bit as much as yours."

"What bothers me," said Adam, "is that the company is in such bad shape that you stand never to get your money back. Maybe if we hadn't lost the harvest . . ."

"But that's precisely the point!" said Meriel. "If we are only going to have fifty or sixty thousand bottles to sell this year, we must find other ways of earning some income. Don't you see? It's precisely because of our present financial situation that my idea merits serious consideration!"

"As I've already said," Adam replied, "I'm beginning to doubt whether we can ever turn this company around to the stage where we are bringing money in rather than always paying out. We'd probably have been OK if we hadn't replanted, but that decision alone has cost us more than we're ever likely to recoup. So, frankly, Meriel, I'm sorry, but I doubt whether the sale of a few cups of tea is going to make much difference."

"Adam," said Vivienne wearily, "we're all aware of your views on our replanting programme, but that particular decision is well behind us. What we have to do now is plan for the future."

"That is exactly what I'm doing," said Meriel. "Please, please do let's at least discuss my idea in a little more detail!"

"All right, Meriel," agreed Vivienne. "Tell us what you have in mind. Exactly what sort of facilities are we talking about, apart from lavatories, that is? For myself, I'd have thought the present shop was perfectly adequate for the number of people likely to need it."

"Since you've mentioned it, let's take the shop first. As it happens, I don't agree that it's adequate, even for our present needs. In fact, it's not a shop at all, it's a corner of an office and it feels like it. People seem to think that if they come in, they'll be under an obligation to buy, and that puts them off."

"I would have thought," put in Jonathan at this point, "that the sort of people who buy English wine – which, after all, is not the cheapest vino on the market – are serious buyers, connoisseurs, even, who aren't so easily influenced by their surroundings."

"Absolutely!" agreed Vivienne. "And in any case, even with a new shop there wouldn't be that many more people calling."

"And I think that's where you'd be wrong," countered Meriel. "I've been talking to the owners of the vineyard over at Yelland. As I expect you know, it's a small vineyard, less than ten acres, yet they had twenty-five thousand visitors last year."

"Twenty-five thousand?" exclaimed Adam in disbelief. "Meriel, they're having you on! That can't possibly be true."

"Oh, yes, it is! And they reckon they'll get even more this year, when they open a children's zoo – "

"There I draw the limit!" exclaimed Vivienne, with an expression of such profound alarm that everyone, even Adam, smiled.

"I wasn't seriously suggesting we should have wallabies at Amberfield," continued Meriel, "but I believe we are in danger of significantly underestimating public interest. The number of visitors to English vineyards is going up, and shows no sign of stopping. As for the English Wine Festival at Alfriston they're having to limit the number of coachloads they can take. English wine is big business now. Unfortunately, we shan't make much money from our wines this year, but we could most certainly turn in a profit if we were to diversify."

By now, Meriel could see that she was definitely making an impression. You could almost hear the cash registers ringing inside Vivienne's head.

"Even so," Vivienne said after a moment's pause, "the thought of all those people tramping across the courtyard, peering into the house, invading our privacy – it's just too ghastly for words!"

"Mother's right," put in Adam, who was beginning to sound impatient. "We simply can't have hordes of people running amok all over the place."

"The sort of people who are interested in visiting a working vineyard and winery are hardly likely to run amok, Adam. They're most likely to be old age pensioners, women's guilds, amateur wine-growers, young families

254

who want a bit of an outing. And in any case, they wouldn't need to cross the courtyard, or go anywhere near the house."

"I don't see how they're going to get to the barn any other way," retorted Adam.

"We could make an opening on the far side of the barn, and install a new door. Visitors could then park their cars right out of sight of the house on that flat bit of field that leads to the ridgeway. We wouldn't see them *and* they'd be that much closer to the vineyard."

"I suppose that might work . . ." said Vivienne doubtfully. "What else?"

"Why not open out the area downstairs? We could build a sales counter along this wall here – " Meriel took a pencil and quickly sketched the details onto a piece of paper " – then give the rest of this space over to tables and chairs and to displays of items for sale."

"Whatever do we want tables and chairs for?" asked Vivienne. "All people need to do is to come in and taste a few wines at the counter and, hopefully, buy lots of bottles and leave."

"I don't agree," said Meriel. "I think people need to be encouraged to take their time when they come here. Make an afternoon of it, particularly if they come by the coachload. And that means they will want teas, sandwiches, cakes, maybe even salads or some other light snacks . . ."

"Oh, now you really *are* joking!"

"Absolutely not. We need the income these people can generate, and it is only fair to make them as welcome and as comfortable as possible."

"A further small point," said Jonathan. "What makes you think there would be enough profit from serving cups of tea to make the attendant hassle worth while?"

"The aim is to make a small profit on everything we sell – that's what other vineyards are doing, and you'd be amazed at how quickly it adds up. The trick is to give people what they want. For instance – " she rummaged in a plastic carrier bag and spread an assortment of items on the table. "These are some of the things I've found on sale at other vineyards in this area. T-shirts, tea-cloths, place mats, books and leaflets, pottery, not all of it irresistible . . ." at this she held up an ashtray bearing an explicit and particularly unattractive naked Bacchus, the sight of which provoked horrified laughter from the other board members ". . . this, for instance, is a good example of the sort of thing we can most definitely improve on. Then there are spin-off items, like wine vinegar and wine mustard, which sell very well, even to people who wouldn't normally buy wine . . . and finally, we can make money by taking people on conducted tours of the winery. We would charge a couple of pounds per person for that, though of course entrance to the tea shop and sales area would be free."

"I'm still not convinced you've thought this through," remarked Jonathan. "You mustn't forget that a scheme of this kind involves considerable overheads. Heating, lighting, wages for counter staff and cleaners, maintenance costs . . ."

"Thank you, Jonathan, but I have taken all those facts into consideration," replied Meriel tartly. "However, I do appreciate that this is a big step, and that you will want time to think about it. Meanwhile, I need to go over my figures and do some double-checking in other areas. So, I suggest – "

"No," interrupted Adam, suddenly. "Er, I'm sorry," he added, "I didn't mean to sound so dogmatic . . . it's simply that I think it's unfair on Meriel to let her spend more time pursuing this . . . this . . . idea. I suggest we put it to the vote. Mother?"

"I have to confess I am too astonished to think straight," said Vivienne, "and I suspect that goes for all of us. For my part, I can't pretend I actually like the idea, but we do have to face the fact that running a vineyard is an extremely expensive business, and unless we do something, heaven knows what will happen. So, if you can demonstrate to me that our income will be significantly increased if we branch out into cups of tea and guided tours, then I'm willing to consider the matter further."

"I'm afraid no amount of demonstrating would convince me," stated Adam. "Rather the contrary, in fact. In my opinion any money put into the building of a shop is money down the drain. But don't just listen to my opinion. Let's take a vote."

"The only problem with that," remarked Vivienne, "is that Jonathan now has full voting rights within the company. It is therefore possible that the result will be a tie."

"In which case," said Adam, "I think the idea would have to be dropped. This is far too important a matter to pursue if we're divided down the middle."

"Perhaps you're right," agreed Vivienne, doubtfully.

"However, I don't think it will come to that. I think we can settle the question here and now."

"Very well, then," agreed Vivienne. "We'll vote. All those in favour?"

Meriel raised her hand. After a moment's hesitation, Vivienne did likewise. Adam's tense features began to relax into a smile. He was opening his mouth to speak when Jonathan, with an ironic glint in his eyes, raised his right hand also.

15

Adam took the stairs up to Jonathan Fox's office two at a time, and responded to Ruth Protheroe's friendly greeting with an abrupt mutter. He then swept past her into the larger office.

"For God's sake, Jon, what do you think you're playing at?"

"Adam! Sit down, do! Coffee – ?"

But Adam would not be stopped.

"Did it not occur to you that voting for Meriel's shop is the worst thing you could possibly have done? Frankly, I can't imagine what possessed you!"

"Yes, I think coffee would be in order. Ruth can always make some fresh when Bert turns up." Jonathan murmured into the intercom, then turned to face Adam.

"Haven't you heard a word I've been saying?" the latter demanded, almost shouting.

"You agreed that I should have full voting rights," observed Jonathan smoothly. "You and Vivienne and Meriel. It may be naïve of me but I assumed you meant what you said. I assumed I could vote as I thought best."

"I'll remind you that it was my idea to have you join the board!" said Adam. "Without me, it would never have happened! I did *not* expect you to take the first opportunity to act against me. You *owe* me!"

"Oh, I think not!" replied Jonathan. "As I recall, you offered me a directorship in return for finding a way of getting rid of Dan. I did my bit, and you did yours, with a bit of prompting. So now we're quits."

"Yes, well, of course there is that . . . Incidentally,

258

how *did* you manage to track down Dan's vineyard in Australia? If he had ever managed to produce any wine it would have been easy – the tax people would have had an address for him – but as things were . . . ?"

The lawyer returned Adam's questioning glance with a cool stare. There was no way he was going to admit that all he had had to do was read a card sent to Dan, at his vineyard, by some woman called Laura.

"You're right, it wasn't easy," he replied. "In the end, I put one of my people on the job. That didn't come cheap, I can tell you."

"I'm grateful, of course," said Adam, "but all the same, you had no right to go against me at the meeting!"

"Let's just get this straight, shall we? I had every right to vote as I did, Adam. And I shall continue to vote as I wish, for as long as I am on the board of Amberfield Wines. Besides, I think you're overreacting. The scheme is still very much in its infancy. And as they say, there's many a slip 'twixt the cup of bright ideas and the lip of planning consent."

"Thanks to Bert Hollyfield's effective little backhanders, I think that's one thing we can safely depend on," agreed Adam, beginning to calm down. "But I can promise you one thing, Jon! That scheme goes ahead over my dead body!"

"Talk of the devil!" said Jonathan as Bert Hollyfield was announced, adding swiftly so that only Adam could hear, "I think it might not be a bad idea to show a united front at this juncture. Besides which," he added for the newcomer's benefit, "Bert has come up with a rather interesting little idea."

"Can't think what it might be," grumbled Adam. "I've already told both of you that Mother refuses to sell. Even though we lost the harvest, even though we've got rid of Dan, even though the money gets tighter and tighter, she will keep clinging on to every little hope. And now Meriel's

259

gone and put her oar in again. With help from certain other members of the board."

Jonathan ignored the taunt. "Come on, Bert," he said. "Tell us about this new plan of yours."

Another man in the same position would probably have opened his briefcase, extracted a document or two, maybe handed duplicated sheets to his audience. Bert Hollyfield was not such a man. Instead, he lit a cigar and leaned amply back in his chair, filling rather more than the available space with his bulk.

"As I see it," he began, "the situation is as follows. You, Adam, want to sell some land. I want to buy that land. And Jon here wants to get his hands on the handsome legal fees to be had in any such deal. Would that be correct?"

"Absolutely," replied Adam.

"I don't think I'd describe my fees as *handsome* – " Jonathan sounded aggrieved.

"Well, that's where we'd differ," Bert interrupted. "Anyhow, we're not here to argue about that. What we're here for is to put an end to all this stop-go, stop-go. I don't know about the rest of you, but I want to see some action."

"I'm sorry, Bert, but delays have been inevitable. You know how everything comes to a standstill over the Christmas period – "

Bert interrupted again. "Christmas was over weeks ago, so maybe now we can finally get things going."

Adam shrugged. "Like I said, earlier, it's all a matter of convincing my mother."

"Listen to this then. While you've been gallivanting about having Christmas holidays, and Jon here has been sitting on his backside getting nowhere – "

"Not fair!" put in Jonathan.

" – I, meanwhile, have been doing something useful. I have put together a consortium – couple of bankers and a financier or three – who are willing to put up the money to buy the land."

"Bert, what *is* the point of all this?" asked Jonathan sharply. "Adam has already explained that Vivienne will not sell. Read my lips, Bert. She. Will. Not. Sell."

Bert, serenely ignoring Jonathan's statement, continued. "As I was saying, my consortium buys the land – " here he paused for maximum effect, hoping no doubt to elicit a further show of irritation from one of the other two. But, seeing the glint in Bert's eye, they kept quiet.

" – my consortium buys the land, and then leases it back to the company at a peppercorn rent. How does that strike you?"

"I don't think I understand," said Adam. "What would be the point in that?"

"What would be the point of that? There'd be several points in that, if you must know! First of all, I'd be buying the land at a very good price – "

"What may seem a good price to you is scarcely going to seem a good price to me," said Adam.

"Adam, Adam," sighed Bert. "You can't have it all ways, you know. I'll grant you that if the land were to be sold on the open market it might fetch more than I'm willing to pay. But that isn't the case, so there's no point fretting about it, is there?"

Adam did not respond immediately, so Jonathan put in:

"I think what Bert is saying is that the leaseback scheme probably represents the only way of exchanging the land for money. In a sense, the consortium are in a position to offer as little as they like."

"Instead of which our offer will be more than generous, given the delays and other problems we've encountered, not to mention the fact that we shan't have the use of the land for some time."

"That bothers me too," said Adam. "The fact that there doesn't seem to be anything in it for you in the short term."

"Well, we'd have the money coming in from the leasing arrangement . . ."

"You're talking peanuts, Bert, and you know it! You've already said you'd only be asking a peppercorn rent! Come on, level with me! You know the board will never sell to you in the knowledge that you're planning to put up a housing estate. And I know you can't make money out of this scheme unless you *do* build houses. So. What are you actually proposing?"

"Let me explain," offered Bert. "What happens is that my consortium gets its hands on a piece of land which can only keep going up in value. Even if I never lay a single brick it can only be a very nice little investment for me. For all of us."

"Mother won't wear it," said Adam. "She'll smell a rat."

"I don't see why," countered Bert. "It's quite a common arrangement nowadays, this leaseback business."

"I've never heard of it," muttered Adam. "Jon?"

"Bert is right, in point of fact. What with EEC quotas being reduced, farmers all over the place are selling land to investment companies and then renting it back. The thinking behind the idea is that in an island as small as Britain, almost any land must of necessity constitute a worthwhile investment in the long term."

Adam hesitated before continuing. "I have to admit, it's an interesting idea."

Bert chuckled and rubbed his podgy hands together. "That's the beauty of this little scheme," he said gleefully. "Everyone gains by it! Nobody loses! The amount my consortium is willing to pay will get your mother out of trouble once and for all. As well as netting the three of us a tidy profit into the bargain – in due course, it goes without saying. In due course."

"I'm still not sure . . ." began Adam.

Bert held up a hand. "Just listen to me, will you? Or better, still, answer me this. If things at Amberfield go on

262

as they are, how long do you think it will be before you are in such a parlous state that your mother is forced into desperate measures?"

"At a rough guess, I'd say October, November," replied Adam. "When we come to pick the grapes. I can't believe it's going to be a good harvest. Dan wasn't around to supervise the pruning this year, so there's a good chance Jethro cocked things up. With any luck, yields should be poor. Besides, I think we can safely rely on the weather to let us down once again."

"As I thought," nodded Bert. "Well, Adam, I'm willing to bet that by this autumn, your mother will be begging me to take the land off her hands for good and all. Do things my way and she won't need any persuading! She'll be that keen to get out of wine-growing."

For some moments, Adam sat with his head bowed, going through the various aspects of Bert's proposal in his mind.

"What do you think, Adam?" Jon prompted him after a time. "Might that work?"

"Maybe . . ." agreed Adam cautiously. "But – well, let me get one or two things straight before I commit myself. You, Bert, are suggesting that Mother will agree to the sale of the land on condition that it is leased back to her and that she can keep the vineyards."

"That's correct," agreed Bert.

"You are further suggesting that when she is eventually forced to admit that Amberfield Wines can never be a going concern – which, incidentally, happens to be my own view – she will agree to terminate the leasing arrangement, at which point you will be free to build your houses?"

"That is my belief."

"It might work," said Adam thoughtfully. "She might just agree to sell on those terms. But . . . there might be another problem."

"Yes?" asked Bert sharply.

263

"What if the company started to make a profit? She wouldn't sell then."

"That's not very likely, is it?" asked Bert. "From what you've told me I'd have thought that was pretty well impossible."

"Adam is referring to Meriel's scheme to convert the barn and bring in visitors," explained Jon. "On the face of it, it's a first-rate idea. It could well work."

"I'm sorry to say this, Adam," said Bert, "but if the shop idea does turn out to be a problem, it's one you're going to have to settle yourself. This idea has been lying around long enough. If you can't get your mother to agree to a sale within, say, six months, I'm washing my hands of the whole business. I'll find another site, with fewer strings attached. I hope you gentlemen understand me."

Meriel was not getting on well with Martin Kingsley, the architect recommended by Adam. He struck her as both opinionated and obstructive, but when she tried to voice her doubts to Adam, he cut her short.

"I'm sorry to hear you won't make the effort to work with him," he said. "Because I can assure you that Martin is very highly regarded in his field. Why don't you accept what he has to say?"

She could tell Adam was annoyed with her for questioning his choice, and she decided to say nothing more for the time being. Instead, she took out Kingsley's plans once more and spread them out before her.

Martin had told her that the ceiling height of the ground-floor accommodation – the area which would house the restaurant – was too low to comply with fire regulations. He therefore suggested raising the ceiling by some fifteen inches, but this in Meriel's view would cause irrevocable damage to the fine old beams supporting the upper level.

Moreover, if the downstairs ceiling were raised, the upper storey would also fall outside height limits and

264

would be rendered unusable. When Meriel suggested to Martin they might do better to lower the ground floor, he seemed unwilling even to consider the idea.

Eventually she decided another opinion was needed, and took the drawings over to Vivienne.

"I wondered if we could look over these plans together," she said. "I'd be very grateful for your reaction."

Vivienne seemed doubtful. "I've already told Adam I can never make head or tail of architects' drawings . . . but . . . oh, very well then. Tell me what seems to be the problem."

The drawings for the new barn were laid out for her perusal and she made a show of studying them intently.

"So neat!" she observed eventually.

"If I could just explain . . ." Meriel began by detailing her own views on the state of the finished barn. Her aim was to create a single large, airy space at ground level with a sales counter running the length of one of the shorter walls. Some two-thirds of the counter space would be given over to sales of food and drink for consumption on the premises, while the remaining third would be devoted to sales of Amberfield's wines and other vineyard products. These latter would be displayed on stands and tables arranged around the perimeter of the room, the remaining space to be occupied by tables and chairs.

"This all seems perfectly straightforward to me," said Vivienne, at last beginning to make some sense of the drawing. "We've got our counter here, the food preparation over here, the loos downstairs in the cellar area . . . frankly, I can't see what you're complaining about."

"It's simply that Martin keeps telling me I'm contravening some planning regulation or other – "

"Oh, but we must comply with the regulations, Meriel! Otherwise we'll never get planning permission."

"I realise that. I just get the feeling that Martin doesn't like anyone making suggestions he hasn't thought of himself. For instance, he says the ceiling height of the

265

restaurant area is too low to comply with fire regulations. I suggested that, since we have to strengthen the ground floor, we might as well lower it at the same time, but he refuses to discuss the possibility."

"I'm sure he must have very good reasons!" exclaimed Vivienne. "Adam tells me he really is most amenable. What does he suggest instead?"

"He wants us to raise the ceiling – "

"There you are! I knew he must have something up his sleeve!"

"But Vivienne! Raising the ceiling gives us problems with the upper level."

"How, exactly?"

Meriel pulled out a further drawing and laid it over the first. "Take a look at this horror," she urged.

The "horror" in question referred to two vast and disfiguring dormer windows which Martin had seen fit to incorporate into the upper storey. These, he explained in a note attached to the plans, were needed to provide the legally required headroom.

"Oh dear," was all Vivienne said. She was clearly shocked at what she saw. "Meriel," she continued after a long pause, "I do think maybe you have a point. It could be that Martin Kingsley is not the right man for this particular job. After all, his experience is mainly with modern buildings. It takes a special kind of knowledge to deal with tricky conversions like this one."

"Not to mention sensitivity," said Meriel gloomily. Then she added: "What sort of work does Martin usually do?"

"He designs houses for luxury estates, I believe. Adam tells me he works mainly for Bert Hollyfield. Do you know who I mean?"

"I've heard his name mentioned," replied Meriel thoughtfully.

"Dreadful little man," said Vivienne. "Quite appalling. Listen, Meriel, I think it might not be a bad idea if I were to have a word with Adam. See if we can't persuade Martin to find a way round the planning regulations. This simply will not do."

One weekend in May, before she left to join Rory at Melbury, Meriel went in search of Jethro. She found him in the vineyard, hoeing the area round each vine to keep it clear of weeds. The trouble was that weather such as they had experienced over the past two months – mild, often sunny, but with occasional rain – tended to favour the weeds every bit as much as the vines, and Jethro had his work cut out making sure the former did not leach valuable nutrients from the latter.

"Cheer up, Jethro," Meriel said, unable to ignore the troubled look he tended to wear these days. "It's not all bad news."

"Seems a long time since I heard any other kind," he remarked.

Meriel was having difficulty containing herself. "You said yourself, the danger of frost is past. And the vines are in better shape than you've ever seen them . . ."

"True enough," said Jethro. "But . . ." he shrugged rather than continue. Meriel knew what was on his mind. *What use is a good crop*, he was thinking, *if we don't have an expert winemaker to turn it into good wine?* Today, though, she was in no mood to let herself become depressed.

Almost bursting with excitement, she said: "What if I told you we'd got an English Vineyards Association seal of approval? Would that lift your spirits?"

It had been his suggestion that they should submit three of Dan's wines for assessment by the EVA.

A slow smile began to spread across Jethro's face. "That'll be for the Seyval Blanc, I suppose."

"Yes, Jethro. For the Seyval Blanc. And – " she was tormenting him on purpose, a wicked gleam in her eye. "And also – "

"Yes?"

267

"And for the *méthode champenoise*."

"You're not having me on, are you?"

"And for the Schönburger! Jethro, we've got EVA seals for all the wines we submitted! Isn't that absolutely the most wonderful thing ever?"

Jethro flung down his hoe and enveloped Meriel in a vast hug.

"Right, I give in," he said. "That *is* good news!"

"And that's not all!" added Meriel. "Adam got Martin Kingsley to alter his design for the barn, and we've agreed he should take it along to the council without delay. Of course, it will be a few weeks before the application is heard, but with any luck we'll start building in July. Jethro, isn't it marvellous? I think it's going to be all right after all!"

Her elation at these two positive developments – the first in almost a year of worry and uncertainty – lasted right through her weekend in Wiltshire.

"So, tell me," said Rory over Sunday lunch. "What is so wonderful about this seal of approval? How difficult is it to acquire?"

He was watching her seriously, and at first she declined to answer the question, fearing she was boring him. But as he insisted, she replied:

"Very difficult, as it happens! First of all the wine has to be chemically analysed and tested for bacteria and moulds and sulphur and so on. Then it has to be heated right up and then cooled right down to make sure it's stable. And then, and only then, it goes to a tasting panel and if they like it, they give it their seal."

"I see. But . . . forgive me, but does it actually count for anything?"

"Of course it does! It puts Amberfield up with the best English producers. It certainly means I'm going to book a stall at the English Wine Festival in September now that we've got so much to shout about. I feel we need more exposure, more . . . oh, Rory, I'm sorry! I seem to have done nothing but talk about myself all weekend."

"You've talked so much you haven't given me a chance to tell you our good news at Melbury," he said lightly.

"Why, Rory! What's happened?"

"Patsy and Jarvis are getting engaged. They're planning the mother and father of balls here in October to celebrate the event."

"That's wonderful news! Rory, I am so pleased!" She ran round the table to give him a kiss. "There," she said. "That's for Patsy."

"Meriel . . ."

"Mmm?" She had walked across to the window and was gazing out, smiling to herself, almost surprised at her genuine delight at Patsy's news.

"Do you suppose there's any chance that we could make a similar announcement by October?" His voice came from very close behind her.

"A similar . . . ?" She turned towards him, eyes wide with surprise.

"Don't look so astonished!" he laughed. "We can't go on like this for ever, you know, seeing each other so rarely. It's beginning not to feel right, somehow. I think the time is coming when you are going to have to choose between Amberfield and me."

"Ouf!" was all she could manage. She felt almost winded by the suddenness of it all, but she knew Rory was right. She was trying to lead two very different lives, and sooner or later a conflict was bound to arise. Besides, she was both touched and deeply flattered by Rory's interest in her. She also felt grateful for his friendship throughout these last difficult months, and although she said nothing in response to Rory's pronouncement, she could see he was pleased by what he read in her eyes.

"As I may have said to you before," said Rory, holding her hands in his and kissing her fingertips, "you will most definitely do."

16

She knew there was something wrong when she saw Hatta waiting for her at the door one Sunday evening in early summer.

"What are you doing here?" Meriel asked, beginning to be alarmed. "Why aren't you at school?"

Hatta was due to start her GCSE exams within the next couple of weeks, and the thought that she might have decided to drop out of school at this all-important moment was worrying indeed.

"It's Dad," said Hatta, sniffing as she spoke. "They don't think it's going to be much longer. Adam came to get me."

"Oh, Hatta, I'm sorry!" Meriel hugged her before following her down the corridor towards the sickroom.

At Miss Digby's suggestion, Hatta took her cello to her father's room and played to him, hesitantly at first, for she found it hard to concentrate, then with greater confidence. Edward, who had been restless earlier in the day, his breathing painfully racked and wheezing, seemed suddenly to relax. It did not take much convincing on Miss Digby's part to persuade Hatta that her father had simply been waiting for her to come and say goodbye. By the time she had finished playing, the old man's breathing was shallow and almost soundless; his body still.

This certainly was how he appeared to Meriel when she entered his room to find Edward's wife and son seated by his bedside. But when Meriel offered to sit with him for a while, Vivienne refused. "I couldn't leave him," she said.

That night, Vivienne, Adam and Miss Digby kept watch

at Edward's bedside. Shortly before two o'clock the following the morning, a long, slow exhalation of breath announced that their vigil was over.

Miss Digby felt Edward's pulse, then said simply:

"He's gone now."

Vivienne and Adam rose, then hugged one another tightly.

"Mother," began Adam, "I think I . . ."

"Not now, darling," she said, shaking her head. "I shan't be able to take any of it in. Why don't you get back to The Lodge? I'm sure Sophie needs you."

There was no denying that the sorrow that followed Edward's death was mingled with relief that his suffering had come to an end. Hatta returned to sit her exams with a renewed determination to do well, and even Vivienne admitted that she found her grief easier to bear than the endless waiting and hoping and not knowing.

The reading of Edward's will took place in Jonathan Fox's office later that week. Vivienne asked Meriel to accompany her and other family members, while making it clear that the document had been drawn up before either Simon or Adam married, and that neither daughter-in-law figured among the beneficiaries.

As expected, there were small legacies to Miss Digby, Jacinta and Jethro, and a number of individual items were separately willed. As Meriel was already aware, Amberfield House and lands formed part of the family company, and the matter of inheritance had already been settled by the setting up of a trust.

It was over sixteen months since Meriel's previous visit to Jonathan Fox's office, and as the lawyer concluded his reading she was suddenly assailed by a sensation of such profound unease that for a moment she had difficulty catching her breath. She instantly recognised the feeling as the one she had experienced in Amberfield Church on the day of Simon's funeral, and then again here, in this very office when discussing her status on the board. On both occasions, and again when the vines were sabotaged and the frost candles mysteriously removed, she had thought she detected a malign influence working to damage Amberfield, but each time, she had after a while convinced herself she was imagining things.

Since she had no evidence to the contrary, she could only assume that this was what she was doing all over again. Once before she had blamed her reaction on a kind of mental computer virus which prevented her brain from functioning fully, and this was precisely the analogy that sprang to her mind now. She had, she decided, programmed herself to respond to imaginary danger signals in a certain way. It was high time she re-programmed herself to accept that nothing untoward was going on. There was a threat to Amberfield, certainly, but it was a purely financial one. One which, moreoever, her barn conversion would surely solve.

Afterwards, there only remained the task of clearing out Edward's room and sorting through his belongings. Miss Digby, who had intended leaving immediately after the funeral, was persuaded that she was still needed, and agreed to stay on for a few more days. Meriel, far too busy with the growing number of jobs in vineyard and winery which had fallen to her, was relieved that this extra support was available to Vivienne. For Vivienne seemed to have aged suddenly, to have become diminished. It was as though she had steeled herself to be strong as long as Edward lived, and now that he was gone, the façade was cracking.

Early the following week, Meriel drove a tearful Miss Digby to the station – now that her task of caring for Edward was over she was returning to her sister's – and waited for an opportunity to ask the question which had been preying on her mind. In the event, Miss Digby got there first.

"You'll be wondering what to do about Mr Barton's notebooks," she said.

"Yes, I was. Do you think I should hand them over to Vivienne now that Edward's dead?"

"Course, it's up to you," replied Miss Digby, but she seemed uneasy, and Meriel, thinking she could guess at the reason, patted her on the arm and said:

"Don't worry. I promise I'll think up some story about how I came by them. I won't tell Vivienne you gave them to me."

"I'm really not sure . . ." said Miss Digby unhappily.

"Honestly, I promise I won't bring your name into it! Besides, don't you think the family would be delighted to read Edward's story?"

"You don't understand," said Miss Digby, weeping openly now. "There's still some pages you haven't seen. Ever since I found them I've been wondering what to do for the best. But I never could make up my mind."

"I see!" said Meriel slowly. "So the notebooks didn't simply fall apart through old age – you actually tore the pages out?" Miss Digby nodded miserably and Meriel continued: "And there are things in them you think will upset Vivienne?"

Miss Digby did not answer this last question. Instead, she pulled some sheets of paper out of her handbag and thrust them at Meriel.

"Go on," she said. "*You* read them. *You* decide what's to be done. I want to pretend I never came across them."

"That's all right, Diggers. I'll take them. I'll read them for myself, and I promise you, if there's anything remotely – well, difficult, I'll tear them up and no one will be any the wiser. There. That's a promise. Is that better?"

When the train had pulled out of the station, Meriel returned to the car park, intending to drive back to Amberfield before reading what Edward had written. But the moment she climbed into the car, she knew she could not wait. Opening the window wide to let in the warm early summer air, she bent her head to the now familiar handwriting.

In some ways, I suppose you could say that we have never fully recovered from the hurricane of October 1987. To a certain extent, the physical signs of damage are still with us, and, if I have my way, always will be. Certainly, it is my wish, and it was my suggestion – or could it possibly have been Vivienne's idea? – that the great oak should remain where it fell as a reminder of the awesome force of nature and the helplessness of us mere mortals in the face of such power. When we become too proud, it does us no harm to be reminded of our weakness.

As far as the company is concerned, we lost enough production to land us in financial difficulties for the foreseeable future, and at this stage I cannot guarantee that we will ever fully recoup the income lost in this way. But money, and, for that matter, trees, are replaceable, however desirable they may be. A young oak was planted almost immediately after the storm, though in a different part of the field. In centuries to come, I hope that our descendants will thank us for this gift. Even if they take it for granted, it will surely mean that the world is still full of oak trees, in which case things will not be all bad.

No. It is not the damage to our finances, or to our plants, or to our property which has caused me to alter my previously optimistic approach to the business of growing vines and to see the great hurricane as the cause of my present despair. That mighty wind, which took lives as carelessly as it plucked roofs and cars and tossed them over its shoulder, will surely take one more: mine. For earlier today – this very day, though already I feel as though I am relating something that happened many, many years ago – I

274

made a discovery that has, literally, blown my world apart.

I am writing these pages with no clear idea as to whether I shall keep them, or simply destroy them the minute they are written. But write I must, for I am convinced that only by setting pen to paper can I rid myself of my terrible burden.

As I have mentioned before, it was clear from the very beginning that whereas Simon had enthusiasm and dedication in abundance, Adam was always lacking in commitment. I have to admit that this has been a disappointment to me on occasions, yet it has always been my belief that both Vivienne and I have loved our children equally, and that we have respected their individuality. None the less, I must say it again: in matters viticultural, it was invariably to Simon we turned rather than to his brother.

This explains why, in the months that followed the hurricane, I was neither too surprised nor too upset when Adam began hinting that we should cut back on our vineyards and invest the money elsewhere. When asked whether he had anything particular in mind, he said he had not gone into the matter in any detail, but that in his opinion we were on a hiding to nothing: one more disaster like that of October 1987 and we risked losing everything, he informed us.

He repeated all this at the next board meeting, and argued the point at some length with Dan Courtney. When I finally turned to Simon for his opinion, in the belief that, for once, he would back Dan Courtney, he shocked me by expressing deep misgivings about our financial viability. He had recently begun to compare our products and our prices with those of our competitors and, though he grudgingly admitted that Dan had brought about considerable improvements as far as the former was concerned, he believed that without some extra form of income, we were in real danger of

275

pricing ourselves out of the market. He too felt that diversification was the answer, though, like Adam, he would not or could not be specific.

Somehow, I managed not to spot the warning signs that might have led me to expect what eventually happened. In fact, this morning's events caught me utterly unprepared and shocked me so deeply that even as I write I can still feel my heart pounding and the sweat starting on my brow. Returning from a routine check-up unexpectedly early, I was halfway up the drive when Simon drove past me going in the opposite direction. I was surprised to see him, as I had thought he was leaving for London at round the same time as I was being taken for my check-up.

Once home, I wandered over to the office to see what was going on there. Nothing much, it seemed. Adam was nowhere to be seen, and Michelle was busy plucking her eyebrows, which I considered to be an interesting variation on the theme of filing one's nails.

The phone rang almost the moment I put my head round the door. Michelle answered it, told the caller that no, the person he wished to speak to was not available, and asked whether Mr Edward Barton would do instead? Apparently, he would and seconds later I was seated at Adam's desk talking to – or at least, listening to – a Mr Crowden, of Crowden and Leech, valuers and surveyors, who told me how sorry he had been to miss me earlier that morning and would I mind if he asked me to sort out a couple of minor matters which he failed to raise with the younger Mr Barton?

Now, Mr Crowden is one of those people who talk on and on without letting anyone else get a word in edgeways, which at least gave me an opportunity to try and work out what on earth the man was going on about.

He began by saying he realised I wouldn't have been expecting to hear from him so quickly, but that one or two things had occurred to him while he was on his way back to the office. For a start, would I remind him exactly how much of the land I was thinking of selling?

I started to tell him I didn't know what he was talking about, but he was off again, explaining that no developer worth his salt would be interested in a site under about five acres, not in this neck of the woods, where people liked to have a bit of peace and quiet. He talked throughout as though he were simply repeating things we had discussed earlier, and it was not for some time that I realised he was discussing the possibility of building three-bedroom semis on my land.

Well, the idea was so preposterous I refused to take it seriously and even enquired, in a deeply sarcastic tone, which particular site would be most suitable for the development he had in mind.

I shan't forget his answer in a hurry. "No problem there, Mr Barton," he said. "As I suggested to the other Mr Barton earlier, that site where you've got the vines would be ideal. Perfect for a scheme of this sort."

And on and on he went, while I felt the blood drain from my face and a dreadful understanding entered my brain. So "the younger Mr Barton" was getting my land valued and surveyed, was he, with a view to developing it into some ghastly housing estate? The idea was so ridiculous that under other circumstances I might have laughed. But there was no doubt that this wretched little man was serious, and with reason.

Now at last I understood what Adam had meant when he suggested we sink some money into something more solid than grapevines. Nothing more solid than bricks and mortar, I suppose, but the idea of it!

Hearing me utter a harsh, and probably upsetting, laugh, Michelle came into the office and asked me if everything was all right. I told her not to worry, that I was simply amused by something Mr Crowden said. I also told her not to bother to leave a message for Adam as I would be having a word with him myself.

Seeing the look of confusion on Michelle's face, I asked if something was wrong. And that was when she told me that it was not Adam Mr Crowden had asked to speak to. It was Simon.

Simon! No, I said to Michelle, trying hard not to show how shocked I was, it couldn't have been Simon. She meant Adam, surely? But she was insistent. She was certain beyond all doubt that it was Simon Barton Mr Crowden had asked to speak to.

I don't remember much of what happened between that particular moment and the present, less than twelve hours later, except that when I tried to find Vivienne, she had gone out, and that in any case I then decided not to burden her with the knowledge of Simon's deception. Not at least until I have had time to discuss the matter with Simon after the weekend. For the time being, this is something I must face alone.

Meanwhile, my last forlorn hope that Michelle was somehow mistaken has now been shattered. We dined tonight with Adam and Sophie, though I had little appetite and Vivienne asked me more than once if I was sure I felt well enough to be up.

At one point, still unable to believe what I had earlier been told, I informed Adam that some chap called Crowden phoned and asked to speak to him. But Adam's reply could not have been plainer.

"Jim Crowden?" he said. "He wanted Simon, Father. Not me."

So there it was. The final confirmation. I finally conceded that I did indeed feel unwell, and retired to my bedroom. Unable to sleep, I rose after I heard Vivienne going to bed and returned to my diary. I notice now that my hand – indeed my whole body – has begun shaking and sweating, and there is a swimming feeling in my head which is most unpleasant. Soon, I shall stop and

278

hide these pages so that they do not fall into Vivienne's hands before I have finally decided how to deal with this appalling situation.

The idea that Adam might have harboured secret dreams of making a fortune for himself (and, to be fair, for the rest of us too) by selling my precious vineyards for housing land is distasteful but laughable, as I have said. I can believe that Adam has it in him to begrudge the fact that we respected Simon's opinion over his, and that his sense of alienation might have been heightened by the appointment at Amberfield of Dan Courtney.

But what I find unbearable is that Simon shared his brother's opinions. Not openly, like Adam, but secretly. I had thought Simon was above such behaviour. Yet there was the proof. It was he, and not Adam, who had been scheming in this treacherous and underhand way. How far would things have gone, I wondered, before Vivienne and I eventually discovered the truth? Would Simon have succeeded in persuading Vivienne that I was no longer capable of running the company, and that this sale must go through?

A part of me wants to blame the hurricane for all this. Surely it was that violent act of nature which so shook Simon's confidence in our future, and caused him to turn his back on all that had become so dear to us? And then, another part of me mutters darkly that no single event, however extraordinary, could have brought about such a change in anyone. I am therefore forced to the heartbreaking conclusion that his entire life – his relationship with his mother and me, not to mention that with Adam and Hatta, his commitment to the company, everything – has been nothing but a lie.

Now that I know what is afoot, it remains only for me to tackle Simon tomorrow on his return. What am I to say to him? Will he lie again to me? It is an encounter I dread more than anything . . .

Meriel, reading these last pages with increasing distress, was finally aware of the way Edward's writing had deteriorated, not gradually, but suddenly. A few more words followed, spread haphazardly across the page, but they made no sense. The sheet was partly crumpled, too, as though Edward's hand had seized it involuntarily. And after that, nothing. She knew, even without checking back to the date on which this last entry had been written, that it was done on the night Edward suffered his second stroke.

17

Meriel was trying to remember what it was Shakespeare said. Something about problems coming all at once . . . then, all of a sudden, she had it. "When sorrows come, they come not single spies, but in battalions." That was it exactly. After the double blow of Edward's death and her discovery of Simon's alleged duplicity, she supposed she should have been expecting this further setback, but the truth was that she was quite unprepared.

Ever since reading Edward's account of his betrayal by Simon, she had thought about little else. She had to get it into her head, she kept telling herself, that Simon, in plotting to sell the vineyards, had not only deceived his close family: he had deceived her too, and that was almost the hardest part of it. If it was true, it meant that she had loved him under false pretences. That her attempts to carry on what she thought was Simon's work – to take over his mantle, as Vivienne once put it – had been a cruel mockery of the truth.

She kept asking herself what made him do it. Why did he have to pretend? If he honestly believed the company could not succeed, why had he not shared his fears with her? Together they could have worked to find a way out of their difficulties. She wondered how long it would have been before he admitted to her that he no longer had any interest in growing vines, and that he had instead switched his interest to covering that glorious landscape with overblown mansions.

Each time she reached this point she was brought up short. Try as she might she could not imagine Simon condoning such desecration, nor that he was capable of such deception. Edward *must* have made a mistake: he was ill, and maybe he sometimes became muddled. That must be it.

In the end, Meriel realised that whatever her instincts told her about Simon's fundamental honesty and goodness, she had to accept the evidence of the notebooks. She could only guess at the torment that had forced Edward to write these terrible pages. As he himself put it, he had begun his account with the dual aim of refreshing his memory and of furnishing his heirs and successors with a history of the planting of the vineyards. Sadly, somewhere along the way these aims had become lost as what Edward termed the "great adventure" turned sour and his writing took on an increasingly embittered and disillusioned tone.

Again and again she had read the final sections of Edward's memoir in the hope that they might suddenly come to mean something different, but they had not done so. On the contrary, repeated reading had merely served to convince her that the pages must never be allowed to come into Vivienne's possession. No wonder Miss Digby had hesitated before handing over such a potential time bomb! Better by far if she had destroyed it, and left Meriel with her illusions intact. And as if that weren't enough, she now had this latest setback to contend with!

It was little wonder that it was anger she felt, not surprise, as she sat between Adam and Martin Kingsley in the visitors' gallery at the Council Chambers and heard the planning application by which she had set such store, and on whose details she had worked so hard, being thrown out with the very minimum of discussion.

"Application for Conversion of Listed Building, etc., etc.," murmured the man who Martin Kingsley told her was Mr Grateley of the planning department. "I think we are agreed, are we not, that this submission violates our regulations in several important respects?"

There was a murmur of agreement from his colleagues. Then:

"Application dismissed," said Mr Grateley. "Next?"

Meriel could scarcely wait to get out of the building before rounding on Martin.

"I thought you were supposed to be good at your job!" she said, struggling to keep her voice under control. "How many times have you promised me you know all there is to be known about restrictions on listed buildings? How many times have you refused to listen to my suggestions on the grounds that you had the planning department in your pocket, and that your way would work best?"

Only the fact that Martin appeared to be every bit as shocked as she was stopped her from hitting him.

"I . . . I really don't know what to say," he said, puzzled. "I thought I'd handled enough applications of this sort not to run into trouble with this one. Maybe I'd better try and have a word with Frank Grateley. Find out exactly what the problem is."

"In that case, I'll come with you," insisted Meriel. "I'm not taking this lying down, I can tell you!"

Adam now joined them. "Martin, Meriel. I think perhaps it might be wiser if you left this with me. You're both too closely involved to look at it rationally – and there's no sense in upsetting any of the council people. Why don't you go on home, Meriel, and tell Mother I'll be in to see her later?"

Meriel found Vivienne in the conservatory, trying to concentrate on the biography of some Habsburg princess. The doors leading into the garden stood open, and the night air was warm and still, filled with the scent of jasmine.

"They turned us down," said Meriel without preamble, flopping into one of the white wicker chairs.

"But that's terrible! Why? I mean, did they say . . .?"

"Adam's gone to find out if he can get any sense out of anyone. He said he'd stop by here later."

283

"Yes. Yes." Vivienne swallowed. She seemed almost too shocked to speak. "Will they change their minds, do you think?"

"No," said Meriel simply. "I don't think so."

"You know what this means?" asked Vivienne. She could not control the tremor in her voice, or the wash of tears in her eyes. "You know Beagley has called in the loan? I managed to stave him off while this planning application was going through, but now . . ." she shook her head and busied herself with finding a handkerchief.

"Yes," replied Meriel. "I know." She realised that whatever she was feeling at this moment could only be a pale version of what the woman seated opposite her was experiencing. Meriel had only recently come to Amberfield: this was Vivienne's whole life. When she glanced across at Vivienne, she was shocked by the change in her. Vivienne sat with her head leaning against the back of the cane seat; from her closed eyes a slow trickle of tears spread down her pale cheeks. She looked utterly, completely defeated.

"Vivienne!" Meriel, overwhelmed by sympathy at the sight of so much suffering, went over and placed her arms around her. After a moment she felt one of Vivienne's small, bony hands grasping her wrist, clinging to her.

"Meriel, I'm sorry . . ."

Things could not be allowed to end this way, Meriel decided, with the bank foreclosing and the vineyards destroyed. Something had to be done, some means found . . .

"But, Vivienne!" she exclaimed, as an idea came to her. "It doesn't have to be the end of the road! We can use the money that was going towards the conversion of the barn to start paying off the loan! We can – "

"No!" Vivienne's voice was suddenly stronger, and she pulled away from her daughter-in-law. "I'm sorry, but that is out of the question."

"But why? I mean, what difference does it make?"

"It makes all the difference, Meriel. All the difference in the world."

"Not to me it doesn't!"

"The difference is this. I agreed to use your money to fund the conversion because I was certain – quite certain – that one day you would get your investment back. If I accept that same sum to keep the bank off our backs the chances are you will never see it again. I cannot live with that knowledge."

"But I don't mind! I want to help save Amberfield! At any cost!"

Vivienne gave a sad smile. "But Meriel, *I* mind, don't you see? I cannot and will not take money I do not think I can repay." She hesitated a moment and then added: "Believe me, I appreciate the offer. You have been very kind, Meriel. More so than I deserve. Now do please pour us both an extremely large Scotch."

We've become friends, thought Merile as she filled the glasses. Vivienne's initial coldness and resentment towards her had gradually been eroded to the point where they could now sit side by side, saying little, drawing comfort from the mere fact of each other's company. Though neither knew it, each of them had something on their mind that concerned the other.

"I needn't have sent Dan packing after all," murmured Vivienne, surprising Meriel with her train of thought. "It's made no difference in the long run, has it?"

"Not financially," replied Meriel.

"Meriel, about Dan – " said Vivienne a moment or two later.

"Yes?"

"Oh, nothing. I've forgotten what I was going to say."

They fell silent again. Meriel stole another look at Vivienne and, seeing her exhausted, downcast expression, knew beyond doubt that she would be unable to bear the knowledge of Edward's accusations against Simon. Whatever the cost, the truth must be kept from her.

Soon afterwards, Vivienne rose to her feet with difficulty and announced it was time she went to bed. Only after she had gone did Meriel wonder what on earth she had meant by saying she did not deserve her daughter-in-law's kindness.

Within days, Vivienne called an emergency board meeting and announced that she was handing over the managing directorship of the company to Adam alone.

"Following the failure of our rescue plans," she said, with a nod in Meriel's direction, "we have to make some important decisions. I'm afraid I do not feel up to seeing them through. Adam, I'd be grateful if you would take charge of the meeting."

It seemed to Meriel that Vivienne found even this short speech difficult to deliver. Adam by contrast looked almost smug. With sinking heart Meriel listened as he began to speak.

He had ascertained, he told them, that the development scheme for the barn was effectively dead. Financially, the company had reached the end of the road. Like it or not, they had to accept that the grubbing up and replanting of the vines had been an expensive mistake: a mistake which would have to be rectified sooner rather than later if Vivienne were not to lose the roof over her head.

Vivienne looked up at this point and said: "Adam. Before you say another word, I must repeat what I have already told you on numerous occasions. I will not destroy the vineyards. Please don't ask me to do that."

Adam flung Jonathan a look. *You see?* it seemed to imply. *Didn't I tell you?* Then, leaning forward with that warm smile in which the eyes were never fully engaged, he said:

"Don't worry, Mother! I've had another idea."

"You say this arrangement is not unusual among wine-growers?" asked Vivienne when her son had finished.

Adam hesitated. "To be perfectly honest," he replied, "I don't know about wine-growers – most of them own too little land to make a scheme of this sort worthwhile. But among farmers, this is certainly the case."

Vivienne shook her head. "I don't know," she said. "The fact that the land would no longer be ours is such a worry. Edward would never have permitted it."

"Father would have had no choice," replied Adam. "None of us has any choice."

The truth of this statement silenced Vivienne for a time, but eventually she said: "If I were to agree to your proposal, are you quite sure we would retain full control of the company?"

"Oh, yes. There'd be no doubt about that. For as long as we wanted."

Vivienne stated the obvious: they must all be given time to think about this latest development, and Adam immediately agreed. What he now proposed to do, he told them, was to get in touch once more with the people he had spoken to earlier, and to inform them that the scheme was a definite possibility. By the time of their next board meeting, he hoped to be in a position to tell them that the money had been raised, and their futures secured.

Meriel had been listening to Adam's proposal with increasing bewilderment. Leaseback, consortium . . . she knew what it all meant, of course, and to a certain extent it all made good sense. Assuming the consortium came up with a reasonable sum of money, the immediate financial worry would be lifted. But what use was that in the long term, she wondered, if the crop were to fail again, and if the company continued to lose money as it surely would without a major change of direction?

"Can you perhaps give us a few details about this consortium?" she asked.

"As I'm sure you'll appreciate, it's early days as yet. I wouldn't want to mislead you by giving inaccurate information at this stage."

287

"I see." The reply struck Meriel as evasive, and she decided to persist. "I'm merely concerned that we shouldn't have dealings with anyone who wasn't entirely above board."

"Meriel," put in Vivienne, "I fail to see what precisely you are objecting to. Surely you are not suggesting that Adam would have anything to do with crooks?"

"No, of course not, but I – "

"Meriel is quite right to worry," put in Adam. "And I think she deserves an answer. Basically, the money has been got together by merchant bankers Goldring Fabre, of whom Meriel will certainly have heard – "

"Of course."

"Members of the consortium are likely to include German and American as well as UK interests. I assure you the money is rock-solid and eminently respectable."

"So," said Meriel. "These aren't such early days after all? You have already spoken to your people in some detail?"

"I've been doing little else all week," confessed Adam. "But then we need to move fast. Beagley is pressing us very hard. What I need now is a quick decision from the rest of you as to whether I proceed or not. Jonathan?"

"I'm basically in favour," was the lawyer's reply.

"Meriel?"

"Undecided."

"Mother?"

"Something tells me we have absolutely no choice in the matter. Go ahead, Adam. Do what has to be done."

Within the space of a few short weeks, Meriel's world had been stood on its head, and she had still not managed to make sense of everything that was happening. Less than a week after their last meeting, Adam called the board together once more to announce that the funding was now in place, and that the sale of the land could go through. It seemed to Meriel that Vivienne, Adam and

Jonathan were so relieved to have found a solution to their immediate financial worries that they had lost sight of possible long-term disadvantages. No doubt this attitude was helping to tide them over such a difficult period, but she wished they had not been rushed into the present situation so quickly.

Above all, Meriel would have liked to talk to Dan about what was happening. At one point she almost thought of asking Jethro for his address, but then changed her mind. She knew he did not want to hear from her, and besides, what point would it serve? There was nothing he could do to help, and the news was bound to be unwelcome. Dan was far too astute not to realise that once the vineyards passed into the consortium's ownership, much of his work would be undone. It seemed inevitable, for example, that mechanisation would be introduced in place of his own more painstaking methods; that high-quality, relatively "difficult" varieties would be replaced by lowlier vines. It was kinder to leave him in ignorance.

On an impulse, Meriel phoned Rory at work and asked if she could see him.

"Now? Today?" he asked, but she could tell he was pleased.

"If that's all right?"

"Of course, it's all right! But come to Melbury, not to London. I'll see you there tonight. It'll be late-ish, but I'll be there."

She was asleep when he arrived, but woke the moment he entered the room. Turning sleepily towards him, she smiled when she saw that he was naked, and carrying his clothes in one hand and his shoes in the other.

"I'm sorry," he said quietly, almost whispering. "I was trying not to wake you."

"That's all right." Leaning on one elbow, she half sat up, letting the sheet slip from her. Rory dropped his clothes in a heap on the floor and moved quietly towards her, admiring. After a moment, he extended a hand and placed it gently on her breast.

"Have you thought any more about what I said?"

She smiled. "I don't remember you saying anything in particular," she said.

"Don't tease, Mrs Barton."

She pulled away a little. "Don't . . . don't call me that," she said, surprising him.

"I'm sorry. How about . . . Mrs Lassiter, then? Would that suit you better?"

"I don't know," she answered truthfully. "Can I sleep on it?"

"No way!" said Rory, sliding into bed beside her. "Absolutely no way. But I'll give you till tomorrow to think about it if you like."

They were awoken early the following morning by the arrival of vans and the whistling of workmen.

"What's going on?" asked Meriel.

"Didn't I tell you?" said Rory. "Heavens, I'm sorry! I decided to go ahead with some redecorating in good time for October! Drawing-room, dining-room, study . . ."

Meriel was surprised. "I didn't think we'd discussed a colour scheme for the study."

"Ah, well . . ." Rory looked embarrassed. "Actually, Meriel, I decided to get a firm in after all."

"A firm of interior designers, you mean?"

"Well, I could tell you weren't really passionate about the whole business . . . and Patsy has a friend who does it professionally, so I thought . . ."

So, thought Meriel. That explained Patsy's puzzlement when she realised Meriel thought *she* was helping Rory.

"Rory, I have spent a lot of my time poring over swatches of materials and samples of wallpaper! You might have told me you were paying someone else to do the job!"

Rory was all apologies. "What can I say?" he conceded, gracefully enough. "I suppose I should have realised you'd

290

be annoyed. Do you know, it never even occurred to me. How's that for the behaviour of an unreconstructed bachelor?"

In the end, she forgave him, though she had to fight hard not to give in to some residual resentment. What finally restored her good humour was the sight of Paloma, saddled and waiting for her in the yard.

"Race you to the hilltop!" she called to Rory as she urged the golden mare to a gallop and sent the dirt flying from the dry lane.

"If you win, will you marry me?" he shouted after her, but she did not reply. She was still not quite ready for that.

Against all the odds, and to the astonishment of all – not just wine-growers, but the nation as a whole – that year's summer looked like turning into one of the most memorable of the century. At first Meriel and Jethro watched in delighted disbelief as warm sunny day followed warm sunny day, the flowers opened on the vines and pollination took place as though there was no question of it ever being a problem.

It seemed too good to be true. And then, as it turned out, it *was* too good to be true.

"I take it you've heard the latest bad news?" asked Jethro one morning. Meriel, who did not know what he was talking about, saw that the old man was close to tears. "You wouldn't credit it, would you? You would think they'd realise what this could mean to the likes of us!"

"What is it, Jethro?" she asked. "What's happened?"

"They've put a hosepipe ban on us!" replied Jethro, with a despairing gesture. "There's to be no watering of fruit or crops! And they say there's going to be no concessions for farmers or fruit-growers. What's going to become of the vines without water, that's what I'd like to know?"

This, thought Meriel, must be the final irony. When Dan told her about the loss of his Australian vineyard, he could never have guessed that an English vineyard would ever be threatened by drought! She might have laughed if the reality had not been so terrifying. The grapes were just at the point where they were beginning to swell. Without water, they simply could not change from hard little green berries into fine bunches of plump, healthy fruit.

"Well, we can't break the law," was all Adam said when she turned to him for advice. "A ban on watering is a ban on watering. It affects fruit-growers and farmers throughout the south-east – gardeners too, for that matter. We'll just have to live with it."

"Anyone would think you didn't care what happened to the vines!" Meriel accused him.

"I see to the business side of this comany," Adam reminded her. "I leave the practicalities to Mother and to Jethro. And to you, of course. In any case, there's nothing we can do, other than wait and see what happens."

For a few days she did as he suggested. She waited and she watched as day after day the sun climbed high into a cloudless sky. But when the leaves began to wilt on the plants she could sit back no longer, and decided to implement a programme of watering from the stream that bordered the vineyard.

It made for back-breaking, time-consuming work: much of the day seemed to be spent carrying bucketfuls of water from the stream up to the vines, with preference being given to the thirstiest-looking plants. At one stage they wondered whether the stream, already far lower than usual, might not dry up also. If that happened, there was no hope of saving the vineyards.

Just when her anxiety was at its greatest, her prayers were answered. For three days and two nights it rained well-nigh continuously. The water level rose in the stream and the parched vine leaves uncurled. Afterwards, the sun reappeared and carried on shining as if it had never been interrupted.

With this latest danger now behind them, Meriel turned

292

her attention to more mundane matters. The proofs had recently arrived of Amberfield's new brochure and price list which she herself had designed. At first, she had had some trouble persuading the other board members that there was a need for some new sales literature.

"Isn't this something of a waste of money?" Adam asked when she first broached the subject. "In the past, we've made do with a duplicated typed list. It seems to have done the job perfectly adequately."

"I'm tempted to agree with Adam," said Vivienne. "What's wrong with what we've got?"

"Nothing, if you ignore the amateur appearance of the thing," agreed Meriel, "and the fact that it's full of errors . . . like saying that the 1899 Seyval Blanc has an alcohol level of 105%."

"Oh dear," said Vivienne, with an embarrassed laugh. "Maybe we should rethink our leaflet after all. Mind you, an 1899 Seyval Blanc would be something, wouldn't it?"

In any case, Meriel told them, it wasn't simply a question of minor errors. There was also the fact that, without the sales space they had hoped to gain by converting the barn, they would need to devote more time to publicising their products. She wanted to try and interest the press, both local and further afield, in what they were achieving at Amberfield, and for that they urgently needed a more eye-catching approach.

Eventually Adam and Vivienne agreed that she should go ahead and produce the new material and, so far, she was pleased with the results. After thoroughly checking the copy, and changing her mind about the gap between entries, she took the proofs over to Vivienne for a second opinion.

"These look wonderful," her mother-in-law told her. "Personally, I can't find anything to criticise. How long will it be before we get final copies?"

"About three weeks," Meriel replied. "At any rate,

they'll be here in plenty of time for the English Wines Festival."

"Good. And, by the way . . . congratulations. I see you've decided to include your rosé on the list."

Jethro had insisted that her Amberfield Rosé, described as a "medium dry wine made from a blend of red grapes, with luscious fruit and a hint of vanilla" be included. At first, Meriel had demurred, on the grounds that it surely couldn't be good enough to stand alongside the quality wines made by Dan Courtney.

"What else are you going to do with five hundred and thirty bottles of the stuff?" asked Jethro. "It's meant to be drunk young, isn't that right?"

"Yes, but – "

"And you're not going to get through it all on your own, are you? Besides, it's a damn good wine for a first effort. If I'm not ashamed to sell it as Amberfield's first rosé I don't see why you should be, either."

So there it was, between the whites and the reds, her very own creation. She should have been delighted beyond measure at what she had achieved, but her joy was tinged with regret. After her ridiculously over-ambitious attempt at making a Pinot Noir rosé, she had dared to experiment with the Triomphe d'Alsace and Léon Millot only because she believed Amberfield would always play a large part in her life.

Simon might have been joking when he told her that the wine-growing bug would get her one fine day, but this was precisely what had happened. She had indeed been bitten. Now, with the knowledge that his commitment had been no more than skin-deep, coupled with the prospect of a virtual take-over by Adam's consortium, she had to face the fact that the roots she had put down at Amberfield might not have taken hold.

The company was, and would remain, desperately short of money. Because of the disappointing size of the previous year's crop, they would once again run out of wine to sell

294

early the following year. Without the hoped-for extra income generated by the new sales area it was hard to see how they could survive more than another year or two, yet Meriel hesitated before putting this brutal fact into words in the face of Vivienne's recent bereavement.

And even if they did survive, Meriel very much doubted whether, without Dan's expert guidance, their products would ever again merit the EVA seal of approval. They would simply revert to their old ways, and go back to making wines that were merely adequate. It seemed a terrible waste of investment and talent, yet she did not see how the situation could be resolved.

An hour or so previously, Kit had requested the keys to the winery so that he could carry out his normal daily chores, and Meriel now decided to check on his progress. As it happened, she met him running back up the cellar steps, having just that minute finished.

"I'll lock up, Kit," she said.

"Thanks," he said, rubbing his right arm vigorously.

"Hard going?" she asked with a smile.

"I'll say! It's those champagne bottles – you should see my muscles!"

She carried on downstairs, past the high, gleaming vats and towards the vaulted area where the bottles of *méthode champenoise* wine rested, necks down, in wooden racks. She calculated there must be several hundred of the distinctive bottles, the oldest of which dated back to around the time she first met Simon. Every single day since then it had been Kit's unenviable task to give each bottle a quarter-turn and a sharp tap to encourage any remaining sediment to drop to the neck of the bottle. No wonder his arms ached.

She bent down to peer more closely at the dusty bottles in the hope of seeing some of the bubbles that resulted from the secondary fermentation this wine was currently undergoing, but the chemical processes were too slow and too subtle for that, and the glass too opaque. On the other

295

hand, she could see the accumulation of debris in the most mature wine. Soon the time would come when the necks of the bottles would be frozen, and the plug of sediment removed, leaving the wine literally sparkling clean.

She felt a tug of alarm at the thought of what would happen now that Dan was no longer there to guide them. If the fine weather continued, Amberfield would enjoy its best ever harvest of Pinot Noir and Chardonnay grapes, the two varieties used in the making of their *méthode champenoise* wine. Between them, she and Jethro could probably manage the early processes well enough. She foresaw no difficulty in milling and pressing the grapes after picking, and the first fermentation in tanks should be straightforward. Equally, she knew they could cope with the later stages, as they were doing at present, with Kit's help.

But it was that vital time in-between that mattered most, the time when the winemaker made the blend – the *cuvée* as the French called it – that worried Meriel. The decisions about what proportions of black and white grapes to use, or how much yeast to add when the newly blended wine was bottled, was one that needed to be made by an expert. It didn't matter how well you looked after a wine if the initial blend was unsatisfactory. And to make a first-rate *cuvée* you needed a first-rate winemaker.

In contrast to the world outside, shimmering in the continuing summer heat, the winery was cool to the point of chilliness, but Meriel was unwilling to leave. Once she did, she knew she could no longer delay giving Rory the answer he was now pressing her for.

"Say yes, Meriel!" he kept urging her. "I love you, you know that. Besides, what is there to keep you at Amberfield now that they've turned down your conversion plans? Your place is with me. We need each other. Surely you can see the sense of what I'm saying?"

And the truth was, she could. Seated on the cold winery steps, hugging her arms about her, she felt a sudden rush of gratitude towards Rory, who had behaved so patiently, and who was promising so much.

That she felt love for him was also not in question. Without love, she would never have let herself be taken to his bed. But as she had been discovering over the past few years, love takes many different forms and what she felt for Rory was unlike the solid, certain glow of her love for Simon, or the brief, joyous abandon she had experienced with Dan.

Then she shrugged. What did any of it mean, when she analysed it all? She had been betrayed by Simon. Dan had not suffered the thrilling shock to the senses that had so affected her during their lovemaking. Her feelings for Rory might be different from those for the other men in her life, but that did not mean they were in any way less important. Besides, she knew he was right when he pointed out that they needed one another. They had both had enough of being alone.

She phoned Rory from the winery, demanding to be put through to him even though he was currently in a meeting.

"Rory?" she said when he picked up the telephone.

"What is it? Are you all right?" He sounded anxious for her.

"I'm fine," she replied. "I just wanted you to know that I've made up my mind."

"And?"

She drew a deep breath. "Yes," she said. "I've decided I would like to marry you."

18

The more Adam attempted to make light of it, the more angry Vivienne became.

"Darling, how *could* you make such a stupid mistake?" she asked him. "And particularly when there was so much at stake!"

"As you say, it was a simple mistake," replied Adam. "I sent the council the wrong plans, that's all."

"Really, Adam! That kind of carelessness defies belief!"

"I know, I know!" Adam shrugged expansively. "I put one set of drawings in an envelope to go to the council, and asked Michelle to file the others away. Somehow they appear to have got muddled up."

"I do wish you would take this a little more seriously! If Martin hadn't been so annoyed at having his plans turned down he wouldn't have checked the matter out with the planning people. In which case we might never have found out what happened!"

"What can I say, other than I'm sorry?" asked Adam. "But I'm afraid that's what comes of having so much on my plate. Anyway, does it really matter now that we've found an alternative solution to our problems?"

Sometimes her son's behaviour baffled Vivienne completely. Did Adam not understand that, even with the consortium's money to tide them over, Amberfield needed to find ways of going into profit if the company were to survive in the long term?

"I want the revised drawings submitted to the council without delay," Vivienne stated. "Is that clear? Martin assures me the application will go through on the nod.

298

With any luck we can begin building within the month. Better still, why don't *I* submit the drawings? That way we can at least be sure the right ones are being considered!"

Adam's tone was still mild. "Mother!" he remonstrated. "You really must remember that I'm in charge, now. I decide what to do. Not you."

"Perhaps I could remind you that we took a vote on converting the barn," Vivienne said. "You were outnumbered by three to one."

She had expected him to be embarrassed at the discovery of his mistake, and anxious to make amends. Instead, he seemed utterly unapologetic and, indeed, angry with her for criticising him. His response made her all the more determined.

"I want that planning permission, Adam," she told him. "And you're going to get it for me."

It was still dark when they left Amberfield for Sussex and the start of the two-day English Wine Festival. After some deliberation, Vivienne had opted to spend the second day, a Sunday, at the Festival, in the company of Adam and Sophie, leaving Jethro, Kit, Meriel and Hatta to set up the stand and hold the fort on the Saturday.

Hatta sat yawning in the passenger seat, complaining every now and then about the unearthliness of the hour until Meriel reminded her that she had insisted on coming too.

"I know that's what I said," agreed Hatta, "but I didn't realise you meant *this* early!"

"We have to allow a couple of hours to get to Alfriston across country," Meriel told her. "And once we're there we'll need a good three or four hours to set up our stand. Why don't you try and sleep for a bit?"

Meriel peered ahead of her through the darkness, but could see no sign of Jethro in the rented van which held their precious stocks of wine. She prayed he had not overslept, or had an accident, or taken the wrong road and driven miles out of his way . . . But she need not have worried. When, in the early light of day, she pulled up behind the vast white marquee that dominated the showground, she saw that he and Kit were already hard at work unloading cases.

"Wake up, Hatta!" she said, shaking the girl gently by the shoulder. "We're here!"

Hatta climbed groggily out of the car, then stretched, shook herself like a dog and was suddenly wide awake. "Right," she said. "What do you want me to do?"

Amberfield's stand was located and pronounced satisfactory in terms of size and position. Already, numbers of other exhibitors – vineyard owners and wine merchants, cheese-makers, local charitable organisations, balloon flight sellers and purveyors of organic bread and muesli – were busily at work dressing their stalls. The atmosphere, though crowded and hectic, was good-humoured and Meriel was cheered to be warmly greeted by some of the wine-growers she had met during her tour of English vineyards in the New Year.

With Hatta's help, she began arranging bottles on purpose-built glass stands and on upturned cardboard boxes cunningly disguised by dark-green felt. Wine coolers, flowers and strings of vine leaves cut out of gold-coloured card completed the table display. Meriel, standing back to cast a critical eye over their effort, was not displeased. The green and gold theme, echoing Amberfield's bottle labels, worked well, even if it could not match the professional effect produced by some of the more established wine-growers.

"We may not deserve the prize for the best stand," she concluded. "But it's not bad for a first attempt."

"What about glasses?" asked Hatta, rummaging around and failing to find any. "We forgot to bring glasses!"

"That's all right," Meriel assured her. "Visitors are given a tasting glass as part of their entrance fee. We don't have to provide them."

300

When the preparation was complete, Meriel took a turn outside the marquee and was surprised to find that the sun was already high in the sky. In the distance, beyond the small experimental vineyard, the Sussex downs rolled smoothly out of sight. White puffs of cloud sat poised above the ridge of hills and a light, warm breeze blew. It was going to be a beautiful day.

Already, cars and coaches were beginning to arrive, and people were making their way into the showground. Kit uncorked a selection of bottles and for a little while they stood around uneasily, wondering whether anyone would stop at their stand. They need not have worried. Within minutes, it was as though they had been swamped by a tidal wave of people clutching glasses, asking questions and busily scribbling comments on tasting sheets.

While Meriel answered questions about Amberfield's wines, Kit was kept busy uncorking and pouring, and Jethro made his way over to the judges' tent with the wines they had decided to enter for the English Wine Centre Trophy.

"You're sure you took all the ones we agreed on?" Meriel asked him anxiously on his return.

"Don't worry!" Jethro assured her. "We've got entries in the Traditional Sparkling Method category, as well as in Medium Dry White."

"In that case, we're bound to win something, aren't we?" asked Hatta.

"They're all wines that Dan made," said Meriel, "so we must be in with a chance."

Outside, under a blue-and-white striped awning, a jazz band struck up. Kit returned from a trip to the food tent with the information that the car park was almost full and that there were queues to enter the ground. Meanwhile, Meriel had sold her first case of rosé, and was trying not to look too pleased about it. Moments later, she took an order for three more, and then for another six. They were also doing a brisk trade in *méthode champenoise*, and, if things carried on at this rate, looked like running out of Seyval Blanc altogether.

"Oh, by the way," said Kit to Meriel, out of the blue. "I think you forgot to lock your car. And there are some very peculiar people hanging about."

She went out to check, and, finding, as she expected, that the MG was well and truly locked, returned to the marquee in time to see Kit and Hatta stifling their giggles.

"What are you two up to?" she demanded.

"Nothing!" insisted Kit, Hatta and Jethro in unison, which merely increased her suspicion that something was being plotted behind her back.

The afternoon wore on. People of all ages, from tiny children to senior citizens, began dancing to the jazz band. From another corner of the ground came the sound of supporters urging on their favourites in the grape-treading competition.

"May I try some of that rosé?" asked a familiar voice. With a start of recognition, Meriel turned to find Dan Courtney standing before her.

"Yes . . . yes, of course," was all she could think to say. Then she added, lamely. "I didn't know you were back . . ."

"As you see . . ." He watched her with amused detachment as she fumbled with bottle and glass and handed him the wine.

"I . . . it's . . . I mean, it's not up to your usual standard, obviously, but I did my best."

Dan, who had just taken a first mouthful of the wine, swallowed it suddenly.

"You mean, *you* made it? Not Jethro?"

"Jethro refused to have anything to do with it," she said.

He was leaner than she remembered him, thought Meriel, glancing nervously at him as he tasted her wine. Also, he gave off an air of quiet confidence that suggested his months in Australia had been wholly

302

successful. Amberfield must seem very unimportant to him now.

He looked again at the label.

"Léon Millot and Triomphe d'Alsace, eh? When did you harvest these?"

"Very late," Meriel replied. "In fact, I came close to leaving it *too* late."

"And after picking? How long did you leave the juice on the skins?"

"I didn't. I used the juice just as it came."

Dan looked surprised. "So this is the juice's natural colour? And you treated it as though you were making a white wine?"

"Yes. I only know about making white wine."

"That certainly explains how you got this nice, fresh taste." Dan seemed genuinely impressed. "I wondered how you'd avoided even a hint of tannin. To be perfectly honest, I'm not sure I'd have thought of making a rosé by this method. Congratulations, Meriel. If my first wine had tasted this good I'd have been extremely proud of myself."

Just at that moment Hatta came gallumphing down the marquee and flung her arms round Dan with a squeal of delight.

"You're back!" she said, "Oh, Dan, I'm so pleased! Are you coming back to Amberfield?"

Dan ruffled the girl's blond hair. "'Fraid not, sweet-heart. I'm just over here to make some wine for a vineyard in Hampshire . . . after which I'm off back to Oz."

"Oh!" Hatta pulled a disappointed face. "That's really rotten of you!" Then she cheered up. "Tell you what. Come and have a dance with me."

She led him out of the marquee, leaving Meriel to deal with some waiting customers and trying to tell herself that it was surprise, nothing more, that had occasioned that jolting internal lurch the moment she turned to find herself staring into Dan Courtney's eyes.

"When do the judges come round with the names of prizewinners?" she asked later, during a brief lull in the proceedings.

Jethro hesitated before answering. "They've been, love," he told her at last. "About an hour ago. You see Carr Taylor over there? And Lamberhurst? Tenterden? They've all won something. I saw the judges giving them their slips of paper."

"Then . . ." Meriel couldn't quite take it in. She supposed she must have been too busy to notice what was going on. "Wasn't there anything for us?"

Jethro shook his head and looked away. "Sorry." There was a strange catch in his voice, and she guessed he must be as disappointed as she was.

Just then the ceremony for the awarding of the trophies was announced, and Hatta insisted that she and Meriel should attend.

"Even if we haven't won anything, we should show what good sports we are," she said. "Don't you agree?"

"Oh, Hatta! I was so sure Dan would get a prize! Do you know where he is?"

"Oh, he's gone," said Hatta airily. "He left hours ago."

The band had fallen silent, and a crowd had gathered around the dais before the striped awning.

"And now for the moment you've all been waiting for," said the announcer, "the names of the winners in our annual competition for the best wines of the show! Class 1, for a Dry White wine, and the winner in this category is . . . Amberfield Seyval Blanc!"

Meriel was too surprised to move.

"Go on!" Hatta was urging her. "We've won! The Seyval Blanc's won!"

"But I had nothing to do with the Seyval Blanc!" protested Meriel. "Jethro should collect it on Dan's behalf!"

"Jethro's manning the stall," Hatta reminded her. "You go."

Meriel had scarcely returned from collecting the prize

when the class winner for a Sparkling Traditional Method wine was announced and she found herself stepping once more up the dais to collect a prize on Dan's behalf.

"What a shame he didn't stay to see this!" she said to Hatta on her return.

"Sssh!" whispered Hatta. "Listen!"

"Winner in Class 4 – any other wine, including Red and Rosé, the winner is – Leestone Vineyard Red, the runners-up Hawkbury Rosé and Amberfield Rosé."

"You *knew* about this!" Meriel accused Hatta, hugging her. "That business about the car not being locked – you just wanted me out of the way while the judges were doing the rounds!"

After that, even the fact that Amberfield did not win the English Wine Centre Trophy outright failed to disappoint her. She returned to the marquee to find Jethro surrounded by reporters and photographers.

"Can you let us into the secret of Amberfield's success?" he was being asked.

"We had a damn fine winemaker in the past," Jethro was saying, "and now it looks as though we've found ourselves another one."

It was only then that Meriel remembered that she would soon be gone from Amberfield. And that unless a miracle occurred their prize-winning days were over.

The news that Meriel's conversion plans for the barn had finally been approved by the local council followed within days. Her reaction was one of relief that she had been able to leave a worthwhile legacy to Amberfield. The quality of their wines could only decrease with Adam and his consortium at the helm, but at least the company, and the vineyards, would survive.

Next month, when Rory publicly announced their engagement, she would finally sever all her links with Amberfield. There was no point thinking about what might happen to the company once she was gone.

Besides, she had other things on her mind. Although she took care not to let her doubts show, Meriel was experiencing mixed feelings now that her decision was made. There were moments when she felt almost frightened about what she was letting herself in for. Despite Patsy's friendliness towards her, and Rory's insistence that she was absolutely right for Melbury, it often seemed to Meriel that she had little idea of what her future life entailed.

One problem in particular bothered her. Given the distances involved, there could be no question of Rory returning home on weekday evenings, yet when she suggested she spend the week in London – maybe even find herself some part-time work – he responded with amazement.

There could be no question of her working, he told her, refusing to discuss the matter at any length. Her place as his wife was at Melbury, running his house, attending functions on his behalf and entertaining the sort of people he needed to impress when he was home at weekends.

When she told him she was worried she would be lonely without him he told her how sweet she was, and looked touched, but she could see he did not take her seriously. Staying at home was what all the other wives in the area did, he told her. She would soon make new friends. There was Paloma to be exercised. And besides, if he had his way she would soon start having children, at least three, and preferably four.

Meriel's first reaction on considering this scenario was one of irritation that Rory was, as she saw it, hijacking her life. But the more she thought about it, the more she came to the conclusion that this was probably just what she needed. Rory would provide well for her; he would continue to be great company and given his frequent absences they would probably not tire of one another as quickly as other couples. She felt a great need for stability in her life, and Rory seemed the one to provide it.

As to the possibility that he might occasionally stray while he was alone in London, Meriel decided to cross that particular bridge when she came to it. It might never happen, and in the meantime there were still one or two matters to be cleared up at Amberfield.

Chief among them related to Adam's extraordinary error with the conversion plans. If it *was* an error . . . At no time had Adam showed much enthusiasm for her scheme, but could he possibly have *wanted* it to fail? And if so, could it have been Adam who spirited away the frost candles and was thereby responsible for the dreadful damage inflicted on the vines? Then she decided that it couldn't be Adam. It was he, after all, who had come up with the rescue package they were about to sign and which, like it or not, represented their most immediate hope of salvation.

The clatter of the office fax machine drew her back to the present. She watched the sheet feeding through, then tore it off and returned to her desk. The fax was from Rory and came in answer to her request for more detailed information about Goldring Fabre and the members of the consortium that were to rescue Amberfield. But she found she could not read it through. The moment she turned the sheet of paper towards her, one name sprang out from the list and hit her with almost palpable force. The name was Bert Hollyfield.

"Meriel!" Adam was waiting for her in the foyer of the Red Lion Hotel in Canterbury. "What on earth is this all about? What are we doing meeting here?"

"Adam." As she kissed him, then led the way into the dining-room, she felt her doubts redouble, but it was too late now to turn and run. "I need to talk to you," she explained as they sat down. "In private. This seemed the most convenient place."

"Suits me," said Adam. "Fire away."

Meriel waited until a waitress had brought their first course before beginning.

"Last year," she said quietly, "on the day your father had his stroke, he discovered that Simon had been plotting behind his back to sell the vineyards at Amberfield for housing. I believe that was what brought the stroke on. What do you think?"

Watch him as she might, Meriel saw no tell-tale signs of any kind in Adam's behaviour. He continued spreading pâté on his toast then took a couple of quick bites before looking calmly across at her.

"I don't know what gave you that idea," he murmured, "but it doesn't sound very likely to me. Who told you all this?"

"I got it from your father, as a matter of fact."

"From my father? Oh, come, Meriel! He lost his speech long before you came onto the scene. No!" he held up a hand, seeing that she was about to interrupt. "Don't tell me! You got it from Diggers, I bet. She always did seem to have it in for Simon and me!"

"Well, I . . ."

"There! I knew it! God!" he exclaimed after a pause. "If that's what Diggers was telling the old man, it must have broken his heart! Simon was always his favourite, you know."

"I know," said Meriel miserably. "That's why I was wondering if maybe you knew anything about it."

"Me? What makes you say that? I don't even think any of it is true!"

Meriel felt her heart sink like a stone inside her. Quite what she had been expecting from Adam she was no longer sure, but it wasn't this. Not this corroboration of her worst imaginings. If this was the first Adam had heard of the plan to sell the vineyards, then Simon must be the guilty one.

"Well," said Adam after the waitress had brought him a plate of chicken in red wine. "It was good of you to tell me what's been happening, Meriel. I appreciate it. But I don't see the need to blacken Simon's memory by spreading this any further, do you?"

At that moment, a woman dressed in a smart grey suit, her dark hair pulled tightly back from her face, Spanish-style, was crossing the hotel foyer. With the proprietorial air of a senior member of staff, she glanced briefly through the open dining-room door as if to check that everything was in order, letting her stern gaze wander over the diners. When she caught sight of Meriel and Adam, a look of disbelief spread across her face, and for a moment she clutched nervously at the high neck of her blouse. Then, almost immediately, she appeared to relax and walked smilingly towards them.

"Nikki!" said Adam, rising to extend a hand in greeting. "Long time no see. May I introduce my sister-in-law, Meriel? Meriel, this is Nikki Rosen, the manageress of the Red Lion . . ."

They shook hands, and Nikki, still showing a touch of confusion, said: "Do please forgive me for staring like that, but for a moment I thought . . ." she left the sentence unfinished.

Of course, thought Meriel, leaning back while the others exchanged pleasantries. This must be Simon's Nikki. The one he had been engaged to before he met her. The one in hotel management. It certainly explained the woman's sudden shock as she caught sight of Adam. She thought it was Simon she was seeing, not his brother. Just as Meriel herself had almost been overcome with dizziness in that London hotel the day she first met Adam. There were moments when the two brothers were so alike, even those who knew them best had trouble telling them apart.

Then suddenly she knew. Knew beyond any doubt.

"Adam," she said when Nikki had moved on, "I know it wasn't Simon who was planning to sell the vineyards behind Edward's back. It was you, wasn't it? I know it was you."

"You don't know anything of the sort," he retorted easily, but with the slightest edge of menace creeping into his tone. "Maybe you'd better watch what you're saying."

Far from putting her off, the implied threat merely fuelled her resolve.

"Adam," she repeated quietly, "I *know*. Edward wrote all about it in his journals."

"What journals? Father never kept any journals! And if he had they'd have gone to Mother, not to you."

"Your father *did* keep a journal, and it came to me. There's no need for you to know how. If you want proof . . . here. Have a look."

Adam wiped his mouth, and angrily threw down his napkin. Then he all but snatched the paper from Meriel's hands and read it through at top speed.

"Really, Meriel!" he observed when he had finished. "If you're going to accuse me of killing my father – which is virtually what you are doing – you'd better come up with better proof than this! All this shows is that Father discovered what Simon was up to. Being Father, he would of course have preferred to believe I was to blame and not his darling first-born. But at last he seems to have been able to accept the truth. Unlike you."

"You're not thinking about what Edward wrote," said Meriel. "What he actually said leaves no room for doubt. It was you, Adam. Not Simon."

"And just how do you work that out?"

Meriel read aloud. "We dined tonight with Adam and Sophie, though I had little appetite and Vivienne asked me more than once if I was sure I felt well enough to be up. At one point, still unable to believe what I had earlier been told, I informed Adam that some chap called Crowden phoned and asked to speak to him. But Adam's reply could not have been plainer. 'Jim Crowden?' he said. 'He wanted Simon, Father. Not me.'"

"Well?" queried Adam, when he realised Meriel had stopped reading. "What of it?"

"If you had never heard of this chap Crowden before, how come you were so certain he wanted Simon and not you? More to the point, how did you know he was called Jim?"

Adam stared at her for a moment, his colour rising. At last she could tell she was beginning to make some impression on him. "It stands to reason, doesn't it?" he blustered. "I mean, I'd have known if the call was for me."

"Really? Are you telling me you have never received a phone call from someone whose name you didn't already know? I find that very hard to believe!"

Adam cornered was a different man from the one who had entered the dining-room at the Red Lion three-quarters of an hour earlier. A network of angry red veins seemed to have sprung up over his face, including the whites of his eyes, which now stared angrily into hers. He looked broader somehow, almost frightening, and Meriel might have retreated at this point if there had not been so much at stake. Instead, she faced him out, until he finally directed his angry glare away from her, and forced a small laugh.

"Honestly, Meriel, it was just a misunderstanding. Crowden had met my brother once before, and he assumed I was Simon. You know how alike we were. People were always getting us mixed up. Maybe I should have put him right, but what did it matter?"

"What did it matter? When you were doing something that went against everything your father had worked for?"

"I was simply having the land valued, that's all. Anyone could see the trouble we were heading for! I was merely looking for a way out. Anyway, what matters is that we've got the deal with the consortium – for which you voted, Meriel – so all is well."

"Oh, no, Adam. All is very far from being well. For example, how come Bert Hollyfield is involved in the consortium? And why have you made such a secret of the fact?"

By now Adam, not knowing the extent of Meriel's knowledge, was replying to her questions with a mixture of bluff and caution.

"Bert? If you knew Bert, you'd know how quick he is at spotting a good deal when he sees one! And I can assure you there's no secret about his involvement! It's simply that he's only just recently come in with us. Within the last week, as it happens. I was going to announce it at the next board meeting."

"Perhaps you should know," Meriel told him, "that I saw Bert at Amberfield soon after I came here. He seemed very anxious that nobody apart from you should know he was there. What was he doing, Adam? Checking out the land on which his houses were going to be built?"

"That's just guesswork, Meriel," said Adam after a pause.

"I also checked up on Jim Crowden," she continued, "and I discovered that he works for Bert Hollyfield on a regular basis. He was the surveyor for Bert's previous development. Do you know what I think, Adam? I think you've been working to make sure that Amberfield Wines fails. Vivienne would then have no choice but to allow the consortium to use the land in whatever way it chose. I suppose there'd be a nice little backhander in it for you. One thing I'm sure of: you wanted to get rid of the vineyards from the very start. Isn't that right, Adam?"

"I tell you, those blasted vineyards have been bleeding us dry! I – "

"And of course it was you who hid the frost candles, wasn't it Adam? Your fault the harvest was all but lost, and the reason why Vivienne got rid of Dan?"

"The man was an expensive luxury," said Adam contemptuously. "Mother's better off without him."

"And is it your opinion that she would be better off without me, too?"

"Sorry?"

"You tried to wreck those vines I'd been pruning, didn't

312

you? Tried to make me look like an incompetent fool in Dan's eyes and Vivienne's."

"There I'm afraid you've lost me," said Adam, but she didn't believe him, not for a minute. "The fact is," he continued, "the fact is, I did what I thought was best for all of us. What is so wrong about that?"

"You know very well what is wrong about it! What's wrong is that you had no compunction about trying to destroy everything your parents and your brother had spent years working to build up. And what is particularly wrong is that you were willing – eager! – to sell your birthright for a few pieces of silver. That's what I can't accept."

"Birthright! What birthright, I'd like to know? Without me, without Bert and the consortium there isn't going to be any birthright for any of us! And I'll tell you something else, in case you were thinking of giving me a lecture on family loyalty, things might have been different if I hadn't always been pushed to the side. All my life it's been Simon this, Simon that. Simon first and last, with never a thought for how poor old Adam was feeling, out there in the cold."

"Spare me the self-pity, Adam! It doesn't suit you!"

But Meriel, thinking back to what she had read in Edward Barton's notebooks, knew there was more than a grain of truth in what Adam said. All along, Edward had criticised his younger son's lack of aptitude as a wine-grower, without once stopping to consider that Adam might have other qualities which could be encouraged in other ways. It was indeed sadly true that Adam had taken second place in his father's esteem and affections, but at the end of the day Adam had wrought a cruel revenge.

"Nothing excuses what you've done," she said at last. "You let your father go to his grave believing that his favourite son had betrayed him."

"Father's dead now. What's done is done. Why don't we try and reach some mutually satisfactory compromise?"

"I can't agree to that, Adam. Because it's not just Edward you hurt, it's me too. If I hadn't put two and two together, I'd have been tricked into believing my marriage to Simon was nothing but a lie and a sham, and I can't forgive you for that. I'd have spent the rest of my life convinced that the man I married was worthless, whereas he was everything that you're not. He was open, honest, warm-hearted and generous to a fault. No wonder Edward preferred him over you! No, Adam, there's no question of reaching a compromise. I don't trust you. I couldn't ever trust you."

"Well, isn't that a shame," retorted Adam, who seemed suddenly to have regained his composure. "Because, quite honestly, it doesn't make much difference what you think of me. I am going to stay on here as chairman of Amberfield Wines, and if you don't like the idea you can hand in your resignation."

"But you've admitted what you've done! You've told me the vineyards are going to be destroyed! When I tell Vivienne – "

Adam interrupted her. "Ah, but you're not going to tell Vivienne, are you? I know you, Meriel. There's no way you could bring yourself to do that to her. Not under any circumstances. I'm right, aren't I?"

There was certainty in his smile. Slowly, Meriel lowered her head, not wanting Adam to see how badly this sudden, unexpected defeat was hurting her. She reached for her handbag and the papers she had brought with her, and would have stood up if her strength hadn't suddenly deserted her. As she shuffled the papers together, she caught sight of Adam's clenched hand on the table before her, the shiny gold wedding ring contrasting with the tan. She looked up sharply.

"Yes, Adam. You are right. I wouldn't dream of telling Vivienne what a crook you are. I don't think she could take it. But Sophie could. Sophie would know how to handle the situation."

314

"*No!*" All traces of confidence vanished from his face, and Meriel saw to her relief that she had hit Adam's weak spot. "Don't tell Sophie, whatever you do," he begged her. "It would destroy her. Just . . . tell me what you want of me."

"Very well, Adam," she replied. "I'll tell you." And she did.

19

On the day the builders moved in to begin the work of converting the barn, Meriel told Vivienne she had accepted Rory Lassiter's proposal of marriage.

"Congratulations, Meriel!" she said. "I hope you'll be very, very happy. You deserve to be."

The words were spoken with such warmth that Meriel was taken by surprise.

"Why . . . thank you," she said.

"I'm only sorry you feel unable to continue as a board member. Wiltshire isn't *that* far away. You could easily return for the odd meeting. Won't you reconsider?"

But Meriel shook her head. She had already decided that a clean break was necessary if she was to make a success of her new life. Apart from anything else, Rory not unnaturally expected her to devote herself to him in future.

"Before you leave us . . ." said Vivienne hesitantly.

"Yes?"

"I feel perhaps there is something I ought to make clear. It's about . . . oh, I don't know how to put these things, but it's about Dan. That is, about you and Dan."

"Oh?" Meriel regarded her warily.

"This really is very difficult," she sighed. "The fact is that when we had the frost . . . when the harvest was lost . . . I saw you. And Dan. Walking down the ridgeway. It seemed fairly clear to me at the time that the two of you were . . . er . . . together. I rather fear I may have given Dan the impression that you told me you were . . . oh, dear, I do so hate this sort of thing."

"So that was how you knew about us," said Meriel.

"Of course, I felt sure you would have set Dan right on that score, and that it didn't really matter. All the same, it's something I felt I should clear up."

"You're right," said Meriel. "In the end it made no difference at all."

For most of the previous month, Melbury Hall had been in a state of near-total chaos. There seemed to be no end to the comings and goings, with scarcely a moment's quiet in-between. First, the house had been overrun by painters and decorators refurbishing the entrance hall, ballroom and other rooms which would be used by the party guests. After them came a squad of cleaners, but these were no mere local ladies with mops. They were for the most part specialists in their trade, who concentrated on carpets or upholstery or wall hangings, ensuring that the curtains did not become discoloured, or the stair carpet shrink as a result of their ministrations.

As one delivery followed another, Meriel had gratefully taken on the task of checking the items when they came. She was relieved to be so busy, and not to have time to think about . . . well, anything, really. Not that Patsy would have allowed her to sit around and do nothing: she, like everyone else at Melbury, had been dragooned into doing their bit. Right now, Patsy was in the kitchens, checking that the recently arrived boxes of strawberries were fit to eat, that the cooked salmon was ready to be skinned and decorated with the thinnest of cucumber slices, and that somebody had remembered to order the crushed ice in which the champagne would be chilled.

A ringing on the doorbell informed Meriel that the hired cutlery had at last arrived, and she heaved a sigh of relief. The thought of five hundred guests picking at their food with their fingers for want of knives and forks was not one that amused her on this occasion, though it might have done at other times. After confirming that the delivery

317

tallied with what had been ordered, she consulted Patsy's written list to see what needed doing next.

Check flowers in ballroom, it said. In fact, she had earlier seen the flowers being carried in by the armful, but by now the arrangements should be nearing completion and Meriel made her way to the ballroom to check that this was indeed so. Here, the chaos of the past week was now settling into something resembling order, though, glancing round at the newly painted walls, Meriel could have wished Patsy had chosen a colour other than pink as her main theme.

Pink was all very well in its place, she reflected, but here there was simply too much of it, and in too many shades. Even the band had been issued with pink jackets: she could only hope they did not clash with everything else. Against the pale pink of the walls, the deeper pink of carnations, long-stemmed roses, lilies and the rest was matched by great satin bows tied round the vases and baskets. More pink bows and swags were draped and tied around chairs and tablecloths and curtains and even on Patsy's full-skirted ball gown. The choice of colour had surprised Meriel, for Patsy was a big, high-coloured, almost florid girl, but one had to realise, Meriel told herself, that all this represented a dream. And if it was Patsy's dream to cavort about in baby-pink flounces, what right did anyone have to try and stop her?

"Well? What's your verdict?" Rory was standing behind her, his chin resting lightly on her shoulder.

"It's . . . astonishing," said Meriel tactfully. "Quite amazing. What you and Patsy have achieved between you is just . . ." She shook her head. "Words fail me."

"Liar," said Rory. "Go on, admit it. You hate it."

"I like the walls. But maybe the rest isn't exactly my taste . . ." she said cautiously.

"Of course it isn't. Nor mine either, for that matter. But this is supposed to be Patsy's day, not mine. And some of the excesses can easily be trimmed afterwards."

"Do you always do that, Rory?"

"Do I always do what?" he laughed.

"Pretend to give in, then change things to suit yourself the moment you get the chance?"

"Darling!" Rory held her at arms' length and studied her for some moments. "That was a remarkably waspish comment, if I may say so!"

She was immediately contrite. For some reason, ever since she had accepted Rory's proposal, she had been on edge. "Oh, Rory, I'm sorry!" she said. "I think I must be feeling rather nervous."

"Why nervous?" he asked. "You've had plenty of time to think things through. Aren't you happy we're properly together now?"

"Yes, of course I am. I'm sure I'll relax once this is all over . . . once I know I've been accepted by all your friends and relatives . . ."

"They'll love you!" Rory assured her. "Just wait and see!"

"Well," she said with a sigh. "I'd better get on with the next job, or Patsy will be after me."

"In point of fact," Rory said, catching hold of her arm as she made to return downstairs, "I was looking for you. I've got something to show you."

From a box lying by the door he took out a dress. A ball dress in gleaming midnight-blue satin that whispered silkily as he held it up to show her.

"Well?" he asked. "What do you think?"

"It's a beautiful colour," she said, not understanding.

"And you are going to look perfectly stunning in it!" he said.

"But Rory!" she laughed. "I've already got a dress! I showed it to you, don't you remember?"

"Of course. And it's very nice, as far as it goes – "

"What do you mean, 'as far as it goes'? Rory, I chose it because I liked it!"

"I'm not criticising your taste, Meriel, so there's no need

319

to get so cross. It's simply that I can't have you wearing a rented ball gown. What if someone else was wearing the identical dress?"

She opened her mouth to say that these days, everyone hired their evening dresses. That in any case she couldn't care less if every woman in the room was wearing the same thing. But seeing how serious Rory was, she changed her mind.

As Rory held the dress up against her, and told her exactly which necklace and which earrings would best set it off, she silently asked herself what else she could have expected of this man who so abhorred designer labels and ready-made clothes. This wasn't some recently developed quirk which she was noticing for the first time. She had always known how Rory felt about matters which would have seemed utterly trivial to the other men she had loved.

"You see?" he was saying. "It's perfect! Now. Run along and put it somewhere safe," said Rory. "I wouldn't want it getting dirty. Oh, by the way. I almost forgot to tell you. There's a message for you to phone somebody. Meant to tell you a while back."

When Meriel saw that the message came from Hatta, her first thought was that she had remembered her forth-coming engagement, and was ringing to congratulate her. Instead, the girl sounded frightened to the point of hysteria.

"Meriel," she said without wasting time on preliminaries, "you've got to do something. I don't think I can cope on my own, especially not from school!"

"Do something? But, Hatta! I'm just getting ready for this big party I told you about. I'm about to get engaged!"

"Oh, yes, I forgot. Sorry," mumbled Hatta. "I didn't know who else to ask. But as you're so busy – "

"Hatta – don't put the phone down, wait! Tell me exactly what's going on."

"It's Adam," she replied. "He's suddenly got it into his head that he doesn't want to manage the company any more, and Mum's in a frightful state about it."

So! thought Meriel. Her bluff had worked. Adam had agreed to do as she asked. He was standing down as managing director of Amberfield Wines. She tried to keep the smile out of her voice.

"Oh, Hatta!" she said, "I wouldn't worry too much about that, if I were you! You know, Adam never was desperately interested in the business. It was a job he did simply to keep his parents happy. I'm sure Vivienne isn't as upset as you think. Given time, she'll probably decide it was all for the best."

"No!" said Hatta, "You don't understand! It's not as if he's simply leaving the company! He and Sophie have decided to go and live in France! They're leaving right away! That's what's upsetting Mum!"

Meriel sank down onto the bed while she tried to gather her thoughts together.

"They're . . . you say they're going to France? But . . . what about the leaseback scheme? The consortium?" she added, sensing that Hatta did not understand what she was talking about.

"I don't know!" wailed Hatta. "All Mum kept saying was that she should never have sent Dan away. She says she's not going to be able to manage on her own, and we'll have to sell Amberfield and live in The Lodge . . . Meriel, I've got to go, now, but please! You've got to *do* something!"

Do something? Meriel asked herself as she replaced the receiver. What on earth did Hatta think could be done at this stage? Did anything need to be done? As far as Meriel was concerned, it could only be good news for Vivienne that the consortium deal appeared to have fallen through. By now, much of the construction work on the barn should have been completed and it could only be a matter of weeks before the shop was open. There was surely no need to be

thinking in terms of selling Amberfield and moving into
The Lodge . . .

The very idea sent a flash of unease through Meriel. And
yet, she should be feeling relieved, she kept telling herself.
With Adam gone, the threat to the vineyards should have
receded once and for all. There was every reason to think
that the new shop would help Vivienne to stay afloat –
maybe even to prosper in the long run. Why, then, did
she still, after all this time, feel that there was something
vital which she had overlooked, a disaster just waiting to
happen?

"Meriel?" Rory was standing beside her. "Not bad news,
I hope?"

She shook her head. "Not really. That was Hatta
phoning me from school. I think she's a bit worried about
Vivienne. Maybe I should – "

"No," said Rory, gently but firmly. "Whatever it is
you're thinking of doing, don't. How do you think I'm
going to feel if you keep putting somebody else's interests
before mine? You've left Amberfield now. You can't keep
looking back."

The hairdresser, who like the interior designer was one of
Patsy's London friends, had set himself up in a spare bedroom and, at Patsy's insistence, was "doing" Meriel first.

"Lovely hair!" he kept saying, as he washed and
snipped. "Lovely auburn tints! It's going to look so
elegant, piled on top of the head . . ."

"I'm sure you'll work wonders," said Meriel, trying to
look as relaxed and happy as she knew she should. These
days she only rarely wore her hair other than loose about
her shoulders, or quickly twisted into a single, central plait
from the crown of the head. But Rory had requested
something more elaborate on this occasion, and she felt
it was only fair to oblige him. She decided he had been
quite right to remind her that her duty lay with him, now.
He did not deserve her snappy irritability.

The young man was quiet for a while, and Meriel could tell he had caught something of her tension. Like everyone except for Patsy and Jarvis, he was unaware that Rory and Meriel would this evening be announcing their own engagement. That particular disclosure was not to be made until fairly late in the proceedings, so as to steal as little of Patsy's thunder as possible.

Soon, to Meriel's relief, Patsy came in to wait her turn and Meriel was able to sit back and listen as the young man, whose clientele appeared to be drawn mainly from the ranks of show business – began telling them about some scandal that had yet to hit the newspapers.

"Meriel, you look *gorgeous*!" exclaimed Patsy when the young man had finished. "I could never look like you," she continued, just a little wistfully. "You're so elegant! So right for Melbury!"

"You're going to look even better," Meriel assured her. "And quite right too."

She made her way back to the room she shared with Rory and gently closed the door behind her. There on the bed was the dress Rory had secretly had made for her. Meriel touched the cool, heavy satin and marvelled at the workmanship of the piece, at the oversewn seams and the hand-covered buttons and hooks. Rory must have spent two thousand pounds or more ensuring that she looked as he wished her to on this special night. Why, then, was her overriding reaction one of resentment?

Rory, as she kept reminding herself, was attractive, generous and amusing. If she sometimes found herself straining at the leash when she was at Melbury, or arguing with him over seemingly unimportant things it was only to be expected. She had grown out of the habit of living with a man, and she was certain that the sooner she settled down as Rory's wife, the better it would be for both of them. Once she was married she would do her best to be the best wife he could ever have hoped for. And then, when there were children –

Nervously, she removed the stiff petticoat and under-skirt from the box and stepped into them, before slipping the dress over her head and standing back to look at herself in the mirror. As Rory had foretold, the effect was stunning, and for a moment she thought maybe he had got it right after all. But the more she looked, the more uneasy she became.

The neckline was low-cut and "sweetheart"-shaped, the bodice boned and close-fitting, so that her breasts were pushed upwards and exposed almost as far as the nipple. From the narrow waistline, folds of satin fell to a gathered hemline studded with tiny self-coloured bows. Puff sleeves finished with a larger bow completed the effect. Seen in the better light of the bedroom, the dress no longer looked midnight-blue, as she had thought, but rather a harsh, almost royal blue, and as she stared at her reflection in the tall pier-glass, her eye drawn from dress to hair then back again, she noticed something that not merely worried, but actually frightened her.

It was as if the area between the dramatically-piled hair and the deep-coloured folds of the dress was no more than a blank. Her face and features seemed to have faded into insignificance, the effect made worse by the fashionably light and understated make-up which she preferred.

Grabbing hold of the darkest lipstick she could find, she rubbed the colour into her lips, then outlined her eyes with a dark kohl pencil. Her hand was trembling now and when she came to add the mascara she came close to jabbing the brush in her eye, but when she looked at her reflection again she was relieved to see that she did at least have a face. She did at least have a personality again. But whose? That was the question.

Was this really what Rory wanted of her, she wondered? To fashion her into his creature? Swaying this way and that before the mirror, Meriel knew that he would be pleased with her. She looked as he wanted her to: a beautiful and biddable appendage for the man who had everything. Only she was not herself. The woman in the mirror was, and would remain, a stranger.

In a minute, she told herself. *I'll finish getting ready in a minute.* But first she had to get some air. On an impulse, and ignoring the startled glances of the staff members she encountered on her way, she ran shoeless down the servants' staircase and out through a side door towards the stable yard.

Hitching the hem of her dress up, Meriel skirted the stables and made her way the short distance to the pony field, grateful that she didn't have to venture further in such unsuitable clothing. When she reached the gate, she paused and leaned on the solid wooden bars, still retaining the warmth of the October sunshine, and breathed in the smells of the rapidly cooling evening. Almost immediately, before she had had a chance to call, Paloma came trotting inquisitively up to the gate.

Ignoring the possible damage to her dress, Meriel placed her arms around the mare's neck and hugged her tightly. Horses were often particularly gentle and affectionate at night, as Meriel had already discovered, and this time was no exception. Paloma nuzzled Meriel's shoulder, then tugged gently at her ball dress with huge yellow teeth, snorting softly.

"What am I doing here, Paloma?" asked Meriel, almost as though she genuinely expected a reply. "And why am I crying!" she exclaimed, as the tears, unbidden but unstoppable, began to stream down her cheeks. "That's right," she continued, feeling the horse's warm breath on her wet cheek. "Go on. Ruin my make-up. Lick my tears away. I expect they're lovely and salty."

But soon, sensing that the mare was tiring of her embrace, she gave her a gentle pat on the rump, and sent Paloma skittering away to the far side of the field. In the near-dark, with her pale mane and tail flowing out behind her, she looked like a ghost horse as she gradually faded from sight.

When she opened the door to the bedroom, Meriel knew at once that Rory had been in to bathe and change while she was with Paloma. The scent of aftershave hung in the air, and there were clothes strewn around his dressing-room. For a while she moved about the room, hanging up the jacket he had been wearing earlier, and stowing jeans and shoes in their proper place. When she had folded the lemon cashmere sweater, she buried her face in it for a moment before shutting it away in a drawer.

Then, returning to her dressing-table, she sat with her head sunk in her hands while she tried to compose herself before reapplying her wrecked make-up. She still needed to collect her thoughts, still needed to make sense of the reasons for the wretchedness which now engulfed her.

When at last she looked up, she saw that Rory had left a present for her on the dressing-table. She lifted the small package, and shook it gently, guessing that it contained a piece of jewellery. Whatever it was, it would be beautiful. Expensive. Probably unique. And it would reflect Rory's taste in all respects. Just as she would, if she married him. Already, possibly without being aware of what he was doing, he was beginning to mould her into the woman of his dreams, but now she knew for certain she could never be that woman.

She should have seen it before: the way Rory liked to have everything in his life designed to his own unique specifications. She should certainly have realised that he would never allow her a free hand in the redecorating of his house, even if he did intend her to share it with him. He had sought her opinion only as an excuse to bring her to Melbury. None of this would matter in the least if his faddiness related only to clothes or carpets, but now Meriel knew better. He wanted to redesign her too, and she knew with sudden blinding clarity that, if he succeeded, she could never be happy with him.

She must find him immediately, she decided, talk to him and try to explain how she felt. But she knew it was hopeless. She had let things go too far for Rory to release her now. Although she despised herself for being so cowardly, she knew beyond doubt there was only one course of action open to her.

When it came to apologising, to offering some explanation that might be acceptable, no words she could think of meant a thing. In the end, Meriel picked up a lipstick and simply scribbled the one word, *Sorry*, over and over on the dressing-table mirror. She left Rory's present unopened on the dressing-table. Then, stepping out of her ball gown and pulling on jeans and sweatshirt, she bundled a few essential items into an overnight bag, and slipped out of the grand house, her departure unnoticed amid the bustle and the music and the laughter.

She tapped lightly on the kitchen door and let herself in before Jacinta had time to turn around.

"Sshh!" she warned her, placing a finger over her lips to stifle the maid's delighted exclamation. "I don't want anyone to know I'm here!"

"Is all right!" Jacinta's stage whisper must have carried for miles. "Mrs Barton, she gone to Canterbury for shopping and for tea. She not back for three hours, maybe more."

This was as Meriel had hoped. Vivienne usually went into Canterbury on a Thursday, and Meriel had waited for this moment before returning to Amberfield. "Is there anyone else in the house?" she asked.

"No. Nobody. Now, what you doing here? Why you not with your fiancé? What you want?"

"I'm not sure how to explain . . ." she began cautiously.

"Come. You tell me," insisted Jacinta.

"Jacinta, do you remember when I first came to Amberfield – I mean, the very first day?"

Jacinta's eyes filled with tears at the memory and she clasped Meriel's hands to her. "Yes, yes of course! The day of Simon's funeral! Such a sad time!"

327

"I don't know if you remember, but when you showed me to my room you said something . . ."

"I said I help you always," said Jacinta. "No?"

"You remember!"

"Of course. And now you want I help you. How?"

Meriel drew a deep breath, hating what she was about to ask. "I know this is none of my business. . ."

"You ask, I tell," said Jacinta. "To you, you understand. Only to you."

"After Edward became ill," Meriel continued, "you signed a document placing Amberfield House under joint ownership between himself and Vivienne. Do you remember that?"

"I not know what the papers say, Meriel," said Jacinta. "I not read private things. But I write my name a few times, sure I remember. Why?" she asked, suddenly anxious. "I no do the right thing?"

"Yes, of course you did the right thing. If that was what Mrs Barton asked you to do . . ."

Jacinta nodded her head vehemently. "Oh, yes. She ask me. I remember so well, because she in a big big hurry to go out, and she say to me to sign when Mr Barton he sign."

"So . . . Mr Barton was still able to write his own signature at that stage?"

"Is right, yes. So Mrs Barton sign, and then Mr Barton, and I sign also, each time. For Mr Fox. So. What you want?"

"If possible, Jacinta, I'd like to see Mrs Barton's copy of that agreement. You don't happen to know where she keeps it, do you?"

Jacinta did not hesitate. "Come," was all she said.

Leading the way to Vivienne's study, she fished a set of keys out of a vase on the display case and opened one of the desk drawers. Inside were a number of household files, to which Jacinta pointed with a shrug. "Here, I think. But which one, I not know."

"That's all right. I'll find it. And Jacinta – thank you."

328

Meriel knew at once where to look. From a box file marked "Deeds" she extracted a number of large envelopes and opened each one in turn. Most of the documents related to the purchase of The Lodge and to the former ownership of Amberfield House and were doubtless being kept for historical rather than legal reasons. But in one long brown envelope she came across the paper Jacinta had signed, and, opening it carefully, began to study it intently.

This was the document which had so disturbed her when she had seen it in Jonathan Fox's office. Now, surely, she would at last discover what it was that had set her antennae twitching. But after half an hour of the most minute perusal, she was forced to admit defeat. Whichever way she looked at it, the transfer of The Lodge from Edward alone into joint ownership with his wife was utterly, perfectly, normal and above-board.

Meriel was so disappointed she could have wept. She was on the point of reading the papers through yet again when, in a fit of irritation she flung them down and sat back, closing her eyes, trying to imagine the scene on that occasion.

There was Vivienne, in a hurry to go out, although why she should have arranged to go out when she knew the lawyer was calling was something of a puzzle. Had she forgotten he was coming? That was not like Vivienne at all. Or was it just possible that she was not expecting him? That he had called on the off-chance? There again, it seemed unlikely when there were such important papers to be signed.

Meriel shook her head with a sigh and returned to where she had broken off. There was Vivienne, in a hurry to go out. Jonathan arrived with the papers. He and Vivienne signed, and Jacinta was their witness. Vivienne then left to keep her appointment, whatever it was, and Jonathan and Jacinta went through the whole procedure again with Edward. It was all here, before her. The signatures all in their right places.

Then, something in the region of her heart suddenly lurched, and set it beating at a faster rate. *That's it!* she said to herself. *That must be it!*

"Jacinta!" she called, only the sound came out more as a croak than a shout. "Jacinta!" she repeated more clearly as she ran towards the kitchen.

"What is it?"

"How many times did you sign your name on those papers? Can you remember?"

"Sure I remember!" laughed Jacinta. "I sign three times. That is good, no?"

"That's very good!" said Meriel. "In fact, it's marvellous!"

20

She lived quietly for the next two weeks, hidden away in an anonymous motel just off the motorway. Her room was comfortable if characterless, and noisy when the morning rush hour pounded its way towards London, but it suited her. Here, she was left alone. In the mornings, when she heard the hoovering chambermaids begin their onslaught on her corridor, she went out for a run, mainly along side roads, sometimes across fields and even as far as residential streets lined with dreary terraced houses.

At night she ate alone in the restaurant, where unaccompanied men sometimes attempted to engage her in conversation until she called the security guard and asked him to make them stop bothering her. She had stopped at this particular motel when she left Rory for the simple reason that she had to stop somewhere, but she could not stay here much longer. Soon her money would run out, and she would have to think about selling her car.

As soon as planning permission for the barn had been granted she had transferred all her savings to the Amberfield Wines account, a decision which had caused her no regrets, either then or later. She could think of nothing so worth while as saving the vineyards Simon had planted. All the same, her dwindling bank balance meant that she now had to find herself a job, fast, and during the past week she had attended a number of interviews in London. As yet, nothing had come from any of them, and the suspicion was growing in her that Rory was exercising what influence he could to black her.

Within hours of leaving him, she summoned up the

courage to telephone him. Her conscience simply would not let her go without saying anything. But he refused to come to the phone, first at Melbury and later at the office when she tried to reach him there. Eventually she left a message requesting that her belongings be sent to a friend's house in London, but they never arrived.

It seemed Rory had decided to cut her out of his life, to pretend that she had never existed, and in her heart Meriel could not really blame him. There were times when she wished he could understand something of what she was going through, but she knew that by behaving as she had, she had thrown away any possibility of friendship.

Today she was due to travel up to London again. This time she would seek humbler employment in the form of general clerical or word-processing work. She had also made an appointment to look at a room not far from her old flat in Battersea. She knew the street: the houses had small rooms and no gardens, but what did she need space for? She owned nothing apart from the clothes she had taken away from Rory's and the suit and shoes she had bought to wear when job-hunting.

While she ate her breakfast, she read her newspaper, starting with the business news, just as she used to do, then working her way back towards the front. Coming unexpectedly across a quarter-page photograph of a vineyard which she recognised as one of England's largest, she felt a rush of almost unbearable longing.

As the article that accompanied the photograph made clear, all over southern England, wine-growers were beginning to gather their crops at the end of what had turned out to be one of the great summers of the century. Now, in late October, Meriel knew they must be starting to pick the grapes at Amberfield. She wished with all her heart she could be there, but she could not ask Vivienne to take her back. Her status as Vivienne's daughter-in-law had surely lapsed when she announced her intention to marry Rory Lassiter.

She wondered whether Jacinta had mentioned her secret visit to Amberfield, although Meriel had asked her to say nothing. Not, at least, until she had time to put together the last missing bit of that puzzle, and that was something that, for reasons entirely beyond her control, she could not do until the following Monday. Until then she could only try and sort out her future life. And wait.

"What I need," said Dan, flattering Hatta shamelessly, "is someone clever and beautiful to take charge of the students who have come to help with the picking. How about it?"

"I'm your man," replied Hatta. "But only if it's true that you've come back to Amberfield for good."

"Who told you that?"

"Mum."

"I'd better not argue with the boss then, had I?"

She followed him across to the waiting group and introduced herself. Not long back from a holiday in Tuscany, she was looking tanned and fit, and Dan noticed with amusement that one of the young men was making no attempt to disguise his admiration for her. Nor, as far as anyone could tell, was Hatta displeased by the attention she was getting.

The pickers were now issued with special grape-picking scissors and plastic buckets. Hatta's admirer, Barney, being anxious to look the part in every respect, remembered now to don the black French beret he had thoughtfully brought with him and, with a cheerful wave to Hatta, made his way towards the first of the rows allocated to him, and set to work.

As the day wore on and the sun shone down hotter and hotter, so the harvesters shed sweatshirts and other items of clothing and gratefully accepted the soft drinks regularly delivered around the vineyards by the younger helpers. Could this really be England, Dan asked himself at one point, wiping the sweat from his brow and deciding which vantage point would most suit the two reporters from the local newspaper who had just turned up to capture this decidedly untypical scene. Then, catching sight of Vivienne, he delegated the matter to her and returned to the winery.

Despite the surprising resilience of the fruit, the pickers knew they had to take the utmost care with the grapes so as to avoid damaging them. First, the newly-cut bunches were placed in plastic buckets, before being tipped as gently as possible into plastic crates, which in turn were loaded onto a trolley and taken to the winery. Nothing must touch the grapes which could possibly taint them, nor must the flow of air be hindered at any point, or the mass of grapes would immediately start to deteriorate and the wine would be spoilt.

Jethro, watching the harvesters at work, was constantly surprised by the degree of care they took, and by how rarely he had to caution anyone against rough handling. Then he remembered that these were mostly local people, with a fierce pride in this relatively new industry, and a strong desire to have a hand in producing the best wines they possibly could.

When the grapes reached the courtyard outside the winery they were weighed, a process supervised by Vivienne, elegant in pleated slacks and a wide-brimmed straw hat. After she had noted the exact quantities in her notebook, the grapes were taken into the building so that they could be processed while still warm from the sun, a factor which Dan insisted would make for a higher yield. Each day, only as many grapes were picked as could be milled within a couple of hours, and Vivienne was under strict instructions not to exceed her given quota. For in the matter of making wine, Dan, despite his long absence from Amberfield, still reigned supreme, and Vivienne would never have presumed to question his decisions.

Inside the winery, the high-tech world of modern winemaking took over. Instead of gangs of men, arms linked, trampling the grapes with bare feet, as would have been the case in a bygone age, there was the last word in stainless steel German technology. This marvel of modern engineering did the same job as the barefoot men, though nothing like as picturesquely, gently bursting all the berries without at the same time breaking the grape pips and releasing unwanted acids into the wine.

Time then to transfer the grapes to the press – another example of Teutonic efficiency – which Dan had insisted be bought instead of the traditional wooden screw presses originally chosen by Edward Barton. The latter were functional and attractive, certainly, but for the sheer volume of grapes now being produced and processed at Amberfield, this new wonder, in which a rubber bladder was slowly inflated to press the grapes against the sides of a perforated cylinder, struck him as both more efficient and kinder to the grape pulp. For with English wines, as he could not impress on his helpers often enough, gentleness was of the essence: any rough handling at any stage and the flavour of the wine would betray it. You could get away with murder with some of those rough, southern red wines, he told them, but at Amberfield, never.

The simple process of transferring the milled grapes to the press was always a critical point, and when Vivienne wandered in to tell Dan that the pickers would soon be stopping for lunch, he shooed her away.

"This is the Pinot Noir I'm milling," he told her. "I daren't take my eyes off it, not if I don't want the skins staining the pulp . . . We could lose the whole pressing if I'm not careful."

Vivienne wisely left him to it.

As usual on these occasions, lunch was provided by Jacinta on trestle tables in the courtyard. Huge quantities of sandwiches, pies, crisps, salads and a variety of puddings seemed to vanish within moments. Meanwhile, Hatta filled paper cups with wine, beer or orange juice and handed them round to an appreciative clientele.

"Zut alors," growled Barney in an atrocious mock-French accent, pulling his beret forward over his eyes, then making squeezing movements with his hands. "Quelle jolie waitresse we 'ave 'ere. I sink eet eez not only ze grapes zat need ze pressing, no?"

"Go away, Barney," said Hatta companionably.

Meanwhile Dan, for whom Jacinta only just remembered in time to save some lunch, was carrying out a further pressing of the grapes.

"Why don't you leave it for a moment and take a break?" suggested Vivienne. "I'm sure the machine can safely be left for half an hour or so now you've finished the champagne grapes."

"*Méthode champenoise*," Dan corrected her automatically. In any case, he told her, he preferred to remain in the winery. What if the machine failed? What if someone inadvertently turned up the dial on the wine press so that the juice was irrevocably tainted with bitter residue? What was at stake was far too important for him to take the slightest risk. This juice flowing out of the press was the result, not just of the morning's harvesting activities, but of years of hard, careful work: it would be tragic to ruin it now.

Dan knew he would be busy for some hours yet, completing up to six pressings on each batch of grapes, then overseeing the transfer of the juice into the stainless steel vats where the first fermentation would take place. And then, when the next load of grapes had been picked, the process would start all over again. It would be another week at least before the final bunches were gathered in and they could all finally relax: he could only hope this unbelievable weather did not let him down at the last moment.

Lunch over, the pickers returned to the fields in mellow mood. Someone started singing, and others picked up the tune and joined in. Those who did not know the words hummed along too, and Vivienne thought how much Edward would have enjoyed this day: the sun, the marvellous crop, the harvesters and their good humour. How sad that he would not taste the wine they were all working so hard to make, for it would surely be the best they had ever produced.

What they would have done if Dan hadn't come back, she did not dare think. She was still puzzled as to the reasons why he had suddenly changed his mind. She first wrote to him, begging him to return, when Adam announced his departure for France. There was a bumper harvest to be picked and processed, she told him, a crop which included his own new plantings.

But Dan was adamant that such a move would not be possible. Then, just as they were about to start picking, he telephoned to tell her he had reconsidered. He said he had been talking to Jethro, though for the life of her Vivienne could not see what Jethro had to do with anything.

She was still standing idly gazing across the vineyard when the first of the afternoon's pickings arrived for weighing. Time to get back to work, obviously. And, shaking her hair out before resettling the straw hat on her head, she marched back with a firm step to her place at the weighing table.

"It's not Vivienne, it's me," said Meriel, entering Jonathan's office.

"Meriel!" The lawyer sprang up in surprise. "I'm so sorry! When Mrs Barton was announced, I automatically assumed . . ."

Meriel sat down swiftly, before being asked to do so. The truth was that she was too nervous to remain standing. If she failed to achieve the aim of her visit, then, in spite of the glorious harvest, in spite of Dan's return, and Adam's departure, Amberfield was lost.

"How was your holiday?" she asked, determined at all costs to appear calm and in control of herself.

"Marvellous!" replied Jonathan. "Wonderful place,

Hawaii. You should try it some day. But I don't suppose you're here to see my holiday snaps. So, tell me. What can I do for you?"

He seemed brimful of confidence, so much so that Meriel's courage very nearly failed her. She had to force herself to speak.

"It's about the documents Jacinta signed," she began, then had to stop to clear her throat.

Although his expression scarcely changed, she could tell that Jonathan Fox was all ears.

"Putting The Lodge in Edward's and Vivienne's names jointly. Go on," he said.

"The transfer related to The Lodge *and its lands*, if I remember correctly."

"Naturally, yes." She could tell he was doing his best to appear noncommittal.

"I've been very slow in putting two and two together," she continued. "What I had forgotten was that virtually all Amberfield's land, including the vineyards, came with the purchase of The Lodge. There would be no vineyards if Edward's father hadn't bought The Lodge."

"I fail to see what's bothering you," said Jonathan. "What happens is that the company – that is, Amberfield Wines – rents the land from the owners – until recently, Edward and Vivienne, but now Vivienne only – for a nominal rent. It's a minor technicality, that's all."

Here goes, thought Meriel. *This is the big one. And if I've got it all wrong . . .* ! She did not dare look any further ahead.

"It would be a minor matter if Vivienne did indeed own The Lodge, as you claim."

"Well, of course she does! You saw the transfer document for yourself!"

She leaned forward, studying him closely. "Tell me something, Jonathan," she said softly. "Why was it necessary for Jacinta to sign three transfer documents?"

Jonathan shook his head. "She's made a mistake,

Meriel. Her English was even worse then than it is now. She can't have understood a word of what was going on."

"That's where you're wrong," Meriel told him. "She distinctly remembers writing her name three times. She only needed to witness the document twice: once for the Bartons' files, and once for yours. What was that third signature for, Jonathan?"

After a pause that Meriel thought would never end, Jonathan returned to the filing cabinet and drew out a further document.

"Very well, I'll show you," he said lightly. "In any case I was going to make this public as soon as I'd obtained probate. As you will see, this is all perfectly legal. There's nothing anybody can do about it."

"Oh, Jonathan!" said Meriel, sickened by what she saw. "How could you do this!"

There before her was what she had feared and sus-pected: Edward's and Jacinta's signatures confirming the transfer of The Lodge and all its grounds to joint own-ership. Only the owners were not Vivienne and himself; they were Edward Barton and Jonathan Fox. And on Edward's death the property and its grounds passed to Jonathan exclusively.

"As you see, this document postdates the one in which Vivienne is named as joint-owner. In other words, I am now the legal owner of the vineyards."

"Vivienne will fight your claim tooth and nail! You'll never get away with this!"

"But what can poor Vivienne *do* other than accept the evidence of Edward's signature?"

"For a start, she'll want to know why you've said nothing about this before now!"

Jonathan sighed. "Oh, Meriel, Meriel! You don't seem to understand what a caring and kind-hearted sort of chap I am! When Edward told me, in the strictest confidence, that he had no faith in his family's ability to run the company, when he begged me to let him name me as heir to the vineyards, how could I possibly refuse him? And then, having agreed to Edward's desperate plea, how could I possibly bring myself to hurt Vivienne by revealing what had transpired?"

"You'll hurt her soon enough! What sort of a monster are you, tricking an old man! It's obvious he didn't know what he was signing! He would never have done anything to harm Vivienne!"

"Vivienne will be fine, believe me! She's got Amberfield House. And that lovely new barn conversion which you were good enough to fund. Such a pity I shan't be needing it when Bert and I grub up the vineyards and start building our nice new houses. Poor Meriel. All that clever detective work and nothing to show for it. On top of which, you won't see your money again, you know. I'm afraid that's gone. All gone."

Silenced at last, Meriel let the document fall onto her lap. Jonathan was right. It was going to be well-nigh impossible to prove beyond doubt that he had tricked Edward into signing those papers. She was filled with such revulsion for the man sitting across the desk from her that she came very close to missing the solution to the problem.

It was so blindingly simple she was astonished it had not occurred to Jonathan. Had it done so he would most certainly have taken remedial action.

"Three times," she said, nodding slowly. "Jacinta told me she signed her name three times."

"So?"

"That would be the two copies of the transfer of Amberfield House and lands into joint-ownership – one copy for the Bartons, and one for you . . ."

"Yes, yes." Jonathan waved a hand impatiently. "What about it."

"But only one copy of the document naming you as co-owner. Only one copy of the document I'm holding here – "

"No!" Jonathan leapt up and flung himself across the desk. But he was too late. Meriel had already pushed her chair back out of reach and had consigned the document to the office shredding machine.

"Oh, the wonders of modern technology!" she remarked as a bundle of neat strips emerged before her delighted eyes. "It seems you don't own a slice of Amberfield after all."

Meriel returned to Amberfield the night of the party to celebrate the successful gathering in of the grapes. She had already decided she would not join in the merriment, but when she learnt from Jacinta that there was to be a dance in "her" barn, she found she could not resist the chance of seeing the progress so far.

She parked her car with the others on the flat grassy area on the far side of the building, in which a new opening had now been made. It looked good, she decided. A wide, high arch with old oak doors which had been salvaged from the former stables. Inside, the cramped offices she and Adam and Michelle used to occupy had been transformed into a vast space which in spite of its size barely contained the mass of people within.

From her vantage point she could also see the band, which consisted of Jethro's son Kit and some of his friends, blasting away amateurishly at electric guitars and second-hand drum kits. She could also see, through a kaleidoscope of flashing strobe lights, a seething mass of people, young and old, gyrating away in evident enjoyment.

It was late, well after eleven o'clock, but the party looked like going on for some time. A movement near the door of the barn caused her to step back into the shadows between the parked cars and, to her surprise, Hatta suddenly emerged from the dance-floor with her arms around a young man Meriel had never seen before.

"Barney!" Hatta was protesting. "People will notice we've disappeared!"

"What does that matter? We're only dancing, aren't we?"

They continued bopping and boogying round the cars, giggling and shrieking whenever they tripped on the uneven ground, sometimes coming perilously close to colliding with one of the vehicles. Eventually, exhausted by their efforts, they departed in search of liquid refreshment, and Meriel was able to escape.

There was no moon tonight to guide her on her way to the ridgeway, but in the darkness broken only by the dusty shimmer of the stars, Meriel could almost believe the harvest had not yet taken place. So careful, so precise was the process of cutting the grapes from the vines that the parent plants at first appeared quite untouched. Only when she walked through the rows did it become evident that the crop was gone, all but a few bunches missed by the pickers which by day would provide a succulent meal for wasps.

"Meriel?"

Dan's voice, coming from so close, startled her so that she stumbled and drew aback in alarm.

"Oh, it's you," was all she could say.

"The same," he laughed. "Can I take it that you got our invitation?"

She shook her head. "What invitation?"

"To the dance! Vivienne and I spent hours trying to track you down."

"No, I didn't get it."

"Well," said Dan. "You're here. That's what matters."

"What brought you back, Dan? Was it Vivienne?"

"Partly," agreed Dan. "Though at first when she asked, I said no. Then I heard that you'd decided not to marry this dreadful man you've been seeing."

"He wasn't *dreadful*," Meriel told him. "But . . . I don't think we'd have been right for one another. I had to get away. Anyway, how did you hear?

"Jethro told me. And in case you're still wondering, Jethro got it from Jacinta. But then, afterwards . . . I was

342

so sure you'd come back here. And then when you didn't
. . . when we couldn't find you . . . oh, stop crying, Meriel.
And come here."

"I don't seem to be able to help it!" she said as she moved
into his arms and buried her face in his chest.

"Hey! What's all this!" His voice was gentler than she
could ever have imagined. "Sophisticated ladies like you
don't go in for this sort of thing!"

"You've got to know," she told him. "I didn't betray
your secret to Vivienne. I still don't know how she found
out."

"Oh, that. Jonathan Fox was responsible for that one.
He . . . er . . . has his spies everywhere, it seems. He was
the one who told Vivienne."

"So all that time you were in Australia, you could have
been here with me. Dan, I have missed you so much!"

"Not as much as I missed you," he said. "And no
arguing!"

"Oh, Dan!" she sniffed, and then his arms tightened
around her and his mouth found hers and all Meriel could
think was that whoever it was once said that kisses were
sweeter than wine got it pretty well right.

Some weeks after Meriel returned to live at Amberfield
House, Vivienne sought Meriel out and found her with
Dan in the now-finished barn. She could tell from the
way they looked at and spoke to one another that they
were now reconciled, and she breathed a sigh of relief.
If this was what it took to keep them both at Amberfield,
then so be it.

"So. Tomorrow's the big day. Is everything ready?"

Meriel could not keep the excitement out of her voice.
"Yes! And it's going to be a huge success, I can just
feel it!"

Vivienne wandered around the room checking the displays of goods for sale, and nodding approvingly at what
she saw.

"And the kitchen staff?"

"They'll be here first thing in the morning."

"All I wish," said Vivienne, "is that Adam could see this. He'd be so impressed! And talking of Adam, you'll never believe this but he phoned last night to say he's going into the property development business. Isn't that extraordinary?"

"Extraordinary." Meriel tried not to let an edge steal into her reply. No one, not even Dan, would ever know what had passed between herself and Adam.

"How come?" asked Dan.

"It seems Sophie's grandfather has agreed to accept EC money and grub up some of his poorer-quality vines. They're going to use the land to build holiday homes. Oh, yes. And Sophie's going to open a restaurant. Apparently it's what she's wanted to do all along. Isn't it amazing how things turn out?"

She left to accompany Dan on his routine inspection of the winery, leaving Meriel to reflect how right she was. It was amazing how things turned out. Take her and Dan, for instance. At the memory of these last few weeks, during which they had scarcely been apart for more than an hour at a time, she gave a soft laugh and hugged herself with something close to glee.

Not that she had any illusions about what it meant to be with Dan. He was not like Simon, who had always been easy to be with for the simple reason that he never disagreed with her about anything. She would even have found life with Rory easy if she had been willing or able to submit to his idea of her. But in her relationship with Dan there was a tension which was new to her, and which she found exhilarating.

What if they did sometimes argue, or misunderstand one another? When reconciliation came, as it inevitably would, their rediscovery of one another would be the more pleasurable because of their differences. Dan, she knew, would never want her to be other than she was. He would always . . . but then she stopped herself. She was making plans again, looking to the future, and her experience had taught her that this was rarely wise. Far better to wait and see what happened. What really mattered for the moment was that the vines of Amberfield were saved. And it was going to be a great vintage.